mental_floss presents:

FORBIDDEN
KNOWLEDGE

Also from **mental**_floss:

mental_floss *presents: Condensed Knowledge*

mental_floss *presents: Instant Knowledge*

mental_floss presents:

FORBIDDEN
KNOWLEDGE

edited by

Will Pearson,

Mangesh Hattikudur,

and **Elizabeth Hunt**

Collins

An Imprint of HarperCollinsPublishers

For anyone who loves a bit of mischief...

HarperCollins books may be purchased for educational, business, or sales promotional use. For information, please write: Special Markets Department, HarperCollins Publishers, 10 East 53rd Street, New York, NY 10022.

FIRST EDITION

Designed by Emily Taff

Library of Congress Cataloging-in-Publication Data has been applied for.

ISBN-10: 0-06-078475-X
ISBN-13: 978-0-06-078475-1

05 06 07 08 09   DIX/RRD   10 9 8 7 6 5 4 3 2 1

Acknowledgments

mental_floss would like to thank the Devil for making a book about sins possible. Also, Napoléon, Caligula, Nero, Boss Tweed (and the entire Tammany Hall gang), Genghis Khan, Atilla and all the Huns, Shanta Hattikudur, the victors who wrote history (you know who you are), and Voldemort. It's your inspiration that truly fills this book.

We'd also like to thank Winslow Taft, Lisako Koga, Sandy Wood, and Kara Kovalchik.

Finally, we thank Greg Chaput at Collins for his expert editorial guidance and support.

now with 20% more evil!

FORBIDDEN KNOWLEDGE

CAUTION!

Contains Seven Deadly Ingredients

Introduction

There's no dearth of great literature in the library here at *mental_floss*. Sure, you've got your heavyweights: Beckett, Proust, even a little section dedicated to obscure Chilean playwrights. But perhaps the most telling title on the rack is a dog-eared copy of the picture book *The Fire Cat*.

From the outset it looks like an ordinary kid's tale. Oversized pages, colorful drawings, easy-to-pronounce words. But if you turn a couple of pages in, you'll learn in giant I Can Read Book print that Pickles, who's under the care of Mrs. Goodkind, is neither a good cat nor a bad cat. He is a good *and* bad cat.

Profound. He also has big paws with which he plans to do big things, but that's neither here nor there.

What we mean to say is that we can relate. See, the cats at *mental_floss* often get pegged as a little too good. You know? All toothy grins and saccharine-sweet reputations. And yeah, we've got the good grades to back it up. Not to mention the clean-cut hairstyles, and the finely honed sense for when to insert a please or thank-you without overdoing it. And then there's the press: endless coverage of us helping old women cross streets and plucking kittens out of trees. But don't let that fool you. Look a little deeper and you'll find there's more than a little yin that comes with all this yang.

The truth is, we're kind of bad seeds. Rebels, baby. Catch us when the media's not around and you might see us doing something c-r-a-z-y. Like standing on a moving bus—you know, just for the thrill of it. Or going into a library and using our *out*door voices. Sometimes we'll even bite into a piece of fruit without giving it a good rinse first. Does it taste a little sweeter? Oh, you know it does.

Okay. While we might not be as bad as we'd like to believe, there is some comfort in knowing that someone's made up of more than just medals and virtues. And history's exactly the same. It's not the hearts of gold and battles won that are interesting. It's the smirks and quirks. It's juicy anecdotes. It's history's greatest figures telling Jiminy Cricket to shove off, then getting caught on the wrong side of their conscience.

Take Ben Franklin, for instance. Doesn't his whole perfect patriot, Renaissance man act get a little more intriguing when you find out he was sort of a man slut? Or Adam Smith's Invisible Hand of Capitalism. Don't the yawns come a little slower when you watch it waving at developing nations with just one finger?

Forbidden Knowledge is exactly that. It's the worst history has to offer, all deliciously broken up into seven sin-tastic chapters. If our first book, *Condensed Knowledge,* was every-thing you feel you're supposed to know, this follow-up is the exact opposite: it's all the stuff you shouldn't. It's every bawdy story and dirty secret your history teacher wanted to tell you, but couldn't for fear of losing his or her job. So thumb through the pages. Find a name, person, or place you used to admire. And then read on. We're betting the naughty ending will make you smile.

Enjoy.
Will, Mangesh, and Liz

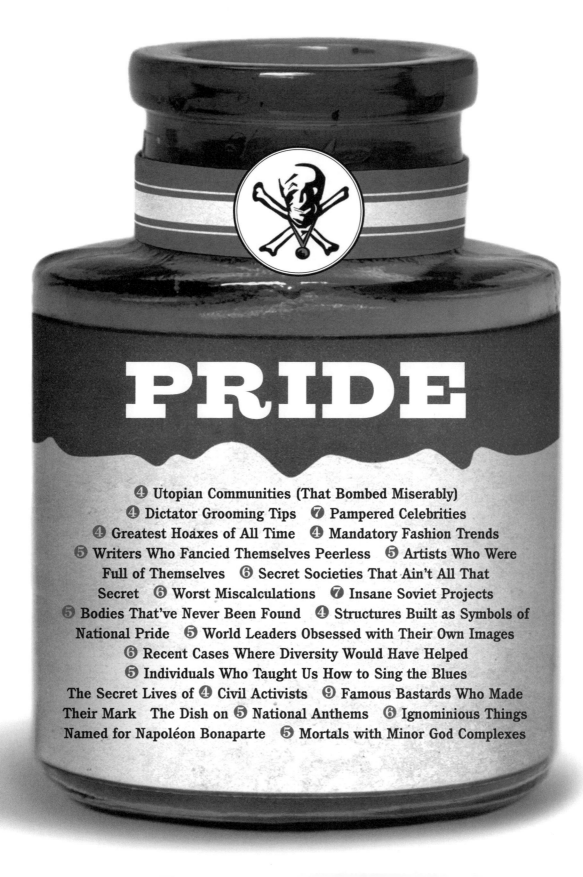

PRIDE

Talk of the Town:
Utopian Communities (That Bombed Miserably)

4

Every once in a while a proud little community will sprout up just to let the world know how Utopia should be run. With chins raised almost as high as ideals, the community marches forth to be an example of perfection. But in most cases, all that harmonious marching gets tripped up pretty quickly. Here are four "perfect" communities that whizzed and sputtered thanks to human nature.

_01:: Brook Farm, or Ripley's Follow Me or Not

Probably the best-known utopian community in America, Brook Farm was founded in 1841 in West Roxbury, Massachusetts, by George and Sophia Ripley. The commune was built on a 200-acre farm with four buildings and centered on the ideals of radical social reform and self-reliance. For free tuition in the community school and one year's worth of room and board, the residents were asked to complete 300 days of labor by either farming, working in the manufacturing shops, performing domestic chores or grounds maintenance, or planning the community's recreation projects. The community prospered in 1842–1843 and was visited by numerous dignitaries and utopian writers. However, Ripley joined the unpopular Fourierism movement, which meant that soon the young people (out of a "sense of honor") had to do all the dirty work like repairing roads, cleaning stables, and slaughtering the animals. This caused many residents, especially the younger ones, to leave. Things went downhill from there. The community

was hit by an outbreak of smallpox followed by fire and finally collapsed in 1847.

_02:: Fruitlands: A Utopian Community (for Six Months Anyway)

After visiting Brook Farm and finding it almost too worldly by their standards, Bronson Alcott (the father of Louisa May) and Charles Lane founded the Fruitlands Commune in June 1843, in Harvard, Massachusetts. Structured around the British reformist model, the commune's members were against the ownership of property, were political anarchists, believed in free love, and were vegetarians. The group of 11 adults and a small number of children were forbidden to eat meat or use any animal products such as honey, wool, beeswax, or manure. They were also not allowed to use animals for labor and only planted produce that grew up out of the soil so as not to disturb worms and other organisms living in the soil. Many in the group of residents saw manual labor as spiritually inhibiting and soon it became evident that the commune could not provide enough food to sustain its members. The strict diet of grains and fruits left many of the members malnourished and sick. Given this situation, many of the members left and the community collapsed in January 1844.

_03:: The Shakers

Officially known as the United Society of Believers in Christ's Second Appearing, the Shakers were founded in Manchester, England, in 1747. As a group of dissenting Quakers under the charismatic leadership of Mother Ann Lee, the Shakers came to America in 1774. Like most reformist movements of the time, the Shakers were agriculturally based, and believed in common ownership of all property and the confession of sins. Unlike most of the other groups, the Shakers practiced celibacy, or the lack of procreation. Membership came via converts or by adopting children. Shaker families consisted of "brothers" and "sisters" who lived in gender-segregated communal homes of up to 100 individuals. During the required Sunday community meetings it was not uncommon for members to break into a spontaneous dance, thus giving them the Shaker label. As pacifists they were exempted from military service and became the United States' first conscientious objectors during the Civil War. Currently, however, there isn't a whole lot of Shaking going on. As the younger members left the community, converts quit coming, and the older ones died off, many of the communities were forced to close. Of the original 19 communities, most had closed by the early 1900s, with only one in existence today.

_04:: Pullman's Capitalist Utopia

Located 15 miles south of Chicago, the town of Pullman was founded in the 1880s by George Pullman (of luxury railway car fame) as a utopian community based on the notion that capitalism was the best way to meet all material and spiritual needs. According to Pullman's creed, the community was built to provide Pullman's employees with a place where they could exercise proper moral values and where each resident had to adhere to the strict tenets of capitalism under the direction and leadership of Pullman. The community was run on a for-profit basis—the town had to return a profit of 7% annually. This was done by giving the employees two paychecks, one for rent, which was automatically turned back in to Pullman, and one for everything else. Interestingly, the utopian community had very rigid social class barriers, with the management and skilled workers living in stately homes and the unskilled laborers living in tenements. Within 20 years the experiment failed miserably. Pullman began demanding more and more rent to offset company losses, while union sentiment grew among the employee residents.

Touch of Evil

Not all cult villages lose touch with pop culture. Reports indicate that, strewn among the bodies of the 900-plus dead at the People's Temple in Jonestown, Guyana, were cassette tapes featuring the vocal stylings of none other than Barry White.

The Totalitarian Style Guide: Dictator Grooming Tips

So, you wanna be a dictator? Sure, you've got the well-equipped, fanatically loyal army, you've selected a country for conquering, and you're ready to murder anyone who stands in the way (what commitment!). But if you want to be taken seriously in the Dictator Game, you'll need to look the part. Lucky for you, we've assembled a handy guide to get you started.

_01:: The Mustache

From Hitler to Mussolini to Saddam Hussein, dictators have long relied on the mustache to give them the illusion of stiff upper lips. And they're touchy about 'em, to boot! In 1923, Hitler's friend Ernst Hanfstaengl encouraged the future Führer to grow his mustache across the entire length of his lip. Hitler, naturally, later tried to have Hanfstaengl killed. Critics of Stalin's 'stache fared even worse. In a poem intended only for a small circle of friends, Osip Mandelstam compared Stalin's mustache to a cockroach. Thereafter, Mandelstam was repeatedly arrested and sent to deadly Soviet work camps—he died, probably in 1939, in one of the gulags. So whether you go pencil-thin or Selleck-thick, remember the mustache—and to crush any who question it.

_02:: Let Yourself Go a Little

Nothing establishes power over the people quite like making it abundantly obvious to them that you have access to more food than they do. Just think of the adorably pudgy (and slightly paranoid) Kim Jong Il, or the rotund Idi Amin. But by far the fattest autocrat is Taufa'ahau Tupou IV, the longtime king of Tongo. But don't let the chub fool you: despite weighing in at a chunky 300-plus pounds, the Tongan king is 100% dictator. In fact, he's led one of the strangest imperialist campaigns of all time to prove it. After an eccentric Nevadan named Michael Oliver piled sand onto a reef in the Pacific and declared his newly built paradise "The Republic of Minerva" in 1972, Tupou and a force of 350 Tongans invaded the one-man nation and annexed it in history's most minor act of colonialism.

_03:: Care for Your Hair, Not Your People

Although it may seem a little too metrosexual for totalitarian rulers, hair care is as vital to a proper dictatorship as erecting statues of yourself and murdering innocents. Historically, dictators lucky enough to have a full head of hair (sorry, Mao) have gone to great lengths to protect it. When he was plucked from his miserable little spider hole outside Tikrit in 2003, it immediately became clear that the suddenly salt-and-pepper Saddam Hussein had previously been using Just For Men. And North

It's a Mad, Mad, Mad, Mad Emperor

NORTON I, EMPEROR OF THE UNITED STATES OF AMERICA

Joshua Abraham Norton (1819?–1880) was just about as crazy as they come. Norton declared himself Emperor of the United States of America (and Protector of Mexico) in 1859, and although he never really left San Francisco to survey his domains, he became such a local celebrity that his "proclamations" were carried in San Francisco's newspapers. Not just that, he ate for free in the best restaurants in town, and stores all over the city accepted the special "currency" he made for his empire of one. Even more impressive, when he passed away, 30,000 San Franciscans turned out for Norton's funeral, perhaps just to see his new clothes.

Korea's Kim Jong Il, whose bouffant may seem out of style to those of us who aren't 70-year-old women, purportedly spends hours on his perms—and spikes his hair into peaks to appear taller than his 5 feet 2 inches (he also wears shoes with lifts).

_04:: Uniforms = The New Black

Durable, washable, and flattering to any build, a military uniform is another essential for any dictator. Suits and ties are for democratically elected pansies—a uniform reminds your citizens who has the guns: You do! When selecting your totalitarian couture, we recommend choosing from one of two classic schools of uniform thought. The Castro—no fancy medals or ornate accessories here—is just your classic, tailored-to-fit green fatigues, with a cigar and a Britney Spears–esque page boy cap to complete the ensemble. Or you can opt for a little more military bling, and fashion yourself in the school of the Amin. Like Idi Amin's bloodthirsty, over-the-top reign, the Amin is ostentatious and intimidating, with dozens of medals, some the size of a hockey puck, adorning a blue double-breasted general's coat. Have your minions sew some gaudy gold epaulets onto your shoulders, and you'll be ready to terrorize the people in style!

Touch of Evil

Some sources claim that Adolf Hitler purposely styled his short mustache after film legend Charlie Chaplin's. The silent film star wasn't exactly impressed and responded by mocking Der Führer in The Great Dictator, *his first "talkie" film.*

7 Ridiculous Contract Riders of Pampered Celebrities

Everyone knows rock and roll is about thrills and excess—we just didn't realize that spirit was supposed to extend to the greenroom buffet. The following are seven very pampered acts that made sure their laundry list of demands got tacked onto their contracts.

_01:: Van Halen and the Whole M&M'S Thing

Van Halen first gained notoriety for their stipulation that, at every gig, their dressing room was to contain a large bowl of M&M'S, but with all the brown ones removed. And while this has often been cited as proof of the band members' towering egos, it was actually included by the tour promoters as an easy way of seeing if the concert venues had read the contract thoroughly (particularly the parts about technical requirements, etc.). But sneaky M&M'S tactics aside, Van Halen's riders are also notorious for the sheer volume of alcohol they stipulate. One rider specified that their dressing room was to contain a case of beer, a pint of Jack Daniel's, a pint of Absolut, a 750 ml bottle of Bacardi Añejo rum, three bottles of wine, small bottles of Cointreau and Grand Marnier, and a 750 ml bottle of one of five specific premium tequilas. Don't forget six limes, margarita salt, shot glasses, ingredients for Bloody Marys, and a blender. Sure, there are only four dudes in the band, but shouldn't you expect this sort of behavior from a group whose bassist plays a guitar shaped like a bottle of Jack?

_02:: JLo's Trailer from the Park

There are divas, there are superdivas, and then there's Jennifer Lopez. That's right, the same sultry soulstress who preaches the "keep it real" street mantra also happens to require a trailer *at least* 40 feet in length, in which *everything* is white. That means drapes, couches, candles, tablecloths, lilies, and roses (she also requires yellow roses with red trim thrown in as well). And if you're hoping to keep a prolonged smile on "Jenny from the Block's" pretty mug, you can't forget the selection of current CDs she requires, chosen from a list of 43 artists, or her three favorite scented candles from Diptyque—Tuberose, Figuier, and Heliotrope. And that's just from her contract for a *charity* song benefiting AIDS victims in Africa! Oh, and did we mention Jenny was only at the event for a total of 90 minutes? It's almost as if her ego's as big as her . . . nope, too easy.

_03:: Guns N' (Long-Stemmed) Roses

They were one of the biggest bands of the 1980s and '90s. Just ask them. And in a band of big egos, the very biggest was lead singer

Axl Rose. He had his own dressing room, stocked with plenty of the things a vocal professional needs: hot water and honey (Sue Bee brand only); a rib-eye steak dinner; a large pepperoni pizza; a deli tray with a heavy emphasis on lean roast beef, ham, and turkey; and a bottle of Dom Perignon. His bandmates had much simpler tastes. Their dressing room was to contain lots of chips, nuts, exotic fruits, and cheese. Of course, they went a little less simple on the drinks. Aside from a few cases of soda, the band also required four cases of beer, two fifths of Jack Daniel's, two fifths of Stolichnaya vodka, two bottles of Chardonnay, and a bottle of Jägermeister. Oh, and don't forget to throw in a couple bottles of . . . carrot juice? Clearly, it's the cornerstone behind every successful rock act. As are the four *cartons* of cigarettes and the assortment of adult magazines you'll need to provide.

_04:: Meat Loaf (Just a Little Overdone)

Yes, *that* Meat Loaf. The man who brought us *Bat Out of Hell* obviously requires quite a bit in return. His rider states that the promoters are to recognize that they are dealing with an international "superstar" and therefore all provisions must be first class, as befits a "superstar." And that's two words: *Meat. Loaf.* Sheesh! His dressing room spread must include, among many other things, a loaf of 100% multigrain bread (preferably Vogel's Flaxseed & Soy), two bags of potato chips, a package of low-fat chicken or turkey wieners, four Gala apples (specifically, hard and crunchy ones), four low-fat fresh-baked muffins *from a bakery,* steamed broccoli and green beans amandine (not too soggy), a sliced roast pork tenderloin, a sliced roast beef tenderloin, and two baked potatoes. And this is supposed to feed two people. Maybe they're both Mr. Loaf?

_05:: Poison's Poison

Pretty standard for a rock band, really. Deli trays, condiments, lots of booze, etc. But what was Poison's poison? Apparently, pyrotechnics. Their contract also required that all the venue's smoke and fire detectors be switched off due to the band's flair for flares. So how do we think the concertgoers would feel knowing that little tidbit? Also very odd, Poison's rider stipulates that an American Sign Language interpreter must be made available on request for the band's deaf fans. And the band will need 24 hours' notice if the ASL interpreter needs the lyrics beforehand. Of course, some disdainful critics would claim that *all* the band's fans *must* be deaf.

Touch of Evil

So, what were the Beatles' demands after a grueling, fast-paced 1965 concert at New York's Shea Stadium? Just a black-and-white TV and some Coca-Cola.

_06:: The Village People's Payment Plan

You might think that a bunch of guys as past their prime as The Village People would just be glad to get a gig. Nope. They still draw a crowd, so therefore they still have demands in their rider. The front page of their rider contains one stipulation: that all balances to The Village People be paid in "CASH" (yes, it's in all caps). It goes on to say that they can only be photographed in costume, that they won't fly in prop planes, and that they prefer certain seats in the plane (as specific as "aisle, rear right side of plane" for the Navy guy) and certain airports of origin. Disco may be dead, but ego certainly seems to be staying alive.

_07:: Various Spoiled Artists

Oh, there are just so many. Celine Dion requires a children's choir with 20 to 24 children of all races. Pavarotti demands that there be no noise backstage or distinct smells anywhere near him; but he does want a golf cart. Cher simply can't perform without a wig room, cable TV that gets Turner Classic Movies, and a room for her massage therapist. "Weird Al" Yankovic is a strict vegan and forbids Dasani water. Elton John demands that his dressing room be kept at 60° in summer and 70° in winter. And Busta Rhymes insists that there be no pork or beef anywhere near his dressing room; but he does want a 24-piece bucket of KFC and a box of Rough Riders condoms (ribbed).

Hoaxing Hoaxers and the Hoaxes They Play: Greatest Hoaxes of All Time

Fool me once, shame on me. Fool me twice, well, shame on me again. But fool me 245 times, come on now! So, why do hoaxes work so well, and why are people always willing to fall for them? Well, maybe it's because there's a sucker born every minute. Of course, if you believe P. T. Barnum really said that, there's a sidebar waiting for you on page 11.

_01:: The "Computer" That Outsmarted Napoléon

Centuries before Deep Blue started whuppin' on Russian grand masters, a chess-playing automaton nicknamed "the Turk" was thrashing all manner of chess players. Atop a wheeled wooden cabinet was a seated, life-sized mannequin made of wood and dressed in Turkish garb. The Turk held a chessboard in his wooden lap, and he beat 'most all comers—including Napoléon Bonaparte and Benjamin Franklin. Premiering in the 1770s, the creation of Wolfgang von Kempelen moved its wooden arms, seemingly without human assistance, around the board. The secret? The Turk's arms were operated by a diminutive chess expert crouched inside the cabinet, who operated gears and pulleys to move the Turk's arms. After traveling the world for almost a century, the Turk ended up mothballed in Philadelphia—where it was destroyed in a fire in 1854.

_02:: Microsoft Buys the Catholic Church!

While the pranksters are still unknown, few press releases have had the impact of the 1994 doozy sent out supposedly by Microsoft, announcing Bill Gates's purchase of the Catholic

Church. As reported, Microsoft not only would get sole electronic rights to the good book, but also would pitch in to the church's efforts, namely by engineering a means for delivering the sacraments online. Needless to say, the prank tricked a few folks. So many customers rang up Microsoft in protest that the distraught company finally felt obligated to clear up the mess via (you guessed it!) another press release. The statement full-out denied the allegations, and further said that it hoped to alleviate customer concerns by declaring that the company had no intentions of purchasing any religious institutions, Catholic or otherwise. Of course, it wasn't long before another "press release" surfaced, this one touting IBM's response to Microsoft: a merger with the Episcopal Church.

_03:: **This Is Your Brain on Bananas**

When the alternative newspaper the *Berkeley Barb* published a satirical article in 1967 claiming that smoking dried banana peels could lead to intoxication, they never expected to be taken seriously. But the oh-so-square national news media didn't get the joke, and publicized the report throughout the nation. Since then, countless wayward teens have been duped into smoking bananas (which can make you nauseated, but not pleasantly so). The hoax really took off, though, in 1970 with the publication of William Powell's *The Anarchist's Cookbook,* which covers all manner of craft pleasantries from building pipe bombs to manufacturing LSD. Not surprisingly, it also provides a recipe for turning your banana peels into "a fine, black powder" suitable for

smoking. Even though no one's ever gotten high from bananas (although they are a great energy fruit, according to Dr. Atkins!), the *Barb*'s hoax has had a stunning shelf life.

Touch of Evil

In 1994, computer users worldwide panicked over the "Good Times" virus, which was spread by an AOL user and was able to "erase your hard drive" if you even read the corresponding e-mail message. Luckily, it was just a big hoax.

_04:: **The *Social Text* Fiasco**

In 1996, the respected cultural studies journal *Social Text* published several complex and dense articles, mainly because that's what respected academic journals do. But one, "Transgressing the Boundaries: Toward a Transformative Hermeneutics of Quantum Physics," was a hoax by NYU physics professor Alan Sokal, who sought to prove that academic journals will publish any paper that uses big words. To the extent that Sokal's article is readable, it makes a grandly silly argument about the political implications of quantum gravity. Among other ludicrous assertions, the article claims that physical reality does not exist, that the laws of physics are social constructs, and that feminism has implications for mathematical set theory. It's hilarious, if you like that kind of thing, but it's also utter nonsense. After Sokal revealed his hoax in *Lingua Franca,* many academic journals beefed up their peer review process.

Mandatory Fashion Trends

If you've ever been in a marching band, the Rockettes, or even a parochial school, you know what it's like to be told how to dress. Of course, getting those orders from a band director or a nun is a little different from being told what to wear by a snazzy dictator and his fashion police. The following are four mandatory fashions, instructed to be worn with pride.

_01:: Queue It Up

The braided pigtail, or queue, which became a worldwide stereotype of Chinese commoners, wasn't so much a Chinese fashion statement as it was a Manchu style. So, why the braid? The initial hairstyle edict occurred during the reign of Emperor Shunzhi in 1654, but since Shunzhi was only eight years old, the law—requiring all Chinese men to wear their hair in a long braid—was actually the work of his uncle and regent, Dorgon. Shunzhi and Dorgon were members of the Qing dynasty, the last dynastic family to rule China (until 1912). But they weren't ethnically Chinese. Since they were from what became known as Manchuria (today a northeastern region of China), forcing people to wear the Manchu hairdo helped indicate who was subservient to the emperor.

_02:: Shaving Grace

Czar Peter I dragged reluctant Russians kicking and screaming into the 18th century after he became sole ruler in 1696. He did not, however, drag them by their beards. Peter's far-reaching reforms involved trade, agriculture, shipbuilding, and more, but Russians became most upset when their "forward thinking" emperor said men should look more like their smooth-faced European neighbors to the west. At the time, the traditional Russian style was a long beard, never trimmed (not even the mustache), worn with close-cropped hair. Beyond the politics of style, though, men were proud of their beards, and many believed that a man wouldn't be admitted to heaven without one. Peter finally decided that every gentleman (nobles, landowners) who kept a beard would have to pay for it: a tax of 100 rubles a year if he kept the bush. A commoner, on the other hand, had to pay a kopek. In other crimes of fashion (or misdemeanors in this case), Peter also taxed traditionally long Russian coats to encourage the adoption of a shorter, above-the-knee French style.

_03:: Suit Yourself

You know the Mao suit: four patch pockets on the jacket front, a turndown collar, five to seven front buttons. And while Westerners link it to China's smiling chairman, its originator was actually Sun Zhongshan (also spelled Sun Yixian or Sun Yat-sen). Dr. Sun, as he was known in the West, ordered the new fashion for the Republic of China (1911–1949) and required civil servants to wear the suit beginning in the 1920s. Among other things, Mao Zedong usurped the fashion statement, and the Communist leader continued wearing it after the 1949 revolution. Millions of Chinese followed suit (literally), as the unisex style became a proud symbol of proletarian humility and Chinese unity. Essentially it became a style mandate: unless you wanted to draw attention to yourself (not the best idea in a totalitarian state), you wore the suit. When Mao died in 1976, though, fashions began to diversify.

_04:: Ankle Management

Throughout history, many religious authorities have dictated proper ways to dress. It's not surprising, though, that when state and religious authorities are identical, as in turn-of-the-21st-century Afghanistan, such dictates become law. The short-lived Taliban government took Muslim social conservatism to such extremes that women and girls could not go outside the home without a head-to-toe burqa—a dark-colored garment with a three-inch rectangle of mesh over the eyes—the only opening. Also on the taboo list: bright colors, cosmetics, and high-heeled shoes. In fact, women couldn't wear any shoes that made noise when they walked. And if an inch of ankle showed under the burqa hem, a woman could be beaten on the street for the violation. Men, meanwhile, could be beaten, jailed, or worse for wearing a beard of insufficient length or otherwise offending the government.

Lies Your Mother Told You

NAPOLÉON WAS A SHRIMP

Momma done led you astray again: While Napoléon wasn't exactly a big man, he wasn't "tiny," either. So, how'd the myth start? Pretty simple, really. The French foot measured 1.067877 English feet, or roughly 13 inches. So, in the French system of measurement, Napoléon was 5 feet 2 inches, but in the British system (which Americans still use today), he stood roughly 5 feet 6 inches, or about 168 centimeters. At the time, that wasn't much shorter than the average man, who stood about 5 feet 8 inches. All the stuff about Napoléon being so "little" may also stem from the fact that his royal guard was made up of 6-footers, making him look small by comparison. Political critics in France liked to perpetuate the idea that he was little (he also had a slight build) while simultaneously making fun of his short, military-style haircut. They called him *le petit tondu* ("the little crop-head"). The exaggerated notion of his diminutive stature may also be rooted in the contempt in which he was held by his enemies. After all, victors do tend to write history.

I Must Be the Greatest—
Writers Who Fancied Themselves Peerless

Book writing requires a certain measure of confidence—even great authors get repeatedly rejected by publishers. Afraid he'd die in World War I, F. Scott Fitzgerald quickly wrote "The Romantic Egotist," which was praised but rejected. But Fitzgerald, something of a romantic egotist himself, persevered. As did these egotists.

_01:: James Joyce (1882–1941)

The only time W. B. Yeats and James Joyce, the titans of 20th-century Irish literature, met, a young, unpublished Joyce told the 30-something Yeats, "We have met too late. You are too old for me to have any effect on you." From the beginning, clearly, Joyce admired his own genius, and his self-admiration only grew with time, as we see in his semiautobiographical masterpiece *A Portrait of the Artist as a Young Man.* Preparing to leave Ireland at the end of the novel (as Joyce did in 1902, at the age of 20), *Portrait's* hero, Stephen Dedalus, announces that he is off "to forge in the smithy of my soul the uncreated conscience of my race." A heady task for a kid who ought to still be in college, but Joyce eventually managed it—*Ulysses* is, most would agree, the Great Irish Novel.

_02:: Dante (1265–1321)

Fortunately for Dante Alighieri, who wrote *The Divine Comedy,* the proud only go to Purgatory. The *Inferno* section of Dante's afterlife epic depicts the poet Virgil taking Dante on a rip-roaring road trip through the nine circles of hell. In Canto IV, they find themselves in the first circle in the company of the greatest poets of antiquity—Homer, Horace, Ovid, and Lucan. In Dante's none-too-humble imagining of the scene, the poets "invited me to join their ranks" (although Dante does save a bit of face by claiming his position as the least among the Greats). In reality, though, Dante could never have chatted with Homer, nor did he ever read Homer's work. At the time, neither the *Iliad* nor the *Odyssey* had been translated, and Mr. Fancypants Dante couldn't read or speak Greek.

_03:: Walt Whitman (1819–1892)

He celebrated himself; he sung himself; he quite clearly liked himself. Walt Whitman's Great American Poem "Song of Myself" features the word *I* a stunning 487 times, so it's perhaps odd that when he self-published the first edition of *Leaves of Grass,* it named neither a publisher nor an author. (In a sacrifice to his ego, however, Whitman placed a sizable portrait of himself on the front cover.) "Song of Myself" is not simply an egotistical poem, of course—it's a celebration of humanity itself—as represented by Walt Whitman. After all, Walt was seeking to both reveal his tender soul and be crowned the great poet of the young nation he so loved. And, indeed, if we are half as confident when we sing of ourselves as Whitman was, America is a proud country indeed.

_04:: William Faulkner (1897–1962)

William Faulkner was not the sort of humble southerner who downplays the difficulty of his work. In his Nobel Prize acceptance speech, Faulkner called his career "a life's work in the agony and sweat of the human spirit." Of course, Faulkner knew his hard work had paid off—whenever asked to name the greatest living writers, he always included himself without embarrassment. In fact, he passionately sought to accomplish the impossible goal of the perfect literary creation, and often attacked lesser writers (we're looking at you, Ernest Hemingway) for having a paucity of "moral courage" when it came to taking chances with narrative style. But while he believed his books were great, Faulkner maintained a strange kind of humility, arguing that the work mattered but the author didn't. "If I had not existed," he said, "someone else would have written me."

_05:: Ayn Rand (1905–1982)

The egoist's egoist, author Ayn Rand (born Alissa Zinovievna Rosenbaum) is the patron saint of Thinking You're Better than Everybody Else. Her most famous novels, *The Fountainhead* and *Atlas Shrugged,* are massive dramatizations of objectivism, an Oscar the Grouch philosophy that champions ego and accomplishment, shuns all religion as folly, and condemns any form of charity or altruism as counterproductive to society. Ever the optimist, Rand created protagonists, invariably men, who were shunned by others because of their genius but then persevered over the foolishness of morons to prove said genius and emerge triumphant. Not surprisingly, she saw humility as weakness and regarded laughing at yourself as "spitting in your own face." So, just how much did Rand believe in her own philosophy? Let's just say a lot. With typical Randian modesty, she ranked herself right up there as a philosophical equal of Aristotle and Thomas Aquinas.

Touch of Evil

The anonymously published novels Zabeebah and the King *and* The Impregnable Fortress *are thought to have been written by Saddam Hussein. Lackluster sales of the latter improved after Iraqi newspapers printed 200-plus glowing reviews that praised the book and its "prodigious author."*

Pre-Madonna Prima Donnas: Artists Who Were Full of Themselves

They say a lot of artistic expression is motivated by self-loathing. Not for these folks. These puffed-up virtuosos didn't just think they could walk on water; they knew they could. Here are a few creative types who raised egotism to an art form all its own.

_01:: Frank Lloyd Wright (1867–1959)

Frank Lloyd Wright may be *the* genius of 20th-century architecture. And boy, did he know it. The designer of the Robie House (Chicago), Fallingwater (Bear Run, Pennsylvania), Taliesin West (Scottsdale, Arizona), the Guggenheim Museum (New York), and countless other buildings was notorious for his belief in his superiority to mere mortals. In fact, the architectural egomaniac frequently acted as if the rules did not apply to him, including the rules of geography and climate. But when you're Wright, you're Wright. After Wright was commissioned in 1935 to design a Dallas home for department store magnate Stanley Marcus, the project quickly went sour when he insisted that his client sleep outdoors year-round on "sleeping porches." He also decreed that the Marcuses' small bedroom "cubicles" would have almost no closet space.

_02:: Salvador Dalí (1904–1989)

"Every morning when I awake, the greatest of joy is mine: that of being Salvador Dalí." Yep, he really said it. Everything about the legendary surrealist (he of the melting clocks), from his whacked-out paintings to his curled-up mustache, was designed to shock, destroy convention, cause scandal, and stir up controversy. If he wasn't getting enough attention, he was known to walk the streets of New York City clanging a handbell. In fact, Dalí once said, "The thought of not being recognized [is] unbearable." Not surprising when you consider that the man criticized for choosing to live in Franco's fascist Spain defended his position by stating that he didn't care about others so long as he himself could be king. Not exactly a man of the people. Need another telling quote? "At the age of six years I wanted to be a chef. At the age of seven I wanted to be Napoléon. My ambitions have continued to grow at the same rate ever since." Apparently, so did his ego.

_03:: Alfred Hitchcock (1899–1980)

Hitchcock was, without question, one of the towering geniuses of cinema. But like many geniuses, he wasn't exactly the best collaborator. In fact, he was particularly trying for screenwriters, who never felt he properly credited them for their work, and notoriously hard on actors (he was very outspoken in his negative opinion of Kim Novak's performance in *Vertigo*). He was even quoted as saying, "Actors are cattle." The quip stirred up such a huge outcry (actors can be so touchy) that he issued this correction: "I have been misquoted. What I really said is: Actors should be *treated* as cattle." Although it began by accident (he was short an actor for the film *The Lodger*), he soon made it his trademark to appear in his own films, amassing a total of 37 such cameos over his career.

_04:: Orson Welles (1915–1985)

When you create *Citizen Kane*—still considered by many the greatest film ever made—at the ripe old age of 26, you're going to get a bit of a big head. But Welles was pretty much convinced of his own importance well before then. In fact, it's said that he created *Citizen Kane* as a withering exposé of newspaper mogul William Randolph Hearst because Hearst slighted Welles at a dinner party. Bruised ego indeed. And as his body grew, so did his arrogance. Do yourself a favor: track down a recording of Welles's outtakes for a TV commercial for frozen peas. You'll hear everything you need to know about his oversized ego. Here's one classic quote from the outtakes: "In the *depths* of your *ignorance,* what is it you want?"

_05:: Al Jolson (1886–1950)

Lots of performers have been labeled "the world's greatest entertainer." But Jolson really, *really* believed it. The greatest star of vaudeville, the singer, actor, dancer, and comedian was born Asa Yoelson in Seredzius, Lithuania (Srednike in Russian), a Jewish shtetl in what was then part of imperial Russia. He was known for hijacking the action in the middle of shows, ad-libbing, or just stopping to talk to the audience. During a 1911 performance of the critically hated *Paris Is a Paradise for Coons* (title not edited for political correctness), Jolson stopped and asked the audience if they'd rather hear him sing than see the rest of the play. They roared their approval, and Jolson ditched the whole program and took over. From that moment on, no one else could really share the stage with him. Unlike some on this list, however, Jolson can be forgiven somewhat for his huge ego; from most contemporary accounts, he really *was* the greatest in the world. Despite the enormity of his contributions to stage and screen, Jolson's image remains a political hot potato because of his use of stage blackface (considered repellent now, but pretty common for the times).

Secret Societies That Ain't All That Secret

Is it possible that so many societies can proudly claim so many powerful and influential people and still be called "secret"? Well, no. Here are six of the most famous of the world's supposedly secret societies. But if anyone asks, you didn't hear this from us.

_01:: The Freemasons

This is the granddaddy of all not-so-secret secret societies. Freemasonry, or "The Craft" as its members call it, most likely has its roots in 17th-century stoneworkers' guilds. Mason lore, however, extends its origins back to biblical times, linking the society to the building of the Temple of Solomon. Freemasonry is split into numerous subgroups and orders, all of which consider God the Grand Geometrician, or Grand Architect of the Universe. At their hearts, these groups are all means of exploring ethical and philosophical issues, and their rituals and symbols are famous (or infamous). Take, for instance, the square-and-compass logo often seen on the backs of Cadillacs. Or the use of secret handshakes, passwords, and greeting postures/gestures called "due guards," all collectively known as the Modes of Recognition. The list of famous Masons is massive, a virtual Who's Who of modern history, explaining the many conspiracy theories regarding the Masons' influence and intentions. Mozart, FDR, Harry S. Truman, George Washington, Mark Twain, Voltaire, Benjamin Franklin, John Wayne, W. C. Fields, and Douglas MacArthur were all Masons. But perhaps the Masons' greatest strides have been made in fast food: KFC's Colonel Sanders and Wendy's founder Dave Thomas knew how to secret-shake with the best of 'em.

_02:: The Illuminati

Over the centuries, lots of groups have called themselves the Illuminati ("Enlightened Ones"), but the one we're talking about here began as the Bavarian Illuminati. A radical product of the Enlightenment and offshoot of the religion-based Freemasons, the Illuminati espoused secular freethinking and intellectualism and proved a threat to Europe's old order. Although they were officially banned by the Bavarian government in 1784, some claim that they live on to this day in other guises (see "The Trilateral Commission" on page 18). So, what's the Illuminati's goal? To establish a new world order of capitalism and authoritarianism, of course! They've been accused of manipulating currencies, world stock markets, elections, assassinations, and even of being aliens. One common myth is that the eye-and-pyramid image on the dollar bill is a symbol of the Illuminati watching over us. Nope. It's a symbol of strength and durability (though unfinished, symbolizing growth and change), and the all-seeing eye represents the divine guidance of the American cause. Or so the government says.

_03:: Opus Dei

This organization has a $42 million, 17-story headquarters building on Lexington Avenue in New York City, claims 85,000 members in 60 countries, and was featured in Dan Brown's bestseller *The Da Vinci Code*. Now that its existence has been significantly unsecretized, this ultraorthodox Catholic sect has definitely raised its share of eyebrows. Founded in 1928 by Saint Josemaría Escrivá (a Spanish priest who bore an uncanny resemblance to Karl Malden), Opus Dei is the short name for the Prelature for the Holy Cross and the Work of God. The sect (some would say cult) stresses a return to traditional Catholic orthodoxy and behavior, especially celibacy, with members falling into one of three levels. Numeraries live in Opus Dei facilities, devote their time and money to the prelature, attend mass daily, and engage in mortification of the flesh (wearing a spiked chain around the thigh called a *cilice*, taking cold showers, or flagellating themselves with a knotted rope called "the discipline"). Next come Associates (kind of like Numeraries, but living "off campus"), then Supernumeraries (the rank-and-file members). The group did gain the praise of Pope John Paul II, and has engaged in a lot of charity work. Yet, critics accuse the group of being linked to fascist organizations like Franco's government in Spain, and of anti-Semitism and intolerance, even of other Catholics.

_04:: Skull and Bones

Top dog among all the collegiate secret societies, Yale's Skull and Bones dates to 1832 and goes by other spooky names like Chapter 322 and the Brotherhood of Death. With a large number of Bonesmen who have attained positions of power, including the president and the head of the CIA, it's no wonder that rumors abound that the society is hell-bent on obtaining power and influencing U.S. foreign policy. The fact that they meet in an imposing templelike building on the Yale campus called (what else?) the Tomb doesn't really help. Bonesmen are selected, or "tapped," during their junior year and can reveal their membership only after they've graduated. But they can never talk about it. The Bones have been accused of all sorts of crazy rituals and conspiracies, including drug smuggling and the assassination of JFK (a hated *Hahvahd* man, after all). It's even rumored that the skull of Geronimo resides in the Tomb, stolen from its resting place by Prescott Bush, Dubya's granddad. In one of the more commonly known rituals, the initiate spends all night naked in an open coffin, confessing all his sexual experiences to the group. So, who's lucky enough to have made such a confession? George H. W. Bush, George W. Bush, John Kerry, William Howard Taft, McGeorge Bundy, William F. Buckley, and Henry Luce are just a few.

_05:: The Bohemian Club

This is a weird one. In the majestic forests of Sonoma County north of San Francisco lies the Bohemian Grove, the 2,700-acre wooded retreat of the Bohemian Club, the nation's most exclusive men's club. Every July since 1879, the "Bohos" have gathered at the Grove for a two-week encampment, where they're divided into more than 100 residential camps with names like Owl's Nest, Cave Man, and Lost Angels. Membership has included, well, just about everybody important: Ronald Reagan, Dwight Eisenhower, Richard Nixon (who once called it "faggy"), Gerald Ford, Colin Powell, Dick Cheney, and many CEOs and wealthy business leaders like Malcolm Forbes. Each encampment opens with a robed-and-hooded ceremony called the Cremation of Care, in which an effigy called "Dull Care" (symbolizing worldly concerns) is burned before a 40-foot concrete statue of an owl, symbol of wisdom and the club's mascot. Throughout the week, plays are staged (called High Jinx and Low Jinx), there's lots of eating and drinking (and, reportedly, urinating on trees), and members are treated to speeches called Lakeside Talks. Some opponents go so far as to accuse the group of Satanism, witchcraft, homosexuality, and prostitution, while more reasonable observers object to the Lakeside Talks as national policy discussions to which the public is not privy. But above all, it's seen as a way that some of the elite meet others of the elite, thereby ensuring that they'll all stay elite. All this makes the club's seemingly anticonspiratorial slogan—"Weaving spiders, come not here"—that much more ironic.

_06:: The Trilateral Commission

While not, on its face, as juicily sinister as some of the other societies on this list, the Tri-

lateral Commission has been accused of all sorts of underhanded shenanigans by its critics. Formed in 1973 by David Rockefeller, the Commission includes over 300 prominent citizens from Europe, Asia, and North America in a forum for discussing the regions' common interests. But conspiracy theorists hold that the Trilateral Commission, along with the Council on Foreign Relations and others, is really just a front for a larger, more sinister order called the Round Table Groups, founded in London over 100 years ago and bent on the creation of a new world order, a global capitalist police state. Yikes! (For the record, some say the Round Table Groups are themselves just fronts for *another* society, the Illuminati, so who knows?) American members of the Trilateral Commission have included Bill Clinton, Henry Kissinger, Jimmy Carter, Dick Cheney, and Dianne Feinstein.

Worst Miscalculations of All Time

To err is human, but to really screw up you need to think you know exactly what you're doing first.

_01:: Columbus and the Indies

Pepper used to be one of the most valuable substances in Europe, mainly because it was

effective in masking the taste of spoiled foods. But since it came from the "East Indies," or the modern-day countries of Southeast Asia, it took forever to get there and back over land. Enter Christopher Columbus, who was sure that the earth was round and that he could therefore sail west across the Atlantic Ocean to the Indies. Only problem: he got the math very, very wrong. Aside from using the calculations of French cartographer Pierre d'Ailly, which vastly underestimated the distance around the globe from the European side to Asia, Columbus also misread maps, believing that "miles" referred to the 5,000-foot Roman mile rather than the 6,082-foot nautical mile. So Columbus believed the circumference of the planet at the equator was 19,000 miles rather than 24,600 miles. Hiding in the missing 5,600 miles, of course, were North and South America.

_02:: Chernobyl

Ironically, the catastrophic 1986 explosion at the Chernobyl nuclear plant began with an experiment to increase reactor safety. As part of the experiment, engineers had to slowly power the reactor down—kind of like "idling" a car engine. But they reduced energy production too quickly, and the reaction was "poisoned" by an increase in neutron absorption. Rather than wait 24 hours to restore energy production, as recommended, the head engineer decided to remove graphite control rods to get power back up because he was impatient, eventually leaving just six rather than the minimum of 30 decreed by operating manuals. Shortly after, when the engineers cut energy to the cooling system, coolant water heated up and quickly began to boil. The water had stabilized the reactor by absorbing neutrons, but when it turned to steam it was less effective. Further, because the rods had been withdrawn they no longer moderated the power production. When the production suddenly spiked, engineers started an emergency process to push all the graphite control rods back into the reactor core and stop the reaction, but because of a small design flaw with the graphite caps on the ends of the rods the exact opposite happened. The reactor overheated almost instantaneously and exploded, and approximately 50 tons of nuclear fuel vaporized into the atmosphere.

Touch of Evil

In 1999, the $125 million Mars Climate Orbiter burned and disintegrated prior to landing. After NASA investigated, simple "bad data" was shown to have caused the mishap. The gaffe? Engineers accidentally mixed up metric units with English units in certain calculations.

_03:: Custer's Last Stand

In 1876, to destroy the Sioux resistance and force them onto a reservation, the U.S. government sent three commanders—Generals Crooks, Terry, and Gibbon—to converge on the Ogalala Sioux encampment at Little Bighorn in Montana. Lieutenant General George Armstrong Custer was serving under Terry's command, and unbeknownst to Custer, by the time he arrived, other Sioux tribes had more than doubled the size of the village, bringing it to 7,000 inhabitants. After an initial skirmish Custer was afraid that the Sioux would retreat before he could attack, so he split up his command of 657 men into three groups—a fatal mistake—and attempted to surround them. When he finally located the village, he led his troops in an all-out assault, saying "Don't worry, boys—there's enough of them for all of us!" Indeed there were. Things turned bad very quickly, as the Sioux spread the alarm. In the end, Custer made his famous "Last Stand" with about 100 men on a small hill near the village, facing 1,500 Sioux warriors. A total of 263 men died that day, the worst defeat ever inflicted by Native Americans on the U.S. military.

_04:: The Big Dig

Boston's "Big Dig" is the most ambitious urban infrastructure project ever undertaken in the United States—but it's become infamous for cost overruns and schedule delays that can be measured in geologic time. Aiming to take Boston's highways and relocate them to tunnels, the Big Dig hoped to spur new development and revitalization. In fact, early on, plans were also added to build a new tunnel under Boston Harbor to Boston's international airport in the east. The price of the project? $2.6 billion, with a project completion date predicted for 1997 or 1998. Because of geologic conditions, design mistakes, shoddy construction work, and frequent public opposition, however, the Big Dig is still going on, with a price tag of over $14.6 billion. What's more, tunnels have sprung hundreds of mysterious leaks, cutting off traffic, and construction has lowered the water table, potentially damaging buildings as they settle. How Boston digs itself out of this one is yet to be seen.

_05:: Draining of the Aral Sea

Shortly after the Russian Revolution in 1917, Soviet planners started diverting water from two large rivers in Central Asia—the Amu Darya and the Syr Darya—to turn Central Asian deserts into fertile cotton plantations. And the project was successful! Except...the

---

It's a Mad, Mad, Mad, Mad, Mad Artist

TALENTS WHO WERE TOO HARD ON THEMSELVES

It's hard to imagine a greater artistic success than Leonardo da Vinci, but the original Renaissance man was a notoriously harsh judge of himself—his last words are reported to have been "I have offended God and mankind because my work didn't reach the quality it should have." The famously depressed Sylvia Plath's will to perfection led to a Leonardian sense of disappointment in her own work. She frequently felt like a failure, and one of her first suicide attempts (at which she also failed) occurred after she was rejected from a fiction-writing class at Harvard. And John Kennedy Toole, author of the brilliant comic romp *A Confederacy of Dunces*, fared no better. Toole wasn't entirely humble (he felt that the book was a masterpiece), but after it was rejected by a publisher, Toole believed he would never be anything but a failed writer, so he committed suicide in 1969. After Toole's death, his mother took the book to the novelist Walker Percy, who reluctantly read it and was surprised to enjoy it. *Dunces* was finally published in 1980 and went on to win the Pulitzer Prize for fiction.

only problem was that the rivers were the sole source of water for the Aral Sea, the second-largest lake in the world. Other rivers were supposed to be diverted to compensate but as the Soviet economy declined, those projects never got under way. By 1960, between 20 and 50 cubic *kilometers* of water were being diverted from the sea every year; during the 1960s, the sea level dropped by an average of 20 centimeters a year, during the 1970s 50–60 centimeters a year, and during the 1980s 80–90 centimeters a year. Currently the sea has lost about 80% of its volume, and 60% of its surface area, and is expected to disappear entirely in the near future.

_06:: Vietnam and Casualty Burdens

One persistent question remains about Vietnam: How could the U.S. government and military make such a bad blunder? Much of the responsibility lies with the top brass at the Pentagon, including Secretary of Defense Robert McNamara, appointed by President John F. Kennedy in 1960, who believed that if American forces killed a certain number of the enemy, their economy would break down and resistance would collapse. However, these calculations proved disastrously wrong. Because they believed they were fighting for their independence, the North Vietnamese absorbed at least one million casualties. After the war, American officials still didn't get it. General William Westmoreland, the highest-ranking American commander during the war, said, "An American commander who took the same losses . . . would have been sacked overnight." Later McNamara himself said, "What I thought was that a very high rate of casualties would soften them up for negotiations. They paid no attention whatsoever to casualties. It had no impact at all militarily, and it had no impact on negotiations."

Bigger Is Better:
Insane Soviet Projects

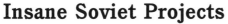

The Soviet Union decided the best way to show up the West was through building the biggest version of any given object. The following are just seven of the largest examples.

_01:: Magnitogorsk

Whether it was for guns, tanks, ships, railroads, or bridges, Stalin, whose name means "Man of Steel," knew he needed one thing above all else for his 1920s Soviet Union: steel. He also knew that to the east, in the southern Ural Mountains, there was a unique geologic oddity named Magnitka—an entire mountain of pure iron ore, the key ingredient for steel. In 1929, Stalin decreed that a city, "Magnitogorsk" (see what he did there?), be built from scratch around said mountain to mine the ore and turn it into steel. So began one of the largest construction projects ever undertaken. With expertise provided by Communist sympathizers from the West, a ready-made city for 450,000 inhabitants was constructed in about five years. Of course, Stalin saved on labor costs by having the heavy lifting done by political prisoners. In fact, 30,000 people died in the effort. Steel production began in 1934, but shortly after World War II the iron ore ran out and the city's economy collapsed.

_02:: The Baltic–White Sea Canal

Ever the optimist, this time Stalin wanted to connect the Baltic Sea, with its key port of Leningrad, to the White Sea's port of Archangelsk. The idea was that he could move the Soviet navy fleets back and forth. So Stalin had more political prisoners sent to work on the canal—there was a seemingly endless supply from the gulags—and after a few brutal years it was completed in 1933. Disease, poor nutrition, and brutal conditions took a huge toll, though, with as many as 250,000 of the slave laborers dead by the end of it. The icing on the cake? The canal was completely useless when finished. For most of its length it was too shallow to admit anything larger than a small barge. Later a book of propaganda detailing the biographies of "heroic" workers and engineers, intended for distribution in capitalist countries, had to be recalled because in the downtime Stalin had ordered all the main characters shot.

_03:: The World's Largest Hydrofoil

The world's largest hydrofoil wasn't really a hydrofoil at all. In fact, it was one of a series of unique machines called "ground effect" vehicles built by the Soviet Union beginning in the 1960s. The Soviets had a monopoly on this fascinating technology, relying on a little-known principle of physics—the "ground effect"—in which a dense cushion of air hugging the ground can provide more lift to a vehicle than air at higher altitudes. Hovering about 3–12 feet above the ground, these vehicles resemble Luke Skywalker's levitating craft from *Star Wars,* and are far more fuel-efficient than airplanes, helicopters, hydrofoils, or cars. And at 58 feet, the largest of these, the "Caspian Sea Monster" was given its distinctive name after CIA analysts saw it at the Caspian port of Baku in photos taken by spy satellites. The craft traveled at speeds of up to 240 mph, had a swiveling nose cone for cargo loading, and could carry up to as many as 150 passengers.

_04:: Avant-garde Design for a Funkier Parliament

Designed by Vladimir Tatlin (1885–1953) in 1920, the *Monument to the Third International* was a gigantic spiraling iron structure intended to house the new Soviet government. Taller than the Eiffel Tower (and the yet-to-be constructed Empire State Building) at more than 1,300 feet, this curving, funnel-shaped structure was meant to encase three successively smaller assembly areas rotating on industrial bearings at different speeds, faster or slower according to their importance. Rotating once a year in the lowest level was a giant cube for delegates attending the Communist International from all over the world. A smaller pyramid, rotating once a month above it, would house the Communist Party's executives. The third level—a sphere rotating once daily—would house communications technology to spread propaganda, including a telegraph office, radio station, and movie screen.

Unfortunately the giant structure would have required more iron than the entire Soviet Union produced in a year, and was never built.

_05:: A Palace for the People

In 1931, Joseph Stalin ordered that the largest Orthodox Christian cathedral in the world—335 feet high, the product of 44 years of back-breaking labor by Russian peasants—be dynamited so he could build an enormous "Palace of the People," to celebrate the Communist Party. Stalin wished to replace the church with a new structure taller than the Empire State Building, and capped with a gilded statue of Lenin taller than the Statue of Liberty, but the "Man of Steel's" mad scheme never came to fruition. Although the first phase was completed (the dynamiting was the easy bit), the construction never took place as necessary resources were diverted to fighting World War II. After Stalin died, his successor—Nikita Khrushchev—ordered a large swimming pool built where the cathedral had stood. Old women who remembered the original cathedral could be seen standing at the edge of the swimming pool, praying to forgotten icons. Recently Yury Luzhkov, Moscow's autocratic mayor, tried to make up for Stalin's mess by ordering the construction of a tacky reproduction of the original cathedral using precast concrete.

_06:: The World's Largest Hydrogen Bomb

Truth is always stranger than fiction, so it's no wonder that Stanley Kubrick's absurd comedy *Dr. Strangelove* is actually premised on fact. The strange truth here was that Nikita Khrushchev and company had actually been plotting to build a "doomsday" device. The plan called for a large cargo ship anchored off the Soviet Union's east coast to be loaded with hundreds of hydrogen bombs. If at any point the radiation detectors aboard the ship measured a certain amount of atmospheric radiation, indicating that the Soviet Union had been attacked, the bombs would detonate. Soviet scientists persuaded Khrushchev to drop this mad scheme. He did, however, order the construction of the world's largest nuclear bomb in 1961, the so-called "Czar Bomba" ("King of Bombs"), which weighed in at about 100 megatons—equivalent to 100 million tons of TNT. The largest nuclear test involved a smaller version of "Czar Bomba" that measured somewhere between 50 and 57 megatons—the Soviets weren't sure themselves.

Touch of Evil

Sociologists, historians, and cultural theorists have all written about the Soviet obsession with making things as big as possible, whether they be factories, vehicles, cities, dams, bombs, farms, or anything else. The large size was intended to convey the might, authority, and technical expertise of the Soviet Union, especially in comparison with capitalist countries.

_07:: World's Largest Icebreaker, the *Yamal*

And it's the world's only nuclear-powered icebreaker at that! Confronted with the world's largest piece of ice—the Arctic Ocean—the Soviets had no intention of letting nature stand in their way. So, they came up with a simple solution: the world's largest icebreakers. The first included the Lenin and Arktika class of nuclear-powered icebreakers, introduced in 1959 and 1975, respectively. The Arktika icebreakers had not one but *two* nuclear reactors, powering 75,000-horsepower engines. None compare with the newest vessel, however—the *Yamal*—launched in 1993. Also powered by two nuclear reactors, it measures in at 490 feet long, displacing 23,000 tons of water, with a crew of 150 and an armored steel hull 4.8 centimeters thick. Recently reoutfitted for tourist operations, it has 50 luxury cabins, a library, lounge, theater, bar, volleyball court, gymnasium, heated indoor swimming pool, and saunas. A helicopter is stationed on the ship to conduct reconnaissance of ice formations.

A Gentleman Never Tells:
Bodies That've Never Been Found

It's tough to have a real first-class funeral, especially when the guest of honor doesn't seem to show up. And whether the following five individuals are smiling down from above or quietly smirking about their fake demises, none of their bodies made it to the lost-and-found box.

_01:: Ambrose Bierce (1842–1914?)

He was wounded during the Civil War, drank with fellow journalists Mark Twain and H. L. Mencken, and kept a human skull on his desk. Bierce was also a devilishly fine writer who lampooned and skewered just about everyone in the American public eye during the last half of the 19th century. One thing he wasn't, however, was found. In late 1913, Bierce went to Mexico to cover the country's revolution. What happened to him when he got there is a mystery. Theories include: he was killed at the Battle of Ojinaga; he was executed by the revolutionary leader Pancho Villa; he shot himself at the Grand Canyon. Any of those ends would have doubtless suited Bierce. Death by bullet, he wrote before leaving for Mexico, "beats old age, disease, or falling down the cellar stairs."

_02:: Joseph F. Crater (1889–????)

On the evening of August 6, 1930, a New York Supreme Court associate justice stepped into a New York City taxi—and became a synonym for "missing person." When Crater didn't show up for court on August 25, a massive search was launched. But no trace of the judge was ever found. There were reports he was killed by the jealous boyfriend of a chorus girl, or by crooked politicians who feared what Crater knew. Conversely, there were rumors that he fled the country to avoid a judicial corruption probe. After 10 years, Crater was declared dead. But by then he'd already become a staple of pop culture: Groucho Marx would sometimes end his nightclub act by saying he "was stepping out [to] look for Judge Crater."

_03:: Amelia Earhart (1897–1937?)

It was the second time around when Earhart and her navigator, Fred Noonan, took off in May 1937 to try to circle the world in a custom-built twin-engine plane. A first effort by the famed aviatrix ended in a crash in Hawaii. Undaunted, however, Earhart had completed all but the last three legs of her second journey when the world last heard from her on July 2, and investigations into her fate have been almost ceaseless since then. U.S. government officials say she crashed at sea. Others claim she died on a South Pacific island, was captured and executed by the Japanese military, or lived out her life as a housewife in New Jersey.

_04:: Glenn Miller (1904–1944?)

On December 15, 1944, it was so foggy that Miller reportedly joked, "Even the birds are grounded." Still, the famed bandleader, who had joined the U.S. Army in 1942, boarded a small plane in Bedford, England, bound for Paris to prepare for a troop concert. He never made it. Depending on your level of credulity: the plane crashed in the English Channel; it was knocked down by Allied planes jettisoning bombs before landing; he was killed by the Nazis while on a secret mission; or he died of a heart attack in a Paris brothel. The big money, though, is apparently on the bomb theory. A Royal Air Force logbook indicating "friendly fire" as the cause of Miller's demise sold for about $30,000 at a 1999 auction.

_05:: Harold Holt (1908–1967?)

On December 17, 1967, the ocean was all motion off Portsea, Victoria, but Australian politician Harold Holt, known as the "sportsman prime minister," plunged into the surf anyway. The man had been PM for only two years, but sadly, he never came out, and an intensive search failed to turn up a trace. The result? 38 years of rumors: had Holt committed suicide; been assassinated by the CIA; been eaten by a shark; or had he swum out to a waiting Chinese submarine and been spirited away? Without a body, no inquest was held at the time. But in 2004, a change in Australian law prompted a formal inquiry to formally close the case of the missing PM. The ruling? A lackluster verdict to say the least: death by drowning.

Touch of Evil

In a 2003 episode of TV's Mythbusters, New York Giants coach Jim Fassel revealed that there was a "bump" at the 10-yard line near the south end zone of Giants Stadium, where many thought that missing labor leader Jimmy Hoffa's body had been buried. Radar indications showed nothing.

A Big Tower? What an Eiffel Idea!
Structures Built as Symbols of National Pride

Sure, any old nation can prove its global might by going out and subjugating the people of an inferior culture, but which of them can simply hint at their supremacy with a piece of art? A few, actually. The following structures weren't constructed just to insinuate their peoples' greatness to the rest of the world; they were meant to flat out proclaim it.

_01:: Colossus of Rhodes

In the third century BCE, the Macedonians had been laying siege to the Greek city-state of Rhodes for about a year when they finally decided that the war was too expensive and called it off. Failing to clean up after themselves, the Macedonians littered the landscape with various siege machines, which the enterprising Rhodesians made use of by selling off the equipment. Then they used their newfound cash to build a mammoth statue of the sun god Helios to commemorate their victory. The hollow bronze statue, which at 105 feet was not quite as high as the Statue of Liberty, took 12 years to complete. The Colossus stood tall for almost 60 years, until it was felled by an earthquake. Then it took to relaxing, lying around for about another 875 years, until the Arabs invaded Rhodes and sold off the statue's remains. Rhodes's scholars claim it took 900 camels to haul the Colossus away.

_02:: The Eiffel Tower

Vilified in the media as a monstrosity—one critic called it "a metal asparagus"—the Eiffel Tower wasn't supposed to stay up very long after it was built. In fact, it was offered for sale as scrap. It was spared only because the French army found its height made it an excellent communications tower. But Gustav Eiffel's 984-foot-high tribute to the 100th anniversary of the French Revolution welcomed its 200-millionth visitor in 2002, and has become one of the most recognizable man-made landmarks in the world. Constructed as the main attraction of the 1889 International Exposition, the tower was also the impetus behind the main draw at the 1893 World's Columbian Exposition in Chicago. Eager to one-up the French, the Americans unveiled a giant amusement ride named after its inventor—George Ferris.

_03:: Mount Rushmore

Meet America's greatest rock group: George, Tom, Abe, and Teddy. But how exactly did this presidential summit come about? And more important, why South Dakota? The fact is, a South Dakota state historian had a big idea in 1924: turn a cliff in the Black Hills into a tribute to heroes of the Old West. And sculptor John Gutzon de la Mothe Borglum liked the idea, but not the choice of subjects. So, the idea morphed a little, and a quartet of presidential busts was opened to the public in October 1941. Mount Rushmore, which cost about $1 million to build and is the largest American artwork ever created, attracts 27 million visitors a year—even though it was never finished. America got into World War II and funds ran dry. That's why Lincoln is missing an ear. Either that or that's van Gogh up there.

_04:: The Petronas Towers

Statues as national monuments are *so* passé, at least in Malaysia. The Petronas Towers, financed by the country's nationalized oil company and a private developer, are basically very tall office buildings, with a twist. They were built quite consciously as symbols of national pride. "We are showing the world we are a developing, industrialized country," the towers' chief operating officer told the Associated Press in 1995. To make sure the world was listening, though, the builders added spires to the towers to ensure they would be the world's tallest buildings. At 1,483 feet, they surpassed the Sears Tower in Chicago. Not to be outdone, however, in 2003, a spire was placed atop the Taipei 101 (Taipei Financial Center) building, in Taipei, Taiwan, just so it tiptoed above the Malaysian structures. And while Taiwan's building may have inched its way taller on a technicality, the view of Kuala Lumpur is still better at the Petronas.

I Want To See My Face in It:
World Leaders Obsessed with Their Own Images

There's no such thing as a face only a mother could love. After all, with the proper coercion (be it a gavel or a gun), a good tyrant can show you just how adjustable your aesthetic sense can be. Here are five world leaders who were obsessed with their own images, and made sure that their subjects were, too.

_01:: Mausolus (?–353 BCE)

For 24 years, Mausolus ruled over the city-state of Halicarnassus in what is now Turkey, and he spent a lot of time building up the city. So, maybe it was only fitting that in his final years Mausolus built a monument to himself. Mausolus's self-styled memorial wasn't finished until a few years after his death—with his wife, Artemisia I, carrying on the work. But when it was done, it was one of the fanciest tombs the world has ever seen: 140 feet high, 12,000 square feet, and tastefully adorned with tons of giant statues. The tomb stood for 16 centuries before it was toppled by earthquakes. But Mausolus's wish to be remembered did come true. His name is at the root of the word for "grand tomb": mausoleum.

_02:: Julius Caesar (100–44 BCE)

Things were looking pretty darn good for Jules in February 44 BCE. He'd stacked the Roman Senate with yes-men and he'd just changed his job title to "dictator for life." So he figured, what the heck, he'd ignore Roman tradition that prevented the images of living persons on coins of the realm. Caesar's portrait soon appeared on silver denari, along with the inscription "Divus Julius," or "Divine Julius." Alas, "divine" did not equate with "immortal." On March 15, Caesar was stabbed to death by a gang of senators. Pride had indeed gone before the fall. Not everyone was daunted by Caesar's recent stumblings, though. Brutus, the most famous of Caesar's killers, issued his own coins shortly after the assassination.

Touch of Evil

Many believe that stuffy old Richard Nixon won the 1968 presidential election largely due to four words he said on television. Those legendary words? "Sock it to me," uttered on America's counterculture comedy show Rowan & Martin's Laugh-In.

_03:: Nicolae Ceausescu (1918–1989)

Starting in 1965, Ceausescu was dictator of Romania, and boy did everyone know it. Portraits of the man hung everywhere, along with billboards extolling him as the "Genius of the Carpathians." Further still, images of him and his wife (the deputy prime minister) adorned postage stamps, and scores of books they allegedly wrote were crammed on bookstore shelves. But Ceausescu's biggest monument to himself was—insert ironic chuckle here—"the

People's Palace." The second-largest building in the world, after the Pentagon, in terms of area, the complex required the razing of a good part of downtown Bucharest in the late 1980s. Not surprisingly, the "people" weren't impressed. After a revolution and a one-day trial, the "people" took the First Couple out on Christmas Day, 1989, and shot them.

_04:: Saddam Hussein (1937–)

For much of Saddam's 30-year-plus reign, it was probably easier to find something in Iraq that *wasn't* named after the dictator or *didn't* have his likeness on it. There was Saddam International Airport, Saddam Hospital, Saddam Stadium, dozens of palaces, and scores of statues. "Saddam has always been obsessed with building," observed *Time* magazine in 2000. So there was poetic justice on April 9, 2003, when Baghdad residents and U.S. marines pulled down a 40-foot statue of Saddam and triggered a symbolic, although as it turned out very premature, end of the Iraqi war. Still, there is something to be said for notoriety: Saddam portraits and bits of his statues are among the hottest souvenirs of the war.

_05:: Saparmurat Niyazov (1940–)

What can you say about a guy who becomes his country's first president and promptly begins calling himself the "Turkmenbashi," or "father of all Turkmen"? That he has a golden statue of himself in the capital city that rotates so the face is always toward the sun? That his image appears on all the currency? That a book he wrote is the foundation of the educational system? That he renamed one of the months of the year after his mother? Well, yes, if the guy in question is Niyazov, who has been president of Turkmenistan since the Central Asian country broke free from the Soviet Union in 1991. Oh, did we mention the palace of ice he wanted to build in the middle of a desert? We're not kidding.

Pride and Prejudice: Recent Cases Where Diversity Would Have Helped

Discrimination in the workplace is a thing of the past, right? Well, not quite. These corporate giants had to find out the hard way that prejudice doesn't pay . . . though lawsuits certainly do!

_01:: Denny's

Usually associated with round-the-clock sausage links and "Moon Over My Hammy" specials, in the 1990s the name Denny's also became a byword for racism and discrimination lawsuits. Accused of making black patrons prepay for their meals, serving them slower than white patrons or not serving them at all, the national restaurant chain was thick in the midst of an investigation when things got even worse. Four black Secret Service agents who were assigned to protect the president reported not being served while their white colleagues were. In 1993, both the U.S. government and Kristina Ridgeway, a then-17-year-old who was asked to pay a cover charge before being served, brought class action suits against Denny's in California on behalf of all minority patrons nationwide. In 1994, the lawsuit was settled for an estimated $54 million and catapulted Denny's into a cultural transformation. Changes included diversity programs from the board membership on down. The results? Today, 50% of the 46,000 employees are minorities, 32% of supervisory positions are held by minorities, and contracts with minority-owned suppliers have increased from zero to $100 million a year.

_02:: Coca-Cola

In 2000, the Coca-Cola Company shelled out $192.5 million and agreed to establish new programs and reforms to settle a racial discrimination class action lawsuit brought by 2,000 black employees. The lawsuit claimed that Coca-Cola discriminated against black employees in pay, promotions, and performance evaluations. The amount (the largest award ever for a racial discrimination class action lawsuit) included $113 million in cash awards, $43.5 million to adjust salaries, and $36 million to establish oversight programs to monitor the company's employment practices. Talk about being the real thing! Coke also paid $20 million in attorney fees and took a fourth-quarter charge of $188 million against their profits to settle the lawsuit. As part of the agreed changes, a seven-member task force was assembled to examine the company to ensure fair hiring, pay, and other human resource practices until 2004. In late 2004, Coca-Cola requested that the task force supervision remain in effect until the end of 2006. Coca-Cola seems to have learned from its mistakes. Just like they did with New Coke.

Touch of Evil

Southwest Airlines broke their pattern as the "fun airline" when they began enforcing a regulation (from 1980) charging hefty passengers for two seats. Despite pending lawsuits, the rule has now been adopted by other airlines. Don't they know the human body swells at high altitudes?

_03:: Boeing

In 2004, Mary Beck and 11 other women filed a gender discrimination lawsuit against Boeing that triggered a class action lawsuit that included approximately 29,000 former and current employees of the company. Boeing agreed to pay $72.5 million to settle the gender discrimination lawsuit. The company was charged with paying female workers less and giving them fewer promotions than their male counterparts, and it actually took four full years to settle the lawsuit. The suit also contained allegations of sexual harassment, retaliation, and racial discrimination. For example, the plaintiffs claimed that they were consistently denied job training and promotions and reported that when they submitted complaints to the internal Equal Employment Opportunity office they were routinely punished with denial of overtime and other forms of retribution. Under the settlement, Boeing agreed to moni-

tor salaries and overtime assignments and to conduct annual performance reviews. Eligible nonexecutive and hourly female workers, from janitors to first-level managers, got $500 or more depending on when they worked and how much they earned. Mary Beck and the 11 other original plaintiffs were each awarded $100,000. The other women received settlements based on the amount of time they had worked and how much they had earned.

_04:: Morgan Stanley

Without admitting any culpability, in July 2004 Morgan Stanley agreed to pay $54 million, out of court, to settle claims that it didn't promote women and that it underpaid them. The financial powerhouse had been accused of passing over senior women employees in its institutional equity division for promotion and pay increases. Even worse, the Equal Employment Opportunity Commission lawyers alleged that women were groped and excluded from male-only outings with clients. Under the conditions of the agreement, a fund of $40 million was established to handle claims from more than 300 women who believed they were discriminated against. A separate payment of $12 million was awarded to the lead plaintiff whose original complaint in 1998 and subsequent firing in 2000 prompted the investigation, and the final $2 million was used to appoint an internal diversity ombudsman and outside monitor to conduct performance and compensation analyses, maintain a complaint database, and implement programs to address the promotion and retention of women.

_05:: Wal-Mart

As many as 1.6 million current and former female Wal-Mart employees alleged gender dis-

ALEXANDER HAMILTON'S HORRIBLE-TERRIBLE, NO-GOOD, VERY BAD DAY

July 11, 1804, Weehawken, New Jersey: Alexander Hamilton met his rival, Aaron Burr, for an "interview" (so called because dueling was illegal). Burr had challenged Hamilton to the duel as a result of years of squabbling and alleged libels that Hamilton could have defused many times but didn't because of his own pride and stubbornness. Both parties seem to have intended for it to be a relatively bloodless affair, simply going through the motions to "satisfy honor." But on July 11, everything seemed to be against Hamilton. First, he chose the north side of the ledge, which meant that the rising sun and glare off the water would be in his eyes. Second, he chose two ornate smoothbore pistols, fancy but highly inaccurate. Historians now believe that Hamilton purposely fired his shot high above Burr, intentionally missing him. Burr, not realizing this, fired back, but probably only to wound Hamilton in the leg. Hamilton's choice of weapon came back to haunt him, though: the inaccuracy of the pistol turned a flesh wound into a kill shot. The huge .54-caliber ball entered above his hip (leaving a two-inch hole), shattered a rib, ricocheted through his liver and diaphragm, and lodged in the second lumbar vertebra. He died at two the next afternoon. It was sort of a bad day for Burr, too. His "murder" of the popular Hamilton made him a villain in the eyes of the public and ruined his political career.

crimination, and a federal judge agreed in June 2004 that the case could proceed as a class action lawsuit. The suit claims that Wal-Mart consistently discriminated against female employees in its manager recruitment and promotion practices. Discrimination lawsuits are nothing new to everyone's favorite superstore, though. In 2001, Wal-Mart was cited and fined $6.8 million by the EEOC for a continued pattern of disability discrimination across 11 states. In fact, Wal-Mart's preemployment questionnaire violated the Americans with Disabilities Act (ADA) by seeking disability-related information from qualified applicants before formal job offers were made. As part of the settlement, Wal-Mart agreed to change its ADA policies and procedures, create an ADA coordinator, provide training in ADA compliance, and offer jobs to certain disabled applicants. Unfortunately, Wal-Mart didn't quite learn its lesson. The company has since paid an additional $720,000 for violating the terms of the agreement and was even ordered to produce a TV advertisement noting Wal-Mart's role in violating the Americans with Disabilities Act.

_06:: Costco

Not wanting to be left out, the Issaquah, Washington, retailer joined the ranks of known corporations embroiled in class action gender discrimination suits in August 2004. The lawsuit, which was brought by approximately 640 female employees, alleged that a "glass ceiling" had been imposed denying women promotions to assistant manager and general store manager positions. Worse still, the claims were well founded. According to company documents, approximately 50% of

Costco's 78,000 employees are female, but less than 1 in 6 managers is a woman. Further, the complaints alleged that the company didn't announce openings for higher-paying managerial jobs. Instead, the selection process resembled a "boys' club"—with top-level male executives routinely selecting other men for the higher-level management positions.

Pride over Prejudice:

Individuals Who Taught Us How to Sing the Blues

Despite all the terrible institutions that have been used to keep African Americans down, they still managed to turn their misery into the beautiful music of the blues.

_01:: W. C. Handy Discovers the Blues

William Christopher (W. C.) Handy was the prototypical bluesman of the early 1900s. Born in a log cabin in 1873, Handy learned to play music at a very young age. But it wasn't until he was 30 that he got his first taste of the blues. While sitting at a railroad station in Tutwiler, Mississippi, Handy heard a local musician playing blues on a guitar, strumming it with a knife and singing about a nearby location where two railroads crossed. At first, Handy thought the sounds emanating were a little too strange, but he soon became intrigued. Over the next few years, Handy collected and copyrighted the songs he'd learned from the rural Delta folk. Then, in 1909, Handy moved to

Memphis and while playing at a political rally, he composed and sang a song about the politician Boss Crump. Three years later, Handy rewrote the lyrics and it became the widely known "Memphis Blues." It was just one of several hits he'd write. In 1914, Handy composed an instant classic, the "Saint Louis Blues," which went on to become the first nationally recognized song of the Delta blues movement and what many consider to be the first jazz recording.

_02:: Mamie Smith's "Crazy Blues" Sells a Million

By the second decade of the 20th century, the blues had gained a strong foothold in the South. Unknown to many, however, is the fact that female blues performers carried more than their share of the load during this time. And while the big names like Ma Rainey and Bessie Smith performed throughout the South, it was a vaudeville singer and dancer, Mamie Smith, who recorded the first blues songs in 1920. While her variety shows always included some blues and jazz numbers, her manager saw a new market for recordings in the large African American populations that had recently migrated to the North. Based on Smith's popularity in New York, her manager was able to persuade Okeh Records to record Smith's version of "Crazy Blues" and "It's Here for You." Not surprisingly, the recording was extremely successful, selling over 1 million copies in less than a year and eventually 2 million copies overall.

_03:: Charley Patton and the "Pony Blues"

Considered the founder of the Delta blues, Charley Patton was the model bluesman. The son of a sharecropper, young Patton moved with his family to the Dockery Plantation in the Delta region in Mississippi and soon began playing gigs around the area. Considered a "superstar" at a young age, Patton was always in demand to play at plantation dances and in juke joints. In fact, his slide guitar stylings became the standard imitated by other Delta musicians. In 1929 he recorded the "Pony Blues," which became a big hit for the Paramount Record Company. But it wasn't his music so much as his stage presence that made him a legend. Diminutive in size (5 feet 5 inches, 135 lbs), Patton became larger than life when he saw an audience. His raw, impassioned voice accompanied by his loud, fluid guitar playing to an unrelenting beat drove audiences into a

frenzy. Of course, Patton's persona carried over into his daily life as well. Loud, boisterous, drinking excessively, and with a woman on each arm, Patton defined the image of the early bluesman. Married eight times and imprisoned at least once, Patton was always on the move.

_04:: Leadbelly Meets John and Alan Lomax

Huddie Ledbetter, known to most of us as Leadbelly, was more than just a blues singer—he was one of America's greatest folk artists. Considered by some to be a murderer and by others a writer of children's songs, Leadbelly's life is legendary for its rumors and inconsistencies. In Texas in 1918, Leadbelly was accused of killing a man in a fight over a woman. And while many witnesses said it was in self-defense, Leadbelly pleaded guilty because he knew that as a black man he wouldn't get a fair trial. In 1930, he was involved in another murder (this time only attempted) and was imprisoned until 1934. Somehow, though, he still came to the attention of John and Alan Lomax, a father and son musicologist team who were commissioned by the Library of Congress to travel through the backwoods and rural areas of the South to record American folk music. The duo recognized Leadbelly's genius and promptly took him on tour with them in the northern United States, but audiences viewed him as more of a curiosity than a performer. Of course, the feelings were spurred by the press. A headline in the *New York Herald Tribune* (January 3, 1935), for instance, read, "Lomax Arrives with Leadbelly, Negro Minstrel/Sweet Singer of the Swamplands Here to Do a Few Tunes between Homicides." Like many a blues star, Leadbelly never achieved commercial success during his lifetime, but his songs "Goodnight Irene," "The Midnight Special," "Cotton Fields," and "Rock Island Line" are American classics today.

_05:: Muddy Waters and the Chicago Blues

In 1948, the blues got ratcheted up a notch when McKinley Morganfield and his Chicago sound hit the scene. Better known by his nickname, Muddy Waters, Morganfield helped create a new high-octane version of the music, which quickly became synonymous with contemporary urban blues. But just because he was pushing the sound forward didn't mean Waters had an easy time finding a label. After cutting some unissued recordings for Columbia, Waters finally persuaded the owners of Aristocrat (a small independent label that later became Chess Records) to put him in a studio. Luckily, one of the singles, "I Can't Be Satisfied/I Feel Like Going Home," became a hit, and the modern Chicago blues was born. Waters's deep, majestic voice, coupled with an amplified guitar, introduced listeners to a sound that was exciting, powerful, and thoroughly compelling. In fact, the new music gave rise to a whole new generation of Chicago blues artists who played with Waters, including Willie Dixon, Otis Spann, Junior Wells, Buddy Guy, and Otis Rush. Later on, Waters was a significant influence on the careers of contemporary artists like Paul Butterfield, Michael Bloomfield, and Johnny Winters.

Disobedience School: The Secret Lives of Civil Activists

4

Sure, you know their names from textbooks. You've seen their statues and heard them praised as heroes for standing up (and sticking it) to the man. Heck, you might even get a day or two off in a year thanks to them. But just because history paints these proud figures heroes, it doesn't mean they didn't come with a couple of blemishes. The following are four civil activists—and a couple of their secrets that history likes to brush over.

_01:: Henry David Thoreau (1817–1862)

A civil activist and the author of *Walden* and "On Civil Disobedience," Thoreau was about as eccentric as they come. In 1837, Thoreau graduated from Harvard but saw little value in the courses he'd taken. After all, old Henry felt that true education came from communing with nature (sadly, the degree isn't widely accredited). Henry, not really fond of the idea of work, once lasted only two weeks at a teaching job because he couldn't keep his students quiet and refused to punish them. So, how'd he get by, exactly? The philosopher survived mainly on odd jobs, though not too many of them. Henry made it his policy to try not to work more than 15 to 20 hours per week. His laziness isn't all this "catch" had going against him; described as "ugly but in an agreeable fashion" by his friends, he once proposed marriage by letter to a young lady only to be rejected. He also took to calling himself Henry David (instead of his given name David Henry) and ticked off his neighbors, who thought this to be unnatural and unseemly. Preferring to live in a small cabin close to Walden Pond, Thoreau was known to spend inordinate amounts of time standing still watching nature. Of course, he did remain active in some aspects of his life. As an uncompromising abolitionist, Thoreau harbored runaway slaves and helped them reach Canada. As for his much-celebrated imprisonment for refusing to pay a poll tax, though, that only lasted one day.

_02:: Ralph Waldo Emerson (1803–1882)

To most of us, Ralph Waldo Emerson was the quirky sidekick and mentor to Henry David Thoreau. And while you might think of Ralph as the consummate Renaissance man, you probably don't consider inventing a religion to be one of his many talents. It's true, though. When Emerson started believing his Unitarian faith was a bit too limiting, he set out to create his own religion based on the relationship among nature, man, and the divine. Known as the Sage of Concord, Emerson was years ahead of others in understanding nature and its role. For example, his ideas on evolution preceded Darwin's, and his thoughts on matter and energy were 80 years ahead of Einstein. In fact, his discussions on the hierarchy of human needs even anticipated the work of Abraham

Maslow in the 20th century. It's too bad most of this Renaissance thinking was lost during Emerson's time—and mainly because he took such a strong stance against slavery. His attacks on the morally bankrupt institution regularly got him in hot water, and calling John Brown a saint and a martyr didn't exactly help. In fact, it strongly curtailed his speaking engagements and left poor Emerson just that, poor.

Touch of Evil

While it's said that Dr. Martin Luther King Jr. had many secrets, things started with the name on his birth certificate. It wasn't Martin but Michael, which his father said was a mistake made by the attending physician.

_03:: Tom Hayden (1939–   )

The poster boy for radical 1960s political movements, Tom Hayden was a chief ideologue of the student movement and the founder of Students for a Democratic Society. Gaining international attention as one of the Chicago Seven (who stood trial for disrupting the 1968 Democratic National Convention), Tom quickly became a celebrity, even marrying fellow political activist and movie actress Jane Fonda in 1973. Although he lost when he ran for the U.S. Senate in 1976, Hayden stayed involved in local California politics and ran unsuccessfully for mayor of Los Angeles in the late 1990s. Interestingly, this self-proclaimed defender of the poor and politically oppressed bought a 120-acre retreat with Fonda in 1977 to be used to train young political activists. The problem was, before they could move in Tom and Jane had to evict a number of low-income tenants.

_04:: Harriet Beecher Stowe (1811–1896)

Known as a moody, absentminded child, Harriet Beecher Stowe grew up to be one of the most influential social critics of the 19th century. Moving with her family from Hartford, Connecticut, to Cincinnati, Ohio, she soon came into contact with the mentality of the Mason-Dixon Line and with fugitive slaves. The effects were clearly profound. In 1851, Stowe became famous for her book *Uncle Tom's Cabin,* which depicted the evils of slavery.

When the novel was attacked as being inaccurate fiction, she published "A Key to Uncle Tom's Cabin" in 1853 to refute the critics. Not only did the book make her an international celebrity, it actually made her quite wealthy during a time when writing wasn't viewed as a lucrative profession. Still, she managed to create arguably the most controversial piece of literature of the 19th century. In fact, when she met Abraham Lincoln in 1862, the president exclaimed, "So you are the little woman who wrote the book that started this great war!"

Who's Your Daddy?
Famous Bastards Who Made Their Mark

Accusing someone of illegitimate birth has long been one of the greatest insults possible, so it's not at all surprising that some of history's greatest shoulder-mounted chips have been securely fastened to people with murky parentage. In fact, by the look of the names on this list, it just might be a recipe for success.

_01:: Sargon the Great (ca. 2360–2279 BCE)

In his autobiography (recorded as *The Legend of Sargon*), Sargon admits, "My father I knew not." And while we don't know his genealogy, we do know the guy was "Great." Supposedly the son of royalty (at least that's what he told people), Sargon was actually abandoned in a basket on the Euphrates River and found by a gardener. Somehow, the clever kid worked his way up to cupbearer (sort of a prime minister) to the king of the Sumerian city of Kish, but his ambition didn't stop there. Eventually, Sargon founded his own kingdom among the

Semitic peoples of Akkad. Of course, anyone who laughed at his supposed illegitimacy probably lived to regret it; in the span of a few decades Sargon conquered Sumeria and built one of the first true empires in world history, stretching from the mountains of southern Anatolia to the Syrian coast and the Persian Gulf. His Akkadian name, Sharru-kin, means "The King Is Legitimate." We think . . .

_02:: Confucius (ca. 551–479 BCE)

The early life of K'ung-Fu-tzu, better known in the West as Confucius, is largely a mystery. Born in the feudal kingdom of Lu, Confucius served as an adviser on political matters and court etiquette to several Chinese leaders during the mid- to late 500s BCE. The circumstances of Confucius's own birth, however, are hardly up to any Emily Post standards. According to the first complete biography of Confucius, the *Shiji,* his dad, a warlord named Shu Liang He, and his mom, a member of the Yan clan, "came roughly together," indicating either a rape, concubinage, or some other sort of extramarital shenanigan. His low birth, however, didn't stop him from attracting plenty of highborn followers, many of whom protected him when his outspoken manner offended his various employers.

_03:: William I of England (1028–1087)

Billy the Conqueror, as he liked to be called, was the son of Duke Robert of Normandy and a tanner's daughter named Arletta, who had a thing for guys in armor. By his early 20s, Billy had defeated his rivals for the throne, conquered the rich province of Maine, and become one of the most powerful men in France. But even after being crowned king of England, "William the Bastard" didn't stop his conquests—he died in Vexin during an attempt to seize control of the French province. Interestingly enough, though, little Billy wasn't the only great king of England to be a bastard; Athelstan (ruled 924–939), maybe the greatest of the Anglo-Saxon monarchs, was also the product of a somewhat less than legitimate union.

_04:: Juchi (ca. 1180–1227)

It almost sounds like a fairy tale: the bride of a young Mongol herdsman named Temudjin was kidnapped by an enemy tribe, but rather than abandon her to her fate (the custom at the time—Temudjin's own mother had been kidnapped by his father), Temudjin gathered an army and risked his life to get her back. When she came back, though, she was pregnant. Amazingly, Temudjin accepted the child as his own, but named him Juchi, "the Guest," just to make sure everyone knew that he didn't regard the kid's paternity as totally kosher. Temudjin soon became known to the world as Genghis Khan, and his son Juchi began the conquest of Russia, possibly to get away from his brothers, who, according to Mongol sources, taunted him and called him a bastard. The kingdom he carved out was ultimately known as the Golden Horde, the longest lived of the Mongol successor states.

Touch of Evil

It may not have been coincidence how Debbie Harry of the band Blondie resembled Marilyn Monroe. The adopted Harry used to dream that Monroe was her birth mother. Of unknown parentage herself, Marilyn would have been 19 when Debbie was born.

_05:: Leonardo da Vinci (1452–1519)

Everyone knows of Leonardo da Vinci, the *Homo universalis* who could be a painter, a naturalist, an engineer, a metallurgist, or a philosopher with equal ease. It's considerably less well known that this personification of the Renaissance was actually the son of a notary, Ser Piero, and a peasant girl of somewhat "easy virtue." In fact, the two simply took a tumble in the hay together before going their separate ways and providing Leonardo, from their mar-

Lies Your Mother Told You

THERE ARE PEOPLE BURIED IN THE HOOVER DAM

It's a good, spooky story. And with more than 100 fatalities occurring over the five years of its construction, there's a pretty good chance that at least one of them fell into the wet concrete and now rests there for all eternity, right? Nope. The construction of the Hoover Dam was notoriously devoid of safety considerations for the 16,000 workers who built the incredible structure. Men died from falls, rockslides, carbon monoxide poisoning (from the gasoline-powered dump trucks in the tunnels), and heat prostration (during the summer of 1931, the temperature routinely reached 140 degrees). But, oddly enough, the pouring of the 3,640,000 cubic meters of concrete went relatively smoothly. Nobody fell in. Well, nobody who didn't get out again, anyway. So the next time someone tells you there are people buried in the Hoover Dam, look them in the eye and tell 'em with confidence it's just a dam lie.

barrassment, and on his father's death in 1503 they conspired to deprive him of his share of the estate. Leonardo had the last laugh, however, when the death of an uncle led to a similar inheritance squabble, leaving him with sole custody of the uncle's lands and property.

_06:: Thomas Paine (1737–1809) and _07:: Alexander Hamilton (1755–1804)

Two of the best-known fathers of the American republic, Thomas Paine and Alexander Hamilton, were the results of extramarital bedroom high jinks. Paine, whose *Common Sense* helped bring widespread support to the American Revolution, and whose other writings, like the anti-Bible tract *The Age of Reason,* scandalized all and sundry, had to flee England a step ahead of treason charges. In the end, however, he died penniless in the United States. Hamilton, on the other hand, was the illegitimate son of West Indian colonials, and made a name for himself as a brilliant orator and writer. He eventually became one of the leaders of the American Federalist Party, but had the misfortune to be challenged to a duel by Aaron Burr. He also had the even greater misfortune of accepting, bringing his career to a dramatic close one fine New Jersey morning. (See "Alexander Hamilton's Horrible-Terrible, No-Good, Very Bad Day," page 31.)

_08:: Thomas Edward Lawrence (1888–1935)

The illegitimate son of a knight and his children's nanny, T. E. Lawrence became the model for generations of British diplomats blindly idolizing all things Arabian. One of the organizers of the much-touted (but in reality

riages to other people, with 17 half brothers and sisters. Needless to say, these assorted half siblings were none too fond of their renowned relation, whose birth was something of an em-

fought more on paper than on the battlefield) Arab revolt against the Turks during World War I, Lawrence later became embittered with Britain's imperial policy and spent the last few years of his life sulking and tinkering with motorcycles (he died in a motorcycle accident). Though he largely tried to keep a low profile, his much-exaggerated accomplishments led to him being dubbed "Lawrence of Arabia."

_09:: Eva Perón (1919–1952)

"Saint Evita" was the daughter of an adulterous relationship between two villagers in an impoverished part of Argentina. She made a name for herself as an actress before marrying Juan Perón in 1944, but, being illegitimate (and a peasant), she was never really accepted in the social circles in which he routinely traveled. As a rising military officer, Perón quickly found himself dictator of Argentina, and "Evita" was by his side. In fact, she was there to do more than just wave at crowds and manage the mansion. Evita actually ran several government ministries and almost became vice president in 1951 (the military bullied Perón into making her drop out of the campaign). And though she's best known to many from the musical and movie that bear her name, you really shouldn't feel obligated to cry for her. While the flick plays up the glamour and romance of her career, it largely ignores her corruption, oppression of political rivals, cozying up to Nazi war criminals, and other questionable doings.

Oh, Say Can You Sin: The Dish on National Anthems

A national anthem is supposed to symbolize everything that is good and true about a country. But these five patriotic songs have a slightly more disturbing past. Read on, and we guarantee you'll never watch Olympic medal ceremonies the same way again.

_01:: A Star-Spangled Drinking Song

What better place to start than with America's own national anthem? Every third grader knows the story of Francis Scott Key penning the great poem while watching the siege of Fort McHenry during the War of 1812. But that's just a poem. So where exactly did all this music hoo-ha come from? When Key wrote the anthem, he had a song in his head as a reference for the poem's meter (a song from *England,* ironically enough). The tune, notoriously difficult to sing, is from a drinking song written by John Stafford Smith originally titled "Anacreon in Heaven." It was the theme song of a club of rich London men who got together to eat, drink, and then—for good measure—drink some more. The Anacreontic Club took its name from Anacreon, a Greek poet who wrote about such things. Perhaps it's fitting, then, that the song is usually sung before sporting events, after fans have been tailgating (translation: drinking) for several hours.

_02:: The U.K.'s Illegitimate Anthem

Most Americans recognize the tune of the United Kingdom's national anthem as "My Country 'Tis of Thee," but the Brits clearly had it first. Like the U.S. anthem, "God Save the Queen" (originally "King," but they switch it depending on the gender of the current monarch) was first sung to commemorate a military victory: the capture of the South American port of Portobelo during the War of Jenkins' Ear (1739–1742). At least, that's what we think. Other traditions link it to the Jacobite rebellion, when George II's troops sang it to restore morale after losing to Bonnie Prince Charlie at Prestonpans (verse 5, now almost never sung, refers to crushing the rebellious Scots). Oddly enough, the well-known tune is the U.K.'s anthem only by default. It has no authorized version and has never been officially sanctioned by either royal decree or an act of Parliament. And get this—it's also the national anthem of Liechtenstein.

_03:: Australia's Beloved Sheep-Stealing Tune

Americans poke fun at themselves for not knowing all the words to the national anthem. But Australians share the same affliction. In fact, "Advance Australia Fair" has two official verses, but the second is usually a mumbled shadow of the first. And maybe it just comes down to the fact that Australians aren't really all that crazy for their national anthem. While most feel that it properly encapsulates good Australian values and whatnot, there are still mixed thoughts about it. So what song do Aussies really identify with? The correct answer is "Waltzing Matilda," a lovely and universally recognizable folk tune written by Banjo Paterson in 1895. There's a tiny problem with "Matilda's" lyrical content, though. It's about a *swagman* (itinerant worker or hobo) who steals a *jumbuck* (sheep), hides it in his *tucker bag* (food sack), and avoids arrest by drowning himself in a *billabong* (stagnant pool). Oh, and it's not about dancing with a gal named Matilda. In Australian slang, to "waltz Matilda" is to bum about from place to place looking for work, carrying your Matilda, or a blanket with all your possessions in it.

_04:: A Dutch Song of Defeat

The national anthem of the Netherlands, "Wilhelmus van Nassouwe," ranks as the world's oldest official anthem. Dating from around 1568, a turbulent time for the Dutch as they struggled with longtime enemy Spain, it's also one of the only anthems that's about a specific person, not a nation. But here's the really cool, borderline creepy part. If you take the first letter of each of the fifteen verses of the anthem, they spell WILLEM VAN NASSOV, the Dutch name of Prince William I of Orange-Nassau. And they did this on purpose. Amazing, huh? Well, maybe the content's a little less inspiring. The song recounts Prince William addressing the oppressed people of Holland after he tried—and failed—three times to free them from oppression under the Spaniards.

_05:: South Africa's Song: Something for Everybody!

Every time you struggle a bit with "The Star-Spangled Banner," just be glad that you're not from South Africa. Like the nation itself, the anthem is a combination of several different ethnic groups. During the apartheid era, the white government had its anthem, "Die Stem van Suid-Afrika" ("The Call of South Africa"). Nelson Mandela's African National Congress had its own separate but unofficial tune: "Nkosi sikelel' iAfrica" ("God Bless Africa"). Then, when apartheid finally ended, blacks and whites (and their anthems) were legally forced to coexist. That is, until 1995, when the pieces were melded to form the current national anthem in all its disjointed glory. Just how awkward is it? The anthem changes key in the middle and uses *five* different languages. Starting as "Nkosi," the tune goes on to sample the more prevalent of South Africa's many native languages. Verse 1 is in Xhosa. Verse 2, Zulu. Verse 3 is Sesotho. Then the key switches and "Die Stem" powers through. Verse 4 is in Afrikaans, and verse 5 is in English. Phew!

Ignominious Things Named for Napoléon Bonaparte

No matter what you think of him, Napoléon certainly did a number on this world. And whether it's as the savior of revolutionary France or the scourge of Western civilization, the little guy's name keeps on keeping on. Of course, not everything "Napoléon" adds luster to his legacy...here are a few examples to prove it.

_01:: His Son: Napoléon II

Sadly, Napoléon François Joseph Charles Bonaparte (aka Napoléon II, or, as we like to call him, "the Deuce"), never had a chance to fill his father's tiny shoes. Despite being the son of Emperor Napoléon I, and garnering the title King of Rome at birth in 1811, poor Napoléon II never ruled anything. By the time of his fourth birthday, the First French Empire had already collapsed. Then, after Napoléon I's brief return to power and his final military defeat at Waterloo in 1815, the emperor abdicated in favor of his son. This proved a futile gesture, however. The brilliantly resourceful statesman Charles-Maurice de Talleyrand, a high official in Napoléon's government, had arranged for Louis XVIII to take over a new royalist government. Napoléon's escape from exile on the island of Elba and his short-lived return as emperor didn't convince the French senate to anoint young Napoléon II instead of Louis XVIII. That wasn't the worst of it for junior, however. Under formal terms of the treaty ending the Napoleonic Wars, young Napoléon also was barred from ever ruling his mother's Italian lands. As duke of Reichstadt (a title based on his mother's Hapsburg lineage), Napoléon the younger spent his short life essentially under guard in Austria, where he died of tuberculosis in 1832. He wasn't confined to Austria forever, though. In 1940, a fellow with an even more nefarious name, Adolf Hitler, disinterred Napoléon's body and sent it packing to Paris, where it could be entombed beside his father's.

_02:: His Quirk: The Napoleon Complex

A Napoleon complex is nothing more than an inferiority complex that vertically challenged individuals self-treat with an unhealthy dose of belligerence, a healthy pursuit of achievement, or both. Think of the tough little brawler, eager to take on all challengers, especially big ones. Think of singer-songwriter Paul Simon (5 foot 3) and actors Judy Garland (4 foot 11), Danny DeVito (5 feet), Michael J. Fox (5 foot 4), and David Spade (5 foot 7). Then there are basketball's Earl Boykins (5 foot 5) and football's Wayne Chrebet and Doug Flutie (both 5 foot 10). Overachievers all. Think of Britain's prime minister Winston Churchill, for that matter, or Soviet dictator Joseph Stalin. At 5 feet 6 inches each (the same, by modern measure, as Napoléon I—see "Lies Your Mother Told You: Napoléon Was a Shrimp," page 11), either of the World War II–era leaders could have had the complex named after him if Napoléon had not gotten there first. The idea of a psychological "complex," by the way, wasn't around in Napoléon's time. It arose in 1899, with the publication of Sigmund Freud's *Interpretation of Dreams*. In that groundbreaking book, Vienna's pioneer of psychoanalysis introduced the

term "Oedipus complex," referring to a child's repressed sexual desire for the parent of the opposite gender. Freud can't claim "Napoléon complex," however. It seems to have arisen in the early 1900s as a casual term, more a backhanded insult than a psychological diagnosis.

_03:: A Pig Named Napoleon

George Orwell's 1945 novel *Animal Farm* tells of a revolt strikingly close to the one that transformed the Russian Empire into the Soviet Union. That is, except for one minor detail: Orwell's rebels and revolutionaries are a bunch of animals (in the farm sense of the word). Feeling a little oppressed, Mr. Jones's barnyard creatures turn against their owner, drive him off the land, and begin running things themselves under an "all animals are equal" banner. However, idealism crumbles pretty quickly as an unscrupulous pig named (you guessed it!) Napoleon wrests control, turns on his comrades, and becomes more tyrannical than old Jones ever was. In fact, the sacred "all animals are equal" mantra quickly finds itself warped into something significantly less utopian: "all animals are equal, but some animals are more equal than others." In an allegorical sense, Napoleon stands for the USSR's Stalin. But the evil porker's name, after the little corporal who hijacked the French Revolution, certainly fits.

_04:: Napoleon Solo (1964–1968 Vintage)

The Man from U.N.C.L.E. premiered in 1964 as TV's answer to the James Bond movies, and each episode was packed with espionage, intrigue, sophistication, and action. With Robert Vaughn in the role of Napoleon Solo, a dashing secret agent and ladies' man, the

A Row Is a Row Is a Row

BEN YOSEF V. BEN ZAKKAI

In this corner: Sa'adya ben Yosef, one of the greatest minds of 10th-century Jewry—and he knew it. He authored dozens of philosophical, religious, and linguistic works (including the *Agron,* a Hebrew dictionary written when he was 20, an Arabic translation of the Bible, one of the first Hebrew prayer books, and the monumental *Book of Beliefs and Opinions*).

In the opposite corner: David ben Zakkai, the Exilarch (leader of Middle Eastern Jewry).

Round 1: David appoints Sa'adya as Gaon (rabbinic head) of the Talmudic academy of Sura (in modern Iraq) in 928.

Round 2: In 930, Sa'adya refuses to sign a court verdict that David issued, announcing repeatedly and loudly that he believes the decision unjust.

Round 3: David orders Sa'adya deposed from the academy.

Round 4: An outraged Sa'adya excommunicates David and announces that his brother Hasan is the new Exilarch (even though appointing Hasan wasn't really within his power).

Round 5: Sa'adya and David fight a decade-long war of foul words until they ultimately reconcile, but the experience makes Sa'adya a bitter man.

Round 6: In 933, Sa'adya pens the *Sefer ha-Galui,* a theological work in which he makes clear his belief that he is the most brilliant man who has ever lived.

show's popularity grew through the first two seasons. In season three, however, the producers fell under the spell of the competing TV series *Batman,* starring Adam West. Impressed by the ratings *Batman* was drawing with its tongue-in-cheek comedy approach to action-adventure, they began taking *The Man from U.N.C.L.E.* in distinctly comic book directions. The lowest comic denominator didn't work out for the show's ratings, though, and Solo quickly degenerated from sophisticated to camp. In the worst episode, Vaughn danced with a man in a gorilla suit.

_05:: An Anthropologist Named Napoleon

Until 2000, Napoleon Chagnon was known as author of the best-selling anthropology text of all time: *Yanomamö: The Fierce People.* But since then, his research has been mired in controversy. The anthropologist, along with geneticist James Neel, inoculated many of the Venezuelan tribe's members. Unfortunately, it was right about this time that the Yanomami experienced their first-ever measles epidemic, leading to thousands of deaths in the region and reducing the tribe to half its original size. Coincidence? Perhaps. Allegations against Chagnon have divided the anthropological community. Many defend the expedition, claiming it would be impossible for a vaccine to spark such an outbreak. Critics, however, point to the expedition's financier, the Atomic Energy Commission, as proof that the accused were using the Yanomami as human test subjects. Either way, the scandal raised serious questions about the practices of studying indigenous peoples.

_06:: The Napoléon Complex Martini

What's terrible about one part Napoléon Mandarin Liqueur to three parts vodka with an orange peel twist? Nothing, we guess, unless you're a martini purist. No offense to Chez Napoléon on West 50th Street in Manhattan, where the Napoléon Complex is a bartender's specialty, but we'll take ours classic: fine, juniper-scented gin (not vodka); the merest suggestion of dry vermouth (wave the vermouth bottle in the general vicinity of the shaker); and a fat, green, pimento-stuffed olive on a toothpick.

Seriously Holier Than Thou: Mortals with Minor God Complexes

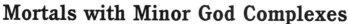

Sure, power corrupts, and absolute power corrupts absolutely, but what about Absolute power with a capital A? Here are four mortals who let their holier-than-thou attitudes go to other people's heads.

_01:: Narmer or Menes, or One of Those Really Old Egyptian Guys

Around 2925 BCE, Narmer united the upper and lower Nile Valley into Egypt. Pretty nice feat. Unfortunately, it was so long ago that historians don't know if Narmer is the same person as Menes, considered the founder of the First Dynasty, or if Menes was Narmer's son.

What they do know is that the ruler we're calling Narmer here definitely had a god complex—not that it wasn't merited! In unified Egypt, kings were considered gods. So, did that mean he was born divine? Early on, that seemed to be the idea. But during the First Dynasty, cunning priests did have a bit of veto power. If they deemed an ill king unfit, they were perfectly justified in killing him and making way for a more potent god (a practice done away with around 2659 BCE, presumably by a self-interested ruler). Slowly, though, Egyptian priests devised a better way to delay those holier-than-thou attitudes in their royalty. Instead of decreeing kings gods at birth, they created a ceremony in which a mortal royal heir was merged with his spiritual counterpart, or *ka,* to become a god only upon coronation.

_02:: Alexander the Really, Really Very Great (aka Almighty to You)

After his best friend (and presumed lover) Hephaestion died in 324 BCE, Alexander the Great demanded that his subjects (who by that point included the populations of Macedon, Greece, Persia, Egypt, and more) honor Hephaestion as a fallen hero. He also decided it was a good time to let people know that they could finally honor him as the god he was (or at least now claimed to be). Never a victim of modesty, Alex had been fond of comparing his accomplishments to those of the Greek gods for years. But, his newfound attitude adjustment indicated that he now believed he was equal to the immortals. Greek cities, which under his rule retained some semblance of self-government, complied with the order, but not necessarily with the spirit. The less-than-enthused Spartans, for instance, issued a decree that said, "Since Alexander wishes to be a god, let him be a god."

_03:: Augustus Caesar: Like Holy Father, Like Son…

On August 19 of the year 14 CE, Augustus Caesar died at age 77. Two days later, the Roman senate enrolled him among the gods of the Roman state. And while being deemed a god by committee isn't exactly the same as claiming godhood while alive, the emperor had the keen foresight to plan his ascension to divinity years before. How so? Just after his great-uncle and adopted father Julius Caesar's murder in 44 BCE, the young man interpreted a comet as evidence that Julius had entered the company of immortals. The strategic proclamation worked in his favor. Later, as a member of Rome's ruling triumvirate, he issued coins with his own image and the inscription "Son of a God." Then in 27 BCE, the "first citizen," as he'd dubbed himself, had a compliant senate name him Augustus, meaning "superior to humanity" or "godlike."

_04:: Caligula Declares Himself a God

Although he was emperor for just four years, Caligula (37–41 CE) was still able to take Rome on a wild ride, according to the ancient historians Suetonius and Flavius Josephus. The adopted son of the previous emperor, Tiberius, Caligula was initially very popular with Roman commoners. You can chalk it up to his spontaneous distributions of gold coins to them or his wacky, unpredictable sense of humor. Whatever the case, the public's opinion quickly turned when (according to Suetonius) Caligula began cross-dressing in public, impregnated his own sister, declared war on Poseidon (bringing back chests full of worthless seashells as "booty"), and topped it all off by declaring himself a god—the classical definition of "hubris." Poor Caligula. The seashell sovereign was assassinated by his own disgruntled bodyguards not long after.

_05:: Carl Jung, Full-time Psychologist, Part-time "Aryan Christ"

One approach to psychology is bringing your patients together to live with you, declaring yourself a god, and suggesting that they worship you. And as unconventional (read: cultish) as it may seem, that's the approach taken by famed Swiss psychologist Carl Jung (1875–1961). In fact, his mystical theory of a mass collective unconscious that unites the human race propounded that human psychological problems are caused by a separation from the divine. Further, he claimed the malady can only be treated through interpretation of visions, dreams, and the occult. Fleshing out some of his ideas when he temporarily lost his mind during World War I, Jung embraced the Hindu concepts of karma and reincarnation and began advocating polygamy. In the end, however, Jung claimed that the only way to reconnect with divine forces was to deify *yourself*, and he practiced what he preached, encouraging his followers to think of him as their connection with the sun god.

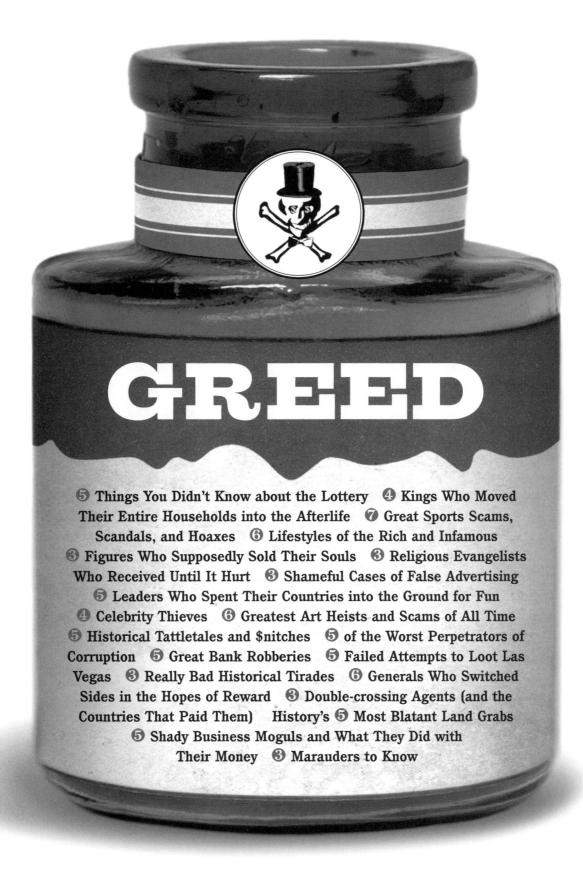

GREED

⑤ Things You Didn't Know about the Lottery   ④ Kings Who Moved Their Entire Households into the Afterlife   ⑦ Great Sports Scams, Scandals, and Hoaxes   ⑥ Lifestyles of the Rich and Infamous   ❸ Figures Who Supposedly Sold Their Souls   ❸ Religious Evangelists Who Received Until It Hurt   ❸ Shameful Cases of False Advertising   ⑤ Leaders Who Spent Their Countries into the Ground for Fun   ④ Celebrity Thieves   ⑥ Greatest Art Heists and Scams of All Time   ⑤ Historical Tattletales and $nitches   ⑤ of the Worst Perpetrators of Corruption   ⑤ Great Bank Robberies   ⑤ Failed Attempts to Loot Las Vegas   ❸ Really Bad Historical Tirades   ⑥ Generals Who Switched Sides in the Hopes of Reward   ❸ Double-crossing Agents (and the Countries That Paid Them)   History's ⑤ Most Blatant Land Grabs   ⑤ Shady Business Moguls and What They Did with Their Money   ❸ Marauders to Know

Ticket to Ride:
Things You Didn't Know about the Lottery

Call it the poor man's dream, a casino without walls, or a tax on the stupid, the lottery has deep and widespread roots. Here's a look at five stories about the numbers game.

_01:: Lotteries of Yore (It's Older Than You Think!)

Lotteries have been around as long as arithmetic. According to the Bible, God ordered Moses to use a lottery to divvy up land along the River Jordan (it's in the Book of Numbers, naturally). And that ain't all the "good book" has to say about it: lotteries are also mentioned in Joshua, Leviticus, and Proverbs. The lottery can also be traced back to China, where a warlord named Cheung Leung came up with a numbers game to persuade citizens to help pay for his army. Today, it's known as keno. Other famous lotteries? The Chinese used one to help finance the Great Wall; Augustus Caesar authorized one to raise money for public works projects in Rome. And in 1466, in what is now the Belgian town of Bruges, a lottery was created to help the poor—which lotteries supposedly have been doing ever since.

_02:: The Founding Fathers Took Their Chances

Displaying the astute politicians' aversion to direct taxation, early American leaders often turned to lotteries to raise a buck or two. John Hancock organized several lotteries, including one to rebuild Boston's Faneuil Hall. Ben Franklin used them during the Revolutionary War to purchase a cannon for the Continental Army. George Washington ran a lottery to pay for a road into the wilds of western Virginia. And Thomas Jefferson wrote of lotteries, "Far from being immoral, they are indispensable to the existence of Man." Of course, when he wrote it, he was trying to convince the Virginia legislature to let him hold a lottery to pay off his debts.

_03:: Louisiana: A Whole Lotto Love

By the end of the Civil War, lotteries in America had such bad reputations, they were banned in most states. But not in Louisiana, where a well-bribed legislature in 1869 gave an exclusive charter to a private firm called the Louisiana Lottery Company. The company sold tickets throughout the country, and for 25 years, it raked in millions of dollars while paying out relatively small prizes and contributing chump change to a few New Orleans charities. Finally, in 1890, Congress passed a law banning the sale of lottery tickets through the mail, and eventually all multistate lottery sales were banned. What's a corrupt U.S. company to do? Move offshore, of course! The Louisiana Lottery moved its operations to Honduras, and America was lottery free until

1963, when New Hampshire started the lottery cycle anew.

_04:: "Inaction" Jackson: Lottery's Biggest Loser

Clarence Jackson's luck began to run out on Friday, the 13th of October, 1995, when the Connecticut Lottery picked the numbers on Jackson's lotto ticket, making his family the winners of $5.8 million. Only he didn't know it—and he didn't find out until 15 minutes before the one-year deadline to claim the prize, despite a whole slew of lottery ads seeking the winner. Jackson, a 23-year-old who'd taken over the family's struggling office cleaning business from his ailing father, didn't make it in time, and lottery officials rejected the claim. In 1997, the Connecticut General Assembly voted to award Jackson the prize, but the state senate refused to go along. Up until 2004, Jackson was still trying each year to convince the legislature. And still losing.

_05:: And Some Other Jackson: Its Biggest "Winner"

Andrew Jackson "Jack" Whittaker was already wealthy when he won the multistate Powerball lottery in December 2002. A millionaire contractor from West Virginia, Whittaker became the biggest single lottery winner in history after snagging a $314.9 million jackpot. But the dough seemed to carry more curses than the Hope Diamond. And when Jack decided to take a $170.5 million lump sum instead of payments over 20 years, it wasn't the only lump coming his way. Whittaker was robbed three times, once of more than $500,000 at a strip club. He was also sued for assault, arrested for drunk driving, and even booked for getting into a bar fight. And in September 2004, three burglars broke into his house and found the body of a friend of Whittaker's granddaughter, whose death may have been drug related. The sad truth? Simply that money doesn't guarantee peace of mind.

You Can Take It with You: Kings Who Moved Their Entire Households into the Afterlife

4

We've all heard the old cliché "You can't take it with you." But that didn't stop a good number of royals from trying. Here are four examples of folks who didn't want just a thin slice of heaven—they wanted it served on the same silver plates they'd grown accustomed to.

_01:: Hauling Jeeves to the Afterlife

It might not have been the most profligate tomb in history, but considering that it was built only a few centuries after the idea of cities came into fruition, Pu-Abi of Ur didn't make out too badly. We know little about her except that she lived and died sometime in the 26th or 25th century BCE. The most ornate of Ur's royal tombs, Pu-Abi's *post vivos* abode was excavated in the 1920s and '30s by Leonard Woolley. Among the artifacts discovered there were a complex headdress of gold leaves, a solid gold comb, and a dress covered with gems and beads. Of course, Pu-Abi didn't go alone into the next world; a number of servants poisoned themselves after being sealed in (possibly willingly) with their late mistress. Still, we're guessing that whatever service the queen was getting in the afterlife, it probably wasn't coming with a smile.

_02:: Here Comes the Sun (King)

Since the Japanese traditionally revered their emperors as gods, it comes as no surprise that they spared no expense in preparing their rulers for the afterlife. Emperors of the Yamato era, particularly, were known for their enormous burial mounds. One grave in Sakai City, traditionally assigned to the late-fourth-century-CE emperor Nintoku, is especially impressive. If you think the Great Pyramid is the swankiest tomb around, well, you're gravely mistaken. Just the sheer scale of the mound dwarfs Khufu's resting place; the artificial hill marking the grave site is the length of five football fields and has an internal volume twice that of the Egyptian's pyramid. And as if that weren't enough, the keyhole-shaped tumulus is surrounded by a triple moat! Twenty years were spent building the massive structure and thousands of funerary offerings are enshrined inside.

_03:: Big Soldiers in Little China

In Chinese culture, death and dying are perceived as just another phase of life. So, it's no

Just the Facts

INCLUDED IN FORMER GE CEO JACK WELCH'S 2001 RETIREMENT PACKAGE

(Trimmed in 2003 in Response to Stockholder Outrage)

$9 million-plus: Annual pension

$86,535: Consulting fees for first 30 days of work each year

$17,307: For each additional day

$11 million: Resale of Trump Towers luxury apartment

$291,869: Unlimited use of corporate jet per month

$600: Leased luxury Mercedes-Benz per month

Priceless: Unlimited use of company limousine, security-trained chauffeur and bodyguards, country club memberships, full health and life insurance coverage, tickets (season courtside to New York Knicks at Madison Square Garden; season box seats at Yankee Stadium; season grand tier Metropolitan Opera; U.S. Open tennis; Wimbledon tennis; VIP seats at all Olympic events)

wonder that the emperor and other royalty have burial chambers that are designed to mirror their former opulence and prosperity. In fact, some tombs are so elaborate that construction begins *really* early. In Emperor Ch'in Shih Huang Ti's case, for instance, construction on his site started when he turned just 13 (the same age he was crowned king of Qin). Of course, the site was also filled with plenty of goodies the good king could appreciate in the afterlife: food supplies and utensils, carriages (just in case he got restless), pets, favorite objects, and more than a few subjects (aka dead servants) just in case something needed to be fetched. In fact, the emperor's large harem also accompanied him to his burial chamber while the majority of his servants and animals were spared and replaced with terra-cotta figures. The practice of human sacrifice eventually disappeared thanks to continued objections by notable philosophers like Confucius, Mozi, and Xunzi. Their arguments not only elaborated on the inhumanity of the sacrifices, but also pointed out that the preparations were extravagant, wasted time, and interfered with the daily labor needed to generate wealth. Pretty wise indeed.

_04:: Good Reason Not to Be a Mourning Person

On August 18, 1227, Genghis Khan, the most feared leader of the 13th century, was buried with a simple procession of 2,500 followers and a mounted bodyguard of 400 soldiers. Anyone unfortunate enough to happen upon the procession was immediately put to death by the soldiers. When the procession arrived at a remote mountain location in Mongolia, 40 virgins were killed to provide Khan with the needed pleasures in the afterlife. Then, at the end of the funeral ceremony, the soldiers killed all 2,500 members of the procession. When the 400 soldiers returned to Khan's capital city, they were immediately put to death by another group of soldiers so that no one could reveal where Khan's final resting place was. Since Khan was considered a god, it was important that no one know his whereabouts and plunder the site. In fact, only recently have archaeologists found a site that they think may be Khan's burial place. So did anyone survive the onslaught? Well, yes—a camel. The creature was spared since she could find her way back to the site if Khan's family needed to visit. Family members had to be led blindfolded—if they knew the whereabouts, they also would be put to death.

Take the Money (or the Gold Medal or the Notoriety or the Potato) and Run:
Great Sports Scams, Scandals, and Hoaxes

Some say the U.S. national pastime is baseball. Others say it's football. Or basketball. Or jai alai. But you can forget all those, because these seven examples prove that when it comes to sports, mankind's favorite pastime is lying, cheating, pulling pranks, and spreading hoaxes. Play ball!

_01:: A Black Pox on the Black Sox

This is pretty much the mac-daddy of all sports scandals. The 1919 Chicago White Sox was one of the greatest baseball teams ever to take the field, including superstar left fielder "Shoeless" Joe Jackson. But two gamblers, "Sleepy Bill" Burns and Billy Maharg, backed up by gangster Arnold Rothstein, changed that by bribing eight players with $100,000 to throw the World Series. The fix was a success, the Sox lost, and nobody really suspected a thing until late in the next season, when the eight players were indicted. Commissioner Kennesaw Mountain Landis suspended them all from baseball for life, and they all had it coming. Except one. "Shoeless" Joe did all he could to avoid being involved: he told Sox owner Charles Comiskey about the scam, but was ignored; he asked to be benched for the Series, but was refused; he even batted .375 for the Series and had 12 base hits (a Series record at the time) *and* the only home run. Due to the scandal, Jackson is still not in the Hall of Fame, though many players have supported his induction.

_02:: Stella "the Fella" Walsh

In 1980, a 69-year-old member of the National Track & Field Hall of Fame was shot and killed outside a Cleveland shopping mall. Police immediately ascertained that the victim was Stella Walsh, the greatest female track-and-field athlete of her day. Stella, born Stanislawa Walasiewiczowna in Poland, won a gold medal for Poland at the 1932 Olympics and a silver in 1936, and set 20 world records. But when the police took the body to be autopsied, they found something very unusual on the 69-year-old woman: male genitals?! Further studies showed that she . . . er, *he* . . . had both male and female chromosomes, a condition called mosaicism. When the shocking news got out, it took approximately 2.7 seconds for the great runner to get a new nickname: Stella the Fella.

_03:: Mighty *Sports Illustrated* Fans Strike Out

The greatest baseball pitcher of all time was actually a figment of George Plimpton's imagination. His article for the April 1, 1985, issue of *Sports Illustrated* was entitled "The Curious

Case of Sidd Finch." It told the story of an English orphan, raised by an archaeologist, educated at Harvard, and trained by a yogi in Tibet, who showed up at the Mets training camp in Florida. He could throw a fastball at 168 mph (the record at the time was a comparatively sluggish 103) and preferred to pitch with one foot bare and the other in a large hiking boot. As of the magazine's publishing date, Finch hadn't yet decided if he was going to play for the Mets. The response was massive. *Sports Illustrated* received over 2,000 letters immediately following the story, many expressing their hopes that Sidd would play. Two weeks later, the magazine fessed up to their hoax. Of course, the clever Plimpton had included a subtle clue in the article's subhead: "He's a pitcher, part yogi and part recluse. Impressively liberated from our opulent lifestyle, Sidd's deciding about yoga...." Confused? Just take the first letter of each word: "happyaprilfoolsday."

_04:: Rosie the (Underhanded) Runner

On April 21, 1980, a young woman crossed the finish line to win the 84th Boston Marathon in the record time of 02:31:56. For someone who had just run over 26 miles, Rosie Ruiz looked notably sweatless and un-rubbery in the legs. Race officials checked photos and video from various spots in the race, and Ruiz appeared in none of them. So how did she do it? Here's the prevailing theory: She started the race with the others, then left the course, *hopped a subway,* then reentered the course about a half mile from the finish line. She was disqualified and stripped of her title. So, how'd she fine-tune her con? By cheating in another mara-

thon, of course. Rosie had sneaked her way past New York Marathon officials, and her time qualified her for the Boston race.

_05:: Simonya Popova: aka How the Women's Tennis Association Got Served

With the advent of computer-generated imagery, the art of the hoax really came into its own. Take the case of Simonya Popova, a female teenage tennis sensation from Uzbekistan who made Anna Kournikova look like Billy Jean King. In the fall of 2002, a Jon Wertheim article in *Sports Illustrated* profiled Popova, proclaiming her the next great phenom on the tennis circuit. It covered five pages and even had a picture. But Popova was a complete fiction; her image was computer generated. Even the name Simonya was chosen as a reference to *SimOne,* a movie about a computer-generated actress who becomes a star. The story was done as a fictional what-if, intended to be a comment on tennis's need for a hot new superstar to give the sport some mojo. But the Women's Tennis Association wasn't exactly amused. A spokeswoman for the organization lambasted the magazine, claiming they should've used the five pages to cover *real* tennis players. And, for the record, they said, "We have tons of mojo."

_06:: The Great Potato Caper

The date: August 28, 1987. The scene: Bowman Field in Williamsport, Pennsylvania. The AA Reading Phillies were in town to play the hometown Williamsport Bills, when Bills catcher Dave Bresnahan decided to pull a stunt he'd been thinking about for weeks. With a runner on third, Bresnahan threw the ball over the head of the third baseman and into the outfield. The runner jogged home, thinking he had an easy run. But unbeknownst to him and the 3,500 fans at the game, Bresnahan still had the ball. The object he had thrown was a potato, meticulously peeled and shaped to look like a baseball. Everyone got a chuckle out of the hoax. Everyone, that is, except Williamsport manager Orlando Gomez, who promptly ejected Bresnahan and fined him a whopping $50. Bresnahan had the last laugh, though: Instead of the money, he gave Gomez 50 potatoes.

_07:: A Rose Bowl Is a Rose Bowl Is a Rose Bowl (Except When CalTech's Involved)

It seems fitting that what is widely regarded as the greatest college prank of all time was pulled off by the college where pranking is practically a major: CalTech. (Students once changed the well-known "Hollywood" sign to read "CalTech," despite the massive security around the joint.) Since the Rose Bowl game is played in CalTech's backyard of Pasadena, the students and their head pranksters, the Fiend-

ish 14, were miffed at the lack of publicity the event generated for their school. So they finally decided to take it out on the game's participants in 1961 (neither of which happened to be CalTech—the game was between the University of Washington and the University of Minnesota). The students learned of an elaborate halftime spectacle planned by the Washington cheerleaders that involved 2,232 flip cards. One CalTech student, disguised as a high school newspaper reporter, interviewed Washington's head cheerleader to learn their plan. The CalTech students then stole one of the instruction sheets, made 2,232 copies of it, altered each one by hand, then swapped them with the real cards while the cheerleaders were visiting Disneyland. The next day, live on national television, thousands of Huskies fans held up cards to make a picture of a Husky. Instead, viewers saw a Beaver, CalTech's mascot. One of the next card formations read "Seiksuh" (read it backward and you'll get it). And finally, the *pièce de résistance:* The cards read, in giant letters, "CalTech."

Crime Does Pay:
Lifestyles of the Rich and Infamous

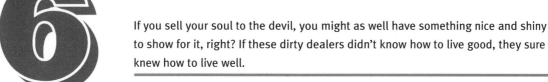

If you sell your soul to the devil, you might as well have something nice and shiny to show for it, right? If these dirty dealers didn't know how to live good, they sure knew how to live well.

_01:: John Palmer (ca. 1947–   )

British bad boy John Palmer suckered over 16,000 people in a phony time-share scheme. Currently ranked Great Britain's wealthiest criminal, having amassed ill-gotten wealth of over £300 million, the notorious Mr. Palmer owns a fleet of cars and several houses all over England, including a huge estate at Landsdown in Bath. He even has a cool nickname: Goldfinger. Which doesn't mean he has a golden rep. Palmer defended himself in the fraud trial, lost, got eight years in the clink, and has so far been slapped with fines of £5 million. But this wasn't his first criminal activity. In 1983 he took part in the U.K.'s greatest-ever robbery, in which he and a partner stole £26 million in gold bullion from a cargo storage company at Heathrow Airport. He smelted the gold himself and was arrested when police found two gold bars, still warm, under his sofa.

_02:: Pablo Escobar (1949–1993)

Picture every stereotypical South American drug dealer you've ever seen in a movie. They're all based in part on Pablo Emilio Escobar Gaviria, head of the Colombian Medellin cartel. Escobar ran his empire from a lavish pad complete with Arabian horses, a miniature bullfighting ring, a private landing strip, a Huey 50 helicopter, and a private army of bodyguards. Clearly, money wasn't an object for the man. After all, he could afford to pay local authorities $250,000 each to turn a blind eye. Plus, he used his money to build schools and hospitals, and was even elected to the Colombian senate. But eventually the pressure from authorities, including the American DEA, got to be too much and he turned himself in. Of course, incarceration didn't stop him from living the lush life. Escobar used some of his loot to convert his prison into a personal fortress, even remodeling all the bathrooms and strengthening the walls. Once he left, he was a fugitive again, but he wasn't hard to track down. An obsessive misophobe, Escobar left a conspicuous trail of dilapidated hideouts with shiny, expensive new bathrooms. In the end, the cocaine kingpin was killed when the secret police tracked his cell phone to an apartment, stormed the building, and shot him. Many, many times.

_03:: Mother Mandelbaum (1818–1894)

One of New York City's earliest criminal godfathers was actually a godmother. Frederika "Mother" Mandelbaum, or "Marm" to her friends, was the top "fence" (buyer and seller of stolen goods) in post–Civil War New York. From 1862 to 1882, she's estimated to have processed almost $10 million in stolen stuff. In fact, Mandelbaum made enough money to purchase a three-story building at 79 Clinton Street. Running her business out of a bogus haberdashery on the bottom floor, and living with her family in opulence and comfort on the top two floors, "Mother" often threw lavish dinners and dances for the criminal elite, which included corrupt cops and paid-off politicos. Ma Mandelbaum could afford to eat well, too, and allegedly tipped the scales at over 250 pounds. But like any good criminal, she gave back. Well, kind of. Mandelbaum ran a school on Grand Street where orphans and waifs learned to be professional pickpockets and sneak thieves. She was finally arrested in 1884, but fled to Canada with over a million dollars in cash before the trial. She remained there in comfort and safety until her death in 1894.

Touch of Evil

Meyer Lansky was the syndicate crime boss who financed Bugsy Siegel's Flamingo Hotel in Las Vegas. While his cohorts died or went to prison, Lansky eventually retired in Florida with a cool $400 million.

_04:: L. Dennis Kozlowski (1946–)

OK, so he's not a criminal in the classic "bang bang, shoot 'em up" kind of way. But this scumbag still has it coming. The former CEO of Tyco International, along with CFO Mark Swarz, allegedly embezzled an estimated $600 million from his company, its employees, and its stockholders. He borrowed $19 million, interest free, to buy a house, a debt that the company then forgave as a "special bonus." He got an $18 million apartment in Manhattan and charged the company $11 million more for artwork and furnishings, including a $6,000 shower curtain and $2,200 garbage can. He even threw his wife a little 40th birthday soiree on the island of Sardinia that cost the company over two million clams. Special musical guest: Jimmy Buffett. And while a mistrial was initially declared in April of 2004, the best lawyers couldn't keep Kozlowski and his cohorts from changing residences from their very big houses to *the* Big House.

_05:: Leona Helmsley (1920–)

The famous New York real estate mogul and class-A witch lived the American Dream. Well, except for the whole prison thing. Leona was a divorced sewing factory worker with mouths to feed before she met and married real estate tycoon Harry Helmsley (the fact that he was already married mattered little). In 1980, Harry named Leona president of his opulent Helmsley Palace Hotel, which she ruled like a despot. Her tendency to explode at employees for the smallest infraction (like a crooked lampshade) earned her the title "Queen of Mean." The tyranny didn't exactly last. In 1988, Leona and Harry were indicted for a smorgasbord of crimes, including tax fraud, mail fraud, and extortion. And after numerous appeals, Leona served 18 months in prison and was forced to pay the government $7 million in back taxes. A healthy dose of irony for the woman who once said, "Only the little people pay taxes." Of course, that doesn't mean things turned out that badly for poor Leona. Said to

WILLIAM THE CONQUEROR'S HORRIBLE-TERRIBLE, NO-GOOD, VERY BAD DAY

Despite conquering England in 1066, William I spent more time back in Normandy, where greedy neighboring rulers tended to grab his lands if he left. In 1087, William, who had grown fat in his 50s, was on his way to take a "cure" (like going to a fat farm) when he made good on a threat to attack Mantes, taken from him by Philip I of France a decade earlier. The attack went well until the aftermath. As the village burned, a spark spooked Will's horse. It reared and the king lurched into the ornate saddle horn. Ugh! The painful result? It took William five agonizing weeks to die of internal injuries. Worse still, at his death, his attendants—including sons Henry and William Rufus—rode out quickly to defend their own properties as word got out. Meanwhile, servants robbed the unguarded body, stripped it naked, and dumped it on the floor.

---

be worth over 2.2 billion bucks, the dreaded Ms. H. still owns the lease to the Empire State Building and lives in luxury with her aptly named dog, Trouble.

_06:: Al Capone (1899–1947)

He killed people. He bought cops by the precinctful. He bootlegged liquor. He ran Chicago like his own personal kingdom. He was damn good at what he did, and he did it with style. Al Capone (aka Scarface) maintained a swank Chicago headquarters in the form of a luxurious five-room suite at the chic Metropole Hotel (rate: $1,500 a day). And when those Chicago winters proved a little too chilly for him, he bought a 14-room Spanish-style estate in Palm Island, Florida, which he spent millions turning into a well-decorated fortress. Capone's total wealth has been estimated at over $100 million (not a penny of which was kept in his vaults, as Geraldo Rivera learned on live TV). Not bad for a guy whose business card said he was a used furniture dealer. Of course, he didn't pay taxes on any of it, which is what eventually sent him up the river.

Friends of the Devil:
Figures Who Supposedly Sold Their Souls

If you really can't get a gig, and you're desperate to become a star, there's only one person who can help you out for sure. Of course, it's probably gonna cost you more than the standard 10%.

_01:: Robert Johnson at His Crossroads

Considered to be one of the most influential bluesmen of all time, Robert Johnson was also one of the most turbulent. And few musicians have achieved Johnson's mythical status, whether the devil had a hand in it or not. As the story goes, one night Johnson happened upon a large black man while walking near the crossroads of Highways 61 and 49 outside of Clarksdale, Mississippi. The man offered to tune Johnson's guitar, and as the story has it, claimed Johnson's soul in return. Within a year, Johnson was in demand throughout the region. Actually, the story may have started when Johnson sat in on a gig with Sun House and Willie Brown. House and Brown were so impressed with Johnson's playing they thought the only explanation was that he'd sold his soul. Of course, mythic lives require mythic endings. Known for his womanizing,

Johnson was fatally poisoned when he sipped some whiskey laced with strychnine—the act of a jealous husband. Johnson died in 1938 at the age of 27.

_02:: Led Zeppelin and Their Stairway to...?

Did they or didn't they sell their souls to Satan for the rights to the classic "Stairway to Heaven" hit? While the debate has continued since the song came out in the early 1970s, it basically can be traced back to the allegation that, if played backward, the song makes numerous references to Satan. Even more damning, tons of people have interpreted the lyrics as being demonic. And Jimmy Page's and Robert Plant's interest in the occult didn't really help matters. In the 1970s, Page proclaimed himself a wizard and actually bought a house in Scotland known as "The Toolhouse," reputed to be a satanic temple. Then, when he played the chords of the rock anthem to Plant, Robert immediately sat down and wrote the lyrics right on the spot. Later, in interviews, Plant stated that he didn't seem to be writing and something else was moving his pencil across the page. Three decades later the debate continues, but the question remains as to who the piper ("the piper's calling you to join him")

Touch of Evil

Church of Satan founder Anton LaVey claims to have been born with a vestigial tail that was surgically removed when he was an adolescent.

is. Is it the devil, Jesus, or, maybe, just a plain old piper? Guess the rock world will never know.

_03:: The Darkness Crossover

It now appears that the fast rise of the British group The Darkness in the early 2000s may have had supernatural intervention. After struggling for many years playing in obscure pubs, the group's lead singer, Justin Hawkins, allegedly sold out to the devil. In 2002, Hawkins sought the assistance of Doktor Snake, a well-known British voodoo doctor. And in a scene reminiscent of Robert Johnson's rendezvous with the devil, Snake led Hawkins to a deserted country crossroads one evening at midnight and some unholy pact was consummated. Within the year, The Darkness was one of the hottest bands in the United Kingdom. Having been successful with The Darkness, Doktor Snake (who still hasn't figured out a cure for spelling his name incorrectly) now sells his dark side services over eBay.

I Want to Hold Your Handbag: Evangelists Who Received Until It Hurt

3

It's better to give than to receive, right? Well, that is unless you're one of the following fat wallet preachers. In a pay-to-pray world, this group of standouts would definitely make it into the evangelism hall of fame—one that no doubt has gilded walls and marble floors.

_01:: The Mail Order Order— The Reverend Ike

A forerunner to the televangelist frenzy of the 1980s, Frederick Eikerenkoetter, known as the Reverend Ike, unabashedly preached capitalism for years. In the 1970s, Ike broadcast weekly sermons on approximately 1,700 television and radio stations across the United States. Famous for saying that the lack of money was the root of all evil, Ike definitely practiced what he preached. In fact, it wasn't uncommon for Ike to tell his listeners that he didn't want to hear the sound of change hitting the collection plate, he wanted the folding stuff. Known for his expensive suits and a fleet of mink-trimmed Rolls-Royces, the Rev clearly didn't live the life of a monk. And while his television career appears to have diminished, old Ike continues his very lucrative mail-order business, which is more like a chain letter scam than anything else. Here's the setup: Normally a letter is sent containing a prayer hankie, a charm, or a curse. Then the recipient is told to send it back to Ike along with a $20 or $30 donation within a day and Ike will bless it or you. Of course, the failure to do so could bring about a whole host of unwanted problems, and no one wants that. Talk about the spirit of capitalism. We're not so sure John Calvin would be proud.

Touch of Evil

In 1987, Oral Roberts told viewers he needed $8 million or God would "call him home." He beat the deadline, thanks to a last-minute $1.3 million donation by dog track owner Jerry Collins, who admitted: "I think he [Roberts] needs psychiatric treatment."

_02:: The Miracle Worker— Benny Hinn

A throwback to the tent preachers of the early 1900s, Benny Hinn is a man of miracles, and estimates are that Hinn's organization receives over $100 million a year in donations (a miracle in itself!). Most of these donations, of course, are in response to Hinn's so-called faith healings, and his choreographed services are structured to elicit as much money as possible. In addition to the healings, he's happy to scare a little cash out of wallets as well, often telling his audience that worldwide disasters are going to occur, but only those giving to God's work will be spared. In 1999, Hinn announced that God had ordered him to build a $30 million World Healing Center. However, in 2003, Hinn stated that God still wanted the center built, but told him the time wasn't right. Like the loyal servant he is, Hinn told the Big Man (and all his followers) he'd hold the cash until then. In the meantime, Hinn lives in an $8 mil-

The Evil How-to

TAKING IT TO THE CLEANERS

Most people have a vague idea that money laundering is bad, but like the clueless protagonists of *Office Space*, have no idea what it is or how to do it. The most common method of laundering money is to give illegal income to a legitimate business already taking in large quantities of cash, so that it can be deposited without arousing suspicion. The term probably arose in the 1930s, when gambling rings opened up launderettes to disguise the influx of small change. Other methods in use are ingenious in their complex maneuvering around international financial reporting regulations. International terrorists, for instance, tend to use legitimate charities to funnel money into arms purchases and other nefarious doings. Of course, because of lax reporting laws and corrupt officials, some countries are better for cleaning one's cash than others. China, the Cayman Islands, the United Arab Emirates, Thailand, and Lebanon are generally among the favorites.

lion oceanfront home, travels by private jet, and stays in $3,000-a-night hotel suites. Apparently, for Hinn doing the Lord's work always feels good. Really, really good.

_03:: **You Gotta Pay to Pray—Robert Tilton**

In 1991, ABC-TV's *Prime Time Live* program investigated Robert Tilton's Word of Faith Outreach Center Church. At the time, Tilton's televangelist show appeared on 200 stations and he claimed his church had over 10,000 members. The truth was that his organization was also making $80 million a year through his direct marketing campaigns. The investigation found that prayer requests sent to Tilton were routinely discarded after the cash and checks had been removed—clearly not what Jesus would do. The exposé led to Til-

ton's downfall and in 1999 he sold the church and moved to Miami. However, in 1997 Tilton started buying time on independent stations, showing mostly reruns, in order to rebuild his mailing lists. Today, his mailings include financial prayer cloths, posters of Tilton, packets of oil, and other trinkets all for just the cost of a small donation. But sadly, old habits are hard to break: Reports state that employees are simply told to take out the dough and discard the prayer requests. But all in all, something seems to be working for him. Tilton owns a $450,000 yacht and property worth at least $1.5 million in Miami Beach.

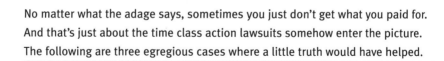

Putting the Wind in Our Sales:
Shameful Cases of False Advertising

No matter what the adage says, sometimes you just don't get what you paid for. And that's just about the time class action lawsuits somehow enter the picture. The following are three egregious cases where a little truth would have helped.

_01:: **BodyFlex**

In 2003, the FTC (Federal Trade Commission) sued BodyFlex, alleging that the company had deceptively advertised that the system caused users to lose 4–14 inches in the first seven days. The complaint charged that the loss of 4–14 inches was advertised as occurring without any reduction in calories, and that users burned enough body fat to achieve the claimed fat loss. In fact, the promotion also cited a clinical study that "proved" that the BodyFlex system caused significant fat and inch loss in the first seven days. No one knows how many

people actually bought into the hype, but according to the FTC, the BodyFlex commercial was one of the 10 most-aired infomercials in weekly U.S. rankings and aired more than 2,000 times from February through September 2003 on national cable channels. Of course, the company spent almost $20 million to promote the product. In September 2004, BodyFlex conceded, and agreed to set up a $2.6 million consumer refund program. They also agreed to stop making false weight-loss claims, effectively proving that not all liars are big, fat ones.

Touch of Evil

While they now do the healthy thing with Flintstone vitamins, when the Stone Age family originally appeared on television, old Fred and Barn were sponsored by (and appeared in commercials for) Winston cigarettes.

_02:: The Wedding

In September 1990, a group of drug crime suspects in Corunna, Michigan, received an invitation to a wedding from a well-known drug dealer in the area. Attendees were asked to check their guns at the entrance, apparently a common occurrence at these events. As part of a five-month undercover investigation, the police staged a wedding on a Friday night, figuring it was easier to make the drug suspects come to them than to round them up. The groom was an undercover investigator, the bride a Flint police officer, and the bride's father (and reputed crime boss) was the police chief. That evening, after the vows, the toasts, and the dancing, the band, called SPOC, or COPS spelled backward, played "Fought the Law," setting off the cue for the evening's real agenda. All the police officers were then asked to stand, and those who remained seated were arrested. A dozen suspects were booked and, by Saturday afternoon, 16 were in custody.

_03:: Sprint

In May 2004, the Florida attorney general charged Sprint with reaching out and scamming someone. Actually, it was charged with scamming many more than one, and to make amends the attorney general spearheaded an agreement with the phone company to pay Florida $2.4 million to settle charges that it switched consumers to their long distance services without permission, a practice known as "slamming." During 2002, consumers were unknowingly converted to Sprint long distance after purchasing unrelated items at electronics stores. The old switcheroo actually occurred when customers reached the checkout counter and were asked to sign what looked like a typical sales receipt but was in fact a letter of authorization. As a result, the customer would leave the store having unwittingly approved a change in his long-distance provider. Investigations that began in January 2002 also uncovered evidence that sales personnel forged consumer signatures on these letters to meet sales quotas and receive bonuses. Nearly 4,000 Florida consumers complained about the unsolicited switches and received restitution from Sprint in response to their complaints.

We Don't Need Another Nero: Leaders Who Spent Their Countries into the Ground for Fun

If you're looking for some bank-breaking works of less-than-staggering genius, look no further. Not only were these five leaders plagued by terrible ideas, they never bothered to get their money's worth.

_01:: Caligula's Bridge (Over Very Troubled Waters)

According to the classical chronicler Suetonius, as he was going mad the Roman emperor Caligula began spending money on increasingly bizarre and extravagant projects to satisfy his megalomaniacal whims. Among Caligula's best efforts: constructing a three-mile pontoon bridge across the Bay of Naples by confiscating merchant ships, having their bulwarks sawed off (making them useless afterward), spreading soil over the planks, and then planting trees, shrubs, and flowers to make the bridge more pleasant. When it was done, Caligula supposedly rode his horse across the bridge at the head of 20,000 troops to prove wrong an earlier prophecy that claimed he could no more become emperor than ride across the bay. After a night of partying, Caligula left and never came back. The bridge itself was destroyed by a storm a short while later. It was this kind of ridiculous spending that broke the Roman bank pretty quickly.

_02:: Nero's Extreme Home Makeover

As everyone's favorite gossip Suetonius tells it, the emperor Nero decided to go Caligula one better by building an extravagant mansion for himself in burned-down neighborhoods of Rome following the great fire of 64 CE. Called the Domus Aurea, or "Golden House," because its exterior was overlaid with gold leaf and mother-of-pearl embedded with gems and beautiful seashells, the building was far and away the largest private residence ever seen in Rome, covering a large part of three of Rome's seven hills. So, just how extravagant was Nero's crib? In the entrance hall stood a 120-foot statue (of Nero); a columned arcade ran for a mile; a pool the size of a small lake was surrounded by buildings shaped like cities and fake farms; exotic animals roamed everywhere; and the ceilings were carved ivory panels that could retract to allow a rain of perfume and flowers to fall on partiers. The Roman poet Martial said of it, "One house took up the whole city of Rome." When it was finished Nero famously said, "Good, now I can at last begin to live like a human being."

_03:: Prince of Thieves (Mainly the White-Collar Variety)

Prince Jefri Bolkiah, the brother of the sultan of Brunei, spent his small country into bankruptcy during the 1990s with a multibillion-dollar shopping spree that puts all the other royal contenders to shame. Clearly, Prince Jefri knew how to treat himself right, as the 300,000 citizens of Brunei found out when his purchases were put up for auction as part of bankruptcy proceedings. Included for sale were a golden toilet roll holder, rows of gold-plated Jacuzzis and showerheads, porcelain flamingos, gold-plated wastepaper baskets, a multimillion-dollar marquee complex, Comanche helicopter simulators, an Airbus jet, a Formula 1 racing car, and a bronze-plated eight-foot-high Trojan horse. Luxury hotels in Great Britain, France, and Singapore were also favorite purchases of Jefri. That's not to say he hasn't been caught with his fingers in more than a few (illegal) pies. Previously, a lawsuit had been brought against Jefri for the theft of approximately $16 billion from Brunei's state-run economic development agency. Needless to say, he didn't develop anything profitable with the funds.

_04:: Versailles and Everything After

Louis XIV was one of the most extravagant kings in French history. A lot of the stuff Louis spent money on was quite respectable—as a famous patron of arts he supported literary and cultural figures like Molière, Le Brun, and Lully, and he spent a great deal of money to improve the Louvre. Of course, Louis' most famous boondoggle was his palace at Versailles, a sprawling 700-room rococo residence on an 800-hectare estate with carefully tended gardens and woodlands about 15 miles to the southwest of Paris. In fact, Louis used so many luxurious materials—including gold leaf, crystal chandeliers and doorknobs, silk and satin window dressings, exotic hardwood furniture, ivory, mother-of-pearl, and precious stones—and his house contained so many famous works of art, that it's actually impossible to calculate a modern cost equivalent. If the spending wasn't bad enough, Louis also foolishly kicked out the Huguenots, or French Protestants, even though they provided many of the country's leading merchants and much of its tax income. Last but not least, Louis launched an endless series of unwinnable wars that were to put the last nail in the coffin of French finances. Who knew the nickname the Sun King referred to was one that was setting?

_05:: Empress Dowager's Ship That Never Sailed

In 1888, China had been on the ropes for a good three decades. Once an international powerhouse, the nation's world rep had suffered greatly since its humiliating loss to Great Britain in the Opium War. Foreign technical advisors told the mandarins who set policy that China needed a modern navy along Western lines if it was going to defend itself from further European and Japanese aggression, and the mandarins duly set aside 30 million taels of silver for new, modern ships. However, the dowager empress Cixi, who had the final say, decided that the money would be better spent on reconstructing the elaborate Summer Palace, which had served as a vacation spot for the Chinese imperial family for millennia.

When advisors complained that the only ship she had purchased was a marble pleasure yacht, she noted that while it was indeed immobile, "it's still a very nice place for a picnic."

Sticky Fingers: Celebrity Thieves

It's not surprising that celebrities steal—the sense of entitlement that accompanies wealth and adulation surely makes for a skewed sense of morality. It's *what* they steal that bothers us. Confederate battle plans? Cosmetics from a *drugstore?* And, most unfathomable, *figs?* Fame does funny things to people.

_01:: Hedy Lamarr (1913–2000)

Hedy Lamarr was a prototypical Hollywood sex symbol. Onscreen, the Austrian brunette sizzled as a femme fatale in movies like *White Cargo* and *Samson and Delilah*. And sure, her personal life was unstable: She married six times (twice more than Marilyn Monroe). But Lamarr was more than just a glamorous face. During World War II, she invented and patented an electronic device that made it more difficult to jam radio-guided torpedoes. Even though she understood the complexities of electrical engineering, Lamarr apparently couldn't outwit drugstore security guards. In the 1990s, she was caught shoplifting cosmetics on two occasions, but was never convicted. In the first case, she insisted on a jury trial and was acquitted by a 10–2 vote. After her second arrest, the charges were dropped.

_02:: Olga Korbut (1956–)

Although the all-around gold medal for women's gymnastics in the 1972 Olympics went to Lyudmila Turischeva, the star that year was Turischeva's teammate, Olga Korbut. Diminutive and adorable, Korbut completed the first back flip on the uneven bars on her way to three gold medals in Munich. And then, a decade after moving to rural Georgia (the American one), cute little Olga Korbut was arrested outside a Publix supermarket. Her crime? Stealing chocolate syrup, figs, and cheese—begging the question: What in the name of God did she intend to cook? Korbut characterized the event as a misunderstanding, but apparently didn't feel strongly enough about it to make a case: She paid a fine of $300 to avoid trial.

Touch of Evil

In April 2005, the New York Post *reported that* Life & Style *star Kimora Lee Simmons not only pilfered props from the show's set, but also "made off with an entire rack of lamb from the lunch buffet table."*

_03:: Dean Martin (1917–1995)

Given the life story of Dean Martin, his kleptomania shouldn't come as a terrible surprise. The former steelworker, prizefighter, and bootlegger never had much promise until he ran into Jerry Lewis at an Atlantic City nightclub in 1946. Martin became the consummate straight man to Lewis's over-the-top clownishness, and it paid handsomely. But old Dean could never go *entirely* straight, even if he never wanted for money again. The Rat Packer once told the *Saturday Evening Post* that he couldn't go to a department store without stealing. His booty? "A necktie or a pair of gloves or a pair of socks. Everyone has a little bit of larceny in them." Indeed. *When pocketing socks/ feels like adrenaline shots/that's amore.* Or kleptomania, anyway.

_04:: Pauline Cushman (1833–1893)

And finally, a celebrity thief with real moxie and a heart of gold! Born in New Orleans, Pauline Cushman became a successful, if minor, actress in New York in the 1850s. At the start of the Civil War, she offered her services as a spy to the Union. Cushman, who reportedly used her feminine wiles to gain favor with the Confederate troops (if you catch our drift), followed General (Braxton) Bragg's army around throughout much of 1863. She was eventually caught red-handed with secret papers and sentenced to death, but a hasty retreat by Bragg's men allowed Union soldiers to save her. Cushman stole for the right reasons, but she was no angel. She abandoned her children, married three times, exaggerated her military exploits, and eventually became addicted to opium. She committed suicide in 1893.

Rome Wasn't Burnt in a Day

SAN FRANCISCO'S BIG BLAST

By the time the Great Earthquake struck San Francisco at 5:13 a.m. on April 18, 1906, the city's fate had already been sealed by years of graft and greed. Corrupt mayor Eugene Schmitz and "Boss" Abraham Ruef had overseen years of shady deals that made the city a tinderbox. How so, you ask? Water mains were built *across* the San Andreas fault. Reservoirs under the city were filled with garbage from construction sites by corrupt contractors. And pillars in major buildings were filled with newspaper, much cheaper than fireproof concrete. When the earthquake struck, fires began in the mostly wooden city and spread like, well, wildfire. What's a corrupt mayor to do? Schmitz turned over authority to General Frederick Funston, who had the (burning) bright idea of creating firebreaks by blowing up buildings with dynamite. Without any water, the demolitions simply spread the fire further. By the time the fires were finally defeated four days later, 29,000 buildings were destroyed and over 3,000 people were dead, many of them shot as "looters" by the U.S. Army. Ironically, Schmitz and his cronies were set to be rounded up by authorities that very day, but the earthquake interrupted the operation.

Lowlife Perpetrates Art:
Greatest Art Heists and Scams of All Time

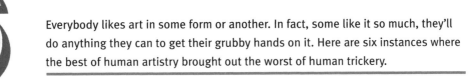

Everybody likes art in some form or another. In fact, some like it so much, they'll do anything they can to get their grubby hands on it. Here are six instances where the best of human artistry brought out the worst of human trickery.

_01:: When Greeks Lose Their Marbles

Since 1832, some of the greatest treasures of ancient Greek civilization have been residing in the British Museum. And the Greeks, who understandably consider themselves the rightful owners of things Greek, want their stuff back. The objects in question are the Elgin Marbles, so called because they were removed by Thomas Bruce, the seventh earl of Elgin, and British ambassador to Constantinople. Elgin claimed to have removed the friezes and sculptures because the Ottomans (who ruled Greece at the time) were neglecting them. Of course, critics are more than happy to tell you the good earl outright stole them. Whatever Elgin's motives, the workers who removed the sculptures did terrible, irreparable damage to the Parthenon. The marbles arrived in England between 1801 and 1805 to a mixture of awe and outrage. A profligate spender (earls just wanna have fun!), Elgin piled up huge debts and ended up selling the collection to Parliament in 1816. Since then, a cold war of sorts has simmered between the governments of England and Greece over the return of the sculptures. In fact, proponents of returning the marbles to Greece have removed Elgin's name and refer to them simply as the Parthenon Marbles.

_02:: "Just Judges" Just Disappeared

The Adoration of the Mystic Lamb, a 24-panel masterpiece by Flemish painter Jan van Eyck, is considered one of the most important Christian paintings in history. One panel, however, known as the "Just Judges," has been missing since it was stolen from a cathedral in the Belgian city of Ghent in 1934. Shortly after the theft, the archbishop received 13 ransom notes signed "D.U.A." demanding 1 million Belgian francs for the painting's safe return. D.U.A. turned out to be a transposition of the initials of Arseen Van Damme (with the "V" unlatinized into a "U"), alias of Arséne Goedertier, an eccentric who allegedly got the idea from a detective novel. Since then, numerous theories about the theft and the whereabouts of the painting have circulated: It was stolen by the Knights Templar; or the painting contains a map to the Holy Grail; or it's buried in the coffin of Belgium's King Albert I; or Goedertier was working for a Nazi spy, who was ordered by Hitler to obtain it as the centerpiece of his new "Aryan religion." The theories and clues have tantalized sleuths for three-quarters of a century, but the painting's location still remains a mystery.

Touch of Evil

In February 2005, two original **Dogs Playing Poker** *paintings by Cassius Marcellus Coolidge went up for auction in New York. Estimated to bring in $50,000, they instead commanded a bid just short of $600,000.*

_03:: The Case of the Missing Munch

The Scream, Edvard Munch's 1893 expressionist masterpiece depicting anxiety and despair, is one of the most famous paintings in the world. In fact, you'd be hard-pressed to find someone who couldn't recognize the ghostly figure on a bridge under a yellow-orange sky, with hands clasped over his (or her?) ears, mouth open in a shriek. And on Sunday, August 22, 2004, administrators at Oslo's Munch Museum were definitely given reason to let life imitate the art. In broad daylight, armed thieves barged into the museum, yanked *The Scream* and another famous Munch, *Madonna,* off the wall, then made a break for it. Police found only the getaway car and two empty frames. Understandably, Norwegians reacted with disbelief and outrage at the theft of two true national treasures. But, oddly enough, this wasn't the first time the painting had been purloined. There are actually *four* versions of *The Scream.* Another version was stolen in October 1994 from Oslo's National Gallery. That one turned up three months later, but the most recently ripped off version remains missing. Weird note: August 22 is a bad day for paint-

ings. On that day in 1911, the *Mona Lisa* was stolen from the Louvre.

_04:: Pahk the Cah, Then Steal Some Aht

On March 18, 1990, in what still ranks as the biggest art theft in U.S. history, two thieves made off with masterpieces worth—get this—over $300 million. The robbery occurred at Boston's Isabella Stewart Gardner museum, where two men dressed as Boston cops pretended to respond to a disturbance. They cuffed the security guards, then helped themselves to 13 paintings, including works by Vermeer, Manet, and Rembrandt. While none of the paintings has yet been recovered, a theory has developed as to their whereabouts: the heist may have been masterminded by the Irish Republican Army, working in conjunction with Irish gangsters in Boston to ransom the paintings, then use the money to run guns to the IRA. Proponents of this theory say the paintings are hidden somewhere in Ireland, but IRA spokesmen vehemently deny this. Nevertheless, the FBI is said to be following this lead. Stay tuned.

_05:: The Disappearing Da Vinci

On Wednesday, August 27, 2003, two men posing as tourists walked into Drumlanrig Castle in Dumfries and Galloway, Scotland. During the tour, they made off with a painting, *Madonna with the Yarnwinder,* a masterpiece by Leonardo da Vinci valued at about £30 million. The thieves were seen on camera casually heading for their vehicle, a Volkswagen Golf GTI (whose slogan, "Getaway Drivers Wanted," seems appropriate), with the incredibly valuable painting tucked under one arm. Over 500 years old, the painting had been in the possession of the family of the castle's owner, the duke of Buccleuch, since the 18th century. In fact, the *Madonna* was the centerpiece of the duke's art collection valued at over £400 million and including works by Rembrandt and Holbein. Despite the theft, the castle reopened to visitors days later. As of this writing, the painting has not been recovered, but it's believed to be too famous to ever be sold by the thieves.

_06:: The Godfather of Fake

What made Elmyr de Hory infamous wasn't the sheer number of forgeries he sold. It was that they were damn *good* forgeries. For 30 years, de Hory sold forgeries of paintings by the world's greatest artists, including Picasso, Chagall, Matisse, Degas, and Toulouse-Lautrec. In fact, his forgeries were so good, so precise in every detail, that they fooled even the most experienced art buyers. So much so that the native Hungarian has even attracted his own cult following, who pay high prices for "authentic" de Hory fakes. Irony of ironies, the forger's forgeries are now being forged and sold by other forgers! Even more odd: today, legitimate museums host exhibitions of de Hory's works. De Hory told his story in *Fake!* a 1969 biography by Clifford Irving (who went on to, yes, forge a phony autobiography of Howard Hughes). But in the end the master forger wound up penniless (just like a real painter) and committed suicide in 1976, although rumors persist that he faked that, too.

Hey Judas:
Historical Tattletales and $nitches

Judas handed Jesus over to the Romans for 30 lousy pieces of silver (about $40 in today's money, by some estimates). And sure, some of the snitches in our roundup got a little more coin than that, but whatever their worth, today they're simply remembered as dirty rats.

_01:: Tonny Ahlers (1917–2000)

In August 1944, the Gestapo raided the warehouse annex in Amsterdam where Anne Frank and seven others had lived in hiding for more than two years. All eight ended up at Auschwitz—with only Anne's father, Otto, surviving. Clearly, someone ratted out the Franks, but only recently has attention started to focus on Anton "Tonny" Ahlers. Dishonest, violent, and virulently anti-Semitic, Ahlers was a business associate of Otto Frank, and knew the Frank family lived in hiding. But just how damning is the evidence? Well, let's put it this way: Ahlers's own son believes that his father betrayed the Franks. He also thinks Tonny might have blackmailed Otto after the war, noting that Tonny received a monthly check from mysterious sources until 1980—

the year Otto Frank died. That part of the story may be far-fetched, but even so, many historians seem to think that the mystery of Anne Frank's betrayal has been solved.

Touch of Evil

Police admitted they probably would not have solved the Manson murders without the help of Susan Atkins, a Manson Family member who spilled her guts to her cell mate.

_02:: Robert Hanssen (1944–)

Widely believed to be the most damaging spy in the history of the FBI, Robert Hanssen snuck secrets to the Russians for millions of dollars in cash and diamonds between 1985 and 2001. His most damaging snitch? In October of 1985, Robbie informed the Soviet KGB that two KGB officers, Sergey Motorin and Valeriy Martynov, had been recruited to spy for the United States. Both men were promptly executed. Despite his handsome payoffs, though, Hanssen—known as Ramon Garcia to his Russian handlers—didn't exactly live like James Bond. The suburban snitch tooled around in a Ford Taurus and was happily married with six kids. And, like all the bad guys in *The Da Vinci Code,* Hanssen was also a member of Opus Dei, a secretive organization within the Catholic Church.

_03:: Richie Rich (1496–1567)

Believe it or not, the name Richie Rich had sinister implications even before Macaulay Culkin made it into a terrible film. After Henry VIII divorced Catherine of Aragon (without the pope's blessing), the devoutly Catholic Sir Thomas More, author of *Utopia,* refused to sign an oath swearing allegiance to the king

above the pope. On trial for treason, More's fate was sealed by the king's solicitor general, Richard Rich, who claimed More had told him that Parliament should have the right to depose the king. Rich, who never missed a chance to suck up to the powerful, was almost certainly lying, but More was convicted. A gentleman to the last, More comforted his executioners, saying, "Be not afraid to do thine office." He died on July 6, 1535—and was canonized by the Catholic Church in 1866.

_04:: Elia Kazan (1909–2003)

Although he directed such classic films as *East of Eden* and *A Streetcar Named Desire,* Elia Kazan is probably most famous for tattling on Hollywood communists to the House Un-American Activities Committee. In the 1930s, Kazan briefly joined the Communist Party but left, feeling betrayed (and rightly so, really) by Stalin's decidedly unegalitarian regime. When Kazan named names, helping to create the Hollywood blacklist, it provoked a firestorm of controversy within the artistic community—and when artists get mad, they do good work. Arthur Miller's play *The Crucible,* which portrays a Puritan who chooses to die rather than make a false accusation, is widely seen as an attack on Kazan. For his own part, Kazan made *On the Waterfront,* a movie about a heroic mob snitch, played by Marlon Brando.

_05:: Doña Marina (ca. 1501–1550)

Conquistador Hernán Cortés might never have conquered much without the able assistance of his slave, snitch, and mistress, Doña Marina. Originally named Malintzin, Marina abandoned her Aztec name after converting to Christianity. And because she understood

Aztec, Mayan, and Spanish (a triple threat!), Marina became a vital adviser and collaborator to Cortés...not to mention his lover. But besides blessing the conquistador with a son, she also aided his efforts in decimating the Aztec empire and people. Known in Mexico as *La Malinche,* Marina's betrayal has become part of the (Spanish, not Aztec) language—a *malinchista* is a person who abandons his or her language and heritage in pursuit of selfish goals.

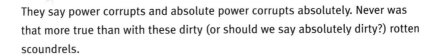

Corruption, Corruption, What's Your Function? of the Worst Perpetrators

They say power corrupts and absolute power corrupts absolutely. Never was that more true than with these dirty (or should we say absolutely dirty?) rotten scoundrels.

_01:: Good Ol' Boss Tweed

The undisputed poster child for graft and greed in American politics, Boss William Tweed raised corruption to an art form. As a member of New York's Tammany Hall, Tweed and his cronies, including Mayor Fernando Wood, ran New York in the Civil War era as their own private money factory. Tweed once bought 300 benches for $5 each, then sold them to the city for $600 a pop. And that's just the tip of it. The building of City Hall was a clinic in graft: the city was charged $7,500 for every thermometer, $41,190 for each broom, and $5.7 million for furniture and carpets. One carpenter even received almost $361,000 for a single month's work. And although he was crooked as a dog's hind leg, Tweed does get a bit of credit from some historians for undertaking many important projects that improved life in New York (albeit at enormous financial gain to himself). Tweed's illicit profits were said to be in the range of $200 *million,* and that's in the 1860s! The law eventually caught up with the Boss, though, and he died in prison in 1878.

_02:: President Grant's Cronies

The 18th president of the United States was a great war general. But he was less skilled at avoiding scandal. To be fair, it wasn't so much Grant himself as the cast of characters around him that caused all the trouble. Grant's period in office (1869–1877) was marred by four major scandals: Crédit Mobilier, a railroad construction scandal during which the federal government and Union Pacific stockholders were bilked out of some $20 million; the Whiskey Ring, wherein over 100 Treasury Department officials were convicted of taking bribes and cutting deals for distillers; the Indian Ring, another scandal of bribes from companies licensed to trade on Indian reservations;

and Black Friday, a scheme involving Grant's brother-in-law that attempted to artificially inflate the price of gold. So, what's buried in Grant's Tomb? Let's just say a lot of dirty laundry.

_03:: The Entire Nation of Bangladesh?

Well, you have to be the best at something. The nongovernment watchdog group Transparency International repeatedly ranks Bangladesh and the regime of Prime Minister Khaleda Zia as the world's most corrupt (the runners-up for this dubious honor are Nigeria at number 2 and Haiti at number 3). You can barely walk a block in the capital of Dhakar without coming face-to-face with graft: you have to pay the postman to get your mail; bus drivers pay cops to let them drive their routes; victims of crime have to pay the cops to have someone arrested; doctors take bribes to dispense medicine; even meter readers get their palms greased for keeping energy bills low. It's estimated that 6% of the nation's GNP is spent on corruption. Not surprising in a place where the unemployment rate hovers around 70%.

_04:: The Less-Than-Honorable Judge Maloney

In the 1970s and '80s, the Cook County Circuit Court system based in Chicago was so corrupt and dirty that two federal investigations, Operations Greylord and Gambat, were undertaken to expose it. Lots of judges went to jail for their underhanded dealings, but the worst of the worst was the not-so-honorable Thomas J. Maloney. During the 13 years he spent on

the bench, from 1977 to 1990, Maloney "fixed" as many as six murder trials, taking bribes from $10,000 to $100,000 from gangs to convict members of other gangs of murder or manslaughter. Eventually, the justice got his own justice as he was indicted and sentenced to 15 years and 9 months in prison. The fact is he's the only judge in Illinois history to be convicted of fixing a trial. Of course, there would have been another in the same Greylord operation, Judge Frank J. Wilson, but he blew his own brains out just before the Feds came a-knocking.

_05:: Alexander the Waste

Sure, there have been some bad popes. With a list numbering 262 and counting, there're bound to be a few bad apples, right? But Alexander VI (reigned 1492–1503) was the baddest apple of 'em all. A member of the Spanish branch of the powerful and corrupt Borgia family, Alexander bought and bribed his way onto the papal throne, and used it to gather wealth and women for himself and influence for his children. By some accounts he had as many as seven illegitimate children and carried on with numerous mistresses while he was pope. Alexander also made a fortune selling indulgences, and married off his beautiful fair-haired daughter Lucrezia three times, each time to someone richer and more powerful. When the pope finally checked out, he was left to rot and turn purple in the Sistine Chapel, until his bloated corpse had to be stuffed and crammed into his coffin—a suitably rotten ending for a very rotten man.

Great Bank Robberies

When the famous bank robber Willie Sutton was asked why he robbed banks, he supposedly replied, "That's where the money is." Sutton claimed he never actually said it. Pity. Someone should have.

_01:: The Great Northfield, Minnesota, Raid

OK, in terms of actual success, this 1876 robbery was a bust. But it had a heck of a cast: legendary bandits Frank and Jesse James; Cole, Jim, and Bob Younger; and three lesser-known outlaws. Their target was Northfield's First National Bank, which the gang settled on after casing a half-dozen other towns. Clearly, not enough casing, as the robbery couldn't have gone worse. The bank's cashier refused to open the safe, an alert passerby sounded the alarm, and townspeople killed two of the robbers as the rest escaped. A week later, a posse killed or captured all of the other outlaws except the James brothers, who escaped home to Missouri. It was the beginning of the end for 19th-century America's most notorious bandits. Worse still? The take from the Northfield bank was a mere $26.70.

_02:: Hitler's Gold

As the German army rolled through Europe in World War II, it ransacked the banks of other countries, transferring the loot to the central Reichsbank in Berlin. But when the U.S. Third Army neared the German capital, the stolen booty was hidden in mines near the village of Merkers. Unfortunately for the Nazis, the Third Army captured Merkers before the treasure could be moved again. And it was truly a treasure: 55 boxes of crated gold, 8,198 bars of gold bullion, and a few tons of artwork. The total value of the precious metals and currency was put at $520 million, and it took 50 years to return the loot to the robbed countries. In 1997, several countries waived their remaining claims, and the funds were used to aid Holocaust survivors.

Touch of Evil

The 1951 robbery of Boston's Brink Express Company headquarters netted seven criminals more than $2.75 million. After the FBI spent nearly $30 million over six years to catch the crooks, less than 2% of the take was ever recovered.

_03:: Thinking Inside the Box(es)

In early 1976, the Lebanese capital of Beirut was in the throes of a civil war. Palestinian guerrilla groups had gained control of the city's aptly named Bank Street and set about knocking off a dozen banks. The biggest prize on the lot? The British Bank of the Middle East. To get to the loot, a PLO-affiliated group blasted through the wall of a Catholic church next door to the bank. Then imported Corsican safe-crackers were employed to open the vault to get to the safety-deposit boxes. Over a two-day period, the robbers loaded trucks with $20 million to $50 million in currency, gold, jewels, and stocks and bonds (not bad for a couple of days' work). The bad guys got away, though all was not lost. Eventually, some of the stocks and bonds were sold back to their owners.

_04:: More Francs Than a Wiener Schnitzel

How many Frenchmen does it take to rob a bank? Well, at least 10, if you're talking about the 1992 Bank of France robbery in Toulon. Using inside information from a bank employee, the gang kidnapped a guard's family and forced the guard to open the bank's doors. But just in case the "we've got your family and we'd be happy to off them" tactic wasn't convincing enough, the group decided to ensure the poor guy's cooperation by strapping explosives to him. Apparently, it was pretty effective. Once inside, the robbers removed the film from the surveillance cameras, emptied the vaults of 160 million francs (about $30 million), and took off in several vans—including one belonging to the bank. Within two months, most of the gang was caught, betrayed by the bank employee (not to be confused with the guard) who'd helped in the job. But several of the robbers still got away, and amazingly, less than 10% of the loot was ever recovered.

_05:: The Trench Coat Job

It was past quitting time when two men wearing buttoned-up trench coats let themselves into the Seafirst Bank in Lakewood, Washington, a suburb of Tacoma. Flashing a

Lies Your Mother Told You

IF THE SLOT MACHINE HASN'T PAID OFF ALL DAY, IT'S DUE

Sorry, Mom. You're a victim of what math professors call the "gambler's fallacy." And while it's possible that some olden-days mechanical slot machines may have responded to continuous play, today's computer chip–driven slots have no "memory" of previous plays. That means every pull is a brand-new game. Slot makers even claim their machines could pay off 19 times in a row, or not for years. A corollary to the gambler's fallacy is that things that happen in the long run should also happen in the short run. It ain't so. Oh, and for those of you still a little green to the machines, a "95% average payback" doesn't mean everyone who puts in $100 gets $95 back. Just think on it for a sec: a player who puts in $10 and wins $100 has a 900% payback. That means a lot of other players on the same machine are going to have a very small, or no, payback just to get the percentage back down to 95. There's a reason the house always wins.

gun, the pair stuffed 355 pounds of cash—$4.46 million—into sacks and made a clean getaway. Insane, right? The 1997 heist was actually the largest bank robbery in U.S. history, but this wasn't the work of amateurs. Nope.

Ray Bowman and William Kirkpatrick were real pros. In fact, between 1982 and 1998, Bowman and Kirkpatrick were believed to have robbed 28 banks around the country for a total of more than $7 million. Even more impressive: only once was there gunfire, and no one was hurt. A special FBI task force was formed, but it was stupidity that finally tripped them up. Kirkpatrick was stopped for speeding in late 1998 by a Nebraska state trooper. A search of the car turned up four handguns, fake badges, two ski masks—and $1.8 million in cash. Meanwhile, Bowman had failed to pay the rent on a storage locker in Kansas City, Missouri. When the owner opened it, and found a virtual armory of guns, he called the cops, and they collared Bowman at his suburban Kansas City home a few weeks after Kirkpatrick's arrest. The dapper duo was convicted in 1999, with Bowman getting slapped with 24 years, Kirkpatrick with 15.

Always Bet on the House:
Failed Attempts to Loot Las Vegas

Not all the bandits in Sin City are one-armed. Here are a few different ways people have tried to beat the odds.

_01:: A Little off the Top

Here's how it worked. In the 1970s, the Mob coerced the Teamsters Union into making loans to a San Diego businessman buying four casinos in Vegas. As hidden partners, Mob bosses then "skimmed" millions of dollars from the joints by rigging slots so they showed winners when there were none, or by fixing scales so they underweighed coins. One estimate had the wise guys swiping $7 million in quarters in just one 18-month period. In the end, though, federal wiretaps and informants broke the scam. The Feds even tapped conversations between mobsters in the visitors room at Leavenworth Penitentiary, and in 1986, a dozen bosses from gangs in Chicago, Kansas City, Milwaukee, and Cleveland were convicted in the biggest Mob-Vegas case ever.

_02:: Playing Your Cards Right

Blackjack is a beatable game—that is, if you can count cards well enough to know when the deck favors the player, not the house. And while solitary card counters are relatively easy to spot for most casino security outfits, it took them six years during the 1990s to tumble to the strategy used by a group of MIT students. Using card-counting *teams,* complete with diversionary players—the cavalier math-letes raked in millions. One player recounted walking from one casino to another carrying a paper hat stuffed with $180,000 in cash.

Amazingly, the MIT ring was never actually caught in the act. Some members retired. A few others were ratted out by a team traitor and banned from the casinos, which learned a lesson about the concept of team play.

_03:: The Genius

Like a football quarterback, Dennis Nikrasch needed his blockers. In Nikrasch's case, however, they were blocking surveillance cameras while he worked his sweet computer magic on slot machines. Once the machines were rigged, the clever hacker vacated the premises, leaving it to confederates to win the jackpots. Cops have reported that the Nikrasch gang raked in at least $16 million between 1976 and 1998, even with a 10-year time-out while Nikrasch spent time in federal prison and on parole. When he was caught again in 1998, Nikrasch indicated that he'd share his secrets in return for a lighter sentence. He got seven years—and apparently refused to talk. "I have no desire to explain anything to the public," he wrote to an Internet magazine in 1999 from jail. "Never smarten up a chump."

_04:: The Mechanic

Starting in 1980 in the back of his TV repair shop in Tulsa, Oklahoma, Tommy Glenn Carmichael invented, refined, then manufactured devices for cheating slot machines. Tommy's bag of tricks ranged from coins on strings to light wands that blinded machine sensors, fooling them into dropping their coins. For most of two decades, Carmichael and his partners raked in millions of dollars. But his luck finally ran out when federal agents tapped his phone and heard him discussing a new device that would rack up hundreds of credits per minute on slot machines. In 2001, Carmichael was sentenced to about a year in jail, and was ordered to stay out of casinos. In 2003, he told an Associated Press reporter he was developing a new gadget, called "the Protector." It was designed to stop slot cheaters.

_05:: And If All Else Fails...

Jose Vigoa was one cocky crook. After doing a five-year stint from 1991 to 1996 for drug dealing, Vigoa decided to change career paths in 1998. Well, only slightly. As the mastermind of a string of armed robberies over two years that rocked the Vegas Strip, Vigoa armed his outfit with high-tech weapons, body armor, and sophisticated planning. In fact, the Vigoa gang hit up the MGM Grand, the Desert Inn, the Mandalay Bay, and the Bellagio. Not looking to slack off, they even robbed an armored car in between gigs, and killed the two guards. Vigoa was tripped up, however, when video cameras at the Bellagio caught him without a mask during the robbery. He was sentenced in 2002 to life without parole, proving crime doesn't pay, even in Vegas.

My Kingdom for a Horse?
Really Bad Historical Trades

3

We've all made deals from time to time that we've instantly wished we could take back. But take heart, friends! Gather round and hear the tales of some of the worst barters in human history. With so much numbskullery to choose from, there's bound to be someone who made a worse bargain than you did.

_01:: Ephialtes Sells Out the Spartans

Nobody really remembers Ephialtes today, but for centuries after his treasonous deeds, Greeks would spit at the mere mention of his name. Here's how the story goes. In 480 BCE, about 7,000 Greek soldiers, led by King Leonidas of Sparta, were holding off King Xerxes' Persian army of over 200,000 men at the narrow pass of Thermopylae. Not exactly the greatest odds, but the troops were buying time for the allied Greek states to gather their armies and oppose the Persians. Enter Ephialtes, a local ne'er-do-well, and now renowned snitch. The Greek traitor decided to show the Persians a secret path around the pass, which would allow them to attack the Greeks from behind. A splendid little secret indeed. Facing attack from both sides, Leonidas sent most of his allies home, and he and his Spartans fought to the death. Of course, Ephialtes was supposed to have been rewarded handsomely for this tattling, no doubt with land, gold, and titles. But when an Athenian fleet destroyed the Persian navy at Thermopylae shortly thereafter, he had to flee the Persian camp without a penny to his name. After all, King Xerxes wasn't exactly in the rewarding mood at the time. On bad terms with the Persians, and wanted by the Greeks for his treason, the rascal fled to the wilds of Thessaly, where a few years later he was murdered.

_02:: The Dutch Buy Manhattan for a Pittance

In 1626, Peter Minuit, a representative of the Dutch government, bought Manhattan Island from an Algonquin tribe for 60 guilders. The old story about the Dutch buying the joint for 24 bucks' worth of beads is unlikely—there is no evidence that beads were part of the deal (iron tools were probably much more valuable to the natives). Nevertheless, considering the fact that a shoebox-sized apartment on the isle today sells for more than most people make in a lifetime, it seems that the Algonquins somewhat undervalued their own real estate. Only in America.

_03:: Cincinnati Gets Hosed: The Christy Mathewson–Amos Rusie Trade

Forget the Curse of the Bambino. Compared with this gaffe by the Cincinnati Reds, Boston's decision to trade Babe Ruth (and the subsequent 86-year curse) looks like a carefully orchestrated work of managerial genius. In 1900, the Reds traded relative newcomer

Touch of Evil

Manhattan for beads? No. The worst trade made between the Europeans and the Native Americans was much more gruesome: Europeans brought smallpox to America, which the Indians traded for syphilis!

and Renaissance man Christopher "Christy" Mathewson to the New York Giants for the ailing "Hoosier Thunderbolt," Amos Rusie. Following this brilliant move, Mathewson won 372 games for the Giants, including more than 20 games in 11 different seasons. He won wide renown as one of the greatest pitchers in baseball history. Rusie, on the other hand, pitched in three games following the trade, losing one and winning none—following which he promptly retired.

An Offer I Can't Refuse: Generals Who Switched Sides in the Hopes of Reward

Military turncoats come in all shapes and sizes, motivated by all sorts of considerations: power, revenge, disillusionment, and, most often, the sound of a little extra coin. But not every turncoat seems to bear the tarnished rep old Benedict Arnold came away with. The following are some of history's lesser-known traitors, but ones who were pleased with the results.

_01:: Flavius Josephus (ca. 37–100)

Revolutionary governments, caught up in the heat of the moment, often make poor decisions. For example, the Jewish rebels fighting against Rome appointed Joseph ben Matthias to be military governor of Galilee. An inveterate coward, however, Joseph surrendered at the first opportunity and became the Roman general Flavius Vespasianus's adviser on Jewish affairs. A nice gig, for sure. And when Flavius became emperor in the year 69, Joseph (or Josephus, as his new pals called him) found himself vaulted to the top of Roman high society. After trying to encourage the surrender of Jerusalem by shouting propaganda at the walls, he retired to Rome and became a famous author. The guilt of his treason may have caught up with old Josephus in his old age; he penned numerous writings lauding Jewish civilization, possibly to try to clear his conscience.

_02:: Alaric (ca. 370–410)

A nobleman of the Visigoths, a Germanic tribe living in central Europe, Alaric fought for the Roman emperor Theodosius I against the rebel

Eugenius. The brilliant decision to hire Alaric, though, gave the cunning nobleman an insider's view of the empire's weaknesses, and he took careful note. When Theodosius died in 395, the empire was divided into eastern and western halves ruled by his quarreling sons— and Alaric decided opportunity wasn't just knocking, it was practically kicking down his door. Alaric marched on Constantinople and ravaged the Thracian countryside, capturing most of Greece before the Roman general Stilicho forced him to withdraw. Soon after, the eastern emperor Arcadius gave Alaric control of most of Illyria, all of which paved the way for his first invasion of Italy in 401. Alaric invaded the nation of his former employment several more times, and in 410 he became the first "barbarian" king to sack Rome in over 500 years. Though Alaric died in a plague in his 40s, his descendents carved out an empire of their own in what is now southern France, Spain, and Portugal.

_03:: Rodrigo Díaz de Vivar (El Cid, Campeador) (1043–1099)

His very title speaks of a checkered past: *El Cid* comes from the Arabic *al-Sayyid,* or "the lord," while *Campeador* is Spanish for "champion." Back when it all started, El Cid was a commander in the army of Castile. Of course, the cocky commander wasn't all roses to work with, and the Cid was forced to flee in 1080 after angering King Alfonso. What's an out-of-work commander to do, though? El Cid quickly decided to shack up with the enemy, joining forces with the Muslim emir (king) of Zaragosa. Despite the emir's cantankerous relationship with Castile, El Cid fought valiantly with his former foes for several years. That is, until Spain was invaded by Berber fanatics from

North Africa. Bathing in schadenfreude, El Cid was summoned back by Alfonso, profusely apologized to, and begged to defeat the seemingly invincible invaders. El Cid accepted, and in the course of the fighting, "the Champion" maneuvered himself into the top spot in Valencia, the gem of Spain's Mediterranean coast. He died in 1099 fighting off a new wave of North African attackers, but even after his death proved useful. The city's defenders strapped the Cid's rapidly-assuming-room-temperature form to the back of his horse and managed to trick the enemies into thinking El Cid, Campeador, was still in charge.

_04:: Francesco Sforza (1401–1466)

Warfare in 15th-century Italy was dominated by the *condottieri,* mercenary generals who commanded motley crews of hungry soldiers. Of course, the soldiers for hire weren't exactly loved by everyone, and were seen as particularly uncouth by those gallant few who fought for land instead of money. The son of one of the most successful of the condottieri, Francesco Sforza was known for his great strength: reportedly, he could bend iron bars with his bare hands. Of course, as a mercenary, his loyalties were just as easily bent. After signing on with various feudal lords in their endless wars, he settled down in Milan and joined forces with Filippo Visconti, the local duke. On Visconti's death in 1447, however, Francesco turned on the duke's family and exiled or killed many of them. He also broke up an attempt to establish a Milanese republic, and then made himself duke. It's not nearly as bad as it sounds, though. Francesco went on to usher in nearly two decades of the best rule Milan had ever seen.

Touch of Evil

The three Generals who have the most impact on the Department of Defense? General Dynamics, General Electric, and General Motors, all of which are among the companies with the most money tied up in military contracts.

_05:: Albrecht Wenzel Eusebius von Wallenstein (1583–1634)

A minor, though well-educated, Czech nobleman, Wallenstein became an officer in the armies of the Holy Roman Empire. He fought numerous battles against Venice and other powers and gained a reputation for military genius. But when his fellow Protestants rebelled against the empire in 1618, ushering in the Thirty Years' War, imperial generals worked themselves into a tizzy fearing that they would face Wallenstein on the field. They needn't have worried, though. A man whose eye was always on the bottom line, Wallenstein calculated that the rewards of serving the Catholic side of the war were greater. He helped crush Protestant armies in his native Bohemia as well as in western and northern Germany. Removed from command in 1630 on suspicion of preparing to switch sides, he was reinstated shortly thereafter on the rationale that a general thought to be disloyal was probably better than generals known to be incompetent. In retrospect, however, the reasoning was questionable, as Wallenstein was killed in 1634 while attempting to defect to the Swedes.

_06:: Shi Lang (1621–1696)

An admiral in the navy of China's Ming dynasty, Shi Lang came into conflict with Zheng Chenggong, a rival general. Deciding that the grass looked greener up north, he defected in 1646 to the Manchus, and left his family behind to be slaughtered as traitors. Was it worth the (very literal) sacrifice? Apparently so. Lacking experienced naval officers, the Manchu ruler Shunzhi welcomed Shi Lang with open arms, and the officer happily participated in the Manchu conquest of China. In fact, he became an official of the new Qing dynasty, made up of Shunzhi's descendents. Then, in 1681, he even got to lead the conquest of Taiwan, which culminated in the surrender of his old enemies, the Zheng family. In the end, Shi Lang made out pretty well, and was given the title "General Who Maintains Peace on the Seas" by a very grateful imperial government.

Double-crossing Agents (and the Countries That Paid Them)

In the trust-no-one world of espionage, an operative for one government may in fact be working for that government's enemy, and vice versa. Of course, the most successful double agents are the ones no one ever heard of. A few of the rest are listed below.

_01:: Numero Trece

An officer in the American Revolution, James Wilkinson moved after the war to Kentucky, where in 1787 he pledged loyalty to Spain. In return for a Spanish pension, Wilkinson (or "Numero 13" to his Spanish handlers) worked to make Kentucky part of Spanish Louisiana. Of course, Wilkinson had his fingers in a few pies at the time, and was simultaneously being promoted to lieutenant colonel in the U.S. Army. After the Louisiana Purchase of 1800, Wilkinson became a U.S. territorial governor, and began conspiring with U.S. vice president Aaron Burr to found an independent nation in Mexico. But like a good double-crosser, he's the one credited with exposing Burr's plot to President Thomas Jefferson, leading to Burr's trial for treason. Wilkinson emerged from the scandal with honor intact and commanded U.S. troops in the War of 1812. His incompetence, however, ended his U.S. service and he moved to Mexico, where he petitioned for and won a Texas land grant.

_02:: The Family That Spies Together...

In 1967, John Walker Jr., a petty burglar and U.S. Navy radioman, walked into the Soviet embassy in Washington, D.C., and offered to supply encryption keys—tools for decoding classified military messages—in exchange for a regular salary from the KGB. For the next 18 years, during and after his Navy career, Walker continued to work for the Soviets. When a transfer removed his access to classified codes and documents, he enlisted help from others, including his brother and his son. In fact, Walker talked his kid, Michael, into enlisting in the Navy just to pilfer shipboard documents. KGB officers later said that Walker had given them access to the most vital U.S. secrets. When the FBI finally caught up with him in 1984, Walker thought he could avoid prosecution by offering to turn the table on the Soviets. Under interrogation, however, he confessed, and is serving a life term in federal prison.

_03:: For a Fistful of Millions

Before his arrest in 1994, career CIA agent Aldrich "Rick" Ames exposed the identity of every U.S. agent working in the Soviet Union and its successor states. And the leak was used to full effect. Between 1985 and 1994, the Soviets executed at least 10 CIA operatives based solely on the info Aldrich and his Colombian-born wife were feeding them. A 31-year em-

Touch of Evil

Benedict Arnold probably wished he could've had a do-over. He never got even half the money the British promised him for switching sides.

the agency. But like a fox guarding the henhouse, Aldrich betrayed his country and traded the lives of his comrades for a mere $2.5 million. Top government officials said the damage to U.S. security was potentially catastrophic. After pleading guilty to charges of conspiracy to commit espionage and tax fraud, Ames was sentenced to life imprisonment without chance of parole.

ployee of the U.S. intelligence agency, Ames's job had been to discover Soviet spies within

ALAN FREED'S HORRIBLE-TERRIBLE, NO-GOOD, VERY BAD DAY

On March 21, 1952, the Moondog Coronation Ball took place at the Cleveland Arena in Cleveland, Ohio, becoming the first rock-and-roll concert in history. The concert, which was promoted by Alan Freed (known for giving rock and roll its name), was also the event where the first rock-and-roll riot occurred. Why, exactly? Well, the concert hall only held around 10,000 people while over 20,000 tickets were sold. Also, even though most of the artists performing were African American, the fans able to get inside were white while those left outside were black. There was gate crashing and fights broke out between groups of fans and then quickly with the police. When the police finally closed down the concert, fans spilled out onto the streets of Cleveland, causing chaos and damage. As for Alan Freed, he was summarily arrested for inciting the riot. It seems that from day one, rock and roll and rioting were destined to happen together.

To the Victors Go the Soils: History's Most Blatant Land Grabs

God supposedly issued a commandment against it, and yet people have been stealing from each other since the world began. And sometimes on a ridiculously large scale. Here are just a few of the more outrageous instances.

_01:: Prussia, Austria, and Russia Partition Poland

Internal divisions accelerated by a ridiculous parliamentary system led to Poland's decline in the 18th century, and its neighbors—Prussia to the west, Austria to the south, and Russia to the east—were more than happy to bite off a large part of the struggling nation in the "First Partition" of 1772. All told, the nations usurped about half of its territory and a third of its population. In an attempt to save itself, the Polish government tried to institute internal reforms, but it was too little too late. In the "Second Partition," in 1793, Prussia and Russia took even more land, causing Polish rebellions that they quickly crushed. As if that weren't enough, the "Third Partition," in 1797, had Austria participating again, and it finished off Poland as a separate state. The nation wouldn't be independent again until 1918. And shortly thereafter, to add insult to injury, the Nazis and Soviets partitioned the country one last time, in 1939.

_02:: America Takes Most of the West from Mexico

In 1776, the 13 colonies covered about 900,000 square miles along the east coast of North America. Over the course of the next 75 years, the country would expand 300%, to about 2.9 million square miles, through five international treaties, two wars, and the Louisiana Purchase in 1803. Though the Purchase was a legitimate exchange of property—except for the claims of Native American inhabitants, of course, who were never really consulted—much of the later expansion was a blatant illegitimate land grab. The Mexican-American War of 1846, for example, began in part because slave owners in the American South wanted to add Texas as a new slave-owning territory. The war resulted in the transfer of all of California, Nevada, Arizona, Utah, and large parts of New Mexico, Colorado, and Wyoming to the U.S., all for a rather paltry payment of $15 million.

_03:: Japan Invades   and Then the Res

In the decades before 1 ore and coal to outfi military and indust 18, 1931, Japan in mineral-rich provi course, the invasic anese officers fab by blowing up a South Manchu

Sout B

nese saboteurs. The move was just the first in a long series of aggressive actions that would bring much of Asia under Japanese control, including unprovoked attacks on Shanghai, Hong Kong, and Nanking in south China, the occupation of many of China's coastal provinces, the sneak attack on the U.S. Navy at Pearl Harbor, and shortly thereafter the invasion and occupation of the Philippines, Vietnam, Laos, Cambodia, Thailand, Burma, Malaysia, Singapore, Indonesia, and New Guinea! Though estimates vary, it's certain that tens of millions of people died as a result of the Japanese aggression, which ended only with the country's defeat in the Second World War.

Touch of Evil

Colombia rejected a $10 million offer by the U.S. for the rights to build a canal across its land, so a "rebel force" was quickly organized, which broke free and became the country of Panama (with U.S. military support). The rebels got the bucks, and Teddy Roosevelt got his canal.

_04:: Cecil Rhodes, Zimbabwe, Botswana, and Zambia

Cecil Rhodes single-handedly added the modern countries of Zimbabwe, Botswana, and Zambia to British South Africa. Hardly content to stop there, Rhodes once famously declared, "I would annex the planets if I could." Rhodes moved to the British Cape Colony in South Africa in 1870 at the age of 17 and founded the ritish South Africa Company, which began at Africa's diamond-rich Kimberly mine

and is now known as DeBeers. The company began expanding north into the tribal lands of present-day Zimbabwe in 1889, and subdued recalcitrant tribes there by force in 1893. The new territory was called Rhodesia in Rhodes's honor. Meanwhile, in 1890, company agents made treaties with local tribal leaders in present-day Zambia. Botswana was brought under British control after the controversial Boer War from 1899 to 1902. In the end, Cecil Rhodes had single-handedly taken control of an area more than three times the size of France.

_05:: Germany Invades Belgium in World War I

At the London Conference of 1838–1839, all the major European powers agreed to protect the neutrality of the small, newly created country of Belgium. However, as time went on Germany claimed that Belgium was not behaving as a neutral country because it had fortified its border with Germany but not with France. Although Belgium had a sovereign right to do this, a contingency plan for war with France was devised by General von Schlieffen in the 19th century, calling for a pincer offensive closing in on Paris, with one arm coming south across the Rhine—intended as a feint—and another arm launching a surprise attack from the north through Belgium. This plan was finally set in motion during the First World War, meeting with almost universal condemnation because it so blatantly disregarded treaty obligations and the rules of warfare, marking a new low in international relations and heralding the brutality to come.

I Got Mine, Now What?
Shady Business Moguls and What They Did with Their Money

"A man who dies rich dies disgraced," said philanthropic industrialist Andrew Carnegie. And while not that many robber barons would agree, a few did try to give something back to society, no matter how unscrupulously their money was acquired.

_01:: An Erie Case of Corruption

Cattleman Daniel Drew turned to the passenger steamboat business in 1834 and prospered. Ten years later, he opened the Wall Street brokerage firm Drew, Robinson and Company. Then a decade after that, when a financial panic hit in 1857, Drew snapped up the undervalued Erie Railroad stock and became a company director. Not a bad few years. Although Drew routinely manipulated stocks, his old steamboat competitor Cornelius Vanderbilt outfoxed him in 1864 with company infighting and Drew lost heavily. Seeking revenge, he and two partners issued enormous amounts of Erie stock, driving down the value of Vanderbilt's investment. Both sides bribed judges in the "Erie War," which ruined thousands of investors, but never really hurt Vanderbilt. Then, in an unexpected twist, Drew's partners turned on him, leaving him ruined. Although dishonest in business, Drew did have a few good qualities. As a devout Methodist, he founded the Drew Theological Seminary (which later became Drew University) before he lost his money.

_02:: Whistle-stop Prosperity

After a few years of law practice in Wisconsin, Leland Stanford heard about all the money you could make selling equipment (at grossly inflated prices) to gold rush miners in California, so he promptly moved west. Once well established as a merchant, Stanford decided to seek public office and in 1860 he won California's governorship. Never bothered by conflicts of interest, Stanford used his position to secure public money and state land grants for himself and his three Sacramento partners—Mark Hopkins, Collis Huntington, and Charles Crocker—who built the western portion of the transcontinental railroad. After one two-year term, Stanford became president of the Central Pacific Railroad. A consummate (and ridiculously corrupt) businessman, Stanford's varied interests were greased with government influence, all of which brought him tremendous wealth. But he did give back a little. In 1885, after the death of his teenage son, Stanford founded and endowed Stanford University in the boy's memory.

DAVID HANNUM'S HORRIBLE-TERRIBLE, NO-GOOD, VERY BAD DAY

Turns out P. T. Barnum wasn't the man behind the memorable aphorism "There's a sucker born every minute." Though nearly always attributed to Barnum, the quote about suckers was actually from a first-rate sucker (and Barnum rival) named David Hannum. In 1869, Hannum and four business partners paid $37,500 for a 10-foot-tall stone giant man. The Cardiff Giant was in fact an elaborate hoax played by a tobacconist named John Hull, who had the stone man carved, then buried in Cardiff, New York, and then dug up again. Theories abounded about the giant (was he a petrified biblical figure? an ancient Native American statue?), and thousands of people paid good money to catch a glimpse. Of course, Hannum was looking to make back his investment easily. But then P. T. Barnum built a giant and claimed that *it* was the true Cardiff Giant. When people flocked to see Barnum's fake, Hannum—who didn't yet know he'd paid almost 40 grand for a fake giant of his own—mused incredulously, "There's a sucker born every minute." Sure is. And it takes one to know one, Mr. Hannum.

_03:: The Art of Making Money

The son of a financier, John Pierpont Morgan bought his way out of the Civil War draft for $300, giving himself plenty of free time to speculate in wartime gold. As Morgan quickly realized, the price of the metal rose against the dollar with each Union Army defeat. As a bank loan agent, J. P. Morgan earned a commission on a deal to buy defective rifles from a Union arsenal in New York for $3.50 apiece, then sell them to the Union Army in Virginia for $22 each. The underhanded deal (in, oh, so many ways) only helped him on his way to becoming a powerful banker, a railroad magnate, and one of the world's top financiers. Of course, he wasn't all bad. J. P.'s giant industrial consolidations reshaped American capitalism and his financial muscle held off national fiscal crises. Further, as a great art collector, Morgan gave many works to New York's Metropolitan Museum of Art. In fact, his book collection and the building that housed it have become a museum and public library in New York.

_04:: Oil Wells That End Well

John D. Rockefeller—originally a dealer in farm goods—got into the oil business in 1863 and founded Standard Oil in 1870. His ruthless competitive practices made Standard Oil a monopoly and made Rockefeller the world's first billionaire. To skirt antimonopoly laws, he reorganized the Standard Oil Trust and made the resulting companies appear in compliance. When the U.S. Supreme Court in 1911 declared Standard Oil to be in violation of federal law, it forced the company's breakup. But by then,

Rockefeller had found a new hobby: philanthropy. Before his death at age 97 in 1937, he had given away $500 million, including $80 million to the University of Chicago, which he had helped found in 1892. With son John D. Rockefeller Jr., the businessman also founded Rockefeller University, the General Education Board, and the Rockefeller Foundation.

_05:: Honeys, I'm Home!

Haroldson Lafayette Hunt speculated in cotton and Arkansas farmland before he became an oilman in the 1920s. As a real-estate operator, Hunt would find out a farmer's asking price, then find a buyer willing to pay a little more. In essence, the slick salesman would cut deals to sell the land before he actually acquired it. In 1930, though, Hunt took his eyes off land and set them on oil. He bought out East Texas oil wildcatter "Dad" Joiner and reaped hundreds of millions in profits. And while Hunt was pretty fond of money, he was also fond of pretty wives. A bigamist, Hunt was married to first wife, Lyda, throughout his 17-year marriage to second wife, Frania. Then, after Lyda's death, he married secretary Ruth Ray, who had already borne him four children. But even with all the wives, and kids, and business dealings, Hunt made plenty of time to preach about the little things he really loved: like conservative values. The billionaire founded the nonprofit *Facts Forum* radio program, and also hosted the conservative radio show *Life Line*. Among his 14 children, daughters Margaret Hunt Hill, Helen LaKelly Hunt, and Swannee Hunt have been especially active in charitable work.

Touch of Evil

Tabloid and "yellow journalism" king William Randolph Hearst did more than buy flowers for his mistress, Marion Davies. He formed Cosmopolitan Pictures to make films starring only her, and put rave reviews in all his newspapers.

Pilfer While You Work: Marauders to Know

3

Who invented the concept of "take the money and run"? Judging by the dates on these entries, we're guessing it wasn't Woody Allen.

_01:: Fur Pants, Iron Sword

The sketchy facts about Ragnar Lodbrok, prototypical Viking king, were spun into legend so long ago that the truth is elusive. Probably born in Norway, this Danish chieftain wore fur trousers that earned him the name Lodbrok ("Hairy Pants"). A proud pagan, Lodbrok enjoyed attacking the coasts of Europe on holy days, when townspeople were off guard. Legend says Ragnar fought Charlemagne (who died in 814 CE), but it's more likely that he led the 5,000 Norse warriors that besieged Paris in the 850s, until Charlemagne's grandson Charles II paid them off. (Ragnar often demanded and received huge bribes.) The Viking then hit up northern England on his European tour, but the strike proved unlucky. Hairy Pants was captured by the Saxon king Aella, who killed him by lowering him into a snake pit, Indiana Jones–style.

_02:: The Holy (City) Terror

At the culmination of the First Crusade in 1099, fair-haired Godfrey of Bouillon, a direct descendent of Charlemagne, led the first troops over the wall into Jerusalem. Bouillon and his fellow commanders from Western Europe, Raymond of Toulouse and Tancred Hauteville, were intent on taking the Holy City away from its Shiite Muslim rulers. Shortly after Godfrey's advance guard threw open the gates, the rest of the Christian troops stormed in. Immediately, the Muslim governor surrendered, but he was comforted when Tancred told him that those residents who took refuge in the Aqsa Mosque would be spared. Although Tancred may have been sincere, the rest of the Crusaders didn't show any mercy. They slaughtered everybody in the mosque in the name of Christ, and they killed virtually everyone else in Jerusalem as well—Muslim and Jew, grandmother and infant. When the raid was over, Godfrey declared himself ruler of Jerusalem under the title Defender of the Holy Sepulcher.

_03:: Black Beard, Black Heart

During the War of Spanish Succession (1701–1714), the Bristol-born Edward Teach sailed under a privateer's charter from Britain, attacking ships from hostile nations for profit. But in 1716 he began to freelance. Teach, better known as Blackbeard for his raven-colored chin whiskers, converted a captured French freighter into a 40-gun warship. As *Queen Anne's Revenge,* the vessel spread terror across the Caribbean and along the southern coast of colonial North America. Blackbeard raided ports and forced bribes from other sea captains in return for safe passage. He also cut deals with unscrupulous officials, including the colonial governor of North Carolina. The lieutenant governor of Virginia, however, called for a British naval force to put the pirate out of business. After a tough sea battle, the Brits killed Blackbeard, cut off his bearded head, and fastened it to the bowsprit of his ship.

Touch of Evil

Know which Marauder helped the Allies win World War II? The B-26 Marauder bomber. Thousands of them combined to drop 150,000 tons of explosives on Hitler and his cohorts.

LUST

④ Famous Scientists Who Shared More Than Equations ⑥ Sinfully Amusing Snippets ⑤ Infamous Female Spies ⑤ Facts on Harems ④ Original Cities of Sin (None of Which Had Elvis Impersonators) ④ Self-proclaimed Casanovas ⑤ So-called Virtuous Figures Who Got Caught with Their Flies Down (or Skirts Up) ⑥ Presidential Affairs (Cigar Not Included) ④ Victorian Tricks for Retraining That Mojo ④ Royal Mistresses Who Made Good ⑤ Risqué Ad Campaigns That Got Canned ⑥ Crazy Historical Trades for Brides ⑥ Historical Dudes with Lots of Illegitimate Children ⑤ Famous People Who Died in the Act World's ⑧ Strangest Aphrodisiacs ④ Historical Eloping Tales ⑤ Greatest Syphilitics of All Time ④ Not-So-Straitlaced Reformers of Victorian Times ⑤ Artists Who Did More Than Portray Their Models ⑤ Divinity School Dropouts ⑥ Portraits of Artists as Young Perverts ⑤ Sex Rumors About Royalty

The "Get Around, Get Around, I Get Around" Awards: Famous Scientists Who Shared More Than Equations

The nerdy scientist stereotype hardly presents the recipe for hot romance. After all, equations, beakers, and Bunsen burners rarely set the stage for love scenes except in the most absurd of parodies. And yet sometimes, while heating things up in the laboratory, scientists have been known to, well, heat things up in the laboratory.

_01:: Frederick's Hypothesis

To his friends, Frederick von Hohenstaufen was the *stupor mundi* ("wonder of the world"). To his enemies, he was the Antichrist. Of course, to the people of Sicily (1197–1250), Germany (1212–1250), and the Holy Roman Empire (1220–1250), he was simply the king. As a skilled warlord, Freddy kept power by overwhelming his enemies with his military expertise. As a clever linguist, he wrote scientific tracts in a dozen languages (including one of the first detailed manuals on the anatomy of birds). Not to mention that the guy was also an early advocate of the experimental method and performed some rather interesting (though highly unethical) experiments—such as raising children in silence to see if they would speak a "natural language." But Fred was best known for his decadent lifestyle—enamored of Islamic culture and philosophy, he kept a harem of nubile young ladies at his beck and call. And why shouldn't he? It's good to be the king.

_02:: Swingin' Ben Franklin

The kite-flying, bifocals-inventing, library- and post office–establishing Renaissance man of the American Revolution was a self-taught meteorologist, printer, inventor...and ladies' man? That's right, old Ben Franklin loved to get his groove on. And though he appears to have been faithful to his beloved wife Deborah during the years of their marriage (from 1730 until her death in 1774), historical records show big Ben was quite the man slut both before they married and after her death. In fact, Franklin fathered at least one illegitimate child, William, in 1728. While on diplomatic missions in Europe for the Continental Congress, Franklin developed a reputation that led more than one worried father to lock up his daughters when the American delegation was in town. And even in his old age, Franklin had so many affairs that we wonder if he might not be literally, as well as figuratively, the "Father of Philadelphia."

_03:: Einstein = Ladies' Man Squared

While he never had an actual harem like von Hohenstaufen or a gaggle of French mistresses like Franklin, old Al Einstein earns his place in the Horny Scientist Hall of Fame just the same for his work in seducing his colleague, Serbian scientist Mileva Maric. The lewd scientist snared more than just her heart when the two were graduate students working together in a lab. And Maric actually gave birth to an illegitimate daughter, whom the couple gave up for adoption, before marrying Einstein in 1903. Though the two went on to have more children (before divorcing in 1919), some have suggested that Maric made significant contributions to Einstein's theories. Albert didn't give up on love, though—he married his second wife, Elsa (not before contemplating marriage with her 20-year-old daughter, Ilse), shortly after his divorce, but maintained numerous affairs with other women throughout the 1920s and 1930s. Whether or not you consider it ethical, of course, remains a matter of relativity.

_04:: Alfred Kinsey Gets Kinky

An entomologist by training, Kinsey's tastes soon strayed far from insects. In 1947 he founded the Institute for Sex Research at Indiana University, single-handedly creating the academic field of sexology. In fact, his well-known Kinsey Reports were among the first scientific studies of human sexual behavior. It's little wonder that the guy was attacked by traditionalists, who accused him of promoting immoral behavior and sexual perversion. And though the first charge is a matter of opinion, they may have been more accurate on the second than they knew at the time. After Kinsey's death it became known that he was a masochist and a fan of group sex. Both Kinsey and his wife regularly engaged in sex with other men, but they stayed married for 35 years and remained devoted to each other until his death in 1956. Kinsey was also infamous for encouraging his assistants and grad students to engage in unusual sex acts with one another, which no doubt made for some rather interesting staff meetings.

Touch of Evil

After the death of her husband, Marie Curie began a scandalous affair with her married lab assistant. Despite her two Nobels and everything she did for science, the tryst ultimately cost her admission into the prestigious Académie des Sciences.

Biblical Girls Gone Wild: Sinfully Amusing Snippets

It's part of the genius of the Bible that most of the great biblical figures aren't portrayed as supermen or saints. Abraham doesn't appear to have been in any danger of winning Father of the Year, Moses had serious anger management issues, and King Solomon's love of the finer things is criticized in the text, particularly his harem filled with 1,000 women. And because they're human, we can relate to them—well, most of the time. Here are a few biblical stories you probably didn't hear about in Sunday school.

_01:: Lot's Daughters Bark up the Family Tree (Genesis 19)

As they hid in a cave somewhere in the wilderness near the Dead Sea, Lot and his daughters were the only survivors of God's rampage through the streets of sinful, sinful Sodom (luckily, as the only righteous man in town, Lot was spared). Suspecting that they were the last people left on earth, and unwilling to die alone and childless, Lot's crafty lot got their father drunk and then had their way with him, making the previously righteous figure his own son-in-law and his two sons' father also grandfather and uncle at the same time. And while this probably made Lot family reunions a tad more interesting, sadly the details are lost in the mists of time. As for the kids, though, they did pretty all right for themselves. Lot's sons grew up to be the ancestors of the Moabites and Ammonites, two very powerful tribes of the highland region east of the Jordan River.

_02:: Jacob's Women (Genesis 29–30)

Need something even more Jerry Springer for your scandal-loving palate? Then get a load of the story of Jacob, grandson of Abraham. Things started off rocky for the kid as Jacob had to flee to his uncle's place after royally screwing his brother Esau in an inheritance swindle. Safe in the warmth of his uncle's home, he fell in love with his cousin Rachel, and married her, but not before his uncle Laban duped him into marrying Rachel's sister Leah as well. (For the privilege of all this cousin-marrying Jacob had to work 14 years, though some might say marriage is hard time enough!) More chaos ensued when Rachel, the beloved wife, was barren while her sister, Leah, (to whom Jacob was presumably relatively indifferent) produced kids with alarming regularity. Not to be outdone, Rachel gave her servant, Bilhah, to Jacob as a concubine, taking the kids produced as her own. Leah upped the ante by giving the probably exhausted Jacob her servant, Zilpah. All told, the competitive fivesome produced 13 children, 12 of which became the ancestors of Israelite tribes and the last of whom (see below) had the poor taste to be born a girl.

_03:: Dinah's Brothers Get Overprotective (Genesis 34)

Dinah was the only known daughter of the extraordinarily fertile Jacob. One day while her family was camped outside the town of Shechem, Dinah went to get some water and had a run-in with a local prince. Whether she ran off with him willingly (as feminist authors like to claim) or was raped by him (as the text seems to suggest) is unclear, but her 11 older brothers (the 12th, Joseph, was by this time in Egypt) had a rather dim view of such goings-on. After convincing the prince's buddies that circumcision was a great idea, Dinah's older brothers slaughtered the lot of them while they were recuperating from their ordeal. Dinah's ultimate fate has gone unrecorded, but folks who heard the tale were probably careful around girls with that many brothers for some time thereafter.

_04:: Tamar Tricks Judah (Genesis 38)

Another of Jacob's kids, Judah, married off his oldest son, Er, to a woman named Tamar. Er, who was "wicked in the eyes of the Lord," ended up dying young. The custom of the time (codified into law later in the Bible) was that his next oldest brother should "go in unto" his widow, and the child from that union would carry on the line of the dead man. Judah's second son, Onan, wasn't exactly up to the challenge, however. Unwilling to fulfill his obligation to his brother, Onan instead "spilled his seed on the ground" (hence "onanism," or masturbation). For the sin of refusing his brotherly obligation (not, as is often stated, for spanking his proverbial monkey), Onan too met an untimely end. So, what was a proud parent (albeit an embarrassed one at this point) to do? Unwilling to risk his youngest son's life, Judah sent Tamar home to her folks. But Tamar one-upped Jacob. Disguising herself as a prostitute, she tricked her father-in-law into performing the neglected duty himself. In fact, she bore him two sons, one of whom, Perez, was an ancestor of King David.

Touch of Evil

A 1631 printing of the King James version of the Bible was missing a rather important word. It became known as the **Wicked Bible** *for leaving "not" out of Exodus 20:14, which as a result read "Thou shalt commit adultery."*

_05:: Jael "Nails" Sisera (Judges 5)

Jael was the wife of Heber, the chieftain of a clan allied with the Israelites. After the Israelite chieftainess Deborah defeated Sisera, who was a general for the king of Hazor, Sisera made a hasty retreat that took him right by Jael's tent. The clever Jael, went on to play it just right. She invited him in, fed him and, in a scene reminiscent of bad porn, may even have had sex with him. Once he was sound asleep, though, she took a hammer and drove a tent peg through his skull. Who knew the chieftain's wife would be so handy with a hammer? Or thoughtful? Jael went on to present Sisera's carcass as a gift to Deborah's army when they turned up shortly thereafter.

_06:: Bathsheba Nonchalantly Goes Skinny-dipping…in Plain Sight of the Royal Palace (2 Samuel 11)

One day King David glanced out his window and just happened to see a beautiful, completely naked woman taking a bath on a rooftop. She had no idea that David was going to be watching (and if you believe that, we have a river in Egypt to sell you), but he was immediately smitten. Just one problem: The woman, Bathsheba, was already married to a Hittite mercenary named Uriah. In one of David's less than stellar moments, he conspired to have Uriah moved too close to enemy lines and, with her husband out of the way, rushed to the altar with Bathsheba. Good thing, too, as it was just in time for her first son by him to be born. In an episode that is part tragic, part comic, and all shocking, the prophet Nathan exposed the adulterous union before the court. And though David and Bathsheba's first son died, their story takes an upswing as David and Bathsheba's second son eventually became King Solomon.

Weapons of Mass Seduction: Infamous Female Spies

Behind every good war are many good women. Using their feminine (and in at least one case masculine) wiles, the following five spies would make James Bond proud.

_01:: Mata Hari

While Margaretha Geertruida Zelle MacLeod (1876–1917) may not have caused World War I, she sure as heck kept it going. Having spent time in Java with her husband, Captain Campbell MacLeod, Margaretha returned to Holland and sued for divorce. To make ends meet she took up exotic dancing and the name Mata Hari (meaning "the light of day" in Malay). With her sensual performances becoming the attraction of the major European cities came the men and the gifts for her favors. Many of these favors came from royalty and high-ranking French and German military officers. As World War I progressed, both sides became suspicious that Mata was spying for the other side. The French eventually put her on trial and, although the charges were never proven, Mata Hari was convicted of espionage and was executed by a firing squad on October 15, 1917. Playing the seductress up until the end, Mata refused a blindfold, smiled, and blew a kiss to the firing squad as the fatal shots were fired.

_02:: Sarah Emma Edmonds (or Was It Frank Thompson?)

Born in 1841 in New Brunswick, Canada, Sarah ran away from home in her early teens. In order to survive she became an itinerant Bible salesman, by calling herself Frank Thompson and dressing like a man. In 1861, Frank (Sarah) enlisted in the Second Michigan Infantry and over the next two years not only fought in a number of Civil War battles, but also served as a spy for the Union Army. Solders in her unit called Frank "our woman" because of his feminine mannerisms and his extremely small boot size. However, none of her comrades ever figured out that Frank was really Sarah. This boded well for her spying, where she dressed as a young boy serving in Confederate camps, as an immigrant Irish peddler and, most interestingly, as a woman. In 1863, Sarah caught malaria and deserted the army out of fear that hospitalization would reveal her true identity. In 1884, though, Sarah applied for and was awarded a veteran's pension in which the secretary of war acknowledged that Sarah was a female soldier who had rendered faithful services to the ranks.

_03:: Noor Inayat Khan

Khan was born in the Kremlin in 1914 and at a young age moved with her family first to England and then to France. In 1940, Khan, along with her mother and sister, escaped back to England just before France surrendered to Germany. While in England she joined the Women's Auxiliary Air Force (WAAF), but her ability to speak fluent French soon caught the attention of the Special Operations group and Khan agreed to become a spy. Khan was flown to Le Mans, where she teamed up with other female spies and traveled to Paris. There they joined the French Resistance Prosper Network. Soon after their arrival, the network was infiltrated and many were arrested. Khan was ordered to return to England, but instead she stayed on and continued to pass information on to England. Eventually she was arrested again and interrogated by the Gestapo. When she refused to speak, she was sent to a prison in Germany and then to the Dachau concentration camp. On September 13, 1944, Khan and three other female British spies were executed by the Nazi SS. In 1949, Khan was posthumously awarded the George Cross.

_04:: Belle Boyd (aka "La Belle Rebelle")

Born Isabelle Boyd in Martinsburg, Virginia, in 1844, the beautiful Belle soon became the star attraction in Washington, D.C., social circles prior to the beginning of the Civil War. With the outbreak of the war, she returned to Martinsburg. When the Union soldiers occupied the city, Belle mixed with the officers and soon gathered information on troop movements, which she passed on to the Confederate forces. However, she is probably best known for warning Stonewall Jackson that the Union intended to blow up all the bridges around Martinsburg. With this information, Jackson, with a small number of troops, was able to surprise the Union troops and drive them from the area. In 1864, Confederate president Jefferson Davis asked Belle to carry letters for him to England. The Union Navy captured her ship, but the officer in charge fell in love with Belle and let her escape. The officer, Lieutenant Samuel Harding Jr., after being court-martialed and discharged from the Navy, traveled to England, where he married Belle. After the war, Boyd toured the United States as an actress under the stage name of La Belle Rebelle.

_05:: Elizabeth Van Lew

Crazy Bet, as she was known, was born in Richmond, Virginia, in 1818 but educated at a Quaker school in Philadelphia. After developing a hatred for slavery, Elizabeth returned to Richmond and freed all her family's slaves. She also went so far as finding where her freed slaves' relatives were and purchased and freed them also. After the Civil War started, Elizabeth asked to visit Union prisoners being held captive in Richmond. The Union prisoners gave her information, which she then passed on to the North. Among the slaves she freed was Mary Elizabeth Bowser, whom Van Lew got a job as a house servant in the home of Jefferson Davis. This allowed Bowser and Van Lew to collect and pass on information directly from the Confederate president's mansion. Elizabeth effectively used the Crazy Bet moniker to make the residents of Richmond think she was mentally ill. She would wear old clothes and bonnets and talk to herself. Because of this, most people thought that her Northern sympathies were just a part of her craziness. After the war, President Grant named Elizabeth the postmaster for Richmond. When the citizens of Richmond found out that Crazy Bet was an act, they shunned her. However, at her death, the state of Massachusetts placed a memorial marker on her grave.

Just the Facts

PORN BY THE NUMBERS

70: Percentage of visits to porn Web sites made between 9 a.m. and 5 p.m.

5.3 billion: Estimated number of dollars U.S. companies lost to recreational Web surfing during business hours in 2000

14 million: Number of porn pages on the Web in 1998

260 million: Number of porn pages on the Web in 2003

68 million: Daily number of pornographic search engine requests on the Web

25: Percentage of total daily Web search engine requests that are related to porn sites

12 billion: Number of dollars in revenues the U.S. porn industry gathered in 2003

33: Percentage of visitors to adult Web sites who are women

253: Number of arrests for pornography/obscenity violations by the U.S. Postal Service in 2002

11: Average age at which men first see a copy of *Playboy* or *Penthouse* magazine

Harem Scarem: Facts on Harems

You've heard about them. You've fantasized about them. You've dreamed about one day owning your own. But are you really mature enough to have your own harem yet? After all, who's going to cook for your harem? Who's going to feed 'em? And a harem doesn't just walk itself, you know. With great harems comes great responsibility. You might want to read the following five facts before you decide to invest in one.

_01:: The Primer: Just a Couple Harems to Know

Under Islamic law, a man can have as many wives as he can support, with the traditional number topping out at around four. However, concubines are unlimited and many harems grew into the thousands. Following are some of history's largest recorded harems. At the top of the list is the 6th century BCE's King Tamba of Banaras, whose harem numbered some 16,000 women. Not to be outdone, the 15th-century Sultan Ghiyas-ud-Din Kilji's harem numbered 15,000 and required him to build a separate walled city to house them. Next, during the 1800s, King Mongkut of Siam housed his 9,000 women in a totally contained city with its own government, recreational facilities, and a theater. Kublai Khan, the Mongol leader in the 13th century, had four empresses and around 7,000 concubines. Every two years he would get rid of a couple hundred concubines and replace them with a fresh supply. Finally, Emperor Jahangir of India maintained a harem of over 6,300 women during the early years of the 17th century. However, Jahangir also kept close to a thousand young men-in-waiting for those times when his appetite tended toward the other gender.

_02:: Getting Some Order in Your Harem

Contrary to the Hollywood view of scantily dressed beautiful women lounging around pools waiting for their romantic interlude with the sultan, harems were actually very elaborate and complex communities with rigid administrative and disciplinary systems. A harem was under the leadership of the Valide Sultan, or the sultan's mother. Directly responsible to the mother were the superintendent of the harem and a number of other female officials. Each of these officials had a number of younger harem members under them training for this and other future administrative assignments. Next in the pecking order after the sultan's mother was the mother of the sultan's heir apparent. After this came the mothers of the sultan's other children, who were ranked by the favor they held with the sultan. These female relatives and other officials were responsible for recruiting new harem members and annually presenting them to the sultan, usually on the 15th day of Ramadan.

Touch of Evil

Nizam Sir Osman Ali Khan Bahadur was perhaps the world's richest man in the early 20th century. He ruled Hyderabad both independently and as part of India, and his fat wallet helped him collect an enviable 42 concubines for his harem.

_03:: So You Want to Be a Eunuch?

Sounds like an exciting life being left to live among hundreds, if not thousands, of the most beautiful women in the empire. Let's look at some of the requirements. The first priority is castration. Most likely you'll want to have this procedure done during your childhood. Next, expect to be a part of a dowry offered by your master when his daughter is given in marriage. Okay, you've passed the entrance exam, now expect to spend years working your way up the ranks of eunuchs. Finally, you gain favor with the sultan and he makes you the chief eunuch. Your sole reason for being is meeting your master's needs. You need to know the master's mood and select his appropriate bedmate for the evening. You must also instruct the young lady on the master's whims and fantasies and have the appropriate aphrodisiacs ready. As the chief black eunuch you have become the sultan's most trusted servant and the third highest ranking official in his empire. You can enter the harem apartments, command the imperial army, and meet with the sultan. If you are the chief white eunuch, you get to run the bureaucracy and control all petitions, messages, and state documents sent to the sultan,

but you cannot enter the harem. Why? Because unlike the black eunuch, who lost everything (anatomically), you still have bits and pieces left and pose a threat.

_04:: How to Furnish Your Harem

The Arabic word *harem* means "the place of the women." The most important part of the harem was the zenana, or the inner sanctum where the sultan's fantasies were played out. The zenana was designed to replicate paradise. Each woman was given her own ornately decorated apartment with its own garden, waterfalls, and running streams. Because the ladies of the harem came from many different cultures, the apartments were furnished to make them feel comfortable and satisfied with their position in life. After all, one must be ready and willing for an unexpected visit from the master. Similarly, the attire was erotic and arousing. The goal was to remain naked while being dressed by wearing translucent muslin and silk garments. The material was so light that many outfits weighed about an ounce. In keeping with the opulence, the garments were adorned with diamonds, gold, rubies, and pearls. Shoes were also covered with precious stones. Finally, the outfit was topped off with an ostrich feather headdress with ruby-covered plumes. Many a sultan spent most of the empire's treasury keeping the ladies-in-waiting happy.

_05:: Keeping Your Harem Under Control

During the late 1500s, Mehmed III ascended to the throne of the Ottoman Empire. His mother, Safiye, as the Valide Sultan or leader of the harem, became one of his most important advisers. While not allowed to be directly involved in state politics, Safiye was able to influence the sultan's decisions, sometimes openly and directly. On one occasion, Safiye sat behind a curtain as Mehmed held a heated discussion with a leading mufti (religious cleric) and openly defended her son. As Safiye's influence increased so did the ire it raised among the vizier, the mufti, the chief black eunuch, and the sultan's favorite wives and concubines, who saw Safiye's excessive influence as overstepping her role of Valide Sultan. Mehmed found himself having to restrain his mother and, on at least one occasion, had her removed to another palace. Safiye's excessive greed, coupled with the ever increasing costs of the harem under her control, helped to bring about riots in Istanbul in 1600 over the devaluation of the empire's currency.

Original Cities of Sin (None of Which Had Elvis Impersonators)

Are you tired of Vegas and Havana? Is Bangkok just not providing the immoral rush you're looking for? Well, there's a quick fix for those of you with access to time machines. Just fasten up and warp your way back to some of these sin-sational locales. Judging by what we've heard (you know—what happened there but didn't stay there), it's a rollicking good time.

_01:: Sodom and Gomorrah

Who wouldn't want to check out the original cities of sin, Sodom and Gomorrah? Located in the beautiful arid wasteland around the Dead Sea (today in central Israel), the twin cities were near valuable mineral deposits, probably the sources of the cities' renowned wealth. Somehow, though, these locales became a byword for sin and corruption, in spite of the fact that the crime that supposedly led to the cities' destruction may not have been homosexuality at all, as some have suggested, but inhospitality—the worst of all sins in the ancient world. According to the Bible, God rained fire and brimstone on the region and destroyed the towns after promising Abraham that He would spare them if 10 righteous men could be found in their region. Apparently, only one could be found: Lot. Luckily for him, Lot offered hospitality to angelic visitors and was warned of the catastrophe. Oddly enough, the original sin cities sit on a seismically active gap between tectonic plates (where earthquakes and volcanic activity are possible), and the biblical account could be describing some sort of geological upheaval.

_02:: Pessinos

If you're looking for a wild night filled with religious ecstasy, you might want to set your time machine for the classical age, and check out Pessinos, in Asia Minor. As the center to a mother/goddess-oriented cult since the Stone Age, Pessinos was known for its worship of Cybyle, an Anatolian goddess dedicated to fertility. So, just how fertile was Cybyle? Well, to give you an idea, her statues are pretty easy to recognize since they feature an inordinately large number of breasts. And while the rites practiced by Cybyle's worshipers are poorly documented, the records tend to suggest that they included priests who castrated themselves while in a drug-induced trance, while presiding over midnight dances culminating in wild orgies.

Touch of Evil

The 12,000 citizens of Monaco are denied the right to enter Monte Carlo's casino rooms; that privilege is only allowed to visitors. Of course, the income helps keep the locals free from paying taxes, so the trade-off isn't that bad.

_03:: Münster

If you're looking for a polygamous good time, you might want to transport yourself back to 1530s Münster, a city in Westphalia, in what is today western Germany, which was a hotbed of Anabaptist agitation. A Christian sect that believed in rebaptizing people once they became adults (their theological descendents today include the Amish), the Anabaptists were persecuted mercilessly elsewhere in Europe both by Catholics and by more conservative Protestants. But in February 1534, the Anabaptists seized Münster in a relatively bloodless coup d'état, and had their way with the city. One of the Anabaptist leaders, Johann Matthys, declared himself a prophet. Unfortu-

nately, he seems to have believed in his own divinity: when the bishop of Münster arrived with an army, Matthys led 30 followers out to fight and, of course, was slaughtered with his men. Then his disciple, Jan Leiden, took over the town's defense, declared *himself* the Messiah, and introduced the townsfolk to polygamy (he took 16 wives). The party didn't last forever, though—after a solid 16 months of multiwife fun the city was taken by the bishop's army, which killed thousands, and tortured and executed the leaders of the revolt.

_04:: Port Royal

The original capital of British Jamaica, Port Royal, is certainly one town that's located on the wrong side of the tracks. The area was a hotbed for rascals, including plenty of pirates, and Limey officials who were happy to look the other way . . . for a piece of the action, of course. In fact, when pirate crews rolled in to town they could enjoy a wide array of vice to whittle down their profit margins, including prostitutes, gambling, liquor, and drugs smuggled from the Orient and the Middle East. If that doesn't sound like enough fun for you, the streets literally echoed with the sounds of sin: from raucous brawls to the incessant nursery rhyme "Sing a Song of Sixpence" (actually a recruiting jingle for the pirate Blackbeard). And just to prove how corrupt it was, Henry Morgan, an infamous pirate admiral, was actually made lieutenant governor of Jamaica in 1674. Of course, such dens of sin can't last forever, and Port Royal was destroyed in 1692 by an earthquake that dropped three-quarters of it into the sea. An initial attempt at rebuilding burned to the ground in 1704, hurricanes stopped several attempts at rebuilding in the early 1700s, and finally a 1907 earthquake caused the remaining parts of the city to sink.

It seems someone upstairs had a grudge against this humble burg.

Self-proclaimed Casanovas

"How do I love thee?" Well, these guys were big fans of publicly counting the ways...just loud enough that *everyone* could hear it.

_01:: Clark "the Shark" Gable (1901–1960)

Despite sporting a pair of ears that were potential obstacles in revolving doors, silver screen legend Clark Gable was the leading male sex symbol of his generation. Known as "the King of Hollywood," Clark the Shark bragged that he had made love to women in a fire escape, a duck blind, a canoe, and a telephone booth. Apparently his choice of locations also said a lot about his technique. "God knows I love Clark," Gable's wife, Carole Lombard, once said, "but he's the worst lay in town. If he had one inch less, he'd be the Queen of Hollywood." As if Lombard's press release wasn't bad enough for his rep, Gable's *Gone With the Wind* costar, Vivian Leigh, complained that the "King of Hollywood's" breath had been atrocious on set. From his dentures, no less!

_02:: Frasier the Sensuous Lion (1951–1972)

This guy didn't actually do much bragging about his amorous exploits, but then again, he didn't have to—his proof was walking all around him! Frasier was about 20 years old, ancient for a lion, when he came to a wild animal park in southern California. The Mexican circus refugee was so doddering he could hardly walk, and his keepers figured his demise would occur any day. But that didn't stop the old lion from tomcatting about. Frasier hung on for 18 months and sired a stunning 35 cubs in his spare time. Amazingly, the press about the fertile feline was so widespread that Frasier fan clubs started sprouting up across the country. Wives even began writing in to find out what park rangers were feeding the beast. In fact, the lion's fame grew so much that a popular song was written about him, and a film was made. When the old cat's time finally came, it's said, Frasier the Sensuous Lion went with a smile on his face.

_03:: Good Wilt's Hunting (1936–1999)

When it came to basketball, very few people could take it to the hoop any better than Wilt the Stilt. But it's a wonder he had the stamina. In his 1991 autobiography, Chamberlain claimed to have slept with about 20,000 women

Lies Your Mother Told You

ALL AUTHORS ARE CADS

No matter what your momma (or your swooning lit teacher) told you, not all authors suffer from odd fetishes or omnivorous appetites. D. H. Lawrence, whose *Lady Chatterly's Lover* was so scandalous that it was banned in Britain until 1960, was happily and faithfully married (although his wife was, briefly, a bigamist, having failed to divorce her first husband before eloping with Lawrence). And some noted authors barely had sex at all. Most notable among them was the playwright George Bernard Shaw. Shaw didn't lose his virginity until his 29th birthday (July 26, 1885), when he slept with a 44-year-old widow. It may have been the only sexual encounter of his life. He married Charlotte Townshend in 1898, not because he loved her but because Shaw thought he was dying and wanted to offer his friend Charlotte the social and financial benefits of widowhood. As it turns out, the two were married—happily, but most likely celibately—for 45 years.

over a 38-year period. Of course, Chamberlain was roundly criticized for everything from propagating sexual stereotypes about African American men to having sex with women outside his race to just plain flaunting his conquests. But the lifelong bachelor said that, whatever else he might be doing, he wasn't bragging. "If you look at it," he said in a 1997 interview, "you can say that I had so many women because I was such a bad lover, they never came back a second time."

_04:: Hugh Hefner: Playboy Original (1926–   )

When Hugh Hefner was 75 years old, a reporter asked about his recent love life, and Hef replied it was "a natural one—except it involved five people." The founder of *Playboy* magazine and patriarch of the Sexual Revolution, Hefner virtually lives in his pajamas, and even a stroke in 1985 didn't slow him down. In 2001, Hefner told *Vanity Fair* magazine that thanks to Viagra, which came on the market two months after his second divorce, he was sleeping with seven women between the ages of 18 and 28, usually simultaneously. "And here's the surprise bit," Hefner said. "It's what *they* want." Hefner's mom lived to be 101, and he says his goal is to stay frisky at least that long.

They Did a Bad, Bad Thing:
So-called Virtuous Figures Who Got Caught with Their Flies Down (or Skirts Up)

This quintet of folks didn't exactly practice what they preached. Please bless them, Father, 'cause they've most certainly sinned.

_01:: Aimee Semple McPherson (1890–1944)

By the mid-1920s, evangelist McPherson was packing them in at her Angelus Temple in Los Angeles, preaching hope and warning against the sinful life. But in 1926, she disappeared while swimming at a local beach. She turned up a month later with a fantastic story about being kidnapped and taken to Mexico. Unfortunately, the evidence said otherwise: It appeared li'l Aimee had been shacked up with a married man. The evangelist was charged with perjury, but she stuck to her story and was eventually acquitted. Her popularity waned after the scandal, but you gotta hand it to her for chutzpah: instead of apologizing to her confused flock, McPherson bobbed her hair, bought some short skirts, and began dancing and drinking in public.

_02:: Jim Bakker (1941–)

Simple people with a simple dream, Jim and Tammy Faye Bakker started out hosting a children's religious puppet show. By the mid-1970s, however, the fabulous Bakker duo had become the toast of televangelism. They pulled in millions of dollars in contributions to their PTL (Praise the Lord) ministry, and even built a sort of fundamentalist Disneyland called Heritage USA in South Carolina. But Jim had a couple of dirty little secrets. He had paid a former church secretary named Jessica Hahn to keep quiet about a sexual encounter they had in 1980. But when the scandal broke in 1987, questions began to be raised about Bakker's financial dealings. In 1989, he was sentenced to 45 years in prison for fleecing his flock of $158 million. In the end he only served five, and moved forward with his life, eventually opening a new ministry in a restaurant in Branson, Missouri.

_03:: Jimmy Swaggart (1935–)

Swaggart was one of Jim Bakker's fiercest critics when the Bakker scandal broke, telling an interviewer he himself had never even kissed a woman other than his wife. Maybe not. But the bombastic and fantastically successful television preacher—and cousin to rock-and-roll legend Jerry Lee Lewis—was doing *something* with that prostitute in a cheap New Orleans hotel room in early 1988. Swaggart's tearful, televised confession kept his $12-million-a-year, 10,000-employee religious empire together—until he got caught with his pants down again. That's right, swingin'

Jimmy Swaggart was linked to (brace yourself!) another hooker in 1991. A couple of lost lawsuits, an IRS tax lien, and that was the end of the line for Jimmy Swaggart. Well, not exactly. As of mid-2004, he was still hurling rhetorical fire and brimstone on TV, albeit on a much smaller scale.

_04:: Amrit Desai (1932–)

A onetime art student, Amrit Desai came to the United States from India in 1960. He began giving yoga lessons on the side and ended up training several thousand people, who in turn became yoga instructors around the country. With his followers calling him "guru dev," or "beloved teacher," one of the things Desai taught at the yoga center he founded in Massachusetts in 1972 was that celibacy was spiritually mandatory for unmarried people. Desai even took a vow of celibacy himself in 1974, despite being married with children. No wonder it was something of a shock (perhaps greatest to his wife) when in 1994, the beloved teacher admitted to having affairs with three of his followers. The scandal forced Desai to resign his $150,000-a-year post. He eventually moved to Florida, but kept up the yoga.

_05:: Paul R. Shanley (1931–)

In the 1970s, Shanley was known as "the hippie priest"; he was a Roman Catholic clergyman whose specialty was ministering to kids struggling with their sexual identity. By 2002, however, Shanley was a central figure in the greatest scandal ever to hit the Catholic Church in the United States. Shanley was accused of molesting more than two dozen boys over a 35-year span. Thrown out of the priesthood, Shanley was still awaiting trial at the end of 2004 on rape and indecent assault charges. Subsequent investigations into other allegations in the Boston archdiocese resulted in the Church paying $85 million in 2003 to 552 people who claimed to have been abused by priests. It also triggered similar probes, and similar results, in other areas of the country.

Presidential Affairs (Cigar Not Included)

Contrary to popular belief, Bill Clinton wasn't exactly the first president to get caught in the act. The following are some of the past presidents who helped unite the country in more ways than one.

_01:: The Many Loves of a Founding Father

Known for his extreme intellect and skills at diplomacy, Thomas Jefferson is truly one of America's founding fathers, but in more ways than just patriotic. Considered a loving and faithful husband to Martha during their 10 years of marriage before her death, Tom Jefferson was actually a bit of a tomcat. In fact, the Virginia statesman had a notorious penchant for other men's wives. While on a trip to New York in 1768, John Walker asked Tom to look after his wife, and that he did, literally. Later, in 1786, as ambassador to France, Jefferson fell deeply in love with Maria Conway, the wife of portraitist Richard Conway. Legend has it that one day while walking through the countryside, Tom tried to show off for the blushing (Conway) bride and fell while jumping a fence only to break his wrist. But Tom's best-known relationship was with Sally Hemings, his slave and his late wife's half sister. Their relationship went on for 35 years and provided Jefferson a number of heirs.

_02:: Grover Cleveland, the Honorable Gentleman from New York?

In 1873, a young, politically aspiring bachelor named Grover Cleveland met Maria Halpin, a 35-year-old widow with two children. Maria's looks and personality made her the talk of Buffalo and Grover soon found himself among Halpin's many suitors. Well, more than just a suitor. In 1874, Halpin bore a son and insinuated that old Grover was the pop. Grover, not sure that he actually was the father, and not intending to marry Maria, decided to do the right thing and bear financial responsibility for the child. He also helped Maria get treatment for her alcoholism and actually set her up in her own business. During the 1884 presidential campaign, however, Cleveland's opposition dug up the old story and printed it in the press. Interestingly, a number of clergy members supporting Cleveland did a study of the case and found that after the "preliminary offense" Cleveland had done the responsible and honorable thing. More important in their minds, he'd shielded many married men in

Buffalo (and their families) from public scandal. Oddly enough, because of this, even many of Grover's opponents supported his run for the presidency.

Touch of Evil

FDR seemed like a ripe fit for The Jerry Springer Show. *Not only did he marry his cousin, but he was involved in multiple affairs, which his wife, Eleanor, countered by having a rumored 30-year lesbian affair with a reporter named Lorena Hickok.*

_03:: Warren G., Carrie P., and Nan B.

Far from the run-of-the-mill tales you hear of political ambition, Warren G. Harding was a small-town Ohio newspaper editor who ran for senator because he liked the gentlemen's club atmosphere and the light workload of the U.S. Senate. However, his wife, Florence, had bigger plans, and Warren somehow found his way to the presidency in 1920. Not at all equipped to run a nation, Harding preferred to let Congress lead while he golfed and had sex with his mistress in closets throughout the White House. But Harding's philandering began well before his run for president. For 15 years, Warren maintained an active love interest with Carrie Phillips, the wife of his close friend. But when Harding ran for president, the Phillipses threatened to go public. So to secure their silence, the Republican National Party came to the rescue and sent Mr. and Mrs. Phillips on a world trip, plus they threw in $20,000 to boot. But it appears Warren didn't quite learn his lesson. Soon after winning the White House he began a secret relationship with Nan Britton, 30 years his junior. With the Secret Service ordered not to inform the First Lady, Nan was routinely ushered into the White House and many a West Wing closet became their intimate playground.

_04:: FDR and His Wife's Secretary

Best known as the president who brought the United States through the Great Depression, Franklin Delano Roosevelt is also known for his longtime affair with Lucy Mercer, his wife, Eleanor's social secretary. In 1918, upon FDR's return from a trip to Europe as assistant secretary of the Navy, Eleanor confronted Franklin with the love letters she'd found and offered him a divorce. Knowing that a divorce at the time would destroy his political ambitions, Franklin said he'd stop seeing Lucy if Eleanor would agree to remain married. Unfortunately, he didn't keep to his new deal. Lucy continued to visit the White House with regularity, especially when Eleanor was out of town. Years later, the widowed Lucy even became a frequent visitor to the South Carolina plantation where FDR was recuperating from his bad health. In fact, it was Lucy, not Eleanor, who was with FDR on April 12, 1945, when he was struck with the cerebral hemorrhage that killed him.

_05:: Ike and Kay— Did They or Didn't They?

Many a book, movie, and television show have portrayed the close relationship during World War II between Dwight Eisenhower and his Irish driver, Kay Summersby. As the Supreme Commander of the Allied forces, Ike found himself responsible for millions of lives, but not having anyone he could share his close thoughts and feelings with. With Ike's wife

Mamie over 3,000 miles away, the young, witty, and attractive Kay capably filled that role. But once the gossip columns got wind of this, talk of their so-called relationship spread on both sides of the Atlantic. With constant reassurances from Ike, Mamie believed that no sexual liaisons ever occurred between Ike and Kay and at the end of the war Ike returned to the States and Kay remained in England. Their lives moved forward, and Ike was elected president in 1952. As the decades proceeded, though, the private lives of the 1940s and '50s quickly became the public domain of the '60s, and the rumors of the affair again surfaced though no evidence of a sexual relationship was ever found. Years later, before her death, Summersby wrote that her relationship with Ike had been close, flirtatious, and intimate, but had never been consummated.

_06:: JFK and the Other Mistress

It's common knowledge that President Kennedy and Marilyn Monroe were an item. Less known, however, is the relationship that John F. had with Judith Campbell Exner, an affair that definitely falls under the category of dangerous liaisons. The extremely beautiful Exner was introduced to Kennedy by Frank Sinatra in 1960. However, Miss Exner was also romantically involved with Sam Giancana, one of the most powerful Mafia bosses of the time. And while their relationship remained secret from the public, it was well known around the White House and by Jackie Kennedy. FBI director J. Edgar Hoover, as he'd done with other presidents, had Exner tailed so that he had information to blackmail Kennedy with. In fact, Exner's affair with JFK remained a secret long after Kennedy's assassination, until in 1975 a number of Republican members of the Senate

Select Committee to Study Governmental Operations with Respect to Intelligence Activities (aka the Church Committee) leaked the information to the press. With the secret out of the bag, it quickly fueled the fires of conspiracy theorists wondering if the relationship in any way had played into JFK's assassination.

Crackers, Corn Flakes, and Chastity Belts, Oh My! Victorian Tricks for Restraining That Mojo

4

Ever play the game where someone tells you to picture anything in the world but an elephant? Anything but an elephant. And as you struggle to concentrate, all you can see are visions of Dumbo, Babar, and Snuffleupagus. Well, that's kind of what everyone in the Victorian age did with sex. It's a wonder they didn't produce more kids.

_01:: Fanning the Flames

In the Victorian age, an eligible Victor couldn't just cruise up to a Victoria and put the moves on her. No, in the extraordinarily prudish age proper etiquette had to be maintained at all times. A man, for instance, needed to be formally introduced to a woman before he could approach and talk to her. However, that didn't exactly mean that flirting was off-limits at social events. In fact, it was pretty en vogue. And one of the most subtle ways of demonstrating interest or disinterest was through the use of hand fans. In fact, a whole sign language was created around fan movements and placement. If a young lady let her fan rest on her right cheek, it meant she was interested; if she placed it on the left, however, it meant the guy was being passed over (subtle, but harsh!). Similarly, if she moved the fan slowly it was a signal that she was already engaged or married. If she held the fan in front of her face with her right hand, it was a signal for the young man to follow her. Finally, if she moved the fan across her forehead, it meant they were being watched. Whew! With all the mixed signals, restrictions, and rites of courtship, it's amazing anyone found time to procreate.

_02:: A Flaky Approach

If in the 19th century Victorians were very concerned about curtailing sexual urges, they were fanatic over masturbation. Dr. John Harvey Kellogg, a lecturer and so-called health "expert," proclaimed that masturbation caused a whole series of medical problems including enlarged prostate, kidney and bladder infections, piles, nocturnal emissions, and general exhaustion (guess blindness wasn't added until later). Kellogg actually came up with a list of 39 signs that could be used to spot masturbators running the gamut from sleeplessness to biting one's fingernails to using obscene lan-

Lies Your Mother Told You

CHASTITY BELTS

So, about those chastity belts...did they really exist or are they nothing more than a Victorian myth? Well, the fact is, the jury's still out. Thought to have been invented in Italy during the 14th century, the urban legend of the belts became popular in the rest of Europe. The antithesis of anything PC, the belts were basically used to maintain sexual control over women by covering the private area and keeping it under lock and key. And while many a suspicious husband may have lauded the invention, there's recent evidence that suggests the chastity belt may have been more of a Victorian myth than a reality. In 1996, two British historians reported that there was no medical evidence from the time of Chaucer through the Victorian period that chastity belts existed or were commonly used. Of course, they had the weight of the British Museum of London behind them. Agreeing with the two historians, the museum removed an alleged chastity belt that had been on exhibit since 1846.

guage. Like other thinkers of his time, Kellogg saw a connection between one's bowels and genitals with the proper diet being the answer. So he created a cold breakfast cereal, which he

originally called Granola. Unfortunately, another masturbation expert had already used that name so Kellogg changed the cereal's name to Corn Flakes. However, it should be mentioned that Kellogg never consummated his own marriage, preferring yogurt enemas instead.

_03:: Trojan Wars of the 19th Century

A number of mechanical methods of birth control were created and used in the 1800s, but they were only affordable for the wealthier Victorian women. Of course, they weren't exactly effective. The first generation of vaginal diaphragms and cervical caps were developed but the quality of the rubber was poor—that is, until the invention of latex in 1884. However, in keeping with the Victorian ethos, a law, known as the Comstock Law, defining condoms as obscene went quietly into effect in 1873. That didn't keep prophylactic science from making advances, though. Toward the end of the 19th century, the forerunners of IUDs (intrauterine devices), intracervical stems, or pessaries, became available. However, the devices were unpopular from the start, as they often led to infections. Oddly enough, the courts wised up to the fact that diaphragms and condoms were effective for disease prevention, and made them legal as medical treatment. However, they still weren't so fond of the idea of birth control, and the courts maintained that using the products as contraceptives should remain illegal.

_04:: Protection au Naturel

While not everyone could afford the premier forms of birth control, it didn't stop less affluent Victorians from jerry-rigging their own homemade remedies. In fact, one of the most commonly used "natural methods" of birth control was the injection of fruit juices or naturally produced chemicals into the vagina, known today as "douches," shortly after intercourse. Of course, that wasn't the only recipe. A variety of mixtures were used, including baking soda, alum, vinegar, and quinine. Other birth-controlling techniques involved using small, natural sea sponges dipped in acidic or naturally spermicidal mixtures with a ribbon or string attached. And there were cheap solutions for the men, too! Condoms made of sheepskin, also known as "French letters," were particularly popular, and a notorious favorite with men who frequented brothels. After all, the rubbers didn't just aid in birth control, but also kept the syphilis at bay. In fact, it's this sordid use for birth control that gave condoms such a bad reputation and made them taboo in the eyes of the general public.

From Wags to Riches:
Royal Mistresses Who Made Good

It's no surprise that a lot of kings have kept a lot of ladies-in-waiting. Of course, not all of these gal pals were content just to wait. In fact, the following mistresses quickly found their way from the bedroom to the boardroom, making sure they were involved in more than just one of the king's affairs.

_01:: Diane de Poitiers (1490–1566)

Considered one of the most powerful women of the 16th century, Diane de Poitiers was the mistress to French king Henri II. And what a mistress! Although married to Queen Catherine, Henri basically let Diane run France by his side. In fact, she got all sorts of executive perks, from signing official documents to appointing ministers and handing out titles, to even dabbling in estates and pensions. And as a member of the Privy Council, Diane even routinely gathered money for the royal treasury. But for those skeptical few who want proof of her power in writing, just inspect any one of the numerous official documents the good king and his gal pal literally cosigned: they actually read "HenriDiane!" Of course, this dubious union did not exist without protest. When church officials questioned Diane's role, she simply had them sent to Rome. When Henri passed away, he was calling out Diane's name. However, Queen Catherine (pretty understandably) prevented Henri's mistress from attending the funeral and, in fact, demanded that she return any crown jewels. Strangely, though, Diane was not arrested for treason as expected—mainly because she was popular with the French people for helping Henri rule so well.

_02:: Nell Gwynne (1651–1687)

During the reign of Charles II of England, mistresses weren't exactly few and far between. In fact, less-than-chaste women were almost as plentiful around the palace as were catfights between them, and Charles was basically an equal opportunity cad. In fact, his favorite mistress was a prostitute from London's slum known as Kindhearted Nell. Renowned for using her influence with the king to help others, Nell also harbored a wicked sense of humor. For instance, when she heard that Charles planned to bed another mistress, Nell offered the gal a bunch of sweets. Little did the lady know Nell had laced the goodies with a laxative and an evening of bedding quickly turned into an evening of chamber-potting. But while Charles frolicked with Nell he let another mistress, Louise de Keroualle, run the country, and there was no love between the two. During a period of anti-Catholic sentiment, Nell's coach was surrounded by a mob thinking it contained the Catholic Louise. The quick-thinking Nell exclaimed, "Pray, good people, be civil, I am the Protestant whore." Amused, the crowd laughingly let her move on.

Touch of Evil

Camilla Parker-Bowles's family has been trying to get into the royal pants for decades. Her great-grandmother was reportedly the mistress to King Edward IV, Chuck's great-great-grandfather.

_03:: Madame de Pompadour (1721–1764)

Probably the most powerful of all royal mistresses, as King Louis XV's lady on the side,

Madame de Pompadour served as the unofficial French prime minister for 13 years. It worked out well for both parties. Louis, being a ridiculously lazy king, wasn't all that fond of making decisions, while Pompadour reveled in the power. All messages to the king and all requests for an audience had to go through her. Not just that, the Madame also controlled all titles, court positions, and honors and quickly began replacing high-level officials with her supporters. She even took over as France's minister of war during the Seven Years' War (1756–1763), and cleverly chose to appoint all the generals more on their social standing than their experience. Pompadour died of a lung disease in her early 40s, but for all her power-tripping she remained faithful to Louis till the end. In fact, court etiquette wouldn't allow Louis to attend Pompadour's funeral, but the casket was made to pass by his castle. Upon viewing the cortege, Louis reportedly cried, saying that tears were the only thing he could give her.

_04:: Mary, Countess von Waldersee (1866–1941)

Unlike most royal mistresses, Mary played the role of the matronly adviser. The daughter of a wealthy New York grocer, Mary was married to Colonel Alfred von Waldersee, the quartermaster general of the German army. As such, Mary opened a salon in Berlin and soon found herself entertaining German royalty, including young Prince William. Enamored of the old gal (she was, after all, two years senior to his mother), William decided to make her his private adviser. In 1888, William became Kaiser Wilhelm II, and he started referring all political matters to Mary before making decisions. However, the power went to Mary's head, and she attempted to get Wilhelm to re-place Chancellor Bismarck with her husband. Wilhelm did remove Bismarck, but not for Alfred. Instead, Wilhelm began to view Mary as his biggest competition and to get rid of her he demoted her hubby and moved them both to Hamburg. Without mother Mary's sage advice, though, Wilhelm was lost, and his weak, egocentric decisions helped bring about World War I.

When Sex Doesn't Sell:
Risqué Ad Campaigns That Got Canned

There are two cardinal rules in advertising: "Sex sells" and "There's no such thing as bad publicity." Here are a few advertising missteps that proved one or both of them wrong.

_01:: Abercrombie and Flesh

It may sound odd for a clothing manufacturer to use nudity to sell clothes, but that's exactly the strategy campus mainstay Abercrombie & Fitch employed in their catalog/photo magazine *A&F Quarterly*. Over a series of years, the models somehow got younger and younger and began wearing fewer and fewer clothes. In fact, nudity wasn't uncommon, and consumers complained of suggestions of pedophilia, sexual irresponsibility, underage drinking, and homoeroticism. But the Winter 2003 edition was the one that went too far. The catalog featured over 100 pages of photos of young men and women frolicking naked in streams and waterfalls (in a *winter* catalog?), and one spread espoused the joys of group sex in both photos and text. The outcry from angry parents was so loud that sales for November 2003 dropped over 13%, and the company discontinued the *A&F Quarterly* altogether soon thereafter. Despite the hubbub, though, A&F has been a lit-tle slow to learn from their mistakes. Since then, they've been criticized for marketing T-shirts with ethnically insensitive slogans and for marketing thong underwear bearing phrases like "Kiss me" and "Eye candy" to teen girls.

_02:: Calvin and Kiddies

Designer Calvin Klein has always used sex to sell his clothes, and it's usually worked. After all, who can forget the slinky Brooke Shields proudly proclaiming "Nothing comes between me and my Calvins"? But in 1995, CK creeped out just about everyone with its ads for jeans and underwear. The commercials featured teen-agers wearing almost nothing, standing in what appeared to be a poorly lit basement in front of cheap wood paneling. What's more disconcerting than cheap paneling? Well, maybe the fact that the models are being inter-viewed with eerie questions, like "That's a nice body. Do you work out?" Or "Why don't you open that vest up?" Although the resulting controversy did increase sales, it also prompted an investigation by the FBI to see if the ads qualified as child pornography. In fact, the campaign is still referred to in the industry as the "kiddie porn" campaign.

_03:: PETA's Sex Kittens (Literally)

It seems logical: What better use for sexual imagery than to promote…having your pets fixed? People for the Ethical Treatment of Animals, long known for their publicity stunts, tried it in 2001. The ad by industry giant Saatchi & Saatchi depicted animatronic cats "doing it" in all sorts of positions while their owner is away, while the copy reminded us that over 2.4 million unwanted kittens are born every year. It's actually very funny and effective, and PETA even tried to run it as a paid ad, not as a free public service ad. But MTV rejected it, saying they do not allow the depiction of "fornication" on their networks. Umm, excuse me? Apparently MTV's (s)executives have never actually *watched* MTV. And the aforementioned fornication wasn't even being done by real cats. They were *puppets*.

_04:: Candie's Bathroom Humor

Lots of companies use models to sell their shoes. But only Candie's used models *going to the bathroom*. A controversial series of ads from the late 1990s showed *Playboy* model Jenny McCarthy wearing a pair of Candie's shoes while sitting on a toilet, panties around her calves, reading a newspaper. So, just how racy was the spread? Both *Vogue* and *Cosmopolitan*

pulled the ads from their pages. Another series featured child-star-turned-sex-symbol Alyssa Milano in a bra and panties, rifling through a lover's medicine cabinet full of condoms. But she's stopped by an unexpected find: a bottle of Candie's perfume. Another has Alyssa about to be mounted by a naked man in the back of a limo. The ads weren't just suggestive, they were downright obvious. In fact, the ads were considered so risqué that they were banned in several countries, and the TV versions were even rejected by the WB, the network that carried Alyssa's hit show *Charmed*.

_05:: Miscellaneous: The DisGraceful Awards

At the height of the late 1990s dot-com boom, Silicon Valley professional Sylvia Paull founded GraceNet, a San Francisco–based networking group for the ever-growing number of women in high-tech fields. Every month GraceNet hands out the DisGraceful Awards for ads that crossed the line into sexism or offensiveness. And back during the boom, with all that ad money flying around, they had plenty to choose from. DisGraceful "winners" include an IBM Lotus ad showing a man using Lotus to learn "discounted cash flow techniques with 40 other analysts," while a woman uses it to finish her crossword by finding "a five-letter word for 'bellybutton'"; and an ad for Hong Kong–based games maker Lik-Sang International, featuring a young girl licking her lips over the line "We don't have young Japanese girls on sale right now, but we do ship more than 300 products directly from Hong Kong!"

Dear Dowry:
Crazy Historical Trades for Brides

Before the whole "old, new, borrowed, and blue" wedding tradition hoo-ha, there was another must-do part of any nuptials: the dowry. And through the years, lots of things have been given or received to sweeten the blessed deal. Here are a few things that have changed hands in exchange for (or in addition to) brides.

_01:: Foreskins: David and Michal

If you know where to look, you can find all kinds of crazy stuff in the good book. So grab your King James Version and flip to chapter 18 of the first book of Samuel for the story of David (yes, *that* David, with the stone and the sling and the Psalms) and Michal. After David smote the heck out of Philistine badass Goliath, he went to live with King Saul of Israel. Saul, afraid of David and troubled by evil spirits, began to plot his murder. When Saul's daughter Michal revealed her love for David, Saul made her a deal: Have David bring back 100 Philistine foreskins, and he can marry you. Now Saul had no particular affinity for foreskins; he just wanted David to get killed trying. But Dave and his posse, with God's help, brought back *200* for the good king. Saul couldn't help but bless his daughter's marriage to such a go-getter.

_02:: Heads: The Dayak of Indonesia

Journey to the Indonesian island of Borneo and you'll find an indigenous tribe of people called the Dayak. But try not to overstay your welcome, as the Dayak were historically headhunters and cannibals. In fact, their economy seems to have been predominantly skull based. If, for example, someone wanted to marry a chief's daughter, the suitor would have to impress the chief by presenting him with three or four enemy skulls. This modern tribe had given up their headhunting ways—that is, until recently, when settlers from the overpopulated Indonesian island of Madura were caught encroaching on the Dayak's traditional land. The late-1990s ethnic struggle proved that old habits die hard. Thankfully, though, things seem to have simmered down since, as the Dayak have figured out better ways to get a head.

_03:: Political Prisoners: Ramses and the Hittites

In the 13th century BCE, there were two superpowers in the Middle East: the Egyptians and the Hittites. And, as rival superpowers are wont to do, they hated each other. The main bone of their contention? The city of Kadesh, which served as a strategic linchpin located in modern-day Syria. After decades of fighting, King Hattusili III ascended to the Hittite throne, and he saw the wisdom of bargaining with the great Egyptian pharaoh Ramses II. So, he proposed a treaty. Ramses agreed to marry Maat-Hor-Neferu-Re (or Manefrure), Hattusili's eldest daughter, and in exchange he got an alliance with the Hittites, control of Kadesh, and the release of all political prisoners. Not a bad deal. But what did the blushing bride get out of it? Well, the lucky gal got only what every princess dreams of...to be the primary consort in a harem of more than 200 wives and concubines.

Touch of Evil

It was suggested that Henry VIII marry Anne of Cleves to help form a bond between England and Germany. After viewing a flattering portrait of Anne he agreed, but upon first meeting her he made it clear that he was disappointed by her looks, saying she resembled "a horse."

_04:: 100 Knights and a Table: Guinevere

The story of King Arthur has been told by many, and one of the best-known versions is Sir Thomas Malory's *Le Morte d'Arthur*. In his version, the famous Round Table was given by Uther Pendragon, its original owner, to a fella named Leodegrance, who happened to have a daughter by the name of Guinevere. When Guinevere was married off to a certain King Arthur, she brought to the marriage a most unusual dowry: the Round Table and, just for good measure, 100 knights to sit around it. But this was one serious table: it could seat 150. So magician Merlin threw in the rest of the knights to fill it. One hopes the happy couple registered for 150 place settings at Ye Olde Crate & Barrel.

_05:: England: "The Dowry of Mary"

Of all England's nicknames—Jolly Olde, Blighty, etc.—perhaps one of the most obscure is "the Dowry of Mary." At first blush, this may seem to refer to some medieval queen who married a king and got England as a wedding present. But it actually refers to the *Virgin Mary*. The story is linked to England's pious King Edward the Confessor, who, upon dedicating Westminster Abbey in 1055, allegedly offered England to the Virgin Mary as her "dowry" with the words *Dos tua Virgo pia, haec est, quare rege, Maria* (Thy Dowry this, O Virgin sweet, then rule it, Mary, as is meet). Legend has it that, a few years later, Mary responded to this piety by appearing to Lady Richeldis de Faverches in the tiny village of Walsingham, asking her to build a replica of the House of the Anunciation. This house became a major pilgrimage destination until it was destroyed unceremoniously during the Reformation.

_06:: India and Tea: Catherine of Braganza

In 1661, Catherine of Braganza, the daughter of Portugal's King John IV, was married off to King Charles II of England. The marriage was meant to cement an alliance between the two countries, and in exchange for taking Catherine's hand, Charles (and therefore England) received Tangier and Bombay. And while the natural deepwater harbor at Bombay became the headquarters of the British East India Company and a perfect foothold for England's growing colonial ambitions, the cities themselves might not have been Portugal's most treasured gifts in the exchange. Aside from the land (and a bride), Charles was also gifted a chest of tea from the far-flung Portuguese colonies. The present quickly turned him into an enthusiastic "tea" totaler, and drinking the steamy beverage soon became all the rage throughout England.

Eight Is Not Enough: Historical Dudes with Lots of Illegitimate Children

Some men produce many works of art. Or great symphonies. Or inventions that change the world. Other men just produce lots and lots of babies. Here are six examples of men whose sperm counts were obviously as healthy as their sexual appetites. Luckily for these prolific gents, Father's Day hadn't been invented yet.

_01:: Louis XV (1710–1774)

When you're made king of France at the age of five, you tend to grow accustomed to having your way. And Louis XV had his way whenever he could, eventually fathering dozens of illegitimate children. Two of his mistresses, Madame de Pompadour and ex-prostitute Madame du Barry, became famous in their own right as the Monica Lewinskis of their day. He also carried on with *five* sisters of a prominent family and kept several young concubines at a house used expressly for the purpose called the Deer Park. By the time of his death, he had a new nickname: Louis the Well Hated. Aside from all the bastard children, Louis' selfish lifestyle planted another seed: the French Revolution, which would commence just 15 years after his death.

_02:: Ramses II (ruled 1304–1237 BCE)

Of all the pharaohs of ancient Egypt, Ramses II is one of the biggies. When he wasn't commissioning statues of himself, or (as legend goes) forcing enslaved Israelites to build temples, or battling the hated Hittites, he was making babies. Estimates of his brood go as high as 96 sons and 60 daughters. Now, to be fair, many of these were born to the pharaoh's many wives, so they weren't all *technically* illegitimate. But, since he had a harem of around 200 wives and concubines, it's hard to keep track. So hard, in fact, that three of his wives—Bit Anoth, Maryamum, and Nebettawy—were *also* his daughters. And one was—wait for it—his *sister*. All together now: *Eeeeuuuw!*

_03:: Henry IV (1553–1610)

The French are world-renowned for romance, so it would make sense that they would revere a king whose many love affairs inspired the nickname *le Vert Galant* ("the Gay Old Spark"). Henry IV was one of France's greatest kings; he re-created Paris as a center of the arts, expanded France's presence in the New World, and soothed the bloody conflicts between France's Catholics and Huguenot Protestants. But he was quite the ladies' man as well. He fathered six children by his second wife, but only after he'd had three by a mistress named Gabrielle d'Estrée, the true love of his life. He also had five children by his three other principal mistresses. Henry is said to have had as many as 50 lovers over the course of his life, several of whom were his baby-mamas. Unlike many, though, he avoided the accompanying baby-mama drama by providing for his bastard offspring, making sure they were all given lands and titles and were well cared for.

_04:: King Augustus II (1670–1733)

How many Polish kings does it take to father an estimated 365 illegitimate children? Answer: one, and that one is Frederick Augustus of Saxony, better known as Augustus II ("the Strong"), king of Poland. Famous as a man of immense physical strength, unquenchable lust, and, apparently, considerable stamina, old Augustus wasn't called "the Strong" for nothin'. The first of his 300-plus love children was Hermann Maurice, comte de Saxe, a military genius who himself had several illegitimate children. The great female French novelist George Sand is descended from both these men. However, with that many children between them, we probably all are.

Scandalicious

POPE AND DAUGHTER CAUGHT GROPING AT SAME ORGY!

Not many women can claim the pope as her baby's daddy, but Vanozza dei Cattanei could. The mistress of Cardinal Rodrigo Borgia, she bore him four children before he became Pope Alexander VI in 1492. The most famous were Cesare and Lucrezia. Cesare was a ruthless general and politician, known for poisoning his enemies and conquering the cities of Romagna one by one in a three-year campaign (he also served as the model for Machiavelli's *The Prince*). His sister Lucrezia was married off to one noble after another as a pawn in her father's system of alliances. A little too fond of wealth, power, and luxurious decadence, Alexander VI was also accustomed to treating himself well by throwing notorious parties at the Vatican. The most infamous of his galas was the Ballet of the Chestnuts on October 30, 1501. Naked, painted men and women allegedly greeted guests as "living statues," and beautiful prostitutes danced nude, after which the party progressed into an orgy. Lucrezia's attendance reinforced rumors of incest. The pope supposedly lusted after his daughter as his sons Cesare and Juan fought over her as well. Some even claim Cesare murdered his brother Juan out of jealousy.

_05:: Genghis Khan (ca. 1162–1227)

Nobody knows how many illegitimate children the great Mongol conqueror actually had. But modern genetic science has proven that he must have had an *awful* lot, a result of the Mongols' ample raping and harem collecting among their many conquered peoples. By tracing the lineage of modern populations of the former Mongol Empire (stretching from China to the Caucasus) through analysis of the Y chromosome, scientists have determined that roughly 16 *million* men, or about 0.05% of the earth's male population, are descended from Genghis Khan or his brothers. Genghis's eldest son, Tushi, alone had 40 sons. In fact, by the year 1260, less than 40 years after Genghis's death, a Persian historian estimated that he already had 20,000 descendants. Now that's what you call a *conquest!*

_06:: Alexandre Dumas (1802–1870)

One of France's greatest literary figures, Alexandre Dumas brought the world adventures

Touch of Evil

England's king John battled his father, his brothers, and the pope, and was forced to sign the Magna Carta. He still had time, however, to connect with several mistresses and father illegitimate children, including Bartholomew, Eudes, Geoffrey, Joan, John, Maud, Oliver, Osbert, and Richard.

like *The Three Musketeers, The Count of Monte Cristo, The Man in the Iron Mask,* and many others. Turns out he was prolific at more than just writing. Dumas lived as colorful and adventurous a life as any of his characters, taking numerous mistresses and frittering away great gobs of money. He was purported to have fathered dozens of illegitimate children, but he acknowledged only three (by different women). Oddly enough, the one he named after himself went on to renown of his own. So to distinguish him from his son, Alexandre senior is known to the French as *Dumas père* (Dumas the Father). Well deserved, don't you think?

He Never Wants to Cuddle: Famous People Who Died in the Act

It's not really surprising that people die from overexertion when they're having sex. What might shock you is *who*.

_01:: The Pope

Actually, that's "popes," plural. Apparently papal infallibility only gets you so far. First we have Pope Leo VII (d. 939 CE), who died of a heart attack during the act. Then there's Pope John XII (d. 964 CE), who was reportedly bludgeoned to death, naked in bed, by the jealous husband of his sex partner. And who could forget Pope John XIII (d. 972 CE), who remarkably enough departed this earthly existence in exactly the same way as John XII. Then, of course, there's good ol' Pope Paul II (d. 1471 CE), who for variety's sake had a heart attack while being sodomized by a page boy.

_02:: The Duke of Orléans (1674–1723)

In 1723, after serving as prince regent and temporary ruler of France for eight years, Philippe II, the duke of Orléans and nephew of Louis XIV, "the Sun King," yielded the throne to Louis XV, who had finally come of age. And not a moment too soon—on December 23, 1723 (just two days before Christmas), Philippe had a stroke after a particularly strenuous night with his mistress, who was 30 years his junior. His only notable accomplishment had been allowing the mass-printing of paper money, which, by the way, bankrupted France.

Touch of Evil

According to a medical study published by the University Hospital of Johann Wolfgang Goethe University in Germany: "Over a period of 21 years (1972–1992), roughly 21,000 forensic autopsies revealed 39 cases (0.19%) of natural deaths occurring during sexual activity.... In most cases sudden death occurred during the sexual act with a prostitute."

_03:: Félix Faure (1841–1899)

Having served as president of France from 1895, Félix Faure seems to have experienced the "little death" and the "big death" simulta-

neously in 1899 while receiving oral sex from his mistress at the Elysee Palace. The woman's terrified screams alerted the president's aides, who broke down the door and found her still kneeling in front of the sofa where the president's corpse was seated, holding her head in his lap with the strength of a death grip. The aides freed the woman, made the president's corpse decent, and laid it out on a bed piously holding a crucifix. Typically, having caught wind of the truth, French newspapers were having none of this. They dutifully ran drawings of this Christian scene, but with the mocking caption "Death of Faure (Official Version)."

_04:: Lord Palmerston (1784–1865)

After a series of accomplishments that won the admiration of the whole world—including helping Belgium achieve independence, supporting the seizure of the French throne by Napoléon III, establishing friendly relations with France, winning the Crimean War, and criticizing the sale of opium in China—what would be the most dignified way for an English elder statesman to end his long life of public service? How about a heart attack as he diddles a parlor maid on a pool table in 1865? Nuff said.

_05:: Nelson Rockefeller (1908–1979)

Grandson of oil tycoon John D. Rockefeller, former governor of New York and vice president of the United States, Nelson Rockefeller left this world doing what he loved best— engaging in lively intercourse with America's free press. Seventy-one years of age, Rockefeller died while having sex with his mistress, a "thirty-one-year-old former news reporter who was working as his research assistant," according to the *New York Times*. The *Times* treated the sticky subject of just *how* Rocke- feller died rather delicately, saying only that he died as he lived, "with an enthusiasm for life in all its public and private passions." Ahem.

Can I Get Flies with That? World's Strangest Aphrodisiacs

8

If the one-two punch of Barry White and candlelight just ain't doin' the trick, maybe your lust needs some thrust from a less traditional source. Here are a couple of internationally acclaimed remedies from the days before Viagra.

_01:: Basil

If you're desperate for a quick trick to jump-start an ailing love life, just look to the sweetest herb on your spice rack for the remedy. That's right! According to practitioners of the voodoo belief system in Haiti, good ol' basil is the Spanish fly of your kitchen cabinet. Said to be sacred to the Haitian goddess of love, Erzulie, basil is added as an aphrodisiac to a special incense burned to invoke her spirit in voodoo love ceremonies—obviously, for romantic purposes. The Old World herb is also sprinkled liberally on food and eaten to stimulate that tingling feeling.

_02:: Antlers

Perhaps because they resemble erect phalluses, antlers have been considered aphrodisiacs in traditional Asian medical folklore for over 2,000 years. Practitioners of traditional medicine recommend grinding up the soft, velvety skin that covers deer antlers and sprinkling it on food or mixing it into a beverage. In fact, the bony outgrowths are so prized that one species, the Tibet red deer, has actually been hunted to near extinction. Luckily, scientists recently discovered a small herd of 200 of these animals near Lhasa, Tibet, we hope none of which will die in the name of love. Or lust.

_03:: Xanat

The flower of the vanilla orchid was reputed by the native cultures of Central America to be an aphrodisiac, and vanilla still carries this association in Mexico. In native folklore, Xanat, the youngest daughter of the fertility goddess, suffered from unrequited love for a young man of the Totonac tribe. In fact, she was forbidden to marry him because she was divine and he a mortal. Since she couldn't marry a human, however, the benevolent Xanat turned herself into a flower with aphrodisiacal qualities so she could help the human race do its thing.

_04:: Frog Legs

Sometimes you can have too much of a wood—er, good—thing. In the case of an unfortunate group of French Foreign Legion soldiers in North Africa, frog legs proved to be such an effective enhancer of "erectile function" that priapism—a prolonged, painful erection that will not go away—ensued. Subsequently, researchers from American universities found that the frog legs contained enormous amounts of cantharidin, better known as Spanish fly. It turned out the frogs had been eating meloid beetles, one of the main sources of the legendary aphrodisiac, eventually making things hard for the soldiers.

_05:: Nutmeg

Another salacious spice lurking in your pantry, nutmeg has long been thought of as an aphrodisiac by a variety of cultures. The ancient Greeks, Romans, and Hindus ate it for that purpose, and the tradition continued into both the Arab and Chinese civilizations. In fact, in contemporary India, couples eat a mix made of nutmeg, honey, and a half-boiled egg before sex to increase their endurance and make intercourse last longer. However, nutmeg may also have unpredictable hallucinogenic effects, and in large quantities can be fatal.

_06:: Sweet Potatoes

Shortly after Columbus made landfall in 1492, the natives of Hispaniola introduced him to the sweet potato, a member of the morning glory family. Spanish colonizers soon spread the sweet potato lovin' to Asia and Europe, the popularity to cultivate it driven in part by its reputation as an aphrodisiac. In *Health's Improvement,* a medical guide from 1595, Dr.

Thomas Muffet wrote that sweet potatoes increase not only libido, but apparently also the incidence of flatulence, claiming that they "nourish mightily . . . engendering much flesh, blood, and seed, but withal encreasing wind and lust."

_07:: Tiger

Today tigers are one of the most endangered species on earth, with the main population in Asia all but wiped out by poachers. Sadly, this is due in large part to a widespread belief in East Asian cultures that tiger flesh is medicinal for a variety of ailments and complaints. Tiger penis, bone, liver, fat, and whiskers are all reputed to stimulate sexual desire in men, driving the illicit trade and pushing the rare animals ever closer to extinction. Even worse? Despite the fact that its illegal, you can probably find a tiger parts dealer near you: tiger is commonly sold under the table in American cities that are home to large numbers of East Asian immigrants.

_08:: Unagi, Unagi

Served raw in sushi or cooked as part of an *udon* (noodle) dish, sea eel, or *unagi,* is reputed in Japan to be an aphrodisiac. The association likely springs from a rather obvious similarity between the shape of the eel and, as usual, an erect penis. Of course, there might be some science behind the belief as well. Unagi is high in vitamin A, which may help sexual function. Although *unagi* is an increasingly popular item on American sushi menus, most diners are unaware of its erotic associations in Japanese cuisine.

How Do You Solve a Problem Like Our Parents? Historical Eloping Tales

Love, they say, conquers all. But sometimes a little thing like parental permission can put up a tough fight. The following four couples didn't get their permission slips signed before taking field trips to the altar.

_01:: Peter Abelard and Héloïse Leonard de Selva

In 12th-century France, Fulbert, a priest of the Cathedral of Notre Dame in Paris, hired Abelard, a gifted but contrary theologian and Aristotelian philosopher, to tutor his brainy young niece, Héloïse. As you might have predicted, Abelard and Héloïse fell in love. What wasn't predicted, however, was that young Abelard would impregnate her. Understandably, Héloïse's uncle was enraged, shipping her off to Normandy for the duration of her pregnancy. After giving birth to a son, she returned to Paris, where, again defying uncle's wishes, Héloïse and Abelard slipped off for a secret wedding. What's an overprotective uncle to do? Fulbert organized his male relatives into a posse, ambushed Abelard, and castrated him, which effectively stopped history from repeating itself. Abelard became a monk and Héloïse reluctantly entered a convent. All wasn't lost, however, and their love affair continued in the form of letters, later collected in book form. In what can be considered a moderately happy ending (given the circumstances, not to mention the uncle), Héloïse ended her life as abbess of the Paraclete, an abbey that Abelard had founded, and was buried next to him.

_02:: John Scott and Bessy Surtees

John Scott was a graduate student at Oxford in 1722, but banker Aubone Surtees wanted more for his daughter Bessy than a merchant's son—especially one who'd been a notorious scamp as a boy. Yet, as songwriter Bob Dylan would put it more than 250 years later, "Love and only love, it can't be denied." Against the wishes of her father and his own (who thought John would imperil his academic career), Scott used a ladder to snatch young Bessy from an upstairs window, and they ran away to Scotland to marry. (It was easier for English couples to get hitched north of the border in those days.) Luckily for the couple, however, neither daddy knew best. John Scott bettered his father's and father-in-law's predictions by becoming the longtime lord chancellor of England. In fact, today, the once mischievous rascal is better remembered as the first earl of Eldon.

_03:: Henry Fitch and Josefa Carrillo

When sea captain Henry Delano Fitch—later a prominent California landowner—fell for 14-year-old Josefa Carillo in 1826, he fell hard. By the laws of Mexican California, however, the San Diego girl couldn't marry a Protestant foreigner, so the Nantucket-born Yankee converted to Catholicism and had himself rechristened Enrique Domingo Fitch. Josefa's father, after some persuading, agreed to the match. During the wedding, however, before the couple could say their vows, Josefa's uncle arrived with an order from the California governor to stop the ceremony. (She later claimed that the governor wanted her for himself.) At the bride-to-be's urging, Fitch took his gal aboard ship and they sailed off to Chile, where they wed. After they returned to California, Fitch was charged with kidnapping and jailed for three months until the governor could verify the legality of the nuptials.

Touch of Evil

Sixteen-year-old Konrad Falkowski eloped with Joan Kenlay in 1952. But to avoid being tracked down by their parents, the young man changed his name, and it's this moniker we still use to refer to the famous actor: Robert Conrad.

_04:: James Joyce and Nora Barnacle

Budding Irish writer James Joyce convinced his Dublin sweetheart, Nora Barnacle, to run away with him to Austria-Hungary in 1904. It wasn't exactly an elopement, though, because Joyce objected to the institution of marriage on philosophical grounds. So, they skipped the ceremony and dove straight into the happily-ever-after bit, living together and raising two children. Joyce, who had by now achieved fame and notoriety, especially for his complex masterpiece *Ulysses,* only agreed to marry his longtime love when the nagging got to be too much. We're not talking about Nora's whining here, but rather her daughter Lucia's. The young woman's incessant complaints about her parents' domestic arrangement drove them to the altar. In 1931, the couple finally legalized their union during a trip from their home in Paris to London. (So, in the end, they ran away to get married after all.)

Greatest Syphilitics of All Time

From Columbus to Gauguin to Al Capone, who knew that syphilis would be the great equalizer? The following are five notables who might have fared better if they'd kept their belts buckled and their legs crossed.

_01:: The Syphilitic Explorer

The long-held view was that Columbus's crew picked up syphilis in the Caribbean in 1492 and brought it back to Europe, where the "new" disease turned epidemic. But what about Columbus himself? He returned from his third voyage west in 1504 partially paralyzed, suffering edema, and mentally de-

The Evil How-to

HOW TO SPOT "THE SIGNS" (OTHER THAN JUST HAIRY PALMS)

Active physician, health innovator, and, yes, the founder of a cereal company, John Harvey Kellogg wrote a handbook for sexual behavior in 1877 (while on his honeymoon) called "Plain Facts for Old and Young, A Warning on the Evils of Sex." A key focus of this piece was a section containing 39 signs for parents to use to tell whether their children were masturbating or "performing the solitary vice," as it was called. The following are some of the signs that, according to Kellogg, all good parents should be on the lookout for: emaciation, paleness, colorless lips and gums, exhaustion, coughing, shortness of breath, chest pains, disobedience, irritability, a dislike for activity and play, sleeplessness, failure to get lessons done, forgetfulness, inattention, and liking to be alone. Kellogg went on to identify some other telltale signs, including bashfulness, boldness, mock piety, rounded shoulders, weak backs, pain in the limbs, lack of breast development in females, bad positions while sleeping, large appetites and the use of large amounts of spices, sunken and red eyes, and epileptic fits. Finally, especially be on the lookout for acne, bitten fingernails, moist, cold hands, bedwetting, the use of tobacco, and fondness for using bad language and listening to obscene stories. It's a good thing Kellogg was so specific; otherwise we might have started accusing everyone.

ranged. But can anybody be sure what caused those symptoms without examining Columbus's bones? Well, no. He could have had typhus or rheumatic fever, but syphilis can't be ruled out.

_02:: The Syphilitic King

A wound on Henry VIII's leg became a festering sore that wouldn't heal. Ulcers spread over his legs and feet. And as he grew hugely obese, the English king's toes turned gangrenous. Not exactly a thing of beauty, Old Hal had something going on. The latter-day diagnosis: advanced diabetes. So what's with the notion that Henry's late-life dementia came from syphilis? Some say first wife Catherine of Aragon's several miscarriages suggest a sexually transmitted disease. And then there's the sad case of Henry's son Edward VI, the boy king with the terrible skin rash whose hair and nails fell out. Tradition says Eddie died at age 15 of tuberculosis. Many, however, argue that he and his half sister Queen Mary I had congenital syphilis passed on from Henry. Of course, it's all unconfirmed. None of Henry's children, including Elizabeth I (another suspected but unconfirmed syphilitic), produced offspring.

_03:: The Syphilitic Philosopher

On a winter day when Friedrich Nietzsche was 54, the German-Swiss philosopher, clad in only his underwear, ran weeping into a street in Turin, Italy, where he tearfully embraced a horse. Stricken with diphtheria and bacterial dysentery during his service in the Franco-Prussian War (1870–1871), Nietzsche never fully recovered his health. His late-life dementia, however, more likely stemmed from tertiary syphilis. In other words, he had probably picked up the disease in his youth and it had run its course for decades. Nietzsche, a philosopher later admired (and grossly misunderstood) by Adolf Hitler, spent the last 11 years of his life totally mad.

Touch of Evil

One radical cure for syphilitic patients was to give them malaria. *The high fever worked to kill the syphilis, after which the malaria was easily cured with quinine.*

_04:: The Syphilitic Painter

Born in Paris, Paul Gauguin spent his early childhood in Peru before moving back to France. As a young man Gauguin signed on as a merchant sailor to see and sample the sensual riches of the world. Later, after he'd supposedly settled down, Gauguin and his wife moved from France to her native Denmark, where they raised their family and Gauguin had a career as a stockbroker. But then Gauguin chucked his family and his career to live a new life as a bohemian painter in Tahiti. So where did he pick up the syphilis that plagued him in his later years? It could have been in the South Seas, although it's more likely that a Parisian prostitute gave him the pox. Nearly blind, barely able to walk, and in terrible pain, this forefather of modern art died alone in his Maison du Jouir (House of Pleasure) in the village of Atuona in the Marquesas Islands.

_05:: The Syphilitic Gangster

When New York tough guy Alphonse "Scarface" Capone arrived in Chicago in 1919, one of his first jobs in the town where he would become America's most famous gangster was looking after mobster Big Jim Colosimo's string of brothels. So, did old Al sample the service? Well, a gentleman gangster never tells. What we will say, however, is that wherever he picked up the "goods," years later, he was discovered to be suffering from paresis—a psychosis that follows after the late-stage disease eats away a significant part of the brain. Released from Alcatraz Federal Prison in 1939, Capone entered a Baltimore hospital and spent his last years deep in syphilitic dementia.

The Cost of Free Love:
Not-So-Straitlaced Reformers of Victorian Times

4

A glimpse of stocking may have been shocking, but a vocal minority of 19th-century reformers fought for your right to hook up.

_01:: John Humphrey Noyes (1811–1886)

As a theology student at Yale, John Humphrey Noyes declared himself sin free and in a state of perfection. Not surprisingly, Johnny the Pure was denied a license to preach, so he organized fellow perfectionists into a "Bible Communist" community in Putney, Vermont. There Noyes taught a doctrine of free love. In 1846 the Putney group adopted what their leader called "complex marriage," such that all the women were "married" to all the men and vice versa. Arrested for adultery, Noyes jumped bail and fled to New York, where he founded a new community in Oneida. There, the Oneida Community practiced complex marriage up until 1879, when Noyes finally gave in to pressure from outside moralists and abandoned the practice. Oneida, once an agricultural-religious utopian community, reorganized as a joint-stock manufacturer of silver flatware. As for John Noyes? He fled again, this time for Canada.

_02:: Ezra H. Heywood (1829–1893)

Massachusetts liberal Ezra Heywood founded his publication *The Word* in 1872 as a voice for labor reform and other egalitarian causes. Heywood and his wife, Angela Tilton, also a writer for *The Word,* shared four daughters and a belief that traditional marriage amounted to slavery of women—both of the economic and sexual variety. So what did the couple do? They decided to pen their own emancipation proclamations, using *The Word* to advocate free love. "Sexuality is a divine ordinance elegantly natural from an eye-glance to the vital action of the penis and womb, in personal exhilaration or for reproductive uses," Tilton wrote. Of course, such salacious language was bound to offend a few Victorians, and Anthony Comstock, a smut-fighting special agent of the U.S. Post Office, was certainly one of them. Comstock took special offense to Heywood's pamphlet "Cupid's Yokes," which advocated birth control, and arrested Ezra in Boston in 1877. Many argued that Angela, known for her frank vocabulary (she used the "f" word in print) should have been jailed, too, but Ezra's the one who spent time in the slammer.

_03:: Moses Hull (1836–1907)

A gifted Seventh-day Adventist preacher, Moses Hull left the church and began lecturing

Touch of Evil

Despite having the Victorian era named after her, Queen Victoria didn't always act so Victorian. In fact, she was notorious for having a long-term out-of-wedlock relationship with her "personal attendant," John Brown—lavishing him with expensive gifts and constant affection—after her husband, Prince Albert, passed away.

instead on spiritualism in 1863. Well known for his eloquence, he was considered highly respectable. That is, until 1873, when old Moses printed a letter in *Woodhull & Claflin's Weekly* (copublished by Victoria Woodhull, see next item) unapologetically confessing that he'd strayed from his marriage. But he didn't stop there. Hull actually went on to praise sexual variety, claiming: "Many think they are improved . . . by a change of climate and scene, when their principal improvement is caused by a separation from their old sexual mate, and sometimes by the substitution of a new one." Hull and wife, Elvira, dissolved their marriage "by a law higher than man's" and Hull subsequently entered a "contract marriage" (no clergy, no license) with fellow spiritualist Mattie Sawyer. Luckily, the "contract" held until his death.

_04:: Victoria Woodhull (1838–1927)

Believe it or not, the first woman to run for U.S. president actually spent her childhood as a fortune-teller in her family's traveling medicine show. Luckily for Victoria Woodhull, she abandoned the psychic act for loftier goals, including stints as a stockbroker, magazine publisher, women's rights advocate, and, most notoriously, lecturer. Woodhull's talks on free love drew thousands—supporters and scandalized alike. Though few details about her own sex life are known (aside from the fact that she lived for a while with two husbands), Woodhull didn't argue in favor of promiscuity. In fact, she pushed sexual self-determination as essential to women's rights, condemning any copulation without love, inside or outside of marriage. In 1872, while seeking the White House on the Equal Rights ticket, Woodhull smeared clergyman Henry Ward Beecher, probably a former lover, who refused to publicly support her. Unfortunately, the first amendment didn't work in her favor in the Victorian climate. Woodhull's published account of Beecher's adultery with a married parishioner landed her in jail on obscenity charges.

Naked Lust:

Artists Who Did More Than Portray Their Models

Emotionally charged virtuosos plus beautiful nude models plus too many hours spent in the studio? These cases illustrate that high art and simple biology are anything but mutually exclusive.

_01:: Anselm Feuerbach and Nanna Risi

The 19th-century painter Anselm Feuerbach, nephew of philosopher Ludwig Feuerbach, admired and tried to emulate the art of the High Renaissance. That's a big part of the reason why he migrated from his native Germany to Italy. Yet Feuerbach also possessed a cool, northern European sensibility, which he brought with him to Rome when he moved there in 1856. In fact, his neoclassical scenes took on a bit of heat only after Italian model Nanna Risi (also seen in works by Frederick Leighton) began posing for him in 1860. It wasn't just his artwork that heated up, though. The chemistry between artist and model grew, and Risi eventually left her shoemaker husband and her child for Feuerbach. The affair didn't last, however, and she later abandoned the artist. Brokenhearted, Feuerbach tried to replace Risi with another model and lover, but he had little luck. After some time spent teaching art in Vienna, Feurbach moved to Venice, where he died poor and alone in 1880.

_02:: Suzanne Valadon and half of France . . .

Before 1892, when she became a painter, Suzanne Valadon was a teenage circus acrobat and then one of the most popular models in Paris—popular in more than one sense. Henri de Toulouse-Lautrec, Pierre Puvis de Chavannes, and Pierre-Auguste Renoir were among the many artists who depicted her. Toulouse-Lautrec's *The Hangover,* for example, is a portrait of Valadon. Usually, however, this model's relationships went well beyond the depicting stage. Valadon had numerous love affairs with Parisian artists, and perhaps the best documented is that with Renoir. Composer Eric Satie was also an intense lover of hers. More intriguing than a listing of the lovers she kept: Valadon never revealed which man fathered her son, painter Maurice Utrillo. Further, at age 44, Valadon was still on the prowl. She left a wealthy husband for the considerably younger artist André Utter, 23.

_03:: Pablo Picasso and Marie-Thérèse Walter

Picasso met Marie-Thérèse Walter either in 1925, when she was 15 and he was 43, or in

1927. In either case, they seemed to be lovers from early in their relationship, as Picasso's marriage to the former dancer Olga Koklova quickly deteriorated. Although Picasso first approached Walter to comment on her interesting face and his eagerness to paint her, Walter's likeness doesn't show up in Picasso's work until 1935, which is the same year she bore him a daughter. In any case, the reliably unreliable Picasso left Marie in 1936 for photographer Dora Maar, who turned the tables and used Picasso as a model. Sadly, Walter hanged herself in 1977. Even more unfortunate, she wasn't the only one of Picasso's former lovers to commit suicide.

_04:: Man Ray and Lee Miller

In 1929 Lee Miller, a 19-year-old art student from Poughkeepsie, New York, walked into innovative painter-collagist-photographer Man Ray's photo studio in Paris and introduced herself as his new assistant. Ray, who'd made his reputation as a surrealist and a pioneer of the Dada movement, said he didn't need an assistant but she persisted. Miller, already a top model who had adorned the cover of *Vogue* in 1927, was pretty persuasive (or persuasively pretty). The affair lasted for a bit. Lee and Ray were together as lovers and collaborators for three years before she went on to a photo career ranging from studio fashion shoots for *Vogue* to feature spreads in *Life* to wrenching World War II battlefield coverage for the U.S. military.

_05:: Jeff Koons and Ilona Staller

In 1991, stockbroker-turned-controversial-artist Jeff Koons—earlier known for works depicting basketballs floating in aquariums and brand-new vacuum cleaners displayed under glass—took a turn toward the graphically sexual in 1991. The series of pieces included photographic tableaux and small glass sculptures depicting him engaged in sex acts with Italian porn star Ilona "Cicciolina" Staller. Oddly enough, there was nothing left to the imagination in these works—some of them barely distinguishable from the porn that was Cicciolina's career mainstay. Nonetheless, it was "art," just as a basketball in an aquarium was "art," because Koons pronounced it so. The pair married that year and produced a son (perhaps conceived on camera), but they separated in 1992.

Out of Order:
Divinity School Dropouts

Hell hath no fury like a former seminarian. From Hollywood superstars to adulterous dilettantes, several seminary dropouts have managed to find success in the secular world. But they've also strayed from the Christian path—whether it was for the teachings of L. Ron Hubbard or simply to reign terror over a Communist nation. Here's a sampling of the finest in almost-clergy.

_01:: Tom Cruise (1962–   )

In 1976, a deeply religious child named Thomas Cruise Mapother IV enrolled in a Franciscan seminary in New Jersey. Within five years, he'd ditched the church, dropped the Mapother, and landed a part in *Endless Love*. And in spite of his diminutive height (5 feet 7 inches) the man who might have been a priest became one of Hollywood's top leading men. Around 1986, though, he abandoned Catholicism altogether, embracing the Church of Scientology, which he once credited with helping him overcome dyslexia. Wildly popular with celebrities, Scientology is the path of choice to "clarity" for everyone from John Travolta to the guy who played Parker Lewis in *Parker Lewis Can't Lose*. Incidentally, Scientology does have ministers—but while Cruise remains an active member and apologist for the group, he has yet to seek ordination.

_02:: Casanova (1725–1798)

Everyone's favorite 18th-century libertine began his scandalous escapades at the seminary of St. Cyprion, from which he was expelled under cloudy circumstances (we're guessing he slept with someone). And as you well know, his postseminary life was as ungodly as it gets. By the age of 30 he was sentenced to prison for engaging in "magic," but he escaped after only a year to Paris. There, he made a fortune by introducing the lottery to France. But before settling down to write his ribald, self-aggrandizing autobiography, Casanova was expelled from more European countries than most of us ever visit. Along the way, he slept with tons of women, dueled with many of their husbands, and generally sinned his way to the top of European culture, befriending such figures as Madame du Pompadour and Jean-Jacques Rousseau along the way.

_03:: Joseph Stalin (1879–1953)

Lasting longer than the vast majority of divinity school dropouts, noted mass murderer Joseph Stalin studied at a Georgian Orthodox seminary in Tiflis (now Tbilisi) for five years, between 1894 and 1899. He left the seminary either because of poor health (his mom's story) or revolutionary activity (Stalin's story). Either way, Stalin clearly didn't take much of what he learned to heart (assuming he had one). After he became the Soviet leader in

1922, he was responsible for the deaths of thousands of religious leaders, and Stalin did more than any other premier to eliminate the role of Christianity in Soviet life. But his seminary wasn't exactly a study in Christian love, either. Prior to Stalin's arrival, a rector was murdered there—possibly by unruly seminarians.

Touch of Evil

When Charles Darwin hesitated to obtain a degree in medicine, his dad enrolled him in the University of Cambridge to study divinity. It wasn't long, though, before the "father of evolution" quit school (in 1831) to begin taking part in scientific expeditions around the world.

_04:: Michael Moore (1954–)

Controversial documentary filmmaker Michael Moore began studying at a seminary in his hometown of Flint, Michigan, as an eighth grader in 1967. Brought up a devout Catholic, Moore aspired to a career as a priest, but he left the seminary the next year for thoroughly secular reasons. When the Detroit Tigers made it to the World Series in 1968, the seminary refused to let him watch the games—so he quit. Before his successful filmmaking career, in fact, Moore was something of a serial dropout. He dropped out of the University of Michigan because he arrived at school one morning and couldn't find a parking place, and he once got a job at an automobile factory in Flint—but called in sick on his first day and never returned.

_05:: Al Gore (1948–)

Believe it or not, the winner of the popular vote in the U.S. presidential election of 2000 was actually a devoutly religious divinity school dropout. It's true! Al Gore graduated from Harvard cum laude in 1969 (although he earned several Cs and a D during his time in Cambridge), but he'd always been interested in theology, so he decided to continue his studies. It's no wonder, then, that he enrolled in Vanderbilt's prestigious divinity school, where, over the course of three semesters, he *failed* five of his eight classes! Gore's allies claim that the birth of his first child and his duties as a reporter at the *Tennessean* newspaper kept him from his studies. For the record, though, Gore also later dropped out of Vanderbilt's law school (in 1976), but this time for a truly higher purpose—to run for Congress.

Portraits of Artists as Young Perverts

In his memoir *A Moveable Feast*, Ernest Hemingway revealed that F. Scott Fitzgerald once confessed to being concerned about his diminutive penis size. Hemingway replied, "You're perfectly fine," but then of course went on to publish a book recounting the humiliating conversation. And if no less a writer than Ernest Hemingway can go around revealing authors' sexual quirks and insecurities, well, so can we.

_01:: Rousseau (1712–1778)

Jean-Jacques Rousseau, an 18th-century Swiss writer and philosopher, believed that humans were basically good but had been corrupted by the social order. And boy, did he know a thing or two about being corrupted. While you wouldn't know it from the dry prose of *Émile* or *The Social Contract,* Rousseau enjoyed the naughty—so long as he got spanked for his transgressions. "To lie at the feet of an imperious mistress," he once remarked, "was for me a sweet enjoyment." Yikes! In fact, he liked it so much that as a young man, Rousseau would drop trou and moon women in dark alleyways, hoping to get a spanking for his trouble. Surprisingly, the great philosopher's greatest impact might not have been made by his quill, but rather by his quirk. The phrase psychologists use to describe young men who get aroused when disciplined by older women: "the Rousseau effect."

_02:: Lewis Carroll (1832–1898)

The most famous sexual deviant in the annals of literature may, in fact, not have been: Lewis Carroll, children's book author and noted fan of taking little girls' pictures. Carroll, who spent most of his career teaching math, spoke with a terrible stammer around adults, but found it easy to talk to children (kind of like Michael Jackson). In fact, the sputtering author found it remarkably easy to engage his child friends in fantastic stories, which culminated with *Alice's Adventures in Wonderland*. Published in 1865, *Alice* is certainly a study in Freudian sublimation: there's a fair bit of squeezing through tiny holes, for instance. And then there are the pictures: Carroll photographed both adults and children, and also took several nude pictures of kids (he even sent a letter to a colleague at Oxford asking if he could photograph his girls nude without chaperones). Still, no evidence has ever surfaced that Carroll abused anyone—incapable of mature relationships, sure, but probably not an active pedophile.

_03:: René Descartes (1596–1650)

Perhaps the only example of a sexual eccentricity changing the history of Western thought can be found in the life story of the father of modern philosophy, René "I think therefore I am" Descartes. You see, Descartes had a fetish for cross-eyed women—due, he

Scandalicious

RUSSIAN CZARINA AND PEASANT SEEN SMOOCHING BY PALACE STEPS (PHOTOS INSIDE!)

How did an illiterate, raggedly dressed peasant with a well-known reputation for sexual debauchery become a trusted friend to Czar Nicholas II and Czarina Alexandra of Russia? Well, it may have been Rasputin's remarkable ability to heal their hemophiliac son, Aleksei. Or maybe, as many have thought, Alexandra was in love with him. When Czar Nicholas went to the front during World War I, Alexandra stayed behind to run the country, and the sex-crazed holy man Rasputin became her most trusted adviser. Meanwhile, she probably became the most prominent of his many mistresses. Though not the best-looking fellow you'd ever meet, Rasputin did have certain, uh, assets—his penis was supposedly more than a foot long. It's unlikely that Alexandra and Rasputin ever consummated their bizarre friendship, but by December 1916, the mere *rumor* of peasant-on-czarina loving was simply too much to bear for a group of Russian aristocrats, who finally decided to put Rasputin out of their misery. It wasn't easy. He survived poisoning and two gunshot wounds before finally being drowned in the icy Neva River.

believed, to his childhood fascination with a cross-eyed playmate. As he describes it in the *Principles of Philosophy,* Descartes was eventually able to condition his body to find straight-eyed women attractive (good for Descartes, maybe, but a disaster for the hard-up cross-eyed ladies of Europe). It was largely this experience that led Descartes to his belief in free will and to his assertion that the mind can control the impulses of the body.

_04:: James Joyce (1882–1941)

When an admirer once asked if he could "kiss the hand that wrote *Ulysses,*" James Joyce replied, "No. It has done a lot of other things, too." Indeed it had. *Ulysses,* the exemplar of 20th-century literature, was banned in much of the world for its purported obscenity. (For the greatest literary accomplishment of its time, *Ulysses* does feature a lot of smut.) In

Touch of Evil

Before Horatio Alger's rags-to-riches stories inspired a generation of youngsters, he was quietly dismissed as minister of the First Unitarian Church in Brewster, Massachusetts, for allegedly molesting two young boys who were members of the congregation.

America, Judge John M. Woolsey lifted the ban on *Ulysses* in December of 1933 (the same month Prohibition ended), and Joyce's sprawling, brilliant tale of one day in Dublin became an instant sensation. *Ulysses* may not be obscene, but Joyce himself was a bit of a perv. He admitted to finding women's unwashed underwear erotic—perhaps not coincidentally, panties and petticoats pop up in *Ulysses* rather frequently.

_05:: Edna St. Vincent Millay (1892–1950)

Many writers have been unfaithful to their spouses, but few can match Edna St. Vincent Millay. The first woman to win the Pulitzer Prize for poetry, Millay was married for 26 years to Eugene Boissevain. In a reversal of traditional gender roles, Boissevain did most of the housework and Millay most of the philandering. She took many lovers, both male and female, and one biographer described her as having a "megawatt libido." True enough, but so did a lot of male poets (like Lord Byron), and they didn't catch much flak for it. Millay was open, and funny, about her trysts. When she complained of headaches to a psychologist at a party, he wondered whether Millay might have a subconscious attraction to women. "Oh, you mean I'm a homosexual!" Millay replied. "Of course I am, and a heterosexual, too. But what's that got to do with my headache?"

_06:: F. Scott Fitzgerald (1896–1940)

Another great modernist, F. Scott Fitzgerald, had his own quirks. Like many authors (Dostoyevsky and Thomas Hardy, among others), Fitzgerald may have had a foot fetish, at least according to biographer Jeffrey Meyers. In 1917, Fitzgerald became acquainted with the great love of his life, Zelda Sayre, outside of Montgomery, Alabama. They married in 1920, the same year his first novel, *This Side of Paradise,* was published. Then, five years later, his masterpiece, *The Great Gatsby,* hit the shelves. Shortly thereafter, Zelda lost her tenuous grip on sanity—she eventually landed in a sanitarium after she began practicing ballet day and night. All those hours en pointe couldn't have been good for her feet. But Fitzgerald might not have cared: most critics think he was only kidding when he made references to a "pedentia complex," which just goes to show you, be careful what you joke about.

A Pain in the Royal Horse: Sex Rumors About Royalty

Long before Prince Charles proved that love is blind by cheating on his beautiful wife with Camilla Parker-Bowles, bluebloods had already proudly renounced monogamy. Over the centuries, they've coveted their neighbors' wives countless times, sure, but what about their neighbors' livestock? It's time to separate the perverted facts from the perverted fiction about royal sex lives.

_01:: Catherine the Great (1729–1796)

The reign of Catherine II, the German-born czarina of Russia, began when she overthrew her alcoholic, incompetent, and purportedly impotent husband, Frederick (the not so Great), in 1762. If there was one thing Catherine the Great would not stand for, it was impotence. Although grossly overweight, Catherine loved men—a great many of them, in fact—over the course of her 34-year reign. And then, it was rumored, she died during a botched attempt to make love (if it can be called such a thing) to a horse. The rumor may have been spread by Catherine's Polish enemies, who resented her for annexing much of Poland. (On the list of European royalty's lei-

sure activities, "overrunning Poland" has historically been a close second to "sex.") At any rate, Catherine never had sex with a horse, and one wonders why anyone felt compelled to make up such a story, since her actual death was plenty humiliating. While straining on the toilet, she had a stroke.

_02:: A Tale of Two Georges

In what seems to be an outlandish coincidence, England's king George II (1683–1760) also died of a stroke while on the commode. Some sources say that although he was quite happily married to his wife, Queen Caroline, George took mistresses so as to *maintain his reputation*. After all, a mistressless king could be seen as weak or, worse still, impotent. His son, George III, however, broke that streak of monarchial infidelity when he married the notoriously homely Princess Sophia Charlotte of Mecklenburg-Strelitz in 1761. Seeing her for the first time on their wedding day, George is said to have winced in disgust, but the two came to love one another immensely (and frequently—they had 15 kids), and George III was never unfaithful.

Touch of Evil

Supposedly, a priest attending Napoléon's autopsy ended up "saving" certain body parts, including the Bonaparte penis. Later bought by a collector and displayed in a New York museum, the organ was said to resemble "a shriveled sea horse."

_03:: Another Royal Horse

The Roman emperor Caligula (12–41 CE) redefined sexual debauchery during his reign. Aside from fancying himself a god and having an altogether creepy sexual fascination with his sister Drusilla, Caligula supposedly engaged in many orgies (which inspired a famous adult film). Plus, he had a suspiciously intimate relationship with his favorite horse, Incitatus. Some Roman historians claimed that Caligula intended to make his horse consul, but that appears to have been kind of a Roman urban legend. Roman historians despised Caligula so intensely that it's difficult to sort out the actual facts of his reign. And while Caligula did *like* his horse (he apparently built Incitatus a house), there's no reason to believe he "liked him" liked him.

_04:: Jahāngir (1569–1627)

Though there are plenty of excellent candidates for most sexually insatiable king ever, including Hal the Horny (the oft-married Henry VIII of England), our vote has to go to Jahāngir, the fourth Mughal emperor of India. Jahāngir had little to do with the day-to-day running of the empire—that work was accomplished by his favorite wife, Nūr Jahān. (The Taj Mahal was built for Jahān's niece, Mumtaz Mahal.) While Jahān became one of the most powerful women of the 17th century, Jahāngir busied himself with loving. He supposedly had 300 wives (296 more than allowed by the religion, Islam, he supposedly followed), 5,000 female concubines, and 1,000 male concubines. Jahāngir also kept a massive herd of 12,000 elephants, but we won't speculate.

_05:: And, of Course, Prince Charles! (1948–   )

Of all the recent sex rumors about the British royal family, none has been kept quite so quiet as that of Prince Charles's supposed bisexual affair. For weeks in late 2003, the British press printed banner headlines about a royal sex scandal but, conscious of Britain's strict libel laws, never came out and openly revealed the accusations. Instead, they engaged in all manner of hints and innuendo. This led to the strange phenomenon of the royal family issuing a statement denying allegations that had never publicly been made. The rumor: Prince Charles had a love affair with his adviser Michael Fawcett. Scandalous, sure, but unlikely—it seems the prince only has eyes for Camilla. After decades of courtship, they finally wed in 2005.

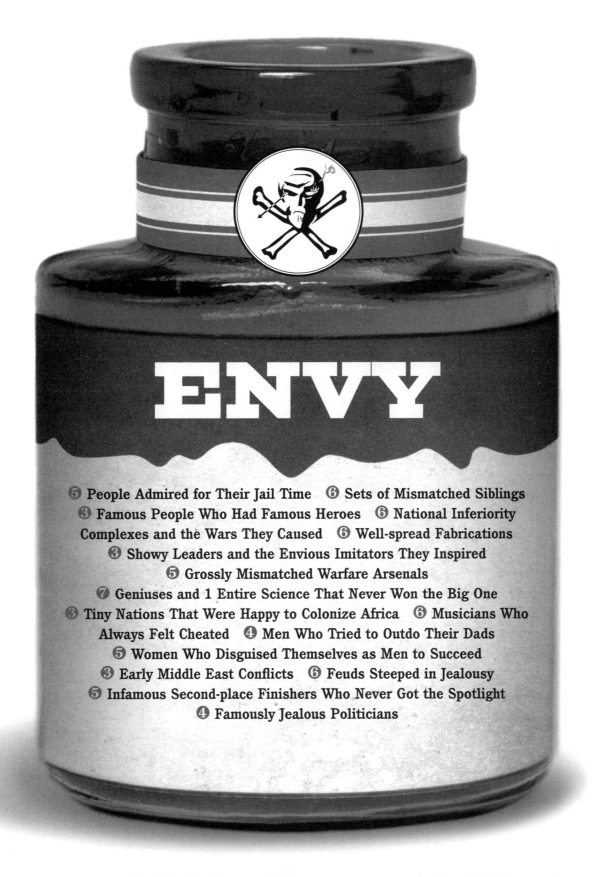

ENVY

5 People Admired for Their Jail Time **6** Sets of Mismatched Siblings
3 Famous People Who Had Famous Heroes **6** National Inferiority
Complexes and the Wars They Caused **6** Well-spread Fabrications
3 Showy Leaders and the Envious Imitators They Inspired
5 Grossly Mismatched Warfare Arsenals
7 Geniuses and 1 Entire Science That Never Won the Big One
3 Tiny Nations That Were Happy to Colonize Africa **6** Musicians Who
Always Felt Cheated **4** Men Who Tried to Outdo Their Dads
5 Women Who Disguised Themselves as Men to Succeed
3 Early Middle East Conflicts **6** Feuds Steeped in Jealousy
5 Infamous Second-place Finishers Who Never Got the Spotlight
4 Famously Jealous Politicians

Does That Come in Stripes?
People Admired for Their Jail Time

Before she began serving her five-month sentence for illegal insider trading in 2004, Martha Stewart came perilously close to comparing herself to a somewhat more noble former inmate. "There's many other good people that have gone to prison. Look at Nelson Mandela." Oh, we'll look at him, Martha. But we're not so sure you'll stack up. While we wouldn't envy the following folks, they certainly earned respect by spending time in the clink.

_01:: Nelson Mandela: The Political Prisoner

The son of a Tembu chief, Nelson Mandela worked as a lawyer (an honest lawyer!) until becoming a leader of the African National Congress in 1949. Today, Mandela has a reputation for nonviolence, but in reality he embraced armed struggle and sabotage after the appalling 1960 massacre of nonviolent protesters in Sharpeville. After admitting he helped found Spear of the Nation, the ANC's military wing, Mandela was sent to prison for life. During his 28 years in jail, the charismatic Mandela became even more popular among black South Africans, and his writings from prison, particularly *I Am Prepared to Die,* galvanized international opposition to apartheid. Released in 1990, Mandela made the most of his freedom. Within four years, he helped negotiate an end to apartheid, won the Nobel Peace Prize, and became South Africa's first black president.

_02:: 50 Cent: The Platinum Prisoner

In the hip-hop world, nothing sells like street cred. Anybody can *rhyme* about prison and shootings and drug deals—but it's the precious rapper who can claim nine bullet wounds and several incarcerations that'll move those albums. For better or for worse, 50 Cent's payment of dues in jail certainly played a role in his seven-figure record contract. After all, the rap world was starving for authenticity, and 50 (aka Ben Jackson) was a true gangster in the Tupac mold. His résumé includes growing up selling crack and surviving being shot nine times in 2000 (he's also been stabbed!). Many critics, and some fellow rappers, have attributed his success more to his life's story than his mediocre rhyming. But it's probably not a trade worth making—most ex-con crack dealers who get repeatedly shot and occasionally stabbed tend not to end up with platinum albums.

_03:: Adolf Hitler: The Palace-Bound Prisoner

These days, Adolf Hitler is perhaps history's least admired individual. But during his reign as Führer, Hitler's time in prison was seen as proof he sacrificed for National Socialism and Germany. In reality, though, his hard time wasn't particularly hard. Sentenced to five years in prison after failing spectacularly to take over the country in 1923, Hitler served only nine months. Also, he was "jailed" in a castle, and all his friends were either in jail with him or free to visit. What's a poor inmate to do? At the castle, Hitler decided to write (or dictate, actually) *Mein Kampf,* his self-aggrandizing autobiography/study in irrational hatred. Hitler originally gave the book the catchy title *Four and a Half Years of Struggle against Lies, Stupidity, and Cowardice,* which Nazi publishers smartly shortened to the catchier *My Struggle.* Soon enough, much of Germany admired Hitler's struggle—even if *he* was the real lying, stupid coward.

_04:: Leonard Peltier: The Pine Ridge Prisoner

While America was extricating itself from Vietnam in the early 1970s, a minor war was brewing on the home front. The American Indian Movement (AIM), advocating a return to Native traditions, was locked in a fierce battle with those Indians who supported, and were supported by, the federal Bureau of Indian Affairs. Some 60 Native Americans died, but the story didn't become big news until June 26, 1975, when two FBI agents were killed during a gunfight on the Pine Ridge Reservation in South Dakota. AIM activist Leonard Peltier was convicted of the murders. Although quite probably guilty, many (including Nelson Mandela, the Dalai Lama, and Amnesty International) have argued that Peltier is a political prisoner. President Clinton considered pardoning him in 2000 but didn't. Perhaps hoping to pardon himself, Peltier ran for president in 2004 as the candidate for the somewhat ironically named Peace and Freedom Party.

_05:: Dietrich Bonhoeffer: The Pacifist Prisoner

The most prominent theologian in Hitler's Germany, Dietrich Bonhoeffer openly and courageously opposed Nazism and condemned the church for "staying silent when it should have cried out." Although a pacifist, Bonhoeffer participated in a lengthy struggle to overthrow the Nazis that culminated in a failed assassination attempt on Hitler. Already imprisoned for helping Jews escape to Switzerland, Bonhoeffer's connection to the group resulted in his execution on April 9, 1945. His brilliant *Letters and Papers from Prison* remains in circulation, however, and is required reading for contemporary theologians. Among the first thinkers to consider the role of Christianity in an increasingly secular world, the suffering Bonhoeffer lived his theology. "God is weak and powerless in the world," he wrote, "and that is exactly the way, the only way, in which He is with us to help us."

Mom Always Liked *You* Best: Sets of Mismatched Siblings

Brothers wrestle; sisters scream. Siblings always compare themselves—how much they're loved, how much they inherit, how they look—and feelings always get hurt.

_01:: Jesus and Who?

The New Testament mentions brothers (*adelphoi* in Greek) of Jesus and even names them. Yet, many Christians teach that Jesus was an only child and that the *adelphoi* James, Simon, Judas (different from apostles James, Simon, and Judas), and Joseph were Jesus' cousins. In fact, according to Catholic theology, Jesus' mother, Mary, never had sexual intercourse and never bore a child other than the Messiah, so the *adelphoi* couldn't have been his brothers. Other lines of thought tell it a little differently, claiming that the Gospel writers used *adelphoi* literally and that Mary was a virgin only until after the birth of Jesus. We don't want to take sides, but if these four guys really were Jesus' brothers, they got the seriously short end of the sibling stick. Imagine—not only is your brother God Almighty, he's also the most famous man in history. Meanwhile, scholars are sitting around arguing about whether you ever even existed.

_02:: Charlotte Brontë and Her Five Siblings

Maria and Elizabeth Brontë couldn't help being eclipsed by younger sister Charlotte; after all, they died in girlhood in the 1820s. Sister Emily, second youngest, was the family's only poetic genius and wrote *Wuthering Heights* (1847). Seen in retrospect as one of the finest novels in English, it was panned in its own time and she produced no more. Youngest sister Anne's novels, *Agnes Grey* (1847) and especially *The Tenant of Wildfell Hall* (1848), were popular, if literarily undistinguished. Branwell, the one brother, drank too much, smoked too much opium, and died a failure in 1848. Emily and Anne died the next year. All of which leaves Charlotte the only Brontë to achieve popular, critical, and lasting success with her novels, especially *Jane Eyre* (1847). In the end, she was the longest-lived of the TB-plagued Brontë siblings, surviving until age 39. She was also the only one to marry (the show-off).

_03:: John and Tom Fogarty: Bad Blood Rising

In 1959, Tom Fogarty, two school chums, and Tom's little brother, John, formed a band. Playing in the Fogarty garage in El Cerrito, California, they called themselves Tommy Fogarty & the Blue Velvets. Then, in 1964, they landed a recording contract with Fantasy Records in nearby Berkeley. Renamed the Golli-

TOM WOLFE'S HORRIBLE-TERRIBLE, NO-GOOD, VERY BAD DAY

The 1998 publication of Tom Wolfe's novel *A Man in Full* brought healthy sales but brutal reviews from literary heavy hitters including novelists John Irving, John Updike, and Norman Mailer. Mailer, a longtime Wolfe nemesis, was particularly damning, comparing reading the book to having sex with a 300-pound woman. "Once she gets on top it's all over. Fall in love or be asphyxiated," Mailer wrote in *The New York Review of Books*. A decade earlier, the pugnacious Mailer had angered the Virginia-born Wolfe by making fun of his sartorial trademark, a natty white suit. At the time, Wolfe replied that "the lead dog is the one they always try to bite in the ass." After the attacks on *A Man in Full*, Wolfe dismissed critics Mailer and Updike as "old bags of bones" and said that all three of his novelist-rivals (whom he often refers to as "My Three Stooges") were panicked by his neorealist fiction. Either that, or his fancy-pants style.

wogs, the band floundered until John suddenly emerged as both a towering talent and a control freak. As lead singer, lead guitarist, lead composer, lead lyricist, lead arranger, and lead (if not sole) band manager, he could do everything but spell. John turned the group, now called Creedence Clearwater Revival, into an "overnight" sensation, cranking out top-10 singles ("Proud Mary," "Bad Moon Rising," "Down on the Corner") and No. 1 albums. Brother Tom? In 1971 he quit in disgust. Worse yet, he couldn't catch a break. He passed away in 1990 as a result of AIDS, a condition contracted from a blood transfusion.

_04:: Jimmy and Billy Carter: Not Like Two Peanuts in a Shell

Twelve years younger than brother Jimmy, Billy Carter found himself cast in the role of clown prince in the late 1970s. A beer-for-breakfast kind of guy who proudly wore a "Redneck Power" T-shirt, Billy sometimes embraced the role of buffoon and sometimes tried to shake the stigma. His bid to become mayor of Plains, Georgia, close on the heels of his brother's 1976 presidential victory, failed. He also failed as manager of the family peanut warehouse. His PR makeover wasn't helped by the fact that he regularly greeted reporters while perched on a stack of beer cases in his service station. It also wasn't helped by his business initiatives: Billy once tried to cash in on celebrity, promoting a brand of beer named for him. His biggest misadventure, however, came when he accepted money from the Libyan government in return for his supposed influence with his brother. Dubbed "Billygate," the episode prompted a congressional investigation and embarrassed Jimmy as his 1980 bid for reelection approached. Billy Carter died at age 51 in 1988.

_05:: Rajiv and Sanjay Gandhi: Who Gets Mom's Job?

Prime Minister Indira Gandhi had two sons: Rajiv and Sanjay. The elder, Rajiv, didn't want to follow in the political footsteps of his family (including grandfather Jawaharlal Nehru, founding prime minister of independent India). So, he became an airline pilot. Sanjay, on the other hand, was groomed by Mom to succeed her as leader of the Indian National Congress Party. Willful and aggressive, Sanjay pushed for his mother's 1975 declaration of a state of emergency—an unconstitutional abuse of power. After Sanjay's death in a 1980 plane crash, though, Rajiv agreed, reluctantly, to run for the Lok Sabha (lower house of the Indian parliament). After his mother's assassination in 1984, though, he was cast full force into the political sphere and elected prime minister. Unlike Sanjay, Rajiv was a reasonable leader, open to compromise. Yet financial scandals plagued his government and in 1989 he resigned as prime minister. He was seeking reelection to the Lok Sabha when a suicide bomber—linked to Tamil separatists in southern India—killed him. Today, his wife, Sonia, is active in Congress Party politics and continues the political legacy.

_06:: Bill and Roger Clinton: Little Rock

Like Jimmy Carter, Bill Clinton brought his own sibling of ill repute to the national spotlight. When Bill Clinton was Arkansas governor, Roger Clinton pleaded guilty to distributing cocaine and served 15 months in prison. When Bill was U.S. president, his half brother, 10 years younger, was supposedly a rock singer. After Bill left the White House, a congressional investigation in 2001 showed that much of Roger's considerable income during his brother's two terms had come from mysterious sources. His "musical gigs" overseas brought him big money from foreign governments, payments that suggest he was playing something other than rock and roll. (Clinton bashers say it was influence.) He also accepted money from organized crime figure Rosario Gambino, apparently in exchange for seeking leniency from a parole board. Hey, take "the work" when you can get it. Since Bill's White House departure, rockin' Roger's music career has fizzled.

If I Weren't Alexander (I'd Be Diogenes): Famous People Who Had Famous Heroes

3

Alexander the Great wanted to be Diogenes, Salvador Dalí wanted to be Napoléon, and J. Edgar Hoover wanted to be a lady. Hey, inspiration comes from strange places, so it's no wonder that even heroes have heroes. The following are three important figures and their unlikely influences.

_01:: Fathers of Their Countries

Growing up in China's Hunan province, young Mao Zedong loved to read. In fact, he liked it so much that his father, who wanted the boy to be a farmer, grew impatient. There was a less dreamy side behind the bookish Zedong, however. His heroes were military leaders, especially those who opposed established order. Though Mao concentrated on Chinese generals and great battles in Asia, he was also fascinated by ideas and stories from the Western world, including, believe it or not, the life of George Washington. In 1911, just before he turned 18, Mao joined a revolutionary army fighting Manchu authority in his province. And although he had yet to embrace the Marxist philosophy that would shape his life and China's history, the young man's stint as a soldier helped him begin to understand that he, like his hero, Washington, could use military force toward political ends.

_02:: A Mother of Innovation

Frank Zappa's early fans—most of them 13-year-old boys mesmerized by the vulgar weirdness of *Freak Out!,* his 1966 debut album—understood little about the artist. After all, Zappa came across like a zany cultural gadfly and wild-haired rock guitar hero—not the serious musician that he turned out to be. But an early clue to what was really going on lay in Zappa's frequent references to French-born composer Edgard (originally Edgar) Varèse. And while Zappa freaks didn't know that Varèse, a pioneer of electronic music, celebrated asymmetrical rhythms and dissonance, or that he died at age 81 in 1965, they did know that Zappa dug him, so he became cool by association. Over the course of Zappa's 30-year career, though—much of it as an ambitious, iconoclastic, and outright weird proponent of musical (and political) experimentation—his debt to Varèse became ever more apparent.

_03:: What'd I Say?

Born in 1944 in Sheffield, England, Joe Cocker went to work at age 16 installing gas pipes, but he was obsessed with rock and roll. And despite his appreciation for the vocal stylings of Chuck Berry, Little Richard, and Jerry Lee Lewis, young Joe fell in love with one voice that would shape his career as a music star of the 1970s and '80s—Ray Charles. Cocker said he got "hung up" on Charles, and French fans later referred to the gravel-voiced rocker as Le Petit Ray Charles. Although the blind genius's

Lies Your Mother Told You

MACBETH WAS A GOOD-FOR-NOTHIN' SOCIAL CLIMBER

Forget everything Shakespeare told you about Macbeth. The real Macbeth was a political genius who united the disparate Scottish lords and set Scotland on the path to nationhood. He was also beloved by the common people for his charity and piety and the fact that, unlike his predecessors, he preferred to rule in peace rather than involve them in disastrous wars abroad. In 1054, Malcolm, son of Duncan I (a hated egotist whom Macbeth had defeated fair and square in battle, not murdered in his sleep as Shakespeare would have it), invaded Scotland with an army of Anglo-Saxon mercenaries looking for land and power. Macbeth fought a three-year war against the invaders but was ultimately killed. As for Malcolm (III), he became one of Scotland's worst kings, and that's saying a lot; he fought numerous wars against England, losing every time, taxed the commoners to ruin, and put hated Sassenachs (Englishmen) in positions of power. Overall, one of the worst trades in the history of the British Isles.

influence can be heard in many corners of popular music, he had a particularly profound effect on boys growing up in the British Isles in the 1950s and '60s. You can note Charles's phrasing and intensity reflected in such Cocker hits as "A Little Help from My Friends" and "The Letter," but also in the vocal styles of Welsh pop star Tom Jones, Irish soul man Van Morrison, and English superstar Elton John, among others.

May I Have a Cup of Culture?
National Inferiority Complexes and the Wars They Caused

If you think Polish jokes are bad, you should hear what they were saying about these other unsophisticated underdogs—that is, right up until they got bitten.

_01:: Macedonia v. Greece

In the fourth century BCE, the rest of Greece disdained the redneck Macedonians, and strangely enough, the Macedonians seemed to agree! Philip II, the king of Macedonia, and his son Alexander both learned the more sophisticated Ionian Greek dialect and aspired to educate themselves in the Greek style. In fact, Philip went so far as to hire the Greek philosopher Aristotle to tutor his young son (nothing's too great for my little Alexander!). The pair also wanted to reshape Macedonian culture and society along "sophisticated" Greek lines. Of course, the most logical way of making Macedonia more like Greece was to make Greece part of Macedonia, and so over the course of their reigns both Philip and Alexander brought the entire Greek peninsula under their control.

_02:: Rome v. Greece

Greek culture still carried its cachet a few hundred years later, when the rising power of Rome began to threaten the Macedonian kingdom from the west. The Romans venerated Greek culture even more than the Macedonians had, with educated upper-class Romans aspiring to read, write, and speak Greek as proof of good breeding. The Greek influence is even more evident, when you notice that Rome's public monuments are total imitations of Greek architecture. It's no wonder then that when Rome was expanding abroad, the Greeks, still resenting their Macedonian rulers, welcomed Roman intervention. At least they did at first. The Greeks figured that the Romans, respectful and assiduous students of their culture, would be honored to liberate Greece and set the Greeks free. Rather than letting the people go, however, the Romans simply took over the administration from Macedonia and incorporated Greece into their empire, marking the end of Greek independence for almost two millennia.

_03:: Arabs v. Persia

When the first Muslim Arabs came out of the Arabian Peninsula to conquer much of the known world in the seventh century CE, they were fairly simple bedouins with an oral tradition and little in the way of art or literature. Luckily, one of the first powers they encountered on leaving the deserts of the Arabian Peninsula, the Persian kingdom of the Sassanids, possessed the oldest and most refined culture in the Middle East. Hungry for Persia's wealth, great cities, material comforts, and beautiful art, the Arabs gobbled up the land beginning in 635. Within 20 years, these bedouin go-getters had incorporated the entire kingdom, including Afghanistan, and since they'd immediately adopted Persian art and literature as the gold standard of education and good breeding, its reach soon extended all the way from the Atlantic Ocean to the borders of India.

Touch of Evil

After General Leopoldo Galtieri seized control of Argentina in 1981, he ill-advisedly took the nearby Falkland Islands by force—a foolish move. Britain's Margaret Thatcher wasted no time regaining the land, and the general was quickly disposed of in a follow-up coup.

_04:: Mongols v. China

In the 13th century CE, the Mongol tribes of Central Asia had no written language, no cities, no knowledge of agriculture, and no real notion of the geography of the globe outside their own small corner of it. China of the Sung dynasty, by contrast, was the oldest continuously ruled empire in the world, with a highly refined culture and a complicated, evolved social structure that was the product of thousands of years of development. After all, Chinese agriculture produced enormous amounts of food—principally rice—supporting an extremely wealthy aristocracy and a Sung emperor who lived in opulent luxury. But all the money and refinement in the world couldn't protect the Sung dynasty from the maelstrom the Mongols unleashed on them. As masters of archery and cavalry combat, the Mongols, led

by Genghis Khan, swarmed over China in 1211 CE, killing millions of Chinese and establishing their bloody rule for decades to come.

_05:: England v. France

In the 15th century, France was the uncontested center of western European civilization. Paris had been the clearinghouse of medieval scholarship with its famous university at the Sorbonne, and France boasted the most productive agriculture; the largest population; the most creative painters, architects, and artists; and the most developed code of chivalry. As for England? During this time the nation was simply a small, poor, damp little backwater ruled by a French royal family descended from William the Conqueror. And believe it or not, the English aristocracy and royal family were all but French—they spoke French, drank French wine, ate French food, wore French clothes, read and talked about books by French scholars, and visited France frequently. So when a dispute over the succession to the French monarchy gave King Henry V an opening to conquer France, he naturally went for it—and won! Henry was crowned king of France shortly before his death in 1422.

_06:: Japan v. China

The Mongols weren't the only people attracted to China's refined, developed culture. In fact, the nation's sophisticated ways were alluring enough to draw the attention of another warlike neighbor, Japan, several times throughout history. And the effects are evident. The Chinese written language was adopted in its entirety by Japan; Buddhism, which dominated Japan for a long period, was a Chinese import, with Japanese Buddhist monks going to study in China; the Japanese borrowed Chinese architectural styles and governmental structures; and literate, well-educated Japanese studied Chinese literature. But as recently as the 1930s, even after Japan had modernized its economy and built a highly efficient armed forces, this Japanese obsession with China manifested itself in the desire to conquer and control the country. Sadly, the brutal attack resulted in the deaths of tens of millions of Chinese in the Second World War.

It's a Slanderful World: Well-spread Fabrications

The fifth-century-BCE dramatist Sophocles once said that "a lie never lives to be old." Clearly, Sophocles never heard the one about suicidal rodents, or about the world-famous animator frozen in suspended animation. Here's hoping that, at the very least, these lies don't live to be any old*er.*

_01:: Elephants and Mice

In spite of what you may have seen at the circus, elephants aren't afraid of mice. Actually, they're not afraid of anything, which is why it's not all that hard for poachers to kill them for ivory. For decades, circuses have featured elephants rearing up and trumpeting with fear upon catching "sight" of a scurrying mouse. But in reality, the elephants probably can't even *see* the mouse in question—they have notoriously poor eyesight. Due to their excellent memories, however, elephants *can* learn a variety of tricks, including rearing up on their hind legs when ordered to do so by whip-brandishing circus trainers. And while we're dispelling elephant rumors: There's no such thing as an elephant graveyard. When elephants are ready to die, they just fall down and do it, like the rest of us.

_02:: Betsy Ross

In all likelihood, Betsy Ross did not design, or for that matter even sew, the first post–Union Jack American flag. Ross, a seamstress who took over her husband's upholstery business after he died fighting in the Revolutionary War, purportedly sewed the flag based on a pencil sketch from George Washington himself. But no evidence has ever been found to back up the Ross family story. In fact, most historians believe the flag was either based on the British East India Company's flag or designed by Francis Hopkinson, a signer of the Declaration of Independence and early member of Congress. Regardless of who designed it, the Continental Congress officially adopted the Stars and Stripes in 1777, on June 14, which, in an amazing coincidence, happens to be Flag Day.

_03:: Disney's Remains

Despite the ubiquitous rumor to the contrary, Walt Disney was not cryogenically frozen after his death. Disney, who won more Academy Awards (26) than any other person, expressed a desire to be cremated, and his wish was carried out two days after his death on December 15, 1966. There's scant evidence, in fact, that Disney even knew that cryogenic freezing existed. At any rate, it's highly unlikely that cryogenic freezing could have saved Walt. Putting aside the fact that most scientists think frozen bodies will never be resurrectable, Disney's lung cancer necessitated the removal of his left lung a month before his death. So even if future scientists could have brought Walt back from the dead, he would have been awfully short of breath.

Touch of Evil

It was a fascinating story how struggling musician Charles Manson auditioned for The Monkees back in 1965. Fascinating, and false! Manson was behind bars when the tryouts took place.

_04:: Lemmings

The poor, oft-maligned lemmings—you couldn't blame them for being suicidal, if they are, which they aren't. The notion of lemming suicide extends back at least to Freud, who in *Civilization and Its Discontents* (1929) explained the human death instinct in the context of lemmings. But the notion didn't really take hold until Walt Disney's 1958 so-called documentary *White Wilderness* hit the big screen. For his film, the lovable animator shipped dozens of lemmings to Alberta, Canada, herded them off a cliff, filmed them falling to their deaths, and passed it off as nonfiction. In reality, though, lemmings aren't suicidal. They're just dumb. Lemming populations explode in four-year cycles in Scandinavia, and when the tundra gets crowded, they seek out new land. Being stupid, they sometimes fall off cliffs, but not on purpose.

_05:: Rice at Weddings

These days, it's become common practice for eco-friendly couples not to feature rice throwing at their weddings. After all, the science-deficient theory claims, birds eat the rice, which expands in their stomachs and causes them to explode. Rice farmers from Thailand to Arkansas probably *wish* that rice-eating birds blew up, but quite simply, they don't. The fact is, nuptial rice poses no more danger to birds than combining pop rocks and soda does to kids. So, how'd the rumor come about? It all started in 1988, when old Ann Landers discouraged readers from the practice. Of course, the USA Rice Federation (motto: "Proving there is a federation for everything") immediately debunked Landers's story, but, surprisingly (and disappointingly), Ann Landers had a broader readership than the USA Rice Federation.

_06:: Van Gogh's Ear

In the fierce competition for the title of History's Most Tortured Artist, Vincent van Gogh certainly makes a compelling case. Impoverished, unloved, and underappreciated in his time, van Gogh led a miserable life, potently symbolized by his missing left ear. We've all heard the story: He chopped it off and Pony Express-ed it to a prostitute in a perverse act of love—here is an artist so tortured, even the prostitutes didn't love him! But wait! He didn't chop off his *entire* ear—just the lower half of it. And it wasn't about women at all. In a fit of rage after an argument with friend and fellow artist Paul Gauguin, van Gogh cut his ear to symbolize the end of their friendship, believing that Gauguin had grown "deaf" to his needs. Some claim van Gogh later visited a brothel to give the half-ear to a prostitute named Rachel (hey, we never said he wasn't crazy), but he certainly never *mailed* anything!

Playing the Palace: Showy Leaders and the Envious Imitators They Inspired

A smaller-than-average castle can give a guy a complex, so it's no wonder so many world leaders suffer from palace envy. The following are three characters who were pretty eager to overspend in an attempt to overcompensate.

_01:: Francis I and Henry VIII

In the first half of the 16th century, the kings of France and England were more than contemporaries, enemies, or allies. They were personal competitors. England's Henry VIII, especially, felt it important to keep up with French counterpart Francis I, and boy did it show. When the two were vigorous young men, handsome Hank fancied that his impressive physique outshone that of flashy Frank. But this was more than just a beauty competition. When Henry went on a state visit to France in 1520, he had an extravagant pavilion of gold cloth (like a luxury tent village) built to match that of Francis, nearby. The three-week diplomatic campout, known as the Field of Cloth of Gold, was a daily orgy of expensively competitive pageantry that nearly bankrupted both countries. The competition didn't end there. Later, Henry spent heavily on arts and architecture, trying not to be outdistanced by the sophistication of Francis's capital.

_02:: Louis XIV and Leopold I and...

If a finance minister builds a house bigger than the king's, the king gets suspicious. That isn't exactly what happened to Nicolas Fouquet, who in 1661 threw a party for his boss, the "Sun King" of France, at Fouquet's magnificent new chateau, Vaux-le-Vicomte. Impressed, Louis XIV moved straight past the suspicion phase, and threw his host in jail. Then, he put Fouquet's former architects and builders to work on the royal estate outside Paris. Completed in 1682, the huge and incredibly ornate Palace of Versailles inspired envy in monarchs everywhere. In response, Leopold I of the Austro-Hungarian Empire commissioned a "hunting lodge" outside Vienna, the

1,440-room Schönbrunn Palace, completed in 1695. Other monarchs who retaliated with a Versailles of their own: "Mad" King Ludwig II of Bavaria (Castle Herrenchiemsee) and Empress Elizabeth of Russia (the Winter Palace).

Touch of Evil

As America's fifth president, James Monroe was so flattered by comments about his resemblance to George Washington that he dressed in the same style the Father of Our Country did. Sadly, that style was way out of date by then.

_03:: Richard Nixon and Queen Elizabeth II

U.S. president Richard Nixon liked a bit of pomp (with occasional circumstance). After all, Tricky Dick often saw other heads of state protected by guards in bright-colored uniforms with shiny trim or tall fur hats (as in Britain's famous Beefeaters outside Queen Elizabeth's official London residence). But what did the White House have? Guys in dark, plain security uniforms. Wanting a piece of the regal action, Nixon ordered a redesign of the outfits worn by White House guards (Secret Service Uniformed Division). Unveiled in 1970, the new duds featured gold-trimmed tunics and rigid, peaked hats reminiscent of 19th-century Prussia. The royalist look didn't go over so well with Americans. Critics howled. Comedians

Scandalicious

CAMBODIAN WIVES LASH OUT AGAINST ADULTERY (WITH BATTERY ACID)

Adultery is frowned upon in most societies, but in Cambodia it can mean taking your life into your hands. During the late 1990s, a rash of attacks by high-society ladies against their husbands' mistresses broke out. In the most famous case, Bun Ray, the wife of Prime Minister Hun Sen, hired hit men to murder Piseth Pilika, a Cambodian film star who was reputed to be assisting the prime minister with his homework after hours. Another infamous incident occured on December 5, 1999, when Tan Chhay Marina, a teenage actress and singer, was horribly disfigured when five liters of battery acid were dumped on her by the wife of Svay Sitha, an undersecretary of state.

snickered. And the White House immediately threw out the Prussian hats. Within a few years the fancy duds (along with their chief proponent) were retired entirely.

Who Throws a Shoe? Honestly!
Grossly Mismatched Warfare Arsenals

We know all's supposedly fair in love and war, but somehow these conditions still seem remarkably stilted.

_01:: Romans v. Celts

At the beginning of their long march to supremacy, the Romans had an early advantage because they knew how to make steel weapons that were much stronger than their opponents' iron weapons. Iron swords and spearheads were relatively simple to make, requiring that the blacksmith melt down iron ore in a furnace, hammer the metal into a blade, and then shape and sharpen it on a forge. To make steel, the Romans understood, the blade had to be put back in the furnace for a long period to allow carbon from the coals to infiltrate the metal, making it stronger. The results for their enemies were often disastrous: in a series of battles the Romans fought against the Celts, who were armed with iron weapons, the Celts' swords became so badly deformed that the Celtic warriors had to bend them back to their original shape over their knees in the middle of combat.

_02:: English v. French at Agincourt

When the English, led by King Henry V, fought the French in the battle of Agincourt, they had a secret weapon: Welsh subjects trained in the use of the longbow. Amazingly, these weapons of war were simply five-foot-high yew arcs that could be used to shoot eight arrows a minute, each arrow about three feet long. And the rapid-fire assault was too much for the French. With a total force of about 5,000 archers, Henry slaughtered the pride of French chivalry before Genovese crossbowmen in French employ were even in range. In fact, it was said that the ground was covered with so many white feathers from the arrow fletching that it looked like snow.

_03:: Spanish v. Aztecs and Incas

When the Spanish invaded Mexico and Peru in the early 16th century, they wielded weaponry far superior to anything the Aztecs and Incas could have imagined. The 600 Spaniards who landed at the site of modern-day Vera Cruz in 1519, under the command of Hernando Cortés, carried firearms—muskets—and small cannons, and rode horses, all of which terrified the Aztec natives. And though the Aztecs fiercely fought back on foot with swords and spears made out of sharp pieces of obsidian, or black volcanic glass, set in pieces of wood, ultimately they were no match for the Spaniards. Despite Cortés's encountering a few setbacks, there was no contest, and he managed to subdue five million Aztecs with his tiny army. Similarly, beginning in 1530, the Spanish conquistador

Francisco Pizarro subdued the Inca empire with 180 soldiers, fighting a native army of about 40,000 men.

_04:: English v. Mahdi in Sudan

When the forces of British general Charles Gordon were surrounded and eventually destroyed by Islamic fundamentalist tribesmen at Khartoum, Sudan, in 1885, the blow to British prestige was tremendous. In fact, the imperialist nation was so embarrassed that it decided the event demanded a total and overwhelming response. To get revenge, the British shipped a well-trained army to fight the native Muslim rebels in central Sudan. But the army wasn't just well trained; they were well armed, and were even carrying Gatling guns— prototype machine guns that drew ammunition from a long straight clip filing through the firing chamber. The result at the battle of Omdurman in 1898 was decisive and horrendous, resulting in the slaughter of tens of thousands of native tribesmen with virtually no British casualties.

_05:: Germans v. Poles

One of the better-known instances of grossly mismatched weaponry in warfare occurred in 1939 when Nazi Germany under the dictatorship of Adolf Hitler invaded Poland. At the time Poland was an underdeveloped nation that had become independent only 20 years before. Itching to get his hands on more real estate, and determined to "restore" Germany's "original" borders, Hitler sent modern German tanks, at the head of regular and mechanized infantry, crashing into Poland. Simultaneously, the Führer sent the German air force to pound Polish cities from the sky. The Stuka dive-bombers railed on the virtually undefended towns, and killed tens of thousands of people in Warsaw alone. It wasn't exactly a fair fight. The impoverished Poles fielded horse-mounted cavalry and peasant brigades armed with old-fashioned muskets in an effort to resist the Germans. Their air effort was even more pathetic: the few antiquated World War I–era biplanes were no match for the Germans. In three weeks, Poland was finished.

They Put the "No" in Nobel: 7 Geniuses and 1 Entire Science That Never Won the Big One

Scientists are supposed to be above petty politics and popularity contests, right? Nope. Here are a few bright bulbs that never got the fancy Nobel gold medallion (or the 10 million Swedish krona that go with it). And you thought the Oscars were bad.

_01:: Joan Robinson, Economics

Great Britain's Joan Robinson may be one of the most exciting figures in the history of "the Dismal Science." An acolyte of the great John Maynard Keynes, her work covered a wide range of economic topics, from neoclassicism to Keynes's general theory to Marxian theory. Not to mention, her notion of imperfect competition still shows up in every Econ 101 class. Add to that the fact that Robinson's greatest work, *The Accumulation of Capital,* was published way back in 1956 but is still widely used as an economics textbook. So why no Nobel? The easy answer is that she's a female, and no female has ever won the Nobel in Economics. Others say that Robinson's work over her career was too eclectic, rather than hyperfocused like that of so many other laureates. Still others claim that she was undesirable as a laureate because of her vocal praise for the Chinese Cultural Revolution, a thoroughly anti-intellectual enterprise.

_02:: James Joyce and _03:: Marcel Proust, Literature

One wrote *Ulysses* and *Finnegan's Wake,* almost universally regarded as two of the most brilliant works of the 20th century (in the case of *Ulysses, the* most brilliant). And the other is, well, Marcel Proust. Proust's towering work, *A La Recherche du Temps Perdu (In Search of Lost Time,* or, sometimes, *Remembrance of Things Past)* is considered one of the greatest literary achievements ever, combining seven novels and 2,000 characters for a celebration of life, consciousness, and sexuality spanning 3,200 pages. James Joyce's works and stream-of-consciousness style are the basis of countless college courses, doctoral theses, and poetic ruminations. But the writings of Proust and Joyce were probably just too controversial and "out there" for the more conservative Nobel committees of their day. And Nobel's stricture against posthumous awards hasn't exactly helped, especially since the influence of these two artists has continued to grow long after their deaths. Most ironic, Proust and Joyce have been major influences on many writers who went on to win Nobels themselves, like Saul Bellow, Samuel Beckett, Jean-Paul Sartre, Albert Camus, and Hermann Hesse. Other literary giants who have gotten the Nobel shaft? Evelyn Waugh, Jorge Luis Borges, Bertold Brecht, Graham Greene, Henry James, Vladimir Nabokov, and Simone de Beauvoir, to name a few.

_04:: Dmitri Mendeleev, Chemistry

Why would this guy deserve a Nobel Prize for chemistry? After all, his only achievement was to devise the entire periodic table of elements, the miracle of organization and inference on which all of modern chemistry is based. Mendeleev's table was so good, it even predicted the existence of elements that hadn't yet been discovered. But here's where politics rears its ugly head. In 1906, Mendeleev was selected by the prize committee to win the honor, but the Royal Swedish Academy of Sciences stepped in and overturned the decision. Why? The intervention was spearheaded by Swedish chemist Svante Arrhenius, who had himself won the prize in 1903 for his theory of electrolytic dissociation. Mendeleev had been an outspoken critic of the theory, and Arrhenius seized the opportunity as the perfect chance to squeeze a few sour grapes.

_05:: Jules-Henri Poincaré, Physics

Although Poincaré was a mathematician, his genius was too universal to be confined to one category. Sure, he came up with all sorts of mathematical theories with crazy names: algebraic topology, abelian functions, and Diophantine equations. But he was into physics, too. Poincaré laid the foundation for modern chaos theory and even beat Einstein to the punch on certain facets of the theory of special relativity. And one of his math problems, the Poincaré conjecture, even remained unsolved for nearly 100 years! So why was Henri overlooked for the Big One? Due to Alfred Nobel's stipulation that his prizes go to those whose discoveries have been of practical benefit to mankind, the Nobel committees have often been accused of rewarding experimental discoveries over purely theoretical advances. Poincaré's work in physics seems to be a victim of that prejudice.

_06:: Raymond Damadian, Medicine

Lots of deserving folks have been passed over for the Nobel, but few were as vocal about it as 2003 runner-up Raymond V. Damadian. He was the brain behind the science of magnetic resonance imaging (MRI), a technique that completely revolutionized the detection and treatment of cancer. But the 2003 Prize for Medicine went to Paul Lauterbur and Peter Mansfield, two scientists who expanded on Damadian's discovery. Enraged at the slight, Damadian ran full-page ads in the the *New York Times* and *Washington Post* featuring a photo of the Nobel Prize medal upside down and the headline "The Shameful Wrong That Must Be Righted." The ad featured quotes from other scientists backing up Damadian's claim, even a letter of protest to be cut out, signed, and mailed to the Nobel Committee. Some claim Damadian was slighted because his fundamentalist Christian belief in creationism made him anathema to the scientific community. Others say it was because his discovery wasn't really useful in medicine until Lauterbur and Mansfield improved upon it. Either way, 2003 left the poor scientist Nobel-less.

_07:: Mahatma Gandhi, Peace

The Susan Lucci of Nobel Peace Prize contenders, Mohandas "Mahatma" (Great-Souled) Gandhi was nominated like crazy: 1937, 1938, 1939, 1947, and 1948. He certainly deserved it, as his nonviolent methods helped kick the British out of India and became the model for future Peace Prize laureates like Martin Luther King Jr. Gandhi's final nomination came in 1948, and he was the odds-on favorite to win it that year. However, the "Mahatma" was assassinated just a few days before the deadline. Since the Nobel Prize is never awarded posthumously, the prize for peace went unawarded that year on the grounds that there was "no suitable living candidate." The decision was also motivated by the fact that Gandhi left no heirs or foundations to which his prize money could go.

_08:: Oh, and Anybody in Mathematics

When dynamite inventor (that's not a comment on his abilities; he really did invent dynamite) Alfred Nobel stipulated in his will that his fortune be used to establish a fund to award five annual prizes "to those who, during the preceding year, shall have conferred the greatest benefit on mankind," he mysteri-

ously left out mathematics. All kinds of theories have popped up to explain the omission, the most salacious of which claim that Nobel hated all mathematicians because his wife was schtupping one on the side. Nope. The most likely reasons for Nobel's ditching math are (1) He simply didn't like math all that much, and (2) Sweden already had a big, fancy prize for mathematics, bestowed by the journal *Acta Mathematica*. Although math is still a Nobel bridesmaid, a prize for economics was added in 1968, thereby giving the extremely boring sciences their due.

Touch of Evil

Before making a bang with dynamite and creating his famous prizes, Alfred Nobel lost his company to bankruptcy and his brother to a nitroglycerine explosion.

The Grass Is Definitely Greener: Tiny Nations That Were Happy to Colonize Africa

3

Historians call the gobbling up of territory at the end of the 19th century "the Scramble for Africa." And while the big European powerhouses—Germany, England, France—got much of the good stuff, there were plenty of scraps left for the little guys, too. Here are a few tiny nations that made out like bandits.

_01:: Portugal

While most people think of Portugal lurking in its big brother Spain's shadows, the tiny nation was quite the world power in the 15th and 16th centuries, and had early established outposts in West Africa. By the 1880s, however, Portugal's star had fallen, and it moved to being a second-tier global player. Still, it was pretty crafty in its imperial ways. While the big countries were occupied with bickering with one other, Portugal decided it was still occupied with, well, occupying. It took over most of both Angola and Mozambique, and by 1900 the nation controlled about 8% of the continent. Because it was a poor country, though, it could do little for its colonies except exploit them, which it did with gusto. In 1961, revolutions that had been brewing for years finally burst out. Five years of war were followed by seven years of unrest, and in 1974, Mozambique won its independence. In 1975, the Portuguese wisely left Angola and turned out the lights on their imperial ways.

_02:: Italy

Amazingly enough, Italy has the distinction of being the only European country to have had its butt kicked by an African nation, when it tried to conquer Ethiopia. How so? Italy had formed a colony in neighboring Eritrea. And while they were negotiating a friendship treaty with Ethiopia, the Italians cleverly decided that simultaneously invading the African nation would be a good way to seal their pact. Not so. In the Battle of Adova in 1896, Ethiopians under Emperor Menelik II soundly defeated the Italians. The loss didn't sit well, obviously, and in 1936, Italy attacked Ethiopia again. This time it was literally airplanes and tanks against spears, and the Italians held on for five years. With the outbreak of World War II, though, British troops and Ethiopian freedom fighters drove the Italians out, and expelled Italy from Eritrea and Italian Somaliland, too. So much for the Roman Empire's comeback.

_03:: Belgium

If there was a single infernal spark to the Scramble for Africa, it was King Leopold II of Belgium. After all, it was Leo who convened meetings of European nations to compromise on divvying up the continent. In fact, the Belgian king was so anxious to build an empire, he used his own money to buy a huge section of the Congo River Basin, 80 times the size of Belgium itself! As exploitation was the name of the colony-building game, Leopold followed the recipe to a T. The monarch literally bled his African kingdom, mutilating and torturing its residents when they failed to meet crop quotas or pay taxes. By 1908, however, the international outcry was so loud over Leopold's excesses that he was forced to transfer control of the Congo to the Belgian government. From then on, the Belgian government ruled the area, mostly badly, until 1960, when it was finally given its independence.

Touch of Evil

In 1821, the politically powerful American Colonization Society literally bought what would become a country. The land purchase in western Africa provided a home for freed slaves from America, and the citizens formed the independent republic of Liberia in 1847.

Musicians Who Always Felt Cheated

Sometimes it isn't just the guitar that's gently weeping. The following six musicians definitely felt they got the short end of the stick as far as their bands were concerned.

_01:: Syd "Wish You Were Here" Barrett (1946–)

During the early 1960s, a London art student named Syd Barrett teamed up with four kids from the Regent Street School of Architecture to form an R & B group. Barrett named the band the Pink Floyd Sound after a blues record by Pink Anderson and Floyd Council, and the group was off and running. Trading their sound in for a psychedelic one, the band became a huge hit around London. By 1968, however, Barrett's excessive drug use and mood swings made his onstage and offstage behavior a little too erratic and strange. The band brought in David Gilmour to cover the performances and Barrett was sacked within the year. Of course, Gilmour brought a heft of talent with him, and in 1973, Pink Floyd became an international success with the release of "Dark Side of the Moon." Some years later, they achieved superstardom with *The Wall* album and movie. At the same time, Barrett was working on solo projects but continued in a downward spiral of bad health. While not much of a consolation, Pink Floyd did dedicate their 1975 hit "Shine On, You Crazy Diamond" to Barrett, a cut off their album *Wish You Were Here.*

THOMAS CARLYLE'S HORRIBLE-TERRIBLE, NO-GOOD, VERY BAD DAY

Political scientist and historian John Stuart Mill showed up at his close friend Thomas Carlyle's house on March 6, 1835, with the only manuscript of Carlyle's *French Revolution*. It was a single burned scrap of paper. Why just one? Because Carlyle's manuscript had inadvertently been thrown into the fire—probably by Mill's maid. Mill apologized profusely, and Carlyle responded with remarkable kindness and empathy. After mourning the lost masterpiece, Carlyle restarted the project and eventually finished rewriting *French Revolution* in 1837. Published in three volumes, its first reviewer was Mill, who may or may not have noticed the abundance of "fire" imagery in the rewritten manuscript. Either way, Mill tried to make up for his maid's carelessness by hailing the book as a great work of genius. (Indeed, Dickens used Carlyle's book extensively when writing *A Tale of Two Cities*.) But their friendship never recovered from the burned manuscript—Mill went on to become a leading progressive member of Parliament, whose *On Liberty* is now required reading in political science courses, while Carlyle became something of an angry bigot.

_02:: Pete "I Want to Hold Your Hand" Best (1941–   )

Having been the original drummer for an up-start Liverpool group called the Silver Beetles, Pete Best was sacked in favor of another, more experienced drummer named Richard Starkey, better known as Ringo Starr. As fate would have it, the Silver Beetles changed their name to the Beatles and became the best-known group in the history of rock and roll. Best's mom, who ran the Casbah Club in Liverpool, was their initial booking agent, landing them a two-month gig in Hamburg. But while in Germany the young group happened upon Ringo, and when they returned to London both Paul McCartney and George Harrison asked their new manager, Brian Epstein, to get rid of Best. On August 23, 1962, poor Pete found out that he was no longer a Beatle, and although he later sued Ringo for libel, he received nothing for his early years with the band. Today he tours with his own group (he even put out an album under the tricky title *Best of the Beatles*) and freely discusses his sacking, although he doesn't accept the theories—Ringo's superior drumming, McCartney's jealousy, or his own unreliability. In the end, it was only John Lennon who ever sent Best a message about the way the Fab Three had treated him.

_03:: Keith "Can't Get No Satisfaction" Richards (1943–   )

Although Keith Richards first met Mick Jagger in elementary school in 1950, it wasn't until 10 years later when they ran into each other that they found they shared a deep interest in American blues and R & B. Within the next two years they formed the Rolling Stones and began to proclaim themselves "the World's Greatest Rock-and-Roll Band." Of course, they backed up the claim with a long string of hits and concert performances. However, by the mid-1980s, Richards had grown resentful of Jagger's fame and the fact that Mick was receiving the majority of the credit for the Stones' success. Richards had always said that while the Stones existed he would never do a solo album and became angry that Jagger was performing outside the group. By 1986, the two were no longer speaking to each other and the group went into hiatus for the next three years. Richards and Jagger publicly went after each other in the press and with songs on their respective solo albums. In 1989, the two decided to end the feud and got together in Barbados to write a new album, which led to the Stones' first U.S. tour in over eight years, grossing over $144 million. Of course, the jealousy's probably still lurking. After all, Mick was recently knighted for his service to the British Empire, while Richards remains a rock star commoner. He just can't get no satisfaction.

_04:: Johnny "I'm a Lazy Sod" Rotten (1956–)

In 1975, the 19-year-old John Lydon met a young entrepreneur, Malcolm McLaren, at McLaren's fashion boutique in London called Sex. McLaren, who was putting a rock group together, was on the hunt for a lead singer. Happy to oblige, Lydon accepted the position even though he'd never sung before...and somehow Britain's most notorious punk group, the Sex Pistols, came into existence. With his outrageously rude manner and his total lack of

personal hygiene, Lydon was soon dubbed Johnny Rotten. Because of their lyrics, the group was soon banned on British radio, but they still garnered a huge following. Of course, they garnered huge egos as well. Rotten soon became disenchanted with McLaren's management style and inability to move the group to a higher level of stardom. At the same time, he didn't feel that he was receiving his just due as a top performer, and after a concert in San Francisco in 1978, Rotten officially broke up the group, claiming that all of rock and roll and been played and now it was officially dead. The legal system, however, was not. Johnny Rotten eventually reverted to his given name and, teaming up with the other Sex Pistols, successfully sued McLaren for $1.44 million in back royalties.

Touch of Evil

As founder and original lead singer of The Supremes, Florence Ballard was more than a little peeved when Berry Gordy moved Diana Ross into the front spot. So, what good did her tantrums do? Ballard was ultimately fired and faded into obscurity, while lady Di became a Motown legend.

_05:: George "You Never Give Me Your Money" Harrison (1943–2001)

Known as "the quiet Beatle," George Harrison, who was the youngest of the lot, was also arguably the best musician among the Fab Four. Having attended school in Liverpool at one time or another with both Paul McCartney and John Lennon, Harrison started jamming with the two, forming a group called the Quarrymen, later to become the Silver Beetles, and eventually just the plain old Beatles. Harrison, who played lead guitar and occasionally sang lead ("Roll Over Beethoven"), was the first Beatle to get involved in Eastern religion. However, over the years, he found it more and more difficult for the group to take his compositions seriously and feature them on the albums. Interestingly, some of Harrison's works such as "I Need You," "While My Guitar Gently Weeps," "Here Comes the Sun," and especially "Something," are considered among the Beatles' greatest hits. By 1970, Harrison's resentment of his second-class status within the group had grown to the point that it became one of the factors that caused the Beatles to disband.

_06:: Big Mama Thornton (1926–1984)

In 1953, while playing at New York's Apollo Theater as part of the "Hot Harlem Revue,"

Thornton was asked by composers Jerry Lieber and Mike Stoller to record a song they had written for her. Thornton recorded "Hound Dog" and the single quickly sold nearly two million copies. As we all know, though, a young rockabilly recording artist with Sun Records named Elvis Presley also recorded said song and the rest is history. For her recording of "Hound Dog" and the two million copies sold, Thornton received one check for a whopping total of $500. Of course, that wasn't her only hit. Big Mama's song "Ball and Chain" became a huge hit for her in the 1950s. However, most of us remember that tune as the version recorded in the 1960s by another booming voice—Janis Joplin's. Like so many African American artists before her, Big Mama Thornton never received the financial and historical rewards she was due.

Oedipus Redux:
Men Who Tried to Outdo Their Dads

It's always tough to follow in your father's footsteps, particularly if Pops had big feet. Here are four guys who observed the massive footprints, and still decided to give it a shot.

_01:: Alexander the Great (356–323 BCE)

If Alexander was great, his old man was at least really pretty good. After all, Philip II did seize the throne of Macedon from his nephew,

reorganize the army, and conquer Greece at the age of 46. "My father will get ahead of me in everything, and will leave nothing great for me to do," Alexander reportedly whined. But Philip was killed during a wedding party brawl before he could put his plan to conquer the Persian Empire into operation. At age 20, Alexander took the throne, and he and his dad's well-trained armies not only conquered Persia, but also India and just about all of the known world. Not bad. And nice of Dad to leave the young Alexander something to do.

_02:: John Quincy Adams (1767–1848)

Unlike Alexander the Great, John Q. had a good relationship with his pa. Not only that, but they seemed to follow similar paths. John Adams had had a long diplomatic career and served as the country's first vice president and second president. Clearly, the apple didn't fall too far from the tree. Like his dad, John Q. was a veteran diplomat. And both fared similarly in their runs for the presidency, as in barely squeaking past their opponents on their way to the big house. But while Dad retired after being defeated for a second term, John Q. was elected to Congress. He served for 18 years, until he was fatally stricken while sitting at his House desk. Unfortunately for the Adams family, two Adamses were apparently plenty when it came to White House material. One of Q.'s three sons, Charles Francis, became a distinguished diplomat. As for the other two, one died of alcoholism and another became a heavy drinker who jumped or fell from a ship in New York Harbor.

_03:: Johann Strauss Jr. (1825–1899)

Junior was the oldest of five sons, and Johann Senior had no interest in his eldest being a musician. After all, he himself was a composer, orchestra leader, and leading Viennese waltz maestro, and he knew the musician's life to be a tough one. Be a banker, Pops said. But Junior wasn't having it. At the age of six Strauss the mouse tried to squeak out his first waltz, but by 19 he was conducting his own dance band in a Viennese restaurant. In 1845, Strauss the smaller became conductor of the city's second militia band, and a bit of father-son rivalry ensued. Pops was, after all, conductor of the first militia band, so for five years the two had a battle of the bands. All ended well enough, though. After Strauss Senior died, Junior was left sans competition at the top of the waltzing world.

_04:: Barry Bonds (1964–)

Whatever else he was capable of accomplishing, Barry Bonds is baseball pedigree, and the kid was born to play America's game. Consider the facts: Not only did his dad, Bobby, play for 14 years in the major leagues, but his godfather was none other than the legendary Willie Mays. As a kid, Barry didn't much care for his father, who played for seven different teams and was often away from home. But whatever youthful ambivalence he had toward Dad was gone by the time Barry made the majors himself in 1986. And there's no question that both nature and nurture must have played a role in Bonds's development. In the 100-years-plus history of baseball, only four men have hit at least 300 home runs and stolen 300 bases in their careers. Three of them are Willie Mays, Bobby Bonds—and Barry Bonds.

Johnson Jealousy: Women Who Disguised Themselves as Men to Succeed

As sharp, determined women, these five gals didn't let the "It's a man's world" mantra dull their ambitions. Instead, they pulled their pants on one leg at a time, just like the guys, then set out to tackle their dreams.

_01:: Anne Bonney (1700–?)

The daughter of a big-shot South Carolina plantation owner, Anne fell in love with a sailor and went off to sea. But then her love life took an unusual turn—she fell in love with a pirate, Captain John "Calico Jack" Rackham. One of the most feared buccaneers of the day, Bonney dressed as a man, and shared Rackham's pirating adventures. But that's just the start of it. Rackham's Bonney, who seemed to be lying all over the ocean, found herself attracted to one of his lieutenants . . . only the officer turned out to be a disguised woman named Mary Read. In 1722, Rackham's ship was captured, and Bonney and Read were sentenced to hang. But—surprise—they were both found to be pregnant, and British law forbade executing pregnant women. Bonney escaped the gallows only to disappear into the mists of history.

_02:: Deborah Sampson (1760–1827)

Standing tall at 5 feet 8 inches and strong from years as an indentured servant, Deborah Sampson didn't have much trouble enlisting in the Continental Army in 1781. That is, until she got drunk and spilled her secret. Undaunted, she reenlisted under her dead brother's name and served with distinction for three years. Amazingly, even bullet wounds didn't prove to be Sampson's undoing. Once wounded in the thigh, she decided to remove the musket ball herself rather than jeopardize her secret. When she caught a fever, however, a doctor finally discovered the truth, and she was honorably discharged. In 1792, the state of Massachusetts paid her back wages for her service, and in 1804, with the help of an old friend, Paul Revere, she was awarded a veteran's pension by Congress.

_03:: Sarah R. Wakeman (1843–1864)

At least 400 women fought in the Civil War as men, but Wakeman got a head start on most of them. A farmer's daughter, she disguised herself as a man to get a job on a coal barge. Then, for a $152 bounty—or about a year's wages—she joined the Union Army in August 1862. Most of her stretch was spent in non-combat situations, but Sarah did fight in at least one battle. In 1864, our young patriot was stricken with dysentery and died in a New Orleans military hospital. But her secret wasn't revealed till years later. Her gravestone reads "Private Lyons Wakeman," and her identity surfaced only when her letters home were brought to light a century later. "I am as independent as a hog on ice," she wrote in one letter. Or as a woman in this man's army.

_04:: James Miranda Stuart Barry (1795?–1865)

Barry wanted to be a doctor in the worst way, which for a woman in the early 19th century meant pretending to be a man. Thus disguised, she enrolled at Edinburgh University, graduating at the tender age of 15. In 1813, Barry joined the British army, and by the time she retired in 1859, she had served all over the world and risen to the rank of senior inspector general. In fact, Barry is credited with performing the first successful caesarean section in the British Empire while in South Africa. Known as a skilled surgeon, and as a grump, she's recorded to have fought at least one duel and also publicly scolded Florence Nightingale. And while there was speculation about Barry's sexual preferences during her life, her gender itself stayed private until after her death.

_05:: Billy Tipton (1914–1989)

Dorothy Tipton wanted to swing, so at the age of 19, the Oklahoma City–born kitten reinvented herself as a jazz cat: the saxophone- and piano-playing Billy Tipton. A popular nightclub entertainer in the Pacific Northwest, Tipton played in big bands and fronted her own trio. More amazing, she had five common-law wives and three adopted sons. According to biographer Diane Wood Middlebrook, Tipton concealed her gender by using a prosthetic male organ, binding her breasts and having sex only in the dark. Even more amazingly, she explained it all away with vague references to "past accidents." Of course, the truth came out after Tipton's death when someone leaked the story to a Spokane newspaper and the dirt started a bitter fight among her survivors, thus ending a splendid deception on a somewhat sour note.

Touch of Evil

In 1950, 12-year-old Kathryn Johnston tucked her hair under a cap and tried out for the King's Dairy Little League team of Corning, New York, under the androgynous handle Tubby Johnston. She made the cut and clued her coach in to her secret two weeks into the season.

To the Victor Go the Oils: Early Middle East Conflicts

3

Sometimes the oil looks greener on the other side. Long before huge reservoirs of oil were discovered in Persia in 1908, the Middle East was prize territory. Massive, waterless deserts, you say? One hundred twenty degrees in the shade in May? Well, sure. But like any good real estate professional will tell you: location, location, location. For millennia, the Middle East was a gateway from Europe to Africa, India, and East Asia. Combine that with the Middle East's cultural and religious diversity, and you've got a place worth fighting for.

_01:: The Battle for Mecca

Unlike Jesus or the Buddha, Muhammad founded a religion *and* a political entity. As the leader of the early Islamic community in Mecca, Muhammad found himself at odds with his clan's pagan leaders. Facing annihilation, Muhammad and his followers fled Mecca for Medina in 622 CE. Over the next eight years, the Muslims periodically engaged in bloody battles over Mecca (in one, the Prophet's uncle was partially eaten by the wife of a Meccan tribal leader). However grand a general he was, Muhammad was an even better negotiator: In 630, the Muslims finally overtook Mecca via a treaty with tribal leaders. After almost a decade of casualties, nary a drop of blood was shed in the final battle for Islam's holiest city.

_02:: The Battle of Karbala (Which Has *Nothing* to Do with Madonna)

Although the fighting lasted only a couple hours and the result was never really in question, the Battle of Karbala has come to symbol-ize the divide between Shia and Sunni Muslims—and, for many Muslims, represents the last stand of Islam's golden age. After the Prophet Muhammad's death, the Islamic community was led by a succession of four "Rightly Guided" caliphs. By 680 CE, however, a ruthless and distinctly Wrongly Guided caliph named Yazid held court, and the Prophet's grandson Husayn set out to defeat him. Husayn and just 72 followers (many of them young boys) met Yazid's massive army at Karbala, in present-day Iraq. And though Husayn and his supporters were slaughtered, the martyrdom is still remembered by Shia Muslims today with passion plays and public mourning.

_03:: The Crusades

Not content to let Muslims fight among themselves, Christian Europe decided to get into the act in 1095 CE. For the following two centuries, European Christians undertook eight major expeditions hoping to conquer Jerusalem and control Christ's tomb, the Holy Sepulcher (which seems like a lot of trouble—waging eight wars over a cave where Jesus spent three measly days). Armed with plenty of manpower, the Crusaders took Jerusalem in 1099, but Saladin then reconquered it in 1187. Long story made short, the back-and-forth kept on until everyone got tired and decided to postpone fighting over Jerusalem until the mid-20th century. Of course, the Crusades had a lasting effect on the therefore fairly peaceful relationship between the Islamic world and the Christian one, but they also deepened the divide between the Catholic and Eastern Or-

thodox churches, particularly when the Catholics decided to sack Constantinople during the fourth Crusade.

Touch of Evil

Italian porn star Ilona Staller tried to save everyone a peck of trouble back in 1990 when she told Newsweek *magazine that she'd sleep with Saddam Hussein "to achieve peace in the Middle East."*

When Opposites Attack: Feuds Steeped in Jealousy

Jealousy has been likened to a green-eyed monster, much like Godzilla, a rampaging creature that leaves destruction in its wake. Unlike Godzilla, however, jealousy and the feuds it sparks are by no means limited to leveling Tokyo.

_01:: Feud like an Egyptian: The Petiese Saga

It was a time of renaissance in ancient Egypt, but for the town of Teudjoy the seventh and sixth centuries BCE were a little less enlightening. The tiny town became the venue for a multigenerational feud, leading to the demise of a noble family. Here's how the tragic happenings kicked off. In 660, the pharaoh Psammetichos I appointed a nobleman named Petiese to take charge of Teudjoy's Temple of Amun. If the local priests were nervous about this appointment, it was for good reason: Petiese punished corruption and incompetence

with beatings and ended up taking personal charge of the temple's affairs. Even worse for the priests, within a few years the place was thriving. With less than holy spirit, the jealous priests took their revenge, murdering Petiese's grandsons in the temple itself. Of course, Petiese tried to get the pharaoh's support, but by then the king was too old and sick to do anything about it. Unfortunately, the vicious pattern of attack, reprisal, and appeal to authority continued for at least four generations, at the end of which the family of Petiese was reduced to utter poverty, still begging officials to take note and restore them to glory.

_02:: They're All Greeks to Me: The Peloponnesian War

In the early years of the fifth century BCE, the cities of Greece, led by Athens and Sparta in a Hellenic League, successfully fought off two separate Persian invasions. But the alliance developed cracks—instead of focusing on what they had in common (like wine, olive oil, and pedophilia), the Athenians and Spartans let their mutual jealousy and political and economic differences split the Hellenic League into two competing blocs, the Spartan-led "Peloponnesians" and the Athenian-dominated "Delians." Although it was difficult for the two sides to actually fight a battle (Athenian military might was mostly naval, while Sparta had few ships but large land armies), they finally worked out all the angles and settled in for nearly three decades of fighting in 431 BCE. Sparta won (sort of), but both sides were so exhausted from the fighting that in the end, both were left as prey for rival states, first Thebes and later the rising star of Macedon.

_03:: Viking Love Triangle: The Tragedy of Laxdaela

The Laxdaelas struggled to succeed in harsh 10th-century Iceland, and their tale (cleverly titled *The Laxdaela Saga*) reads like a veritable catalog full of soap opera–ish jealousy. It starts out with the family fleeing Norway because one of its ancestors, Ketill Flatnose, incurred the envy of King Harald for his able administration and great wealth. A good enough reason to leave, we suppose. But the drama just keeps coming: the tension between jealous half brothers Hoskuld and Hrut almost leads to combat; a chieftain named Olaf "the Peacock" incurs the jealousy of kinsmen and neighbors for, among other things, the ostentatious clothes that gave him his monicker; and a woman named Gudrun goads her husband, Bolli, into a feud against his cousin and foster brother, Kjartan (who had promised to marry Gudrun but later reneged). And if there weren't enough punches thrown in there for your taste, the emotional climax of the tale comes in 1003, when Bolli and some friends ambush Kjartan only to kill his foster brother in a duel. And while Bolli immediately regrets his actions, catching Kjartan as he falls, Gudrun probably does, too; just before her death in the mid-1000s Gudrun reportedly tells her son, "To him I was worst whom I loved best." Hey, sometimes love really hurts.

_04:: Sibling Rivalry among the Children of the Sun

When Inca Huayna Capac, the god-king of the Andes, died in 1525, he left his oldest son, Huascar, as the new king. But Huascar was dismayed to learn that his father had left the rich lands in and around the city of Quito to his younger son, Atahualpa. Apparently, the irritation was directed both ways. Atahualpa envied his older brother's rank and title, especially since Huascar was ugly, ill-tempered, and probably crazy. Fortunately, the two brothers decided to settle their differences like gentlemen. Unfortunately, they were Inca gentlemen, who also happened to have fully equipped armies at their disposal. The two brothers engaged in a brutal civil war in which tens of thousands died. In the end (1532) Atahualpa won, but the empire was so weakened that it was unable to offer serious resistance to the Spaniards, who conveniently showed up a few months later.

_05:: Blood Brothers: Jamuka and the Great Khan

Jamuka was chieftain of the Jadirat, a minor Mongol tribe, but through a combination of military skill and cunning diplomacy, he managed to acquire a large following in the closing years of the 1100s. Among his allies was a young chieftain named Temudjin; the two were so close that they became each other's *anda,* or blood brother. But things turned sour (much like fermented horse milk, the Mongol national drink) as Jamuka watched his little bro gain influence, followers, and herds of precious sheep and horses. The jealousy came to a head when Jamuka took the title of Gurkhan ("Warlord") in 1201 and declared war on his erstwhile buddy, which turned out to be a pretty unwise move. In 1205, after repeated defeats, Jamuka's own men murdered him and declared allegiance to Temudjin, who took the title "Genghis Khan" after rewarding the assassins by executing them.

_06:: Redneck Rampage: The Saga of Douglas County

Apparently, in the mid-1800s in Douglas County, Missouri, jealousy could be a deadly thing. It all started pretty innocently: two rival families, the Alsups and the Sheltons, gathered to engage in a little friendly horse racing. But during the race a Shelton hit an Alsup's horse with his whip. The Alsup then hit the Shelton back, with more fun ensuing. The games ended a few moments later when the Shelton killed the Alsup by shooting him in the heart. The Shelton was immediately blown away by an older Alsup, who in turn was made to resemble Swiss cheese by a hail of Shelton gunfire. The feud went back and forth until the Sheltons were forced to leave the county. Left without any family competition, the Alsups terrorized the region until the angry citizens banded together and killed enough of them to cow the rest into submission.

Born Losers:

Infamous Second-place Finishers Who Never Got the Spotlight

No one remembers who followed the Beatles on *The Ed Sullivan Show*. No one remembers the second dog to go into space, who Secretariat's closest competitor was, or who was the first man to break Roger Bannister's 4-minute mile. Nope, those names have been relegated to the same part of your brain reserved for high school chemistry and diagramming sentences. But we think it's about time you polished off your gray cells and gave some of these second-placers a second look.

_01:: Tenzing "I Could Have Climbed This Without You" Norgay

Tenzing Norgay was a Sherpa, one of the hardy mountain folk of Nepal. Like many Sherpa, he discovered that he could make a nice living guiding Europeans up the mountains of his homeland. In 1952, he led Sir John Hunt's expedition to the summit of Mount Everest, the highest point on earth. But few remember Norgay's name, because a New Zealander, Edmund Hillary, insisted on being the first person to stand on the summit. It took Hillary and company seven weeks to climb to the summit and three days to descend, though one suspects Norgay could have done better *without* the Europeans. In 2004, Pemba Dorji, another Sherpa, reached the peak in just 8 hours, 10 minutes.

_02:: Thorfinn "I Could Have Discovered This Without You" Karlsefni

Most Americans now know that Leif Eriksson was the first European to make a documented landfall in the New World. No one remembers the guy who got there second. In 1010, 10 years after Lucky Leif's expedition, an Icelander named Thorfinn Karlsefni led an expedition of two ships to North America, exploring regions he called Helluland, Markland, Furdustraands, and Straumford (probably the coast of Labrador and Quebec). Thorfinn's men even built a settlement called Hop, but they were forced to abandon it and head back to Greenland after coming under attack by the natives.

_03:: Gottfried "I Figured This Out Without You (and Didn't Even Get a Lousy T-shirt)" von Leibniz

Leibniz was a brilliant mathematician of the late 1600s as well as a philosopher, scientist, lawyer, librarian, and diplomat. Of course, today he is remembered (outside the wacky world of mathematicians) for none of these things. The reason? Independent of Leibniz, Sir Isaac Newton simultaneously developed many of the principles underlying the science

It's a Mad, Mad, Mad, Mad Scientist

MAYBE THAT APPLE *DID* FALL ON NEWTON'S HEAD

There's a fine line between genius and madness, and Isaac Newton skipped back and forth over it like a giddy schoolgirl. Often forgetting to eat, Newton would wake up in the morning and then sit on the edge of the bed for hours. Of course, all that time spent on his mattress didn't really help his attitude: Newton was notorious for being a champion grouch, even with his friends. And despite being one of the greatest scientists the world has ever known, Newton spent countless hours either practicing alchemy (trying to prove lead could be turned into gold) or trying to disprove the Christian religious tenet of the Trinity. That ain't all, though. While studying lights and colors, Newton once stuck a big needle in his eye socket to determine what was back in there, and stared at the sun so long that he had to spend days in a darkened room to recover his vision. It's been suggested he was mildly autistic. Or maybe just nuts.

of calculus. Newton turned out to be the better promoter. When schoolchildren today mutter about having to learn calculus, it's Sir Isaac's name they curse, and Sir Isaac alone they envision roasting in hell. As far as recog-

nition goes, Leibniz definitely got the short end of the stick.

_04:: Claudius

Most people with an interest in classics know that Julius Caesar was the first Roman general to lead an invasion of Britain. Few, however, remember that Caesar's expedition ended without a permanent occupation—he was forced to return to finish up a collection of outrageously one-sided battles in Gaul (which became known as the Gallic War). And it was four generations before a Roman commander again led troops to fair Britannia. In 43 CE the emperor Claudius, thought by many to be an imbecile, led a brilliant lightning conquest of the Britons, coordinating a number of legions and even bringing the first elephants ever seen so far north. In fact, "Claudius the Fool" was given the surname Britannicus in honor of his victories. Not bad for a moron.

_05:: Robert Falcon Scott

Captain Scott engaged in a famous and not-so-friendly contest with Norwegian Roald Amundsen to be the first human to reach the South Pole. Amundsen spent months preparing for his journey, learning cold-weather survival techniques from indigenous people of the Arctic. Scott, on the other hand, believed he needed no such instruction; ignoring sources on Inuit customs, refusing to use dogsleds, and otherwise, as the British say, "making a hash of things." On January 18, 1912, Scott and his party arrived after much hardship at the South Pole, only to discover that Amundsen's party had beaten them by over a month (Amundsen even left Scott a note advising him to help himself to whatever was left at the Norwegian camp). Amundsen returned home a hero; while Scott, well, didn't. Sadly, he and his entire party died on their return trek in weather that was harsh even by Antarctic standards.

It Ain't Easy Being Green: Famously Jealous Politicians

Sure, jealousy isn't exactly the best of traits, but occasionally it'll help a guy get a lot done. The following go-getters found plenty of things (and occasionally people) to cross off their to-do lists when plagued with a bit of the green.

_01:: Nero's Fiddling with Power

Poor old fiddling Nero was an unlikely candidate for emperor of Rome. But after his mother, Agrippinilla, conned her way into the bed of her uncle, Emperor Claudius, Nero was adopted by Claudius as coheir with Claudius's son, Britannicus. When Claudius died in 54, Nero became the emperor in name only. Of course, the real power was concentrated in the hands of his mother and her cronies, and Nero didn't like it. Jealous of his mom's power and her playing favorites with Britannicus, Nero most likely had the boy murdered in 55 and in 59 arranged for a series of mishaps for Agrippinilla (she had a strong survival instinct, so he eventually ordered her to be stabbed to death). Not exactly the best son, he wasn't exactly the best ruler, either. He went on to a reign of terror, killing anyone he perceived as a threat, including most of his surviving relatives. Of course, it all caught up with him in the end. Nero was eventually overthrown, declared a public enemy, and forced to kill himself while on the run.

_02:: Themistocles's Sleep Disorder

Themistocles was a brilliant orator and politician, but his jealousy knew no bounds. Furious after a rival named Miltiades won a victory over the Persians at Marathon (490 BCE), he famously declared "Miltiades' trophy does not let me sleep." And it didn't. Not only did Themistocles force his countrymen to build the largest navy in Greece, but as an expert on both battlefield tactics and psychological warfare, he was also largely responsible for the Greek victory over the Persian navy at Salamis (479 BCE). That was hardly the end of Themistocles' jealousy, however. The ugly green monster reared its head again not long after, and he became involved in a struggle against his rival, Aristides. Unfortunately for Themistocles, allegations of political corruption led to his exile in the late 470s BCE, and the architect of Greek victory over the Persians died in Asia Minor... living off a Persian government stipend. Strange bedfellows indeed!

_03:: The Bonaparte Black Sheep

It's not easy being the little brother, especially when your big sib is a self-made emperor. So it's no wonder relations between Lucien Bonaparte and brother Napoléon were often abrasive and strained. At first a supporter of Napoléon, Lucien became disillusioned by what he saw as the betrayal of the French Revolution. Unfortunately, he was sort of the Fredo Corleone of the family, being stupid enough to let a subversive pamphlet he had written fall into the hands of Napoléon's police. Obviously, it strained their relationship even further and made him one of the few Bonapartes who didn't end up king of something. In 1804, Lucien went into exile in Rome, and the pope named him prince of Canino, largely to annoy Napoléon. Not the brightest move. Napoléon imprisoned the pope in 1809. Lucien on the other hand was America-bound; captured by the British, he remained a prisoner for several years before returning to a comfortable, Napoléon-free retirement on the Continent.

_04:: Jealous Joe

Iosif Dzhugashvili, better known to the world as Joseph Stalin, was a man of complicated psyche, but jealousy was one of his most obvious traits. During the years leading up to and following the Russian Revolution, his idol,

Touch of Evil

Some believe that "sore loser" Richard Nixon might have been in on the plot to assassinate John F. Kennedy. The flimsy theory is based on the fact that Tricky Dick was actually in Dallas at a Pepsi-Cola board meeting mere hours before the tragic event occurred.

Lenin, scorned him in favor of intellectuals such as Leon Trotsky, Lev Kamenev, Grigory Zinoviev, and Nikolay Bukharin. But when Lenin died in 1924, Stalin was quite happy to take his revenge, spending several years playing his rivals off against each other before eliminating them all in the Great Purge of the 1930s. In deciding whom to eliminate, Stalin paid particularly close attention to those whose popularity rivaled his. Of course, his private life wasn't free of jealousy, either; his fights with his second wife, Nadezhda Alliluyeva, whom he sometimes suspected of infidelity, were legendary. After one such incident in 1932, Nadezhda died of a gunshot wound; the official line is that this was a suicide, though there's no dearth of historians who suspect Stalin of pulling the trigger himself. After all, he wasn't exactly of the "never harm a fly" mold.

GLUTTONY

I Eat Therefore I Am: Unusual Food Competitions

The Nathan's Hot Dog–Eating Contest is only the most famous of all eating contests. And the ones on *Fear Factor* are only the most contrived. But if you're looking for a lesser-known chow challenge to show off your plate-cleaning prowess, these gastronomic free-for-alls might be just the place to start.

_01:: Matzo Balls

It ain't easy keeping kosher. Especially for contestants in the Ben's New York Kosher Deli Charity Matzo Ball–Eating Tournament. The contest is a charity fund-raiser for the Interfaith Nutrition Network sponsored by a New York–area deli chain. The record holder for 2004 is Eric "Badlands" Booker of Copaigue, Long Island, who ate 20 matzo balls in five minutes and 25 seconds. If that doesn't sound like a lot, you should know that these matzo balls were roughly the size of *tennis* balls. *Oy!* The winner gets a trophy and a $2,500 gift certificate to a stereo store, while runners-up get various prize packages, all of which involve tickets to a New York Islanders game. Umm...all that matzo for an Islanders ticket? We're thinking we'll pass.

_02:: Live Mice

The MTV show *Jackass* spawned a lot of copycat dumbasses. But two hungry fellas in Brisbane, Australia, win the prize. Participating in a contest at Brisbane's Exchange Hotel in which they were dared to eat a live mouse, the two men competed for a grand prize that was a vacation package worth a handsome $346.

Both men chewed the tails off, and the "winner" actually chewed his mouse whole and spit it out. Needless to say, the RSPCA, Australia's version of our own SPCA, wasn't thrilled about the stunt and got the Queensland police on the participants'—um—tail. If caught, the winner will face fines of $75,000 and two years in the pokey. And just think how many big, fat, edible rodents must be in there!

_03:: Pickled Quail Eggs

Texas may have plenty of barbecue contests and chili cook-offs, but nothing holds a candle to the Pickled-Quail-Egg-Eating Contest held annually in Grand Prairie, a town between Dallas and Fort Worth. Begun as a publicity stunt by a flea market called Traders Village, the contest determines who can down the most pickled quail eggs in 60 seconds. Quail eggs are roughly the size of a large olive, and the rules stipulate that they must be eaten one at a time. In 2003, the contest was won for the seventh straight time by Grand Prairie resident Lester Tucker, who downed 42 in a minute. So, what's the secret to old Lester's success? He swallows them whole.

_04:: Cessna 150

Yes, that's an *airplane*. And the guy who ate it is a French gent named Michel Lotito, who goes by Monsieur Mangetout (French for "Mr. Eats Everything." See what he did there?). Lotito engaged in the stunt to earn a place in *Guinness World Records* (his actual record is for Most Unusual Diet: two pounds of metal per day), but his iron stomach's downed a lot more than just a plane. He's also the proud eater of 18 bicycles, a bunch of TVs, a wooden coffin, and several supermarket shopping carts. Not to mention all the light-bulbs, razor blades, and other knickknacks he's downed on variety shows. Looking for a reason why you shouldn't try this at home (or *with* your home)? Well, Lotito's got a natural advantage because his stomach lining is twice as thick as a normal person's. He's also aided by the fact that he's French, and the French will eat just about anything (*Escargot,* anyone?).

_05:: Black Pudding

It's hard enough to eat a little bit of some English food, much less a lot of it. And black pudding is not a dish you want to overindulge in. But don't let the name of this delicacy fool you. This treat from northern England and Scotland isn't pudding in the yummy, creamy, Bill Cosby sense of the word. It's more like a sausage, and it contains oatmeal, onions, spices, plenty of suet, and a whole lot of pig's blood. Hence the black. In 1998, the Robert Peel pub in the English town of Bury, near Manchester, decided to start a black pudding–eating contest. The first winner was Martin Brimelow, who ate nine black puddings. Though he was ahead, his victory was assured when he ate a special black pudding injected with Tabasco sauce, which counted as two.

_06:: Corned Beef and Cabbage

Mo's Irish Pub in Milwaukee celebrates its very Irish heritage with dignity and class: an annual Corned Beef and Cabbage–Eating Contest. The winner in 2004 was Ed "Cookie" Jarvis, a veteran eating-contest competitor (he holds 29 titles) who weighed in at an intimidating 419 pounds. Jarvis packed away over five pounds of corned beef and cabbage in 10 minutes, beating the closest competitor by almost two pounds. Need an idea of just how fast that is? He packed away his first plate in a mere 80 seconds! As in many eating contests, there are only two ways to get disqualified: cheat or puke. It's a wonder this contest wasn't followed by an unofficial Gas-X Binge-Drinking Bout.

Touch of Evil

In 1990, Guinness World Records *stopped listing records for gluttony or eating contests. They later ended "heaviest pets" records, too, as demented folk were overstuffing Fido and Fluffy to try to gain entry into the book.*

_07:: Vodka

Sure, there are beer-drinking contests, so why not vodka-drinking contests? Well, here's why. In 2003 a bar in the southern Russian town of Volgodonsk decided to hold just such a competition. After all, Russians are famous for their ability to hold their vodka, and annual consumption is over 15 liters *per person*. The winner would get . . . well, more vodka.

Ten liters of it, to be exact. Sadly, the winner never got to claim his prize. After downing 1.5 *liters* of vodka in under 40 minutes (which is about 51 shots), the vodka champ passed away about 20 minutes later. What about the runners-up? The five other contestants got treated to full luxury stays in intensive care. Scary enough, many of the ones who weren't hospitalized actually showed up at the same bar the next night.

3

"Where the Buffalo Roast": Delicious Animals We Charbroiled into Extinction—and 1 That Tasted Nasty but We Killed It Anyway

"Good to the last drop" proved to be a great slogan for Maxwell House coffee. But the "Good to the last existing representation of the species" tagline hasn't worked so well for these delectable creatures. Here are four animals that prove that slow and tasty never wins the race.

_01:: The Dodo

Bigger than turkeys and more naive than happy taxpayers, the dodo didn't exactly have the best survival strategy on the block. Consider the evidence. Not only was the dodo a flightless bird, it also had tiny wings, a small tuft of curly feathers on its bum, and it laid only one egg a year. It's no wonder European sailors who landed on the shores of Mauritius in the early 16th century got a big laugh out of the clumsy bird, which, in addition to its previously lamented attributes, had absolutely no fear of man. The sailors also got quite a few meals out of the *aves,* even though they were said to be close to inedible (Dutch settlers called them *walgvogel,* or "disgusting bird"). No matter. Pigs, rats, and monkeys introduced to the island helped man kill off the bird by 1681. Which is why there aren't any Kentucky Fried Dodos today.

_02:: The Sea Cow

They were big, slow, tasty, and defenseless, all of which is a bad combination around a slew of hungry humans. A cold-water relative of the manatee and dugong, the sea cow was discovered by Europeans in 1741 when the explorer Vitus Bering and his crew were shipwrecked in the area between Siberia and Alaska. And since the adventurous lot couldn't really explore the land, they took to exploring their palate. Our shipwrecked gourmands quickly discovered that sea cow meat tasted like veal and remained fresh for a surprisingly long time. And there was a lot of meat, too, since the beasts reached as much as 26 feet in length and weighed up to 8 tons. They resembled a modern manatee, with looks like your mother-in-law—if your mother-in-law has big expressive brown eyes, a small head, external ears the size of peas, and bristling whiskers. Estimates are that only about 20% of the sea cows shot or harpooned were actually caught, but they all died. By 1768, the gentle, delicious beasts were naught but lip-smacking memories.

Touch of Evil

The Labrador duck went extinct not only because of its meat, but also because of its eggs. The bird could lay up to an egg per day, but that didn't stop humans and other predators from wiping them out by 1875.

_03:: The Great Auk

Rich in protein, chock-full of nutritious fats and oils, and great for baiting fishhooks, this flightless seabird was, well, great. Found on the rocky islands and coastal areas on both sides of the North Atlantic, great auks were like a somewhat smaller version of the dodo, and they had the brains to match. Starting in the early 16th century, sailors began marching the clueless creatures up the gangplank and pushing them into the ship's hold by the hundreds. Unlike the dodo, however, the auk was considered great grub, and the tasty bird was hunted for its feathers, skin, and eggs to boot. Unfortunately, you'll never get to feast on the great auk's tender meat, and you have your European brothers to thank for it. The last pair was killed on an island off the coast of Iceland back in 1844.

_04:: The Passenger Pigeon

The naturalist John James Audubon once reported seeing a flock of passenger pigeons so numerous, it took three days for them to fly over. And he wasn't exaggerating. In the early part of the 19th century, the birds, which were slightly larger than mourning doves, were estimated to make up as much as 40% of North America's entire avian population. But the abundance of the creatures made them easy marks. Effortlessly hunted, the birds were mowed down mostly for food but occasionally for sport, with some "sportsmen" bagging as many as 5,000 in a day. In fact, the birds filled entire train boxcars as they were shipped to markets in eastern cities. Unable to sustain themselves except in large flocks, the pigeons dwindled rapidly. In 1900, a 14-year-old boy shot the last wild passenger pigeon (boys *will* be boys). Fourteen years later, the last one in captivity died at the Cincinnati Zoo. Her name was Martha.

Nothing's Good in Moderation: The Most Excessive Weddings in History

Sure, there's lots to consider in planning a wedding: dresses, cakes, bands, halls... all of which can add up to a hefty bill for the parents of the bride (or, in some cultures, the groom). But perhaps those bellyaching about the substantial hit their bank account is about to take should pause for a moment to consider some of history's most ridiculously, outrageously off-the-wall weddings. Suddenly dropping a few grand on a one-wear gown doesn't seem so bad, does it?

_01:: Attila the Hun and Ildico (453 CE)

Attila the Hun, perennial barbarian bad boy, was apparently also a perennial playboy. Leader of the Huns, Attila somehow also found time to marry 12 women and father an unknown number of children. Never able to quite get enough, Attila still might have wanted to hold off on the last wife. On his last wedding night, in 453 CE, the royalty of every nation under Hun dominion, from the Rhine to the Volga, were in attendance, and thousands of gallons of booze and whole herds of sheep were brought in to slake their appetites. No ordinary nuptials, the drinking and feasting were to last for days, but on the morning after taking his 16-year-old bride to bed, the 50-something warlord was found dead. Whether his death was caused by poison, overdrinking, or just too much fun in the sack, the world will probably never know.

_02:: Margaret of York and Charles the Bold (1468)

Despite the protests of France's Louis XI, who was fearful of an alliance between the English and the Burgundians, Margaret of York was engaged to Charles the Bold, aka the duke of

Burgundy. And in spite of the king's objection, the crazy cats decided to go forth with said ceremony and party like it was 1469. Extravagant even by the standards of European royal weddings, the blessed event was accompanied by a tournament in which the most famous knights in Europe bludgeoned one another for days. And Margaret's crown, covered in pearls and diamonds, was so valuable that it's now on display in the treasury of Aachen Cathedral. Of course, the preceremony celebrations were equally grand. The nuptials themselves were preceded by parades through the streets of Bruges, a pageant reenacted every year during (coincidentally enough) the tourist season. Sadly, Margaret's subsequent life was a little less like a fairy tale: she lived to see the death of her husband in battle (1477) against the French and the overthrow of both Burgundy as an independent duchy (1482) and of her own family across the Channel (1485).

_03:: Prince Rainier of Monaco and Grace Kelly (1956)

Billed as "the wedding of the century," the union between the prince of Monaco (whose family is actually descended from Genoese pirates) and the Hollywood starlet was the talk of the civilized world for much of the mid-1950s. Rainier gave his bride a 10-carat diamond ring, and his subjects gave their new princess diamond earrings and a necklace to match and, for no particular reason, a Rolls-Royce. Of course, the gown was no joke, either, as Grace's dress was designed by an Oscar winner, Helen Rose. The couple had two wedding ceremonies, a private civil ceremony in the Riviera principality's throne room and a public religious ceremony in Monaco Cathedral. Over 600 of the world's rich and famous attended the reception, including Frank Sinatra, Cary Grant, and Ava Gardner. Tragically, Princess Grace was killed in 1982 in a car accident. Interestingly, commemorative U.S. postage stamps were issued in her honor, but they gave her name only as "Grace Kelly." Why? Because U.S. law bans the placement of foreign monarchs on its postage stamps.

Touch of Evil

Mariah Carey wore a $25,000 gown for her wedding to Sony Music Entertainment boss Tommy Mottola, an event that featured fifty flower girls and cost more than half a million bucks. If only the investment had paid off: the couple separated before celebrating their fourth anniversary.

_04:: Muhammad and Salama of Dubai (1981)

Things can be rough when you're constantly trying to "keep up with the Joneses," or the Hamids, as the case may be. Arab weddings are often such bank-breakers that Arab economists frequently bemoan the size and expense that have become culturally expected. But that didn't stop Rashid bin Sayid al-Maktoum, sheikh of Dubai, in planning his son Muhammad's 1981 wedding to Princess Salama. Lasting a mere seven days (seven!), the wedding was held in a stadium built expressly to host the festivities. Twenty thousand guests attended, and the bill came in at just over $44 million.

_05:: The Mittal Affair (2004)

In possibly the most luxurious wedding in history, Vanisha Mittal, daughter of Anglo-Indian steel tycoon Laxmi Mittal, married Amit Bhatia, an investment banker who literally cashed in. The wedding, held in June 2004 in a chateau in France, lasted six days and was reported to have cost over $90 million (yes, that's U.S. dollars). The guest roster included some of Bollywood's brightest stars and some of Europe's deepest pockets. Among the expenditures: $520,000 for a performance by pop diva Kylie Minogue, who performed for a half hour. That's almost $300 per second, a figure even more shocking when you factor in dollars per unit of talent.

Facts about Roman Excess

From insanely large feasts to the lewdest of lewd orgies, Romans certainly loved their excess and ohs. The following are just a few of the areas they really could have trimmed back on.

_01:: The Food

If you're throwing a vintage Roman orgy, you'll need to make sure your pantry's well stocked. For breakfast, the Romans served bread, grapes, olives, with cheese and eggs all at the fourth hour. Then followed a meal at the sixth hour and at the ninth hour, the *cena* (evening meal), when a three-part meal was served. The first part was the *gustus,* which was designed to whet the appetite with shellfish and spicy sauces. Second was the *fercula,* which consisted of many different courses of meats and vegetables, while the third, the *mensae secundae,* was a dessert composed of fruits and pastry. Of course, ancient orgygoers also chowed down on ram's head pies, stuffed fowl, and boiled calf and pastry stuffed with raisins and nuts. Don't forget that atmosphere counts for something, too! Dishes were often made of gold and silver and precious jewels, banquet rooms were strewn with lilies and roses, and the participants lived for the present. Of course, you'll want to make sure you've got an army of slaves wearing costly dresses, just to make sure your guests feel extra welcome. Also, any and all sorts of bodily functions were accepted and even encouraged during dinner: belching, farting, spitting, relieving oneself in slave-borne chamber pots in full view of other guests, and even vomiting to make room for more grub. Don't remember that scene in *Caligula.*

_02:: The Entertainment

Nothing *screams* entertainment, well, like the Roman entertainers of yore. And games, festivals, and gladiatorial shows were just another part of Roman society carried to excessive lengths. Generally speaking, spectators and participants were exposed to unnatural excitements, and somehow developed an entertaining perspective on acts of cruelty and suffering. In fact, historians estimate that over 500,000 people were regular attendees at these forms of entertainment, often staying for days at a time. To sweeten the deal, all concessions (food *and* drink!) were provided free of charge by a generous government. And boy could these people party! The amphitheater at Titus was built to hold 80,000 seated spectators arranged by rank. And from the emperor to the lowest of the population, all seated on marble benches, covered with cushions and protected from the elements by canopies. There, gladiators and political prisoners fought with people or animals to the death. And as the audiences got bored, organizers were forced to find new sources of entertainment. For instance, Pompey let loose 600 lions in the arena with the gladiators one day, while Probus, a wealthy Roman, at one of his festivals once reserved 600 gladiators for extinction and massacred another 200 lions, 20 leopards, and 300 bears (oh, my).

_03:: The Bath

Citizens of the Roman Empire regarded sexual relations and sexual freedom with passionate abandon. In fact, the indolent lifestyle of the rich focused more on pleasure than industry and the Roman baths were a focal point for daily relaxation, socializing, and idleness for both the rich and the poor. Originally designed for cleansing purposes, the baths quickly became hangouts for socializing, relaxing, and ultimately engaging in plenty of sex orgies. The baths were kept open all day and night and sometimes the wealthy classes, attended by armies of slaves, lived in them. Today, the ruins of many of the baths indicate that the inside walls were extravagantly decorated with images made less to excite cleaning activities than the passions and senses.

Touch of Evil

Romans were too posh to commit bulimia themselves, so they actually employed slaves to tickle their throats. Once their systems were clear, they could go back for round two.

_04:: The Fashion

Amazingly, the Romans weren't always so fond of excess. Prior to the dawn of the empire, the Romans were a frugal people and actually dressed with great simplicity, but as the empire grew, so did the flamboyance of its citizens. Men started expecting their women, courtesans and wives, to wear extravagantly ornamented attire every day. And while pearls and rubies were treasured jewels and large amounts of money were spent to acquire them, women were also expected to don woven silk of various colors, with colorful, extravagant embroidery. Dyed hair and exotic cosmetics also came into fashion, as did gold thread, which was fashioned into hair jewelry. The Romans also got an eye for "bling" and more and more stoles were quickly fastened with diamond clips, with jewels being embroidered into clothing, and even footwear, whenever possible. However, there was a constant turnover of clothes and jewelry during banquets, where, depending on the generosity of the host, anything that wasn't bolted down was given to the guests as gifts. A pretty high price to pay for friendship, no doubt.

Diets to Avoid:
Religious Councils through the Ages

Religion means a lot of things to a lot of people. Some consider it to be the source of all compassion, others feel it's the opiate of the masses, and still others view it as a good reason to rent out a village and have a big, old get-together. We're just focusing on the latter.

_01:: Council at Clermont (1095)

By the 11th century, the Christian Church was split into eastern and western factions and the holy city of Jerusalem had been under control of the Muslims for a couple hundred years. Then, in 1095, Pope Urban II summoned the clergy and nobles to a council in the village of Clermont in central France. Urban's PR team had leaked a rumor that Urban was going to make a special announcement at the council, and the effort worked. On the first day the crowds were so large that the papal throne had to be set up in a field so that everyone could be accommodated. After listing a number of alleged atrocities on eastern Christians by the Muslims and arguing the need to recapture Jerusalem, the pope cajoled the crowd into taking up arms against the so-called heathens. And with a flair for the dramatic, the pope stated that "God wills it." He then summoned his followers to take up the cross and head east to fight for Christianity. Of course, Urban did come up with a clever scheme for paying the warriors. For going to the Holy Land and fighting the Muslims, crusaders were offered a heck of a deal: not only would their past sins be forgiven, but present and future ones as well! With free passes to heaven on the horizon, armies of crusaders stormed toward the Holy Land, changing the climate of the region forever.

_02:: Diet of Worms (1521)

While the Diet of Worms doesn't sound particularly tasty, it was definitely historic. Having been excommunicated for his teachings, Martin Luther was invited by the German emperor to attend an imperial diet in the German village of Worms, where he could defend his teachings. And while the emperor expected Luther to recant his beliefs, German princes were actually hoping that the meeting would help loosen Rome's power over Germany. Because Martin hadn't officially been declared an outlaw just yet (as excommunicants normally were), he was allowed to travel freely to Worms and even spent two weeks preaching to large crowds along the way. There was less excitement upon his arrival, however, as Luther appeared twice before the emperor and was told both times to take back his teachings. Luther stated that he saw no reason to do so and simply said, "I am finished" (not the popularly believed "Here I stand. I cannot do other."). Clearly a little miffed, the emperor immediately declared Martin Luther an outlaw, and sentenced him to death. Like the religious fairy tale it was, though, Luther was saved from the sentence by kidnappers, who then hid him for his own safety. The Protestant Reformation was under way.

_03:: Council of Trent (1545–1563)

Arguably one of the most important councils in the history of the Roman Catholic Church, the Council of Trent not only served as the foundation for the Counter-Reformation, it also shaped the traditions and the doctrines of the church that remain to this day. In total, the council actually met three times over the 18-year period. The first two-year session ended abruptly when the city of Trent in northern Italy was attacked, not by the Protestants, but by the dreaded bubonic plague. Then, four years later, the council reconvened and then took the next 10 years off due to a war in Germany. When the third session finally ended, the council issued decrees on Holy Orders, the Mass, the sacraments of marriage, purgatory, and the doctrinal differences between the Roman Catholic Church and the Protestant faiths. And while the decrees from this council set the direction for the Roman Catholic Church for the next 500 years and helped create the chasms dividing the Christian faiths that remain until this day, ironically, the pope had little say or power at the council. Why not? Because the majority in attendance felt the big guy was too corrupt and incapable of fixing anything!

So Hungry I Could Eat a Horse: Delicacies That Make You Gag

Eager to figure out just how thick your stomach lining is? Well, the folks at *mental_floss* rounded up a couple Iron Chef recipes to put your iron stomachs to the test. Of course, you might need a bit of alcohol to work up the courage. The following are six courses to get you in the swig of things.

_01:: The Appetizer: Snails

From the ancient Romans to today's upper crust, snails, or as the French call them, *escargots,* have been a favorite starter of the rich and famous. As the Romans expanded their empire, the tasty little gastropods inched along with them and became a culinary prize, especially in France. In fact, Napoléon was even known to have issued snails as rations to his troops. But if you're about to get your grub on, you should know that a snail is not just a snail. While there are two basic snail groups, the achatine and the helix, you'll be dining on the latter. Helix snails are indigenous to Europe and are the snail gourmets' favorite. The young creatures feed on grapevines with the most famous coming from the Champagne and Burgundy regions. The *petit gris escargot* is considered the best, especially in November when they are the plumpest. And while rumor has it that the best snails are three to four years old, one question always remains for the uninitiated (mainly among the under-10 lot): If you salt the snail, will it disappear before you can eat it?

Touch of Evil

The Summer 1983 issue of Mothering *magazine featured recipes for the human placenta, including placenta stew, placenta cocktails, placenta lasagna, and placenta pizza. Some believe that ingesting the organ is natural and healthy.*

_02:: The Salad: Indonesian Sago Worm and Balinese Dragonflies

The Indonesian sago palm was once cultivated for its starchy substance used to thicken soup and make puddings. Today, however, the tree's extract has taken second place to its inhabitants. In fact, sago palm larvae, which seem to offer the same starchy taste, are a delicacy sold live in the marketplace. And harvesting the sago worm is actually an art form. It starts out by roaming the forest looking for fallen sago palms. If you happen to stumble across one, you knock on it checking for movement. If you hear a little rustling, you should feel free to hack open the tree and collect your jackpot. As for preparation, the worms can be eaten raw or toasted. And back to the salad, just combine the sago worms with deep-fried Balinese dragonflies, add a little coconut paste, fermented fish sauce, garlic, chiles, tamarind juice, basil leaves, ginger, and lime juice. Then, wrap the

whole thing in banana leaf and you have a salad that should tickle your taste buds (literally, if you decided to keep those larvae raw!).

_03:: The Soup: Bosintang (Dog Soup)

What's a full-course epicurean delight without the soup? For course number three, we've chosen Chinese Bosintang, or dog meat soup. Relatively easy to make, assuming Bowser is agreeable, the soup requires taking strips of dog meat and boiling them in a soy paste. Then vegetables like green onions, taro stalk, and perilla are added to the mixture, and the broth is brought to a boil. Finally, a sauce made from mashed garlic, red pepper, and ginger is mixed in. And before digging into your bowl of man's best friend, you should probably season the dish with pepper. Rumor has it that it goes very well with a glass of soju (liquor). Of course, the dish has a bit of versatility. Rice can be served with the soup or the combination can be mixed together to make sumptuous leftovers or a warm meal the kids can take in their lunch box . . . or a doggie bag.

_04:: The Entrée: Horse Meat Pie

Seabiscuit sautéed and simmered? No way! But outside the United States horse meat is accepted in such cultures as the French, Italian, Swiss, and Japanese. That's because horse meat is an excellent source of high-quality protein, vitamin B12, iron, and zinc. Plus, its lean red meat can easily be mistaken for premium beef. As for quality cuts, though, the mare is often considered the best source, followed by the gelding and then the stallion. There are actually numerous horse meat dishes, including horse meat stew, pony Stroganoff, horse parmesan, and chicken-fried horse meat. However,

Profiles in Carnage

IDI AMIN (1924/5?-2003)

Skeletons in the Pantry: Start with his fridge: Probably a big fan of plastic wrap and aluminum foil, Idi Amin kept the heads of some of his victims fresh by storing them in his fridge. Of course, he had plenty to choose from: Estimates are that Idi tortured and murdered up to 300,000 victims while he was president of Uganda.

Idi the Connoisseur: Of course, what good's a fridge if you can't make use of it? Amin once reportedly told his minister of health that he found human flesh "rather too salty." So, maybe Idi wasn't that into dark meat.

Idi the Sharp Dresser: If that isn't enough to make you retch, you should check out his style sense: The guy wore so many medals that his shirts sometimes tore.

Idi the Practical Joker: Amin often sent nonsensical telegrams to other countries' leaders, and he loved to romp about playing his accordion.

Idi "I Am the Most Modest Dictator in the World (and I Have a Medal to Prove It)" Amin: Apparently, he didn't suffer from low self-esteem. By the time Amin had fled into exile to Libya, and then Saudi Arabia, his official title was "His Excellency President for Life, Field Marshal Al Hadji Doctor Idi Amin, VC, DS, MC, Lord of All the Beasts of the Earth and Fishes of the Sea, and Conqueror of the British Empire in Africa in General and Uganda in Particular." Tough to get that on a business card.

today's entrée is Welsh horse pie. Just take strips of horse meat and sear them in a skillet. Next, arrange the strips in a stew pan with layers of potatoes, cheese, and tomatoes. Once tender, just remove the concoction to a baking dish lined with pie dough, cover the top with crust, and then bake until brown. You'll want to serve the dish with a heavy burgundy wine. Of course, caution while cooking is required. Underprepared horse meat can turn the epicurean into the Galloping Gourmet.

_05:: The Pièce de Résistance: Haggis

The crown prize of any culinary feast, haggis is typically served with great fanfare on January 25, or Burns Night, in celebration of the Scottish poet Robert Burns's birthday. In fact, the specially prepared feast is ceremoniously escorted into the room by a bagpiper, and Burns's poem "Address to a Haggis" is then read. So, what exactly is haggis, you ask? How about a sheep's stomach loaded with minced sheep liver and heart. Take one sheep pluck, or stomach bag, turn it inside out, scrape the surface with a knife, and then let it soak overnight in cold salt water. Boil the liver and heart and then parboil an onion. Simply mince this mixture, add toasted oatmeal and suet, and then fill the pluck, making sure to sew closed both ends. Now you just have to place the haggis in boiling water and slow boil for about four hours. For serving, you'll want to slice the haggis and garnish it with neeps (mashed turnips), tatties (mashed potatoes), and nips (sips of Scotch whisky). Actually, you may want to bring the whole bottle.

_06:: The After-Dinner Treat:
Rocky Mountain Oysters

OK, so where does one find seafood in the Rocky Mountains? Well, you probably guessed it. Not really a seafood dish, Rocky Mountain oysters are actually bull testicles. And in fact, this famed western U.S. delicacy has its own testicle festival every September in Clinton, Montana. According to connoisseurs, the deep-fried gonads are best served with hot sauce and a beer. And for the strong of stomach the recipe's really quite simple. First, cut and pull away the skin around the testes, then place 'em in salted water for about an hour. Next, parboil the "oysters" in salt water, drain, and then let cool. Simply slice the delicacy into chip-size pieces and then roll them in a batter of flour, corn meal, and dried garlic. Finally, dip the oysters in red wine and fry 'em up. To serve, just place the oysters in a hot sauce, drain them, then pile on the potato chips and ply your guests with plenty of beer.

Fed Up with People:
Facts on Cannibalism

You are what you eat, or is it who you eat? Following are five facts on the ritual value of cannibalism and some of its biggest gluttons.

_01:: Missionary Accomplished

Remember those cartoons showing natives placing captives in a big caldron of boiling water, tossing in the vegetables, and brewing up a large bowl of missionary stew? In most cultures, this couldn't be farther from the truth. While eating others' flesh may have been, at times, necessary for survival, in most cases it was out of ritualistic respect. In many locations cannibalism was the ultimate honor for the victim—when tribes ate their enemies, they did so to take on valued characteristics of that enemy. Blood was drunk in order to achieve some of the victim's bravery. Likewise, the brain was eaten for knowledge, the heart for courage, and the legs for swiftness. In some cases, a small portion of a recently deceased family member was also consumed out of respect as long as the departed one was not diseased or very elderly.

_02:: The Scottish Mr. Bean

During the time of Scotland's King James VI, later James I of England, there allegedly lived a highwayman named Alexander Bean, who along with his wife, eight sons, six daughters, 18 grandsons, and 14 granddaughters robbed any traveler unfortunate enough to cross their path. In order to hide the evidence and to feed an ever-growing family, each victim was killed and dismembered, with some body parts served immediately and the rest pickled for use later. Legend has it that close to 1,000 victims ended up the meal du jour for the Bean family. When finally captured, the adult male members of the Beans were executed by being dismembered and allowed to bleed to death. The women and children were then burned at the stake. However, there is no mention of what the Bean family had as its last meal.

_03:: Eddie Gein: Hollywood's Favorite Cannibal

On November 17, 1957, the Plainfield, Wisconsin, police began searching the farmhouse of Eddie Gein, a suspect in the robbery of a hardware store owned by Bernice Worden. As the police searched the dark, trash-covered house, they happened across a carcass hanging from the kitchen ceiling. At first they thought it was a deer, but upon closer inspection the officers discovered that it was the decapitated and gutted body of Bernice. But it didn't end there. More ghoulish items were soon found in the house. A bowl was made from the top of a human skull; lampshades, wastebaskets, armchairs, and an entire suit were made from human skin; and, most ghastly, a belt was made

from nipples, a human head, four noses, and a heart. The police could only speculate as to how many female victims were used to make Eddie's collection. Eddie soon became a Hollywood favorite. Norman Bates of *Psycho* fame is based on Eddie, bits and pieces of *The Texas Chainsaw Massacre* are taken from Eddie's story, and the character of Buffalo Bill in *The Silence of the Lambs* was inspired by Mr. Gein.

Touch of Evil

The word "cannibal" came from Christopher Columbus's journeys to the New World. He described the Caribs of Cuba and Haiti, whom he saw making meals of their own kind, as "Caníbalis."

_04:: Jeffrey Dahmer: Milwaukee's Notorious Cannibal

On July 22, 1991, Milwaukee police officers questioned an individual whom they had spotted wandering incoherently down a street with a handcuff on one hand. The individual told them that he had been drugged and handcuffed but was able to get away from his assailant. He then led them to the apartment of a 31-year-old chocolate factory worker named Jeffrey Dahmer. As they searched Dahmer's apartment, the police came across one of the most ghoulish scenes in American history. Upon opening the refrigerator, the officers found a recently severed head staring back at them. They also found three more heads and human meat stored in the freezer along with several hands and a penis in a stockpot. As the case unfolded, it became clear that Dahmer had killed, dismembered, and eaten as many as 17 victims, most of whom were poor transient blacks, Asians, or Hispanics. Dahmer would lure the victim to his apartment to watch TV and drink beer. Once there the victim was drugged and then stabbed or strangled. The body was then dismembered, with the head and genitalia saved as a trophy, the biceps and other muscles frozen to be eaten later, and the rest destroyed by acid and then disposed of. Dahmer was sentenced to 15 life sentences, or 957 years. He'd served only about two years when in 1994 he was murdered by another prison inmate.

_05:: Christian Cannibals and Communion

As with any upstart religion, the powers that be look at it with disdain and ridicule. This was the case with early Christianity. Late-first- and early-second-century Greek and Roman writers, such as Tacitus and Pliny the Younger, viewed the early Christian movement as a small group of superstitious fanatics who were a new sect among the hated Jews. Among both the upper class and common Romans gossip quickly spread about this group, including that as part of their religion they ate human bodies and drank human blood. Obviously a misrepresentation of the Christian ritual of communion, the rumored practice was viewed with disgust by the "civilized" Romans. Not only did this misinterpretation, coupled with other seemingly strange Christian practices, help to sway sentiment against the Christians, it made it easier for the Roman emperors to justify the persecution of the Christians. After all, there was no room in the Roman Empire for such barbarianism.

Too Much of a Bad Thing: Deaths of Famous People Caused by Overindulgence in Drugs, Drink, or Dessert

Before you eat that last french fry, swallow that last dram of Drambuie, or sample a sedative or three, you should probably read on.

_01:: Henry I (1069–1135)

Henry I wasn't exactly given the throne. As the third son of William the Conqueror, Henry became king only after one of his older brothers died and he'd beaten the other out of the throne. He had quite a run of it, though, reigning for a good 35 years—that is, until he was toppled by one-too-many lampreys. If you're not familiar, a lamprey is a nasty-looking beast of a fish with a round mouth that can reach three feet in length. And it's as mean as it looks. Lampreys will attach themselves to other fish, rasp a hole in them, eat their flesh, then detach, leaving an often fatal wound. They are, however, reputed to be great eating (fit for a king, in fact), especially if you like meaty fish with a high fat content, which Henry clearly did. Sometime before Christmas, England's king sat down to a heaping platter of the fatty fish, ate a few too many, and breathed his last.

_02:: Honoré de Balzac (1799–1850)

"Coffee is a great power in my life," this French writer said in his essay "The Pleasures and Pains of Coffee." "I have observed its effects on an epic scale." The thing is, he wasn't kidding. Balzac consumed as many as 50 cups of strong Turkish coffee per day, and we're talking about the days before indoor plumbing! And he was no slouch at eating, either. At one meal old Balzac was reported to have eaten 100 oysters, 12 mutton cutlets, a duck, two partridges, and some fish, along with desserts, fruits, and wine. But coffee was clearly his passion, and he was faithful to the end. When Balzac couldn't get it strong enough, the addict was known to down pulverized coffee beans for the jolt he needed. This produced two results: Balzac was an incredibly energetic and prolific writer, writing more than 100 novels. He also died of caffeine poisoning at the age of 51.

_03:: Zachary Taylor (1784–1850)

Perhaps the most apolitical president in U.S. history, Zachary Taylor was an army veteran of four decades and a hero of the Mexican War, but he never voted or held office before being elected president in 1848. Even more amazingly, the cheapskate refused to accept mail with postage due, so he didn't even know he'd been nominated for the office until weeks after the fact! About 16 months after taking the oath of office, during which time he accomplished very little, old Zach attended a July Fourth celebration at the Washington Monument on a sweltering day, and stood around in the heat for hours wearing dark heavy clothing. To cool off, he wolfed down a bowl full of iced cherries and polished 'em off with a pitcher of milk. Not the best idea. Turns out the milk and/or ice was tainted, and Taylor died five days later of typhoid fever or cholera.

Touch of Evil

Legend has it that the last words of heavy-drinking poet Dylan Thomas before his 1953 death were: "Eighteen straight whiskies... I do believe that's a record." Natural causes? Probably not.

_04:: Ira Hayes (1923–1955)

"It's funny what a picture can do," Hayes once said, but it had to have been said with bitter irony since it was a picture that ruined his life. Hayes was a Pima Indian from Arizona who, with four other U.S. Marines and a U.S. Navy pharmacist, raised a flag on the battle-ravaged island of Iwo Jima on February 23, 1945. The resulting photo made Hayes and the others heroes, but it embittered Hayes because he thought it denigrated the sacrifices of the thousands who'd died in the battle. The sad result? Hayes became an alcoholic who drifted from city to city and was arrested more than 50 times. In the end, the experience turned him into more of a hobo than a hero, and in the early morning hours of January 24, 1955, a drunken Hayes stumbled into a ditch that served as the water supply for his reservation. There the poor veteran froze to death.

It's Good to Be King, Especially If You Like Food: Monarchs Who Tipped the Scales

Throughout history, whether because of abundant food or lack of exercise or both, monarchs have been plagued with largeness of girth (what hardship!). Here are just a few of the fattest kings and queens on record.

_01:: Itey (ca. 1490 BCE)

Sort of an ancient Egyptian punch line, this corpulent queen ruled over the mysterious land of Punt, located somewhere in East Africa. So how exactly do we know of the great monarch's girth? Well, the Egyptian pharaoh Hatshepsut launched a trade delegation to Punt, and carvings on the walls of her temple complex at Deir el-Bahri record the expedition. Itey is depicted as grossly obese and is even pictured standing next to a diminutive husband and a tiny donkey. Under the donkey, in a delightful bit of Egyptian humor, is the inscription "This donkey had to carry the queen." A beast of burden indeed.

_02:: Eglon (ca. 1100 BCE)

According to the Bible, Eglon was the king of Moab (in modern Jordan) who united several tribes of highland and desert raiders to conquer the central Israelite tribes sometime in the 12th century BCE. An Israelite named Ehud gained the king's confidence, got him in a room alone, then killed him. Of course, the murder wasn't exactly a smooth operation. The Bible describes vividly that Eglon was so fat that Ehud couldn't retrieve his blade. Luckily, though, he managed to escape with little

trouble. As he fled, Ehud told Eglon's servants that the king was using the restroom. The stench coming from the room must have been fairly run-of-the-mill, because by the time they went in to check on their beloved king, Ehud had already rallied his followers and formed an army.

_03:: Charles the Fat (Ruled 881–888)

Not many kings actually have "the Fat" added to their names. A series of fortuitous deaths and abdications in the late 870s and early 880s left Charles the ruler of almost all of his great-grandfather Charlemagne's empire, encompassing most of modern-day France, Germany, and Italy. But Charles lacked the energy of his ancestor and namesake, possibly due in part to his obesity. During his reign Arab pirates raided Italy with impunity and Charles couldn't even be bothered to fight Viking marauders in northwestern France (he found it easier to pay them to go away instead). And while the dreaded moniker does have a certain ring to it, Charles wasn't the only French king of notable girth—Louis VI (ruled 1108–1137) also earned the appellation "the Fat."

_04:: George IV (Ruled 1820–1830)

George IV became king of England in 1820 after serving as prince regent while his father, George III, was alive but incompetent to rule. Apparently, though, the plush lifestyle being "Defender of the Faith" provided him seems only to have whetted his appetite. Known as a gambler, a drinker, and a laudanum addict, among other things, George IV enjoyed the dubious distinction of being far and away the fattest king in English history. His favorite breakfast was two roast pigeons, three beefsteaks, a bottle of white wine, a glass of champagne, two glasses of port, and one of brandy...after all, breakfast *is* the most important meal of the day.

_05:: Farouk (Ruled 1936–1952)

Farouk, the last king of Egypt with any real power, was crowned in 1936 and proceeded to live it up. He owned numerous palaces in Europe, hundreds of cars, and thousands of horses. But financing the royal lifestyle turned out to be a bit of a problem, so Farouk turned Egypt into even more of a kleptocracy than it had previously been. He was even renowned as a skilled pickpocket and was known to steal valuable items while on state visits to other countries (including a priceless pocket watch from Winston Churchill and a ceremonial sword from the shah of Iran!). In the end, Farouk was overthrown by a military coup in 1952 and briefly replaced with his newborn son, Fuad. But after a few months of infant rule, Egypt cleverly scrapped the monarchy thing altogether in favor of a very slightly less corrupt military dictatorship under Gamal Abdel Nasser (which degenerated into an arguably more corrupt system than Farouk ever could have dreamed possible). As for ex-king Farouk, he lived out the rest of his life in exile. Eating being one of his few pleasures, he died in 1965, at the age of 45, after gorging himself at the table. He weighed out at 300 pounds.

It's a Wrap:
Fads from the Slimming Fashion Industry

There's always the question of what to do with those extra pounds. Should you squeeze them back, tuck them in, wrap them up, camouflage them, or simply let hang? Well, whatever your preferred method for masking that extra chub, there's a manmade solution out there for you.

_01:: Kirtles, Corsets, and *Coches*

Women and men alike have used bindings either for religious or fashion reasons since time began. The origin of the use of corsets (derived from the French word *corps,* for "body") can be found in drawings discovered at a Neolithic archaeological site in Brandon, England. Not particularly confined to women's wear, the use of stays or corsets is documented back to 1700 BCE, when corsets were used to train small waists on young men and warriors as part of their culture. In the 13th and 14th centuries CE, dress construction incorporated a corseted effect known as "kirtles" into everyday wear. Iron was used in the 14th century to create the first known artificial support known as a *coche* in France and a busk in England. Used as a status symbol, Catherine de Medici, in the French court, ordered her ladies-in-waiting to cinch their waists to no bigger than 13 inches around, prompting the use of a steel framework to achieve this extreme state. In the late 20th century, the corset was resurrected as a piece of fashion outerwear made famous by Madonna in the late 1980s.

Touch of Evil

Some acupuncturists perform "ear stapling," in which a surgical staple is placed partially inside the ear. Why exactly? Because rubbing the device supposedly curbs hunger pangs.

_02:: Jeans and Slimming Cream

The quest to lift and shape our derrieres has become an economic boon for denim jean producers. A select line of jeans, trousers, and skirts produced by Miss Sixty carries an extra ingredient, Skintex, combining retinol, designed to stimulate collagen production, and chitosan, produced from shellfish skeleton bone. The serum embedded in the jeans material is designed to be released upon friction between the skin and fabric when worn. According to Cognis, the German manufacturers, 40% of the "medication" is absorbed after 48 hours and the clothing remains effective for another 30 washings. Hand washing is recommended. Doctors, however, are skeptical. One unforeseen problem is that the retinol reacts to sunlight so sunburn might be an interesting by-product of the slimming exercise. These clothes are not cheap; jeans retail at $139 a pair, pants range from $119 to $149, and skirts are $99 dollars. Already the company has said that it will not reissue this line of clothing next season.

_03:: These Shoes Were Made for Walking It Off

The latest cellulite-busting phenomenon, MBTs, gives a whole new meaning to the song "These Boots Were Made for Walking." Produced by Masai Barefoot Technology, the company's anticellulite sneakers are designed to help you mimic the gait of members of the Masai tribe in Africa. Why, exactly? Well, the lanky Masai are renowned for their perfect posture. Although definitely not a fashion winner, these bulky athletic shoes sit on a sole of rubber, curved thicker and higher in the middle, to force your legs to work harder with each step. Walking like a Masai ain't exactly cheap, though: it's about $255 for a pair of shoes. Despite the hefty tag, the sneakers move off shelves pretty quickly. And while there seems to be little scientific support for the shoes' anticellulite claims, they are credited with improving posture...a slightly pricey way to put some spring in your step!

_04:: Swimsuits

The art of wearing a swimsuit is an acquired technical skill, not necessarily apparent to the naked eye. Every year the agonizing ritual of searching for that ideal magic swimsuit begins. Reality strikes as women start the journey of accentuating the positive and camouflaging the negatives. This focus on body shaping and trend toward exposing more body parts increased in importance at the beginning of the 20th century, spurred in 1902 by the Australian swimmer Annette Kellerman, an "underwater ballerina" who dove into a glass tank clad in a swimsuit that showed arms, legs, and neck. Although she was arrested for indecent exposure, the damage had been done. Today, you can buy a swimsuit with panel-restricting tummy control, underwires to maintain bust shape, bust enhancers using a gel cup, bust reducers, bottom control and support, and even padded bottoms.

_05:: Wrapping It All Up

The fascination (and profit potential) associated with the magical effect of body wraps to reduce inches has survived for more than two centuries. Traced back to the time of the Romans, and used in Cleopatra's court, body wraps have worked by shrinking the size of fat cells to reduce, contour, and slenderize the body shape. Creams, lotions, and gels containing a mixture of either herbal extracts, chemicals, minerals, or vegetable products are applied to the skin before wrapping with terry cloth or cellophane. And while the older European full-body wraps sound closer to a variety of mummification, they promise up to six inches off original body measurements, which might last for a year. Using bandages soaked in sea-clay mud, the entire body is wrapped, starting with the feet and ankles, then going all the way to the jaws, with specialized wrapping procedures for the bustline. Recently,

Scandalicious

FEDS FIND COMMUNIST THREAT IN PUMPKIN!

In 1939, a down-and-out writer named Whittaker Chambers approached Assistant Secretary of State Adolf Berle, describing in detail an underground Communist network in the United States spying for the Soviet Union. Chambers, best known at the time for translating the book *Bambi* into English, was not regarded as a reliable expert on matters of espionage. Of course, it wasn't until 1948 that anyone decided to take Chambers at his word. Richard Nixon, then a congressman, perked up after Chambers provided a list of alleged Communist agents, a list that included Alger Hiss, a State Department lawyer. After first denying that he knew Chambers, Hiss launched a defamation suit. It proved to be a bad idea. Chambers led investigators to a farm where dozens of documents, some of them classified and some of them in Hiss's own handwriting, were hidden in a hollowed-out pumpkin. Hiss was eventually convicted of perjury (the statute of limitations barred trying him for espionage), though some people still dispute his guilt. One thing is sure, however: Alger Hiss lost his taste for pumpkin pie.

at-home body wrap kits sold directly to consumers at a lower price are competing against the high-priced wraps from the luxurious beauty salons.

Turning Over a New Leaf: Plants Known to Cause Hysteria

How about a nice cup of herbal tea? Better check which herbs you're talking about.

_01:: Blue Lily of the Nile

Remember your fourth grade history textbook, with all those pictures and drawings of life in ancient Egypt? If you can jog your memory enough, you might just recall a blue lotus or lily symbol that tended to be a fixture in those drawings. For centuries historians thought the blue lily to be a symbolic flower commonly placed in the sarcophagi of royalty such as King Tutankhamen. However, more recent findings suggest that the blue lily played a more hedonistic role in Egyptian society as a hallucinogen, creating states of ecstasy among the users. The flowers were prepared as a golden liquid tea with a sweet taste. After drinking, the individual entered into a euphoric state. The dried leaves were also smoked, but the favored way of ingesting the herb was mixed with wine. Maybe there is more to the Blue Nile than we thought.

_02:: A Button for Your Thoughts

If you're wondering where peyote comes from, look no further. Take one small Lophophora williamsii cactus and scrape off some of the buttons. Let the buttons dry until they are brown and ugly-looking. Serve in their natural form or grind them into a powder for tea or to mix with other drinks. For maximum effect, vomit early to get over the nausea. You are now ready for your peyote trip. Long a part of Native American culture, peyote was used by the Aztecs as a way to communicate with their gods. By the late 1800s, numerous North American tribes had integrated peyote into their religious ceremonies. In the early 1900s, a number of tribes formed the Native American Church, which still exists today. The basis of their communion is peyote.

_03:: Absinthe, or It's Not Easy Being Green

One of the most popular drinks of 19th-century Europe, especially in France, was absinthe, made from the herbs wormwood, green anise, fennel, and hyssop. The licorice-tasting drink contained more alcohol than wine and soon gained a reputation for causing addiction, excitability, hallucinations, and epileptic seizures. Questionable scientific research (usually funded by the French wine industry) found that the drink caused individuals to become criminally insane and that it brought on other illnesses, such as tuberculosis. In fact, one study found absinthe to be 246 times more likely to cause insanity than wine. By the 1890s, it became the leading target of temperance movements, a cause that reached its zenith in 1905, when Jean Lanfray, a Swiss peasant, murdered his pregnant wife and two daughters after having drunk two glasses of absinthe earlier in the day. What the press failed to mention was that in between the absinthe and the murders Lanfray had also had cognac, several glasses of wine at lunch, a glass of wine before leaving work, coffee with brandy, and a liter of wine after coming home. Absinthe was eventually banned in Switzerland (1910), the United States (1912), France (1915), and other countries.

_04:: Mold and Mass Hysteria: The Salem Witchcraft Trials

Was it sorcery or just a case of mold-induced food poisoning? In February 1692, young Betty Paris became ill and began manifesting hysterical behavior such as contorting in pain, appearing to be in a trance, complaining of fever, running around aimlessly, and diving under furniture. Things only got worse when Betty's playmates started showing similar symptoms. For the small Puritan village of Salem, Massachusetts, this was too strange and, therefore, must be the work of the devil. With this the witch-hunt began. By the time the mass hysteria had subsided over 100 individuals had been arrested and imprisoned on witchcraft charges. Nineteen were executed, four died while in jail, and one 80-year-old man was pressed to death under large rocks. But was it the devil? The winter of 1692 was extremely cold and wet. The main food source was the harvested rye wheat, which is now believed to have been infected with mold. Rye mold contains a chemical called ergot whose effects are similar to those of LSD, including hallucinations and seizures. It seems the devil was one "rye" character.

_05:: Designer Herbs: The Agony of the Ecstasy

The 1990s was a decade of designer drugs. What was a rave without ecstasy, or "X," as it is commonly called? But ecstasy is an illegal hallucinatory amphetamine. Leave it to American ingenuity to come up with a natural herbal alternative, called herbal ecstasy, and sell it as a "designer nutritional supplement." The main ingredients were a natural form of the stimulant ephedrine and the kola nut, a natural source of caffeine. What made the product appear to be more "in" was its slick packaging with pyramids, butterflies, mushrooms, and endorsements from (unknown) publications giving it a psychedelic mystique. Users said that it allowed them to party for hours with no side effects, while hard-core X users found it to be a weak version of the real thing. However, herbal ecstasy had a major problem. Many of its ingredients have been found to cause heart attacks, strokes, and seizures.

Are You Going to Finish That? World's Oddest Cuisines

5

There's no telling what someone's willing to put in their mouth if the right price is involved. Or the right condiments.

_01:: Eskimo Cuisine: Seal Oil

Forget ketchup and salsa, Inuits (often called "Eskimos") consider raw seal oil the king of all condiments. In fact, they're quite happy to slather the excellent sauce on baked salmon, sheefish, whitefish, caribou, moose, and anything else you can catch up north. Inuits also like their seal oil on "frozen-raw" moose or caribou and fish. So what's the secret to this not-so-secret sauce? The oil is produced by cutting up freshly slaughtered seal blubber into chunks and leaving them outside in a bucket for five days, stirring occasionally, until the blubber naturally renders and becomes oil. An adult seal produces about five gallons of usable seal oil. Once ready, just add A-1 or Tabasco to taste (really)!

_02:: Thai Cuisine: Insects I

Though most Americans and Europeans are familiar with Thai cuisine standards—the ubiquitous pad thai and thom yum goong soup—most are unaware of a small epicurean subgroup in Thai cuisine: connoisseurs who appreciate the variety of insect species native to Thailand's tropical jungles. It's true! This lot is quite happy to chow down on cicadas, locusts, mantises, deep-fried crickets, grasshoppers, and bamboo borers (grubs referred to on some menus as "fried little white babies"), steamed giant water bug (which can also be eaten as a paste with chili and sticky rice), weaver ants and their eggs (eaten like the water bug as a paste), bamboo larvae, dung beetles, moth and butterfly pupae, wasp and bee larvae, grilled tarantula, and termite soup. A side of Raid will cost you extra.

_03:: Japanese Cuisine: Insects II

The Japanese also have a little-known gustatory affinity for insects. In fact, the practice of eating aquatic insects in particular probably originated in the Japanese Alps, where a hostile environment resulted in food scarcities. Now, however, insect larvae are considered a delicacy and are served throughout Japan, including the best restaurants in Tokyo. Well-known dishes include hachi no ko, or boiled wasp larvae; zazamushi or water insect larvae; inago, or field grasshoppers in fried rice; semi, or fried cicada; and sangi, or fried silk moth pupae.

_04:: Nigeria: Insects III

Asia isn't the only place you can get someone to rustle you up a couple of bugs. People from Kwara State in Nigeria also have a long-standing appreciation of insects as food. The particular technique used for catching termites is pretty interesting: termites are captured by putting a bowl of water under a bright light, attracting the termites, which then fall into the water and drown. A popular variation is winged termites—female queens and male drones that take flight to mate. Large, mature queens are considered a delicacy and are reserved for developed palates. Generally, the inhabitants of Kwara State roast termites over open coals or fry them in a pot before adding salt to taste. Nigerians also enjoy crickets disemboweled and roasted over open coals, except for the Yoruba because Ogun, their iron god, forbids eating animals that don't have blood. Grasshoppers, however, are the most popular because there's no religious taboo governing them, and field hands can eat them raw.

_05:: Guangxi, China: Live Monkey Brains

Disbelieving Westerners and Chinese have long asserted that the alleged practice of eating the brains of a live monkey directly from its skull in south China is a rumor, but in fact it isn't. Gourmets at Pingxiang, on the border with Vietnam, buy monkeys themselves at market and have them prepared by cooks at local inns. The cooks force the monkeys to drink large amounts of rice wine, and when they are passed out they bind their limbs, chop open their skull, and scoop out the brains into a bowl. Diners can tell the monkey has been prepared well when they can see the blood vessels still pulsing. The brains are eaten with condiments including pickled ginger, chili pepper, fried peanuts, and cilantro, and apparently taste like tofu. In less enlightened times monkeys were bound and gagged and then strapped under a special table with a hole in the center, and the tops of their skulls were sawed off while they were still sober. Thank God the TV show *Fear Factor* didn't exist back then.

They'd Steal Candy from a Baby: Dictators with Infamous Sweet Tooths

After a busy day of oppressing your own people, murdering your enemies, and conquering foreign lands, sometimes a workaholic dictator just needs to treat himself to a little pick-me-up. These were four guys happy to do just that.

_01:: Napoléon: Keeping It Short and Sweet

Though he was originally from Corsica, Napoléon seemed to share the French obsession with pastries. In fact, his cook, Antonin Carême, who would eventually become a globe-trotting celebrity famous for his sugary confections, first made his reputation with an enormous wedding cake for Napoléon, celebrating his marriage to the empress Josephine. Of course, cakes were just the tip of the icing for the squirrelly French commander. Napoléon's favorite dessert was supposedly a pastry that resembled profiterole, made with chocolate and cream, and he was also said to favor a pastry called Turkish delight with pistachio filling. Later, when he was in exile on Elba, the sweet-toothed sovereign consoled himself with copious amounts of a sweet dessert wine from Klein Constantia in South Africa.

_02:: Hitler: Getting His Cake, and Definitely Eating It Too

Old Adolf probably had the most famous sweet tooth on record. And though he was a vegetarian who also abstained from hard alcohol, Hitler's weakness for candy and pastries was well known, and admirers always made sure to bring a box of chocolates or cake or pastries when they came to see the Führer. So, just how sweet were his teeth? Hitler was reputed to put seven teaspoons of sugar in each cup of tea, supposedly added sugar to wine because he found it too bitter otherwise, and plied all his guests with ice cream and candy. In fact, Hitler's favorite dessert chef, Gerhardt Shtammer, claims that Hitler asked him to make delectable desserts right up to the very end, when they were trapped in Hitler's bunker with hard-core Nazi holdouts. According to Shtammer, Hitler's favorite desserts were éclairs decorated with little swastikas and strudel.

_03:: Saddam Hussein and His Spider-Hole Snack Attacks

The bizarre contents of Saddam Hussein's residences—velvet paintings of Elvis and all—have provided endless fodder for cocktail conversations. Amid the revelations of Saddam's incredibly bad taste, it was also revealed that Saddam was a bit of a sugar fiend. In his last rather ignoble residence—the "spider hole" where he was finally apprehended in Ad Dawr in December 2003—American soldiers found a refrigerator filled with Mars and Bounty candy bars and 7-Up. Thank God! No

HIDEKI TOJO'S HORRIBLE-TERRIBLE, NO-GOOD, VERY BAD DAY (AND DENTURES)

General Hideki Tojo, who led Japan to disastrous defeat with his decision to attack Pearl Harbor, apparently enjoyed a lifetime of sweets. In fact, the condition of his teeth was even more abysmal than the condition of his army, because when he was captured he required a full set of dentures! Oddly enough, this led to one of the more bizarre stories of the Second World War: George Foster and Jack Mallory, Navy dentists on loan to the Army, were given responsibility for making Tojo's dentures and, realizing the identity of their famous patient, decided to play a youthful prank on him. Mallory made dentures that were an exact fit, causing no discomfort, but engraved a message— "Remember Pearl Harbor"—in Morse code on his false teeth.

longer relegated to the realm of middle school sleepovers, and Little League pizza parties, these snack foods have finally broken through to a new demographic: dictators evading prosecution for crimes against humanity.

Touch of Evil

In the Soviet Union, the role of Santa Claus was usurped by candy fan Joseph Stalin. Uncle Joe loved sweets so much that they were distributed to schoolchildren all across the country on his birthday (celebrated on December 21).

_04:: Fidel Castro: Near-Death by Chocolate

In a country known for its sugar production, the Cuban strongman's well-known fondness for a particular type of chocolate milkshake might very well have led to his demise had the CIA been a little more on top of its game. Among the approximately 600 assassination attempts the CIA is believed to have set in motion against Castro, one infamous failure called for covert agents to sneak poisoned aspirin into El Presidente's daily chocolate shake. And while they succeeded in getting the poison into the beverage, an overeager servant inadvertently foiled the plan by putting the shake in a freezer to keep it cold. Unfortunately, it froze and Cuba's temperamental dictator dictated a new one.

Servings of Swine:
The Worst Pork Barrel Politics Revealed

Sure, when it's served up as a McRib, or on a platter of chops at Grandma's, pork can be downright tasty. But as soon as a politician gets his grubby hands on the stuff, it becomes a little harder to stomach. The following are six of the worst cases of pork barrel politics, served high with a couple dollops of contempt!

_01:: The Pig Book and Oinker Awards

Every year, a pork barrel watchdog group called Citizens Against Government Waste produces the Pig Book, detailing the year's worst pork in Congress. CAGW picks the most outrageous examples from each year to bestow upon them the facetious Oinker Awards. The 2003 Sometimes You Feel Like a Nut Award went to the National Peanut Festival Fairgrounds in Dothan, Alabama, for the $202,500 allocated to them. The 2004 Soaking the Taxpayers Award was given to an Iowa senator for the $50 million he procured for an *indoor* rainforest in Coralville, Iowa. Montana's senator Conrad Burns took home the 2002 Shear Waste Award, as well as $400,000 for the Montana Sheep Institute. And 2001 had two notable winners: the Taxpayers Get Tanked Award, for $648,000 for ornamental fish research; and the Pillager from Pascagoula Award, bestowed upon Trent Lott for the $460 million he got for his state to develop an amphibious assault ship that the Department of Defense didn't ask for or want. Keep up the good work, CAGW.

_02:: Old Pork: Bonus Bill of 1817

The very first example of pork in American politics comes to us from the legendary and cantankerous South Carolina politician John C. Calhoun. In 1817, Johnny C. proposed the Bonus Bill in Congress, by means of which he planned on using the profits from the Second National Bank of the United States to finance the construction of roads and canals. While his stated objectives were to connect the country and aid all regions, critics said that Calhoun intended most of the money to go to the South, thereby strengthening its economic ties to the North and West and opening new markets for its goods (and considering his future cries for nullification of federal laws and secession from the Union, this argument had some pretty strong legs). After all, the North had already built its own good roads and canals, which was one of the main reasons why it was so far ahead of the South economically. But the whole thing is moot anyway: President James Madison vetoed it as unconstitutional.

_03:: Permanent Pork: The War Finance Corporation

In 1918, as the United States harnessed its economy for World War I, businesses in crucial war-related industries were having trouble borrowing money through bond sales. So Congress authorized the War Finance Corporation, setting aside $500 million to be made available for finance production. But when the war ended, the WFC didn't. Oddly enough, it lived on in various guises: first to finance the postwar European economy, then to help struggling farmers during the Depression. But money this big attracts plenty of opportunists, and through the 1930s and '40s chairman Jesse H. Jones from Texas doled out dough to his cronies in countless industries, including railroads, municipalities, insurance companies, and exporters. During World War II, the WFC payouts ballooned to over $50 billion. In some nifty political sleight-of-hand, the WFC was abolished in 1953 and replaced by the Small Business Administration, which is still with us and does basically the same thing. Same pork, different acronym.

_04:: Porkers-Come-Lately

Seems the two most recent additions to the U.S. community of states are making up for lost time at the pork trough. Alaska and Hawaii have traded the number one and two positions for several years in terms of pork spending per capita. In 2001, Alaska received 30 times the national average of pork spending per person; Hawaii got 15 times. And where did all this money go? It funded vital projects such as the pilot training simulator at the University of Alaska ($2,500,000); repairs on an Aleutian Pribilof church in Hawaii ($1,250,000); a parking lot and pedestrian safety access for the whopping 300 residents of Talkeetna, Alaska ($400,000); marijuana eradication in Hawaii ($2,500,000); and the Native Hawaiian culture

and arts program ($742,000). Not bad for two states with combined populations of under two million people.

Touch of Evil

The Armour brand actually evolved from real *pork barrel politics. Taking advantage of artificially high food prices, P. D. Armour sold futures to pork barrels he didn't own, gambling that the Civil War would end in a year, in which case prices would drop dramatically. The gamble paid off and he netted more than $2,000,000, leaving a bunch of disgruntled traders and government officials in the wake.*

_05:: Out of This World Pork: NASA

With a humongous annual budget of around $14 billion, the National Aeronautics and Space Administration has turned into one fantastic place for pork. In 2000 alone, pork projects connected to NASA included $3 million for the Donald Danforth Plant Science Center's Modern Genetics Project "to permit studies that simulate specialized weather conditions, pathogen attacks, and development and characterization on genetically modified plants in controlled-environment chambers"; $15 million for upgrades to the Life Sciences Building at the University of Missouri–Columbia; and $3 million to enhance the University of South Mississippi's research of remotely sensed data for coastal zone management. The total amount of pork that went to NASA-related projects that year: $140.2 million. Three...two...one ...rip-off!

_06:: The Jumpstart Our Business Strength Act: Coming Soon to a Trough Near You

In a strange way, it's almost comforting to know that war, economic uncertainty, and massive budget deficits have not stopped our government from dysfunctioning normally. Almost. In 2004, a pork-packed piece of legislation called the Jumpstart Our Business Strength Act made its way up the Hill. According to CAGW, the bill was a mother lode of windfall tax breaks for all kinds of corporations: $519 million for makers of small aircraft, including Learjet; $310 million for makers of ships; $189 million for Oldsmobile dealerships (umm...*why?*); $92 million for NASCAR (the number-one spectator sport in the country gets a tax cut?); and, most vital of all in time of war, $8 million in tax breaks for makers of bows and arrows.

8
Let There Be Lunch: Myths from Other Cultures about Gods' Strange Eating Habits

Eve gets a lot of bad press for the whole forbidden fruit incident. After all, who among us hasn't been tempted by a nice, shiny apple? But Eve's garden party foul doesn't even compare with these mythological munchers and their appetites for destruction.

_01:: Kronos and the Kids

If you thought your family was dysfunctional, you oughta meet the early Greek gods. Kronos, a Titan, overthrew his father, Uranus, and had him castrated. But Uranus warned Kronos that one of his children would kill him. So, among Uranus' first batch of offspring, he had the one-eyed Cyclops and the hundred-handed Hecatonchires all imprisoned in the underworld. Fine. But then Kronos' sister and wife, Rhea, gave birth to a bunch of gods and goddesses. Panicky, Kronos ate them whole, one by one: Hestia, Hades, Poseidon, Demeter, and Hera. Chomp! But by the sixth, little Zeus, Rhea got wise. She hid the baby and presented Kronos with a stone wrapped in swaddling clothes. He ate the stone, and all was forgotten. That is, until years later when Zeus tricked Pops into upchucking the rest of the family (gods apparently don't digest so well). The new crew then joined forces with the other Olympians to overthrow Daddy and the Titans.

_02:: Zeus and Metis

Zeus had a lot—an awful lot—of sexual conquests. After all, it's good to be the king—especially of the gods. But his first was Metis, goddess of wisdom and knowledge (who says guys don't like girls with brains?). After much pursuit he finally consummated the relationship, resulting in her pregnancy. But leave it to an oracle to spoil the afterglow. A prophecy said that one of Metis's children would overthrow Zeus (surprising that this didn't sound familiar to big Z, isn't it?). So, naturally, he ate Metis. For a while it worked out: Metis gave Zeus wise advice from his belly. But pretty soon, he started to get wicked headaches. So bad, in fact, that he ordered Hephaestus to split his head open with a hammer and wedge (Excedrin wasn't around yet). Out of his split skull emerged Athena, fully grown and armed.

_03:: Demeter

The Greek goddess of grain and the harvest (the Romans called her Ceres, from whence we get "cereal") also bore quite a temper. When a mortal named Erysichthon foolishly tried to cut down her favorite oak tree, she appeared in the form of a priestess asking him to stop. What did our clever mortal do? Threaten her with his ax, of course. Oh, no you *didn't!* Demeter was, in a word, miffed. Because Erysichthon had wanted the wood to build himself a dining hall, Demeter cursed the man with an endless hunger (goddesses are nothing if not ironic). The more he ate, the hungrier he got. He ate his parents, their house, the dirt in the street, and, finally, himself. Yep. Ate himself, just like that.

_04:: Demeter, the Second Course

We've all heard the ironic punishment tale of Tantalus, the guy with the burning thirst and ravenous hunger who's stuck in a pool of cool water with grapes hanging just out of reach for all eternity. So how'd he get there? Turns out he was a son of Zeus, so he felt like he could have the gods over for dinner. To please

them, he chopped up his son Pelops, boiled him to a nice al dente, and served him to the gods. They were less than thrilled, and no one touched the Pelops platter except poor Demeter. Seems she was depressed and distracted because her daughter Persephone had just been whisked off to be the bride of Hades (and we all remember the pomegranate seeds and how *that* turned out). So, the distracted deity ate Pelops's shoulder. The gods, covering for her, restored the boy to life and gave him an ivory shoulder. Not so good for Dad, pretty good for the son. Apparently, Greek chicks dig ivory prostheses.

_05:: Finn and the Magic Salmon

The Greeks aren't the only ones who can come up with gustatory gems. Straight from the Celtic mythology of third-century Ireland comes the Fenian Cycle, tales of a brave group of warriors called the Fianna. The leader, Finn MacCunaill, was known for his wisdom and intelligence. So how'd he get so smart? Simple. He burned himself while cooking fish. OK, let's back up. Finn's mentor, a Druid, told him of the Salmon of Knowledge that swam in the River Boyne. Eat the salmon, know it all. So, the Druid caught the fish, and Finn dutifully set about cooking it. But salmon, as we all know, are fatty, and some of that fat sputtered from the fire and burned Finn's thumb. He licked the grease, and suddenly he was clairvoyant. The story goes that Finn used this knowledge to warn Ireland of the eventual coming of the Vikings. Lotta good it did 'em.

_06:: Set and the Semen

Every mythology needs a real bad guy, and the Egyptians had Set, the god of evil and darkness, nemesis and occasional homosexual lover of Horus, and slayer of Osiris, Horus's papa. Ever seen that Egyptian god with the head of a jackal? Yep, that's Set. To get revenge on Set, Horus and Isis, Horus's mother, hatched a strange plot: Isis made Horus ejaculate into a jar. She then spread the semen onto a piece of lettuce (a popular aphrodisiac for the ancient Egyptians). Set, suspecting nothing, ate the lettuce. In Egyptian belief, this meant that Set was symbolically "pregnant" by Horus, and thereby subservient to him. When the semen eventually "came forth" from Set, he was humiliated before all the gods. The obvious moral: When having lunch with an Egyptian god, skip the salad.

_07:: Karpakeli

This is an obscure one. Karpakeli is the ancestral god of the Pun Magar tribe of Nepal. One story tells of his nine wicked sons' plot to kill him. While gathering honey on a high cliff, Karpakeli was warned by a honey bird of his sons' scheme, so Karpakeli stored most of the honey in a cave, sending only empty combs down to his sons. They soon cut the rope, stranding him on the cliff, to kill him. But the clever Karpakeli was prepared, and he spent many months living off the honey he'd stored. Eventually, though, it ran out, so he started eating the only other food available: himself. Starting with his arms, then his thighs, then most of his own body. Luckily, the gods sent a series of animals to rescue him: a white monkey, a crow, even ants. Finally, the good god was rescued by a pair of vultures named Khakapati.

_08:: Amaterasu, Sword Swallower

As far as food goes, the Japanese mythmakers were pretty happy to get into the act as well. The chief deity in Japanese mythology was Amaterasu, the sun goddess from whom Japan's emperors were purportedly descended (Emperor Hirohito was forced to renounce this claim to divinity after World War II). She had a bit of trouble with her hot-tempered brother Susanowo, the *kami* (god or spirit) of the sea and storms. So, when she heard he was coming to visit her, she prepared for a battle (don't *any* gods get along with their families?). But they reached an understanding, and he offered her his sword. What's a gal to do? Well, Amaterasu promptly broke it into three pieces and ate them. When she exhaled (some sources say she spit them out), she created several more *kami* out of the pieces. After that, raw fish doesn't sound so bad.

Feeding Frenzies:
Pioneers of All-You-Can-Eat

Despite what you may have heard, the concept of all-you-can-eat wasn't invented by the owner of a Chinese restaurant (they just seem to have perfected it).

_01:: Death by...Hetvägg?

By the time Adolf Frederick came to occupy the throne of Sweden in 1751, a long period of monarchy-weakening reforms called the Age of Freedom left him with very little power. But his appetite didn't seem to suffer. In fact, the old Swede died in 1771 at the age of 61 from digestive problems caused by a giant meal (the dinner table being the only place left to him to indulge his power). His final feast? Smoked herring, lobster, caviar, sour cabbage soup, and a heapin' helpin' of a dessert called Hetvägg, a bun filled with marzipan served in a bowl of milk. It's no wonder the hapless monarch went down in history with an unfortunate (but accurate) epithet: "the King Who Ate Himself to Death." Maybe it's not *always* that good to be the king.

_02:: Mardi Gras' Great-Great-Great-Great-Great-Granddad

Just as the pagan Saturnalia was co-opted by Christmas and the Celtic Samhain got translated into All Hallow's Eve/Halloween, the pre-Lent binge of Mardi Gras has its origins in a pagan festival. On March 15, the ancient Romans celebrated the Lupercalia, a festival commemorating the founding of Rome and the suckling of the infants Romulus and Remus in a cave (the Lupercal) on the Palatine Hill.

While the festival had a solemn religious aspect to it—you know, the standard blood and animal sacrifice—the celebration was marked by much drinking, revelry, and general buffoonery. Boys clad in loincloths and smeared with blood would run through the city, as boys tend to do, lashing bystanders with strips of skin from sacrificed goats. After all, the lashings were said to promote fertility and easy childbirth, so young wives were particularly eager to meet the lash. When Rome became Christianized, the Lupercalia was replaced by Carnivale (literally "Good-bye to the Flesh"), the day before the beginning of the solemn season of Lent. In fact, the day before Ash Wednesday saw so much drinking and feasting that the medieval French dubbed it *Mardi gras,* or "Fat Tuesday."

_03:: The Sumo Diet

Like nearly every aspect of sumo life, the famed Japanese wrestlers' diet is based in centuries of tradition. So, what exactly makes up this traditional food? Sumo wrestlers put on their enormous weight—700 pounds and more—mostly by consuming a simple diet of *chankonabe,* a thick boiled stew containing tofu, carrots, cabbages, leeks, potatoes, lotus roots, daikon radishes, shiitake mushrooms, and giant burdock in chicken broth. Some rec-

Scandalicious

FATTY ARBUCKLE CRUSHES LOVER TO DEATH!

Media circuses around celebrity scandals long predate Michael Jackson and Robert Blake. One of the first involved Roscoe "Fatty" Arbuckle, a major star of silent films. Set around a three-day party hosted by Arbuckle at San Francisco's Saint Francis Hotel in 1921, the case involved a young woman named Virginia Rappe who died of peritonitis during the festivities. While Arbuckle claimed that her death was caused by too much alcohol (other sources say she'd recently had one of several abortions, which may have caused the illness), the papers went wild for the scandal. Based largely on the words of serial celebrity blackmailer "Bambina" Maude Delmont, the papers accused Arbuckle of raping Rappe, crushing her with his nearly 300 pounds, and violating her with various foreign objects. Arbuckle became the public's scapegoat for the amorality of Hollywood, and movie houses stopped showing his films. Even though he was eventually acquitted (he was already back in Los Angeles when Rappe died), Arbuckle was blacklisted by the Hays Office, a Hollywood monitoring organization established in the wake of the scandal. Fatty would eventually have to change his name to get work, directing several films under the pseudonym William B. Goodrich. He died of a heart attack in his sleep in 1933, at the age of 46. It was his one-year wedding anniversary.

ipes call for shrimp, noodles, raw eggs, or beer (interesting note: since falling to all fours in a match means a loss, many sumo wrestlers superstitiously avoid eating any four-legged animals. So there's no beef or pork in their chankonabe). Doesn't sound particularly fattening, does it? By itself, it isn't, even with the side of rice. In fact, chankonabe is actually quite healthy, high in both protein and vitamins. But three factors play into the whole weight-gaining aspect of it for sumo wrestlers: (1) They eat a lot of it—an *awful* lot of it; (2) they traditionally skip breakfast, consuming most of their calories at an enormous midday meal, after which (3) they immediately take a

three- or four-hour nap. As most nutritionists will tell you, skipping breakfast and then sleeping immediately after a meal is a guaranteed way to pack on the pounds.

_04:: The Babe's Bad Day at the Plate

Home wasn't the only plate at which George Herman "Babe" Ruth was a dominator. This guy had a big appetite for everything—food, drink, women, you name it. In fact, "the Sultan of Swat's" favorite breakfast was said to include a porterhouse steak, six fried eggs, and potatoes, all washed down with a quart mixture of bourbon whiskey and ginger ale. The

Babe also had a certain fondness for hot dogs, downing between 12 and 18 one day in April 1925. Shortly thereafter, he blacked out on a train and was hospitalized for an intestinal abscess (recent historians have attributed his hospital stay to gonorrhea, not a tummy ache). Disgustingly enough, one of the Babe's partially eaten hot dogs (now black and shriveled and nasty) is still on display at the Baseball Reliquary in Monrovia, California. And although Ruth became pretty hefty in the last few years of his career, the rumor that the Yankees adopted their famous pinstripes to make him look slimmer is false. The pinstripes first appeared in 1912, when the Yanks were still the New York Highlanders.

Touch of Evil

Realizing that all-you-can-eat buffets would attract customers (who would then pay to be entertained in other ways), the El Rancho casino in Las Vegas began to offer a smorgasbord with lobster, shrimp, roast beef, turkey, and more in 1946.

Crazy Diets from Crazy Times

Whether it's avoiding carbs, trans fats, or solid foods, diets generally ask a lot from you in the restraint department. Of course, when we heard about the following three diets, that meant restraining ourselves from laughing.

_01:: Gustave Jaeger: Don't Eat Animals, Wear Them

By 1885, the British critic and playwright George Bernard Shaw had already been practicing vegetarianism for a few years when he came under the influence of Dr. Gustave Jaeger's "sanatory [*sic*] system." The regimen was as much about what to wear as what to eat, and Jaeger rejected plant fibers such as "unhealthful" cotton and linen in favor of animal fibers such as wool. As a result, Shaw gave up using sheets in bed and took to wearing woolen clothing exclusively. In fact, his knitted "stockinette" suit became a personal trademark. Jaeger also allowed clothing made of hair and feathers—preferably unbleached, unprocessed, and free of dyes. Most of his followers came from Victorian reform movements such as the Fellowship of the New Life, which—like Shaw—preached a strict vegetarianism.

_02:: The Reverend Sylvester Graham: Stay Away from the Ketchup!

Graham crackers today are made from bleached white flour, which means, strictly speaking, that they are not graham crackers. Named for the Reverend Sylvester Graham (who coincidentally *was* a cracker), the sweet cupboard staple was part of a 19th-century diet meant to advocate temperance and vegetarianism in order to fend off excessive carnal desires and thus prevent disease. Graham preached that unsifted, coarsely ground wheat flour was healthier than the white stuff. He was right about that, but most people figured Graham for cuckoo. His regimen, aimed at reining in the sex drive, included sleeping on hard mattresses, taking cold showers, exercising, sleeping with the windows open (no matter the weather), and eating whole grains, fruits, and vegetables. Graham also warned that the use of ketchup and mustard led to insanity. Followers of his doctrine lived in special Grahamist boardinghouses and in an experimental commune near Boston.

_03:: Horace Fletcher: The Great Masticator

Also called "the Chew-Chew Man," Horace Fletcher was an American importer and art dealer who in 1890 donned a white jacket and began lecturing and writing about nutrition. His theme: chew. Fletcher advised that nothing should be swallowed unless it could be reduced to liquid first by chewing. Supported by studies that found chewing every morsel 32 times could be beneficial for weight loss (it slowed down the rate of eating, at the very least), Fletcher claimed such adherents as novelist Henry James and industrialist John D. Rockefeller. Health reformer Dr. John Harvey Kellogg was also a devotee of "Fletcherizing" for a while, and even made up a "chewing song" for patients. Many Fletcherizers spit out anything they could not chew to liquid, which eliminated a lot of dietary fiber and led to constipation.

Hail to the Chef: Presidents Who Overindulged

4

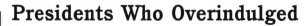

Feeding an appetite for power rarely fills a guy's belly. These four pudgy heads of state were as happy raiding the pantry as they were creating policy.

_01:: Grover Cleveland: The Glass Is Always Half Empty

Large, jovial Grover Cleveland—also known as "Uncle Jumbo"—enjoyed his beer. In 1870 (15 years before he became president), Grover ran for district attorney of Erie County, New York, against Lyman K. Bass. It was a friendly contest. In fact, it was so friendly that Cleveland and his opponent drank and chatted together daily. In the interest of moderation, they agreed to have no more than four glasses of beer per day. But soon they exceeded that and started "borrowing" glasses from the next day and the next until they'd exhausted their ration for the whole campaign—with the election still weeks away. The solution: Each brought his own giant tankard to the tavern, called it a "glass," and went back to the four-a-day ration.

_02:: An Extra-Cuddly Teddy

The standard scoop on Teddy Roosevelt was that he was a scrawny, sickly weakling from New York City who built himself up into a rough, tough cowboy type through vigorous outdoor pursuits. What's seldom mentioned is that Roosevelt went from skinny boy to robust young man to plump (though vigorous) president to obese (though still active) ex-president. While running on the Bull Moose Party ticket in a 1912 attempt to regain the White House, Roosevelt was described as "an eager and valiant trencherman" (it meant he ate a lot). If the main course was roast chicken, TR would consume an entire bird himself, in addition to the rest of the meal. Not to mention the four glasses of whole milk the portly prez routinely threw back with dinner. Photos and films show an aging Roosevelt carrying a decidedly wide load.

_03:: W. H. Taft and His Presidential Privileges

William Howard Taft often dieted because his doctor and his wife told the 290-pound president that he must. But without supervision, Will "the Thrill" didn't just give in to temptation, he sought it. Once while traveling he asked a railroad conductor for a late-night snack. When the conductor said there was no dining car, Taft angrily called for his secretary, Charles D. Norton, who had probably—under instruction from Mrs. Taft—arranged for the diner to be unhooked. Norton reminded the president that his doctor discouraged between-meal eating. Taft would have none of it. He ordered a stocked dining car attached at the next stop and specified that it have filet mignon. "What's the use of being president," he said to Norton, "if you can't have a train with a diner on it?"

_04:: Bill Clinton: With an Assist from Helmut Kohl

President Bill Clinton, who famously frequented McDonald's, was known for eating whatever was put in front of him. He showed a more discriminating, if just as hungry, side in the company of Germany's chancellor Helmut Kohl, though. Kohl was called "Colossus," at least in part because he carried 350 pounds on his 6-foot-4 frame. But, in Kohl, Clinton found a gourmand soul mate. In 1994, Clinton hosted the chancellor at Filomena Ristorante of Georgetown for a lunch at which both consumed mass quantities of ravioli, calamari, and red wine, as well as plenty of antipasto, buttered breadsticks, Tuscan white bean soup, salad, and sweet zabaglione with berries. Each ended the meal by ordering a large piece of chocolate cake to go. Clinton once remarked that he and his German counterpart, though the largest of world leaders, were still too slim to be sumo wrestlers.

Deadly Digestive Problems

On the long list of unpleasant ways to die, it's hard to imagine anything topping "exploding colon." We'll take the stomach flu, heartburn, death by paper cuts even! Just please, please, spare us these fates.

_01:: Farting to Death

Sounds like a third-grade punch line, but maybe it's so funny because it's true. The average person expels about a half liter of gas per day. Put bluntly, that's somewhere between 13 and 17 daily farts. And although any 11-year-old with a matchbook and curiosity knows that gas passed is flammable (since it contains primarily hydrogen and methane), it's not dangerous for the excessively gassy to work around open flames. Once in a great while, though, someone will blow up from gas. The problem usually occurs during colonic surgery, when heat (or a spark) comes into contact with flammable intestinal gasses after inadequate "bowel evacuation." The resulting explosion is sometimes fatal. Anyone who's ever suffered through colon surgery can tell you exactly what "bowel evacuation" entails—you drink a laxative the day before surgery and find yourself in the bathroom with enough

Touch of Evil

The most deadly digestive problem of all may prove to be bovine in nature. Cows emit so much methane in their flatulence that some experts claim it to be a contributing factor to the erosion of the ozone layer.

time to read *Anna Karenina*. Unpleasant, sure, but better than blowing up on the operating table.

_02:: Pica

Pica, an eating disorder in which sufferers feel compelled to eat nonfood items, is usually seen in children. At least 10% of kids enjoy eating dirt or paste or plaster, but adults suffering from pica often develop unusual tastes. Strangely, the same such cravings pop up so often they have their own names. Pagophagia is the compulsive eating of ice; coprophagia describes eating (often animal) feces; coniophagia involves—get this—the pathological consumption of dust from venetian blinds. And pica can be fatal. Too much plaster might lead to fatal lead poisoning, for instance, and consuming clay can lead to a potentially deadly intestinal blockage.

_03:: Roundworms

About 25% of the world's population is infected with roundworms (that's *Ascaris lumbricoides* to the Latin scholars), which is even more disconcerting when you consider that one generally contracts roundworms by swallowing egg-ridden human feces. Once infected, the eggs hatch in the stomach and intestines, then migrate throughout the body.

Although completely disgusting, roundworms are only occasionally deadly—they can cause edema in the lungs; and the female worms, which can grow 18 inches long, sometimes perforate the intestines, leading to peritonitis. But the most terrifying wormy complication involves anesthesia. Because worms find anesthesia irritating, they sometimes migrate up the trachea and nasal passages or down the intestines during surgery. It's been reported, for instance, that one pregnant woman had several of the nematodes worm out of her nose and mouth while she was giving birth.

_04:: Celiac Sprue

Dieters seeking a low-carb lifestyle might do well to seek out celiac sprue, an intestinal ailment that amounts to an allergy to the protein gluten—found in such foods as wheat, barley, and rye. When celiac sufferers ingest the dreaded stuff, the immune system responds by attacking the small intestine, which leads to a sort of intestinal baldness. Villi, hairlike protuberances that line the small intestine, absorb nutrients into the body, but when people with celiac eat gluten, the villi get flattened or otherwise damaged, making proper nourishment impossible. If left undiagnosed, celiac can lead to massive malnutrition, wasting, and even death. But people with celiac can lead perfectly healthy lives provided they forswear gluten. Which means no beer. Which is, frankly, unacceptable.

_05:: Megacolon

A blessedly uncommon but life-threatening disorder, megacolon is characterized by the one-two punch of a massively inflated colon (one), and the accompanying abdominal distension (two). Although generally a complication of bowel diseases like ulcerative colitis and Crohn's disease, megacolon occasionally develops from severe—and we mean *severe*—constipation. One such example is on display at Philadelphia's Mütter Museum, which collects all manner of medical oddities (from John Wilkes Booth's thorax to a tumor removed from President Grover Cleveland's jaw). The crown jewel of the Mütter Museum's collection is a five-foot-long megacolon. Bearing a distinct resemblance to Jabba the Hutt, the monstrosity was removed from a man who, unable to move his bowels, died with 40 pounds of excrement in his gut.

All You Need Is Drugs: Philosophers Who Liked to Get Groovy Thoughts

Philosophy requires precise reasoning and intense concentration on the most complex and intractable problems of human existence. But when your job involves developing elaborate proof about subjects like epistemology (the science of figuring out what we know, and how we can know it, and whether we can really know what we think we can know, and so on), perhaps you can be forgiven for winding down with a bit of illicit pleasure.

_01:: Aldous Huxley and His Rave New World

While no one confuses him with Aristotle, Aldous Huxley *is* considered something of a minor philosopher. Most famous for his tome *Brave New World* (1932), which featured the drug Soma, Huxley became fascinated with Hindu philosophy in the late 1930s, and eventually wrote a book *(The Perennial Philosophy)* and many essays on the subject. By the time 1953 rolled around, Huxley had tried the hallucinogen mescaline, and believed the visionary experiences he'd had reflected a truer world. In fact, Huxley was so enamored with hallucinogens that he dropped acid on his deathbed, passing away on November 22, 1963. For the record, C. S. Lewis, who abstained from drugs, and John F. Kennedy, who took copious amounts of tranquilizers, died on the same day.

_02:: Plotinus and the "Good" Life

Plotinus, the third-century Roman credited with founding Neoplatonism, traveled more extensively than most ancient philosophers. And in those days, the easiest way to see the world was by joining a war. So in 242, Plotinus accompanied Emperor Gordian III in his battles against Persia, where Plotinus likely encountered Persian and Indian philosophies. He also probably encountered opium. Upon his return to Rome, the older, wiser, and definitely groovier Plotinus founded a loosely affiliated school of philosophers who placed great emphasis on union with "the Good," or God. And while it's not clear whether or not he thought it helped him in his search for this union, Plotinus also became a regular opium

Touch of Evil

In 1963, Timothy Leary was fired from his job as a psychology professor at Harvard University due to continued experiments with psychedelic agents.

user. In fact, some scholars have even argued that his opium addiction shaped his high philosophical beliefs.

_03:: Foucault: The Thinking Man's Drinking Man

Being something of a postmodernist, the French philosopher and literary critic Michel Foucault (1926–1984) didn't believe drugs to be intrinsically good or bad, true or false. But he did use them. In addition to drinking heavily, Foucault dabbled in psychedelics and opium, and reportedly grew marijuana plants on the ledge of his Parisian apartment (he also enjoyed S and M, but that's neither here nor there). Luckily, the drugs didn't affect the quality of his intellect—books like *The Order of Things* and *The Archaeology of Knowledge* were the first major rebuttals to existentialism—and Sartre called the latter "the last rampart of the bourgeoisie." Foucault's books are also so exceedingly dense and his definition of "truth" and "knowledge" so nuanced that, frankly, it's difficult to imagine he ever wrote stoned.

Booze Is to Comedy as Pen Is to Literature: Funny Lushes

There's nothing funny about alcoholism. But for whatever reason, there's often something very funny about alcoholics. We can trace the phenomenon back at least 23 centuries, to the ancient Greek comic playwright Aristophanes, who is recorded as having said, "Quickly, bring me a beaker of wine so that I may wet my brain and say something clever." When full-blown alcoholism took hold of the comedians below, it was usually with tragic consequences—but until then, their wet brains made some great jokes.

_01:: W. C. Fields (1880–1946)

Of all the alcoholic comedians, the bulbous-nosed W. C. Fields (né William Claude Dukenfield) was by far the least embarrassed by his indulgence. Fields started his career as a juggler but found fame with his impeccable wit and comic timing, first on Broadway and then in the movies. Although also noted for his dislike of children ("Any man who hates children and dogs can't be all bad") and his ostentatious immorality (he claimed to religiously study the Bible—in search of loopholes), Fields is probably best known for his drinking. At his peak, Fields downed two *quarts* of gin daily. "I like to keep a bottle of stimulant handy in case I see a snake, which I also keep handy," he once remarked. Fields died on his least favorite of days—Christmas—in 1946.

_02:: Lenny Bruce (1925–1966)

Among his many contributions to American culture, we ought not forget that it was Lenny Bruce who coined the term "T and A." Who knows what other witty obscenities he might have added to the vernacular were it not for his prodigious drinking and drug abuse. Attacking everyone from JFK to Dear Abby, Bruce brought social commentary into stand-up (although it didn't always pay well…he once dressed up as a priest and "solicited money for lepers" to supplement his income). After repeated arrests for obscenity and worsening addiction, though, Bruce lost his sense of humor. He took to reading transcripts of his trials onstage, and on those rare occasions when he'd tell a joke, he'd often forget it midsentence. Sadly, Bruce passed away, bankrupt and alone, of a heroin overdose in 1966.

_03:: Bill Hicks (1961–1994)

Considered by many to be the Lenny Bruce of a new generation, Bill Hicks's innovative, ranting stand-up style inspired everyone from Sam Kinison (also an alcoholic, and also dead) to Denis Leary. Raised in Georgia, Hicks abandoned his conservative Baptist upbringing and quickly garnered critical acclaim on the comedy circuit. But his rages, both onstage and off, made him quite a misanthrope throughout much of the 1980s—heavily intoxicated, he once said Hitler "had the right idea, but was an underachiever." Unlike Lenny Bruce, though, Hicks managed to sober up. He never drank after 1988, making his 1994 death from pancreatic cancer all the more tragic.

_04:: Buster Keaton (1895–1966)

Buster Keaton, who was discovered by Fatty Arbuckle (and stood by him throughout his trials), also drank to excess. An innovative filmmaker, Keaton's masterpiece, *The General,* mixed his trademark slapstick comedy with his obsessive fascination with trains. But when Keaton's film company was bought in 1928, he soured on moviemaking, and his alcoholism worsened. In fact, by 1934 he was straitjacketed and placed in a sanitarium. Some claim that Keaton, whose godfather was none other than Harry Houdini, escaped the jacket using his godfather's tricks and then left the sanitarium to find some booze. Maybe so, but Buster eventually sobered up, and continued to be productive, if less famous. He starred, for instance, in playwright Samuel Beckett's only movie, cleverly titled *Film.* In the end, though, liquor didn't beat Buster Keaton; smoking did. He died of lung cancer in 1966.

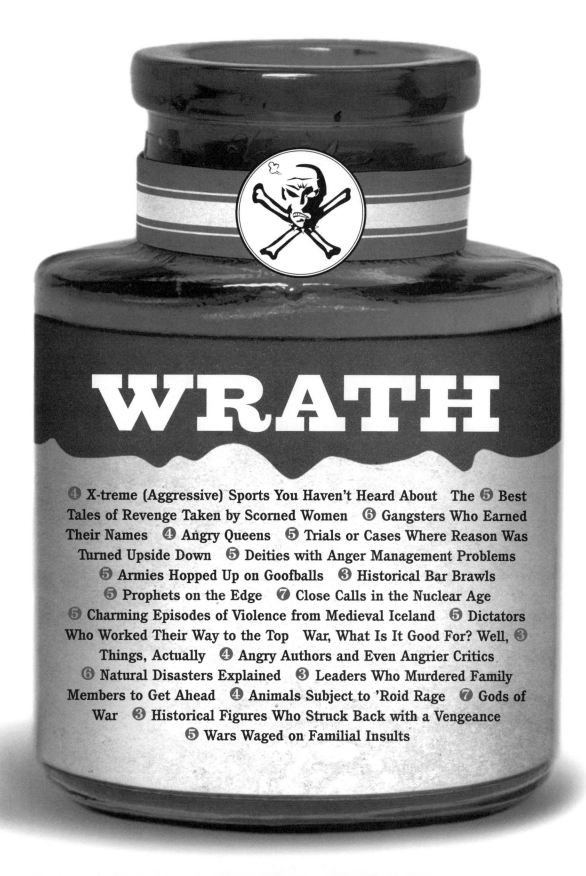

WRATH

④ X-treme (Aggressive) Sports You Haven't Heard About   The ⑤ Best Tales of Revenge Taken by Scorned Women   ⑥ Gangsters Who Earned Their Names   ④ Angry Queens   ⑤ Trials or Cases Where Reason Was Turned Upside Down   ⑤ Deities with Anger Management Problems   ⑤ Armies Hopped Up on Goofballs   ③ Historical Bar Brawls   ⑤ Prophets on the Edge   ⑦ Close Calls in the Nuclear Age   ⑤ Charming Episodes of Violence from Medieval Iceland   ⑤ Dictators Who Worked Their Way to the Top   War, What Is It Good For? Well, ③ Things, Actually   ④ Angry Authors and Even Angrier Critics   ⑥ Natural Disasters Explained   ③ Leaders Who Murdered Family Members to Get Ahead   ④ Animals Subject to 'Roid Rage   ⑦ Gods of War   ③ Historical Figures Who Struck Back with a Vengeance   ⑤ Wars Waged on Familial Insults

Working It Out in Court: X-treme (Aggressive) Sports You Haven't Heard About

Ah, sportsmanship. It summons up images of competition, camaraderie, broken bones, disembowelment, and brutal, disfiguring death. No wonder players have always had fans to cheer them on.

_01:: Dead Goat Polo

The modern game of polo, favorite pastime of English aristocrats and snobbish upper-class wannabes, is usually played with a small ball about the size of a billiard ball, and almost never with a human head or a dead goat. But that's how the sport of kings began thousands of years ago under a different name—"bughazi." In fact, bughazi wasn't so much a leisure activity as military training for Persian cavalry, and it was possibly adopted from tribesmen in what is now modern-day Pakistan or Afghanistan. Aside from the dead goat factor, there were also other differences in play. Instead of four players on a side, for instance, the ancient version involved armies of men—literally—with hundreds or even thousands of players on each side. In fact, it's believed that the first tournament was won by Turkish tribesmen playing against the Persians in 600 BCE. And although the game was often played with animal heads, the Mongol conqueror Genghis Khan made a popular change, instituting the practice of decapitating military opponents and making a game ball of their noggins, still in their helmets.

_02:: Aztec Paddleball

"Ullamalitzli," a ceremonial ball game played by the Aztecs a few hundred years before the European discovery of America, called for players on two teams to don large stone belts or hip paddles. These paddles were used to bounce a small rubber ball back and forth down a narrow court with inclined stone walls. The players used each others' bodies and the walls as they attempted to maneuver the ball into a small stone ring high above mid-court. The game ended when either side scored a goal. Amazingly enough, the game actually enjoyed long popularity among the native peoples of Mexico and Central America before the Aztecs played it, including the Maya some thousands of years earlier. Of course, the stakes were a little greater when the Aztecs came to play. In their version of the sport, at the end of the game one of the captains was sacrificed to the gods, giving even more meaning to the phrase "sore loser."

_03:: X-treme Cricket

As with many aspects of their culture, it's unclear exactly what kinds of games the Vikings played, but one thing is certain—their games were incredibly brutal and violent, since they were considered training for personal combat. From vague descriptions in Icelandic "sagas"—histories of the Vikings that were passed down orally for hundreds of years before finally being transcribed in the 1200s—one ball game sounds a bit like an early and very violent version of cricket. The main difference being that most contemporary cricket players can expect to survive to the end of the game. Vikings, on the other hand, weren't always so lucky. "Egil and Thord played against Skallagrim, who grew tired and they came off better. But that evening after sunset, Egil and Thord began losing. Skallagrim was filled with such strength that he seized Thord and dashed him to the ground so fiercely that he was crushed by the blow and died on the spot."

_04:: Cheese Rolling

Though it's without a doubt one of the most absurd sports on record, the annual cheese-rolling contest at Cooper's Hill in Gloucestershire, England, is also incredibly dangerous. Which is not surprising when you consider how the sport is played: first, a master of ceremonies gives the countdown—"One to be ready, two to be steady, three to prepare, four to be off"—and then up to 20 contestants chase a seven-pound circular block of cheese down a steep, bumpy hillside, trying to catch it before it gets to the bottom 300 yards below. Four games are played over the course of one day, including one for women. Video footage of past events shows contestants breaking bones and splitting heads open, in addition to spectators suffering frequent injuries as contestants lose their footing and hurl themselves into the crowds. No one is quite sure how cheese-rolling started, though speculations include ancient pagan fertility rituals or harvest festivals.

Touch of Evil

Way back in 1984, a Japanese show called Za Gaman *("Endurance") broke open the whole* Fear Factor *TV genre by rewarding contestants who could withstand the most punishment. Physical and mental tortures included events with hot coals, snakes, cacti, and a wide range of scary implements.*

Served Cold: The Best Tales of Revenge Taken by Scorned Women

Who shot J. R.? A scorned woman. Who gave Mr. Bobbitt a belated bris? A scorned woman. Who bested Buttafuoco? You guessed it. Those guys could have picked up a thing or two from these poor saps, who quickly learned it's *never* a good idea to upset a lady.

_01:: "Mrs. Jack Johnson"

Black heavyweight boxing champion Jack Johnson was known for two things: (1) his conquests in the ring and (2) his conquests of the fairer sex. One of his favorites of the latter was Belle Schreiber, a prostitute at Chicago's glitzy Everleigh brothel. And though the Everleigh was for whites only, Johnson knew how to pull a few strings. In truth, Belle was only one of five white Everleigh girls Johnson saw, but when he married not one but *two* white women, Belle was crushed. Her high-class career ruined by her widely publicized affair with Johnson, Schreiber was broke and strung out on absinthe and drugs. Agreeing to testify for the government in their prosecution of Johnson for violating the 1910 Mann Act (which outlawed taking a woman across state lines for the "purpose of prostitution or debauchery") Belle's testimony got him a year in prison and seven years of exile in Canada. She also got her way: The stint put an end to Johnson, ruining his stellar boxing career.

_02:: Boudicca, One Badass British Babe

In the year 60 CE, the Romans were busy bringing Britain under their heel. Since anyone who resisted was crushed, it's no wonder that Boudicca, queen of the Iceni tribe in southeast Britain, decided to cooperate and offered to share her realm with Roman emperor Nero. Instead, Nero had a governor declare the region a slave province, and took Boudicca into custody (did Nero ever do *anything* right?). She was then flogged publicly while her two daughters were raped by Roman soldiers. Not a particularly clever move. In response, Boudicca raised an army, marched on the Roman city of Colchester, and burned it with thousands of Roman colonists trapped inside. Her army grew until it became unwieldy, and was eventually defeated by a disciplined Roman army. Defiant to the end, Boudicca killed herself on the battlefield rather than surrender.

Profiles in Carnage

VLAD THE IMPALER (1431-1476)

This guy was pretty much as bad as it gets. Most famous, of course, was his penchant for having people impaled—skewered alive through the anus or vagina on giant wooden spikes, to be slowly dragged down by their own weight. In fact, he liked the practice so much he once impaled 30,000 people *at one time,* for violations of some trade law or other (those of higher social standing got longer spikes). All told, good old Vlad is said to have impaled hundreds of *thousands* of people. And while his nickname Vlad the Impaler or, in Romanian, Vlad Tepes ("Vlad the Spike") only came about after death, his behavior certainly could have earned him lots of other colorful monikers.

Vlad the Daddy's Boy: As a boy, Vlad's father, Vlad Dracul ("Vlad the Dragon"), traded him to the Turks as a peace offering. That obviously tweaked the kid a bit. Upon his return, Vlad (called Dracula, or "the Little Dragon") invited his father's murderers, the boyars (Romanian nobility) to an Easter dinner. He arrested them all, sending the healthy ones into slavery to build him a palace (which many of them did naked). The rest he had impaled.

Vlad the Utopian: As ruler of Wallachia, Vlad wanted his realm to be a model of order and productivity and tried several innovative tactics to achieve this. He once had all the poor and sick invited to a great banquet. Like a good host, he fed 'em, got 'em drunk, then burned the hall with them all inside. The result: no more poor and sick people. To demonstrate his kingdom's absence of crime, he placed a golden chalice in the middle of a busy square in Tirgoviste and left it overnight. Not surprisingly, no one touched it, knowing what the penalty for thievery was under Vlad's rule (hint: it probably involved a tall spike).

Vlad the Literalist: When Turkish ambassadors said their custom prevented them from removing their hats in his presence, he had their hats *nailed to their heads.*

Vlad the Renaissance Man and Dietary Innovator: Impaling wasn't Vlad's only pastime. He also enjoyed having people physically disfigured, skinned, dismembered, boiled, eviscerated, or blinded while he watched, and frequently while he ate. His supposed habit of drinking his victims' blood and eating their flesh led to the Dracula vampire stories we all know so well. If you happened to be a guest at one of his impaling dinners and you got queasy or expressed disgust, guess what—you got impaled.

_03:: Perfect for the Part of Tyrant: Lady Mao

Before the Communists took power under Mao Zedong, China had a thriving film industry centered in Shanghai. There, as in Hollywood, thousands of young actresses flocked to the city hoping to become stars. One did become a star, but not in the way she'd originally intended. Her stage name was Lan Ping ("Blue Apple"), and as an actress she never got the big roles. Frustrated by her career and increasingly resentful of the system, Ms. Apple fell in love with and married a young revolutionary named Mao. Of course, her demeanor was to change quickly. As Lady Mao, she became the head of the notorious Gang of Four, who presided over their own purge of "unacceptable" elements. This reign of terror, ironically called the Cultural Revolution, is one of the most terrifying and chaotic periods in China's history, where freedom of thought and diverse opinions were effectively outlawed. As a former actress, Lady Mao put herself in charge of the film industry, and banned films that she felt did not exemplify good Communist values— and any film directed by someone who'd passed her over. Many were executed for their so-called crimes, and her ruthlessness earned her a nickname: "the White-Boned Demon."

_04:: Rhymes with "Odious"

Salome gets a lot of misdirected criticism for the death of John the Baptist, but the real villain of the story was her mother, Herodias. The Roman wife of Herod Philip, Herodias had come to Palestine with her beautiful daughter, Salome, and married her husband's brother, Herod Antipas. John the Baptist looked none too kindly on this royal scandal and made no secret of his disdain for the arrangement. In an effort to appease his new wife's anger, Herod reluctantly had John imprisoned. You probably know the rest: Herod threw himself a birthday bash, and Salome danced the oh-so-sexy Dance of the Seven Veils. Delighted, drunk, and probably more than a little lecherous, Herod granted her anything she desired. When she asked her mom what she should ask for, Herodias wasted no time in punishing her least favorite scandalmonger, the poor, locust-eating, camel-hair-wearing John the Baptist. She instructed Salome to ask for John's head on a platter, and Herod reluctantly complied. Even worse, in the historian St. Bede's version of the story, Herodias stabbed poor John's tongue repeatedly with a dagger.

_05:: Cochiti Caught Cheatin'

The Cochiti tribe are one of the native Pueblo peoples of New Mexico. Their colorful folklore and mythology includes the tale of a woman who suspected her husband of having an affair with her younger sister. One day, while the husband and younger sister were out on a rabbit hunt together, the wife looked into a bowl of clear water and saw an image of her husband and sister, umm, "hunting rabbits" under a cedar tree. Repeatedly. She began to cry, sat in the middle of a basket, and sang to the spirits to be turned into a snake. When the two lovers returned, she bit them both, killing them. She then appealed to the tribe's medicine men to be taken somewhere to live in peace. They took her to Gaskunkutcinako ("the Girl's Cave"). This is how the Cochiti explain the tearlike marks on a certain species of snake. And why rabbit hunting is not more popular.

Killing Is My Hobby:
Gangsters Who Earned Their Names

What's in a name? And would a thug by any other moniker still be as dangerous? We're guessing a definite "yes."

_01:: Vincent "Mad Dog" Coll (1908–1932)

His first nickname, "the Mick," was relatively harmless, since he hailed from Ireland and all. But his second one—it proved to be a keeper. The criminal with an ominous moniker, and a rep to boot, Mad Dog Coll was a top mob enforcer for New York bootlegger Dutch Schultz. And among his many talents, the versatile Coll also specialized in kidnapping and extortion. In fact, he had no qualms about torturing his victims. After falling out with Schultz, Coll touched off a gang war in which at least 20 people were killed. One was a five-year-old boy caught in a crossfire. Coll was charged with the shooting, and though he was acquitted, his days on the street were numbered. Mob bosses put a price on Coll's head, and on February 8, 1932, he was shot more than a dozen times while placing a call in a telephone booth. The Mad Dog had had his day.

_02:: Lester "Baby Face Nelson" Gillis (1908–1934)

He wanted to be called "Big George," but at 5 feet 4 inches and with the visage of a choir-boy, Lester Gillis was stuck with "Baby Face." No matter. Starting as a pickpocket, Lester put an even better face on things by graduating to enforcer (for Al Capone), bank robber, and psychopathic killer, sometimes shooting people for no reason midheist. By 1934, Baby Face was the FBI's Public Enemy No. 1. But on November 27 of that year, he went out with a bang. A lot of bangs, actually. In a gun battle with two FBI agents, Nelson killed both Feds, but not before they put 17 slugs in him. Amazingly, Nelson walked back to his getaway car and escaped. Of course, the 17 shots ended up doing the trick. Lester's body was found in a ditch the next day.

_03:: Frank "the Dasher" Abbandando (1910–1942)

Abbandando was one killer who was fast on his feet. A hit man for the New York mob's Murder, Inc., an organization of contract killers, Abbandando may have killed as many as 50 people. In one case, he walked up to a guy and pulled the trigger only to have the gun misfire. With his armed victim in pursuit, Frank "the Dasher" ran so fast around the block that he came up behind his quarry and coolly shot him in the back. Hence his nickname. But even Abbandando couldn't outrun a stool pigeon inside Murder, Inc. Convicted of a single murder, the speedy criminal was awarded a speedy trial, followed by a speedy execution via electric chair.

Touch of Evil

Al Capone was impressed with a story about his new trigger man, Tony Accardo, who took a liking to going to town on his rivals with a baseball bat. "That kid's a real Joe Batters," Capone said approvingly, and Accardo lived up to the moniker.

_04:: Albert "Lord High Executioner" Anastasia (1903–1957)

Also dubbed "the Mad Hatter" for his love of fancy fedoras, the dapper "Lord High Executioner," as his name suggests, was not a man to be messed with. In the early 1920s, Anastasia was sentenced to death for killing a fellow longshoreman. But he was granted a retrial and the conviction was reversed when four of the witnesses "disappeared." And that was just at the start of his career. After helping to kill crime boss Joe Masseria, Anastasia was made head of Murder, Inc. by new boss Lucky Luciano, and was dubbed the mob's "Lord High Executioner" by the press. And while the name stuck, his position didn't, as Anastasia eventually fell out with the other bosses. On October 25, 1957, Anastasia was shot six times while getting a haircut. As one New York paper put it the next day: "He Died in the Chair After All."

_05:: Tony "the Ant" Spilotro (1938–1986)

For the 15 years after he first hit Las Vegas in 1971 to the day he died, the mob's chief Vegas enforcer, Tony Spilotro, never spent a day in jail. Not bad for a guy who was implicated in at least 24 murders. In one case, he was even said to have squeezed a victim's head in a vise until his eyes popped out. Ugh. As for "the Ant" bit, though, li'l Tony hated the nickname, which was a reference to his diminutive stature (he was 5'5"). What he didn't hate, however, was the limelight, and it proved to be his undoing. Tony's bosses in Chicago figured he was getting a little too much press, so they came up with a quick remedy: Tony and his brother were beaten up, then buried alive in an Indiana cornfield. As for the slick lawyer who kept the Ant out of jail all that time? His name was Oscar Goodman, and he was elected Vegas's mayor in 1999, then reelected in 2003.

_06:: Aladena "Jimmy the Weasel" Fratianno (1914–1993)

"When the boss tells you to do something," Fratianno told a reporter in 1987, "you do it. You don't do it, they kill you." That's how he explained taking part in 11 murders. Of course, it didn't explain why he became a government witness in 1977 after 32 years in the mob. Fratianno, who got his nickname after speedily fleeing a crime scene as a kid, explained that he began ratting on his colleagues because they had a contract on his life. Fratianno spent 10 years in the Federal Witness Protection Program before being kicked out because he was costing taxpayers too much. Amazingly, he died peacefully in his sleep at the age of 89. Not bad for a weasel.

Hell Hath No Fury:
Angry Queens

4

Whether they were picking fights with the Arabs or torching all of the nation's heretics at the stake, these royal highnesses were definitely capable of a little rage, and more than a few people felt the burn.

_01:: Nitocris (2200 BCE)

OK, so Nitocris didn't exactly leave an archaeological record, but as far as the story goes, she was brave, beautiful, and married to her brother (which was common among Egyptian royalty). At some point, a mob killed her sib/hubby and put her on the throne, all of which made Nitocris the first woman known to rule Egypt. Her response wasn't exactly sweet, though. According to the Greek historian Herodotus, after a few years in charge, Nitocris built a big underground chamber, and then invited her brother-husband's slayers to a banquet. But just as they were settling in, Nitocris had the chamber flooded, to kill all of them. After the murders, she didn't exactly celebrate. Her life's work having been done, Nitocris then killed herself by jumping into a room full of hot ashes. At least her revenge was inspirational, though. In 1928, a 17-year-old kid had his first story published, in *Weird Tales* magazine. The story was called "The Vengeance of Nitocris." The kid was eventually called Tennessee Williams.

_02:: Dihya al-Kahina (ca. 694 CE)

The Berbers of North Africa were religiously a mixed lot in the last part of the seventh century: pagans, Christians, and Jews. But not Muslims. So when Arabs began pushing into the area with a convert-or-die message, the Berbers pushed back. Their leader was a tough, smart Jew said by some to be a prophetess. Keep the emphasis on tough. Al-Kahina took no mercy on the Arabs, and forced them to retreat almost out of Africa. Convinced they wouldn't come back if there were no riches to take, al-Kahina then mounted a scorched-earth campaign that decimated the region's settled areas. Irrespective of her efforts, the Arabs decided to return anyway, and al-Kahina's army was soundly defeated. It's unclear whether she died in battle or was captured and executed. Either way, legend claims she was 127 years of age when she died, which might be just a tad old to still be on the warpath.

_03:: Mary I (1516–1558)

Mary I had it pretty tough for much of her life, especially for a princess. Her dad, Henry VIII, had married her uncle's widow, which made her mom, Catherine of Aragon, her aunt, sort of. But never mind that. The important thing is that Hal divorced Catherine only to claim that it made Mary a bastard. Despite their religious differences (Henry being a Protestant and Mary an ardent Catholic), however, dad and daughter managed to reconcile. That is, until a crown was placed upon her head. When Mary became queen in 1553, she quickly decided there wasn't room for two religions in England. She was also quick to act on said belief. During her reign, about 300 people were burned at the stake for heresy, earning her a place in history as "Bloody Mary." Shortly after a disastrous war with France, she died alone, having been abandoned by her husband and being childless. Poor bastard.

Touch of Evil

Elizabeth I had known and loved Robert Devereux, the second Earl of Essex, since he was a child. And while she had no choice but to put him to death in 1601 after he had taken part in an uprising against her, the event triggered a bitter depression from which she never recovered.

_04:: Queen Isabella Offs Her Fella

Edward II was, surprise, the son of King Edward I of England. And, not to put too fine a point on it, the Deuce liked boys—particularly a French knight named Piers Gaveston. Although married to Isabella, daughter of the French king, Edward spent most of his time hunting and cavorting with Piers, showering him with gifts and, occasionally, playing some "hide the scepter." But Isabella didn't take kindly to being ignored. Taking a lover of her own, Roger de Mortimer, Izzy decided to oust Edward and proclaim her son the king. She and Mortimer imprisoned Edward II until, in 1327, they decided it would be better to just get rid of him. The method of execution was unbelievably gruesome. Edward was wedged between two tables. Then a hunting horn was inserted into his, ahem, royal exit door. *Then* a red-hot poker was shoved through the horn, cauterizing poor Ed's intestines and killing him. While this method was partly chosen as punishment for Edward's homosexuality, the more practical (and horrifically devious) reason was that it would leave no marks on Edward's body, so Isabella could claim he died of natural causes.

Good Witch Hunting: Trials or Cases Where Reason Was Turned Upside Down

Sometimes Lady Justice isn't blind, she's just massively embarrassed. The following are five cases where the light of truth could have used some more wattage.

_01:: Autun v. the Rats

When the French province of Autun's barley began disappearing in 1521, the local rats were charged with stealing. When they failed to answer a summons (yes, really!), their appointed lawyer, Bartholomew Chassenee, argued that a single summons was invalid because the rats lived in different villages. New summonses were issued. This time Chassenee argued some of his clients were aged and infirm and needed more time. After that, he argued the rats were afraid to come to court because of all the cats along the way. When villagers refused to obey a court order to lock up their cats, charges against the rodents were dismissed. Chassenee later became France's leading jurist. The dirty rats presumably returned to lives of crime.

_02:: Making a Monkey of the Prosecutor

It was a simple case. In 1925, a Dayton, Tennessee, teacher had taught Darwin's theory of evolution in defiance of a new state law. But the charges quickly became international news when Clarence Darrow, the era's most famous liberal lawyer, took up teacher John Scopes's defense. The case only got more intriguing when William Jennings Bryan, the three-time

Democratic presidential candidate, joined the prosecution. During the defense's case, Darrow stunned the courtroom and a national radio audience by calling Bryan to the stand. For two hours, the two dueled over Bryan's literal interpretation of the Bible. It was immensely entertaining, but had almost nothing to do with the case. Scopes was found guilty and fined $100. Bryan died a few days after the trial. And the state's ban on teaching evolution was reversed—in 1967.

Touch of Evil

In 1982, laid-off Detroit autoworker Ronald Ebens literally beat a Chinese-American man to death after mistaking him for Japanese and blaming him for the loss of jobs stateside. In the judicial farce that followed, Ebens pleaded guilty to manslaughter and received three years' probation.

_03:: The Scottsboro Boys

There were 11 of them: nine black male teenagers and two white women, all traveling in a freight car through Alabama in 1931. When they hit the town of Scottsboro, though, all 11

Scandalicious

IROQUOIS WARFARE SPURS LACROSSE GAME!

Think lacrosse is a game for high schoolers in pleated skirts? Despite the sport's growing popularity around the world, the history of lacrosse isn't generally known. Originally dubbed *Gatciihkwae*, or "Little Brother of War," lacrosse began as training for young men from tribes in the Iroquois federation of what is now upstate New York, preparing them for hunting and combat. The equipment resembled that used in the modern game—small baskets attached to the ends of sticks, which were used to catch and volley a small round stone. The game itself, however, has changed pretty drastically. "Little Brother of War" exhibitions lasted for two or even three days on a "field" that ranged from 500 yards to a few miles in length, and involved up to 1,000 players. Needless to say, the game was incredibly violent (no sideline medics or oxygen tanks), and extreme injury or even death was considered just a part of the play.

were arrested for vagrancy—and the two women quickly cried rape. Defense attorneys were given 25 minutes to prepare their case. In the kangaroo court proceedings that followed, all nine boys were quickly convicted by an all-white jury, and eight were sentenced to death. The U.S. Communist Party hired attorney Samuel Leibowitz for the boys, and he convinced the U.S. Supreme Court to overturn the convictions. The nine were retried—and reconvicted, despite the confession of one of the victims that the rapes never happened. Then, a third trial was ordered. This time, four were acquitted. Of the other five, one escaped and the other four were eventually paroled. The whole thing took almost 20 years.

_04:: The Twinkie Defense

There wasn't much question it was Dan White who climbed through a window at San Francisco City Hall in 1978 and methodically shot to death Mayor George Moscone and Supervisor Harvey Milk, one of the nation's most prominent gay politicians. So lawyers for White, who was an ex-cop and county supervisor, relied on a "diminished capacity" defense. They argued White was too depressed to commit premeditated murder. As proof, they briefly mentioned White's recent consumption of sugary snack foods. Oddly enough, the defense worked, and White was convicted of manslaughter instead of murder. The verdict, however, triggered a night of rioting in the city's gay community. White served five years in prison and then killed himself a few months after his release. In 1982, California voters abolished diminished capacity as a legal defense.

_05:: "Can't We All Just Get Along?"

On March 3, 1991, a 25-year-old black man named Rodney King was stopped by Los Angeles police for reckless driving. While a passerby videotaped the affair, several cops began viciously beating King, and four were charged with assault. In a controversial move, the trial was shifted from L.A. to the suburban community of Simi Valley, where a jury of 10 whites, an Asian American, and a Latino acquitted the police, despite the videotaped evidence. And while the ruling made no sense, what happened next was unimaginable. The verdict triggered one of the worst riots in U.S. history, with more than 50 people killed, 4,000 injured, and $1 billion in property damage done. The violence was so great that it spurred King to make his famous query: "Can't we all just get along?" The following year, two of the cops were convicted in federal court of violating King's civil rights. The other two were again acquitted.

My God's More Furious Than Yours:
Deities with Anger Management Problems

There are more than a few deities from world mythology that had serious issues reining in their powerful emotions—and with omnipotence to match, the results were often devastating, as well as really entertaining.

_01:: Artemis:
The Angry Bathing God

The ultimate definition of a woman scorned, Artemis, the Greek goddess of the hunt, of nature, and of chastity, had a temper notorious even by the standards of her fellow anger-prone Olympians. The fact that she killed her follower Maera and changed another friend, Callisto, into a bear was the least of it (in both cases, by the way, the hapless ladies had committed the "crime" of losing their virginity). Along with her brother Apollo, Artemis slaughtered the children of the Theban queen Niobe, for no more than insulting their mother. On two separate occasions young men had the misfortune to stumble upon Artemis while she bathed naked in the forest; one was turned into a stag and promptly killed by his own hounds, while the other got off easy (only being turned into a woman). Artemis even killed a girl named Chione for the sin of being too beautiful—which became more of a sin when the girl's beauty was said to rival the goddess's.

_02:: Kali: The Badly Dressed God

A Hindu fertility goddess, Kali is the female aspect of divine energy and the consort of Shiva, the Destroyer. As the slayer of evil spirits and the somewhat unpredictable mother of all life, she also moonlights as the goddess of death. Not a bad gig, except the uniform's a little scary. To show how many evil spirits she's slain, Kali's usually depicted wearing a necklace of human skulls and a girdle of severed arms, children's corpses as earrings, and cobras as bracelets. The outfit is pulled together, however, by her ferocious grimace and the blood smeared on her face. And in her eight arms she holds weapons or the severed head of a demon, representing both her creative and her destructive power. Some followers honored her with animal sacrifices, though a few even took things to the next level. One India-wide sect, the Thuggee, kidnapped and murdered humans as sacrifices to "the Dark Mother" until they were wiped out by British colonial authorities in the 1800s.

_03:: Huitzilopchtli: The Needy (in a Human Sacrificial Way) God

Huitzilopchtli, the Aztec god of the sun and war, was worshiped with rites so horrific that they probably couldn't be shown in the most demented of horror movies today. As far as the mythology goes, he's been causing a violent ruckus since birth. Right after he was born, Huitzilopchtli killed his own sister, Coyolxauhqui, and hung her head in the sky as the moon. He then killed thousands of his other siblings and placed them in the sky as the stars and planets. Not easily appeased, Huitzilopchtli, like virtually all Aztec deities, demanded constant human sacrifice as his price for not destroying the world. And boy did he get 'em! Every day, people were slaughtered in his temples and their hearts offered to the sun. Of course, during festivals, you could count on Huitzilopchtli's wrath to make sure that thousands of people were sacrificed at a time.

_04:: Thor: The God of Hammer Time

The Norse god of thunder and protector of the common man, Thor wielded a war hammer so

heavy that only he could use it. In fact, the weapon was so unwieldy that he was known from time to time to fly off the handle (no pun intended). Of course, that wasn't his only unusual gimmick. Like any god who commands respect, Thor enjoyed rolling around town in a pimped-out chariot drawn by—what else?—magic goats. And as if that doesn't sound tough enough, his ride also was equipped to scorch the earth wherever it went. But back to his wrath; nothing could get on Thor's nerves like Loki, the divine trickster. And eventually, it was Thor's anger that became the driving force behind Loki's torturous imprisonment, strapped down to a rock under a mountain with venom dripping into his face. Not that the rascal didn't deserve it. You can't, after all, just go around stealing the hair off Thor's wife's head and expect not to have to pay. Aside from cruelty to Loki, though, Thor's anger also emerged when he treated a group of dwarves rather roughly for making advances on the goddess Freya. But then again, Thor was generally on the hunt for a good fight. What more can you expect from a god whose favorite pastime is killing giants and monsters?

_05:: Balor: The Never-Look-Him-in-the-Eye God

Balor of the Evil Eye, as he was called, was the Celtic god of the underworld and king of the Fomorians, a race of giants whom myth assigned to the Emerald Isle. As the story goes, Balor's mere gaze was enough to kill anyone it fell on (though, he normally kept his eye closed). That, of course, didn't keep him from doing plenty of wrong. Among his more nefarious doings was locking up his daughter Ethlinn in a vain attempt to keep her from having her child, a prophesied savior. (Her son, Lugh, eventually became god of the sun and killed Balor by throwing a spear into his eye.) Balor was also pretty fond of picking wars in order to use his evil eye. In fact, in one of them, Balor was thrilled to put an end to King Nuada, the Celtic sea god, using just his fearsome gaze.

Take Two of These and Maul Me in the Morning: Armies Hopped Up on Goofballs

5

The disinhibiting and pain-numbing effects of drugs make them perfect for turning people into killing machines. In fact, criminals on PCP have been reported to withstand multiple shocks with Taser guns, pepper spray, and Mace, and even direct gunshot wounds to the chest, without slowing down. It's no wonder that so many generals have relied on drugs to bring out the so-called best in unwitting soldiers.

_01:: Thai and Burmese Bandit Armies

"The Golden Triangle"—an area straddling Thailand, Laos, and Myanmar, where poppy plants grow particularly well—has long been a center of the international drug trade, and for centuries national armies, revolutionaries, and criminal gangs have waged war for control of the income it generates. Recently, however, bandits and rebels from all three countries have begun recruiting children, feeding them opium, hashish, amphetamines, and tranquilizers to give them courage, then sending them out on "human wave" attacks. The disturbing phenomenon leaves a huge proportion of the children dead. One adult soldier from Burma who had to fight these poor child soldiers recalled, "There were a lot of boys rushing into the field, screaming like banshees. It seemed like they were immortal, or impervious, or something, because we shot at them but they just kept coming."

_02:: U.S. Army "Go Pills"

Though amphetamines are essentially off-limits for the civilian population of the United States, American armed forces have long made use of them to enhance the fighting abilities of pilots, soldiers, and sailors, and to keep them awake for long periods of time. Interest peaked in World War II, when all the major combatants on both sides conducted extensive research and distributed large amounts of stimulants to their soldiers. Surprisingly enough, America's armed forces continue the practice to this very day. The amphetamine most often dispensed to American servicemen and-women is Dexedrine, short for dextroamphetamine sulfate, also referred to as "go pills." In one April 2002 incident in Afghanistan, pilots from the Illinois Air National Guard accidentally dropped bombs on a Canadian unit, killing four and wounding eight. In the inquiry that followed, the pilots claimed that they were disoriented because they had been forced to take Dexedrine "go pills" by their superiors and would have been declared unfit for combat if they had not.

_03:: Nazi Shock Troops

During World War II, Nazi Germany definitely led the pack in its use of amphetamines, cocaine, and other "performance-enhancing" drugs. In fact, amphetamine pills were included in every German soldier's first-aid kit, and Nazi researchers developed chewing gum that delivered a dose of cocaine with each piece. But that wasn't all! According to a book by German author and criminologist Wolf Kemper on the subject, *Nazis on Speed,* one of the substances tested by the Nazis in 1944, D-IX, was actually a cocaine-based compound that included both amphetamine and a morphine-related chemical to dull pain. The experimental drug was tested on prisoners of war, and Nazi doctors found the test subjects could march 55 miles without a rest before they collapsed. The Nazis hoped that the drug could put some fighting spirit into their armies, which were by that time being defeated on all fronts, but luckily the war ended before production could begin.

_04:: West African Child Soldiers

In the brutal civil wars that have bedeviled West Africa over the last two decades, much of the fighting is done by children who are teenagers or younger. Armed with automatic weapons, the children are rewarded with sex, candy, tobacco, or alcohol—anything that encourages them to fight. However, sometimes the temptation isn't great enough, so their adult commanders often find it helps to ply them with more powerful drugs that inhibit their judgment. In Sierra Leone, Western observers met children between the ages of 9 and 16 who had been given amphetamines, while children of similar age in the militias of Liberian president Charles Taylor were routinely given cocaine, opium, marijuana, and palm wine to encourage their killer instincts. Often dressed in outlandish costumes out of a belief that strange clothing would protect them in combat—a wedding dress with fright wig was a favorite—these children were described by the journalists who met them as borderline psychotic.

_05:: Medieval Iranian "Assassins"

In the 12th century CE, the invading Seljuk Turks encountered resistance from a small but fanatical group of Shiite Muslims in Persia. Unable to defend against the attacks, the resisters, known as the Ismailis (ancestors to today's second largest Shi'a community), retreated to the impenetrable mountain fortress of Alamut, where they continued their life as a separate society. To protect his people, the Ismaili prince Hasan-i Sabbah began recruiting young men and training them to be fanatical religious killers. The training wasn't exactly kosher, though. During one part, he supposedly gave his men huge amounts of hashish and other drugs and led them to a luxurious chamber. There they were plied with copious amounts of drugs and sex by beautiful women, who told them that they were getting a preview of the heaven that awaited if they died in battle. The fanatics were then sent out, still lost in a hashish haze, to kill the prince's opponents. Interestingly, the modern English word "assassin" comes from *hash-shashin,* the Persian word for "hemp eaters."

Black Eye for the Straight Guy: Historical Bar Brawls

3

What's a good bar without a good brawl? The following are a few famous fisticuff events and the watering holes where they were thrown.

_01:: Truckee, California

One of the best barroom brawl scenes isn't plucked from an old classic or Western, but rather from a real-life saloon in Truckee, California. In 1891, Jacob Teeter was the constable and James Reed the sometimes deputy of Truckee. But over the years, their friendly rivalry (they always ran against each other for constable) escalated, and the constable-deputy feud finally exploded on November 6. That's the day James Reed and a couple of his pals happened upon Teeter in the local bar. A fight ensued and Reed grabbed Teeter's gun. Embarrassed, Teeter left the bar only to return later on a mission. As Reed walked by, the constable shot point-blank at his deputy. The problem was, he missed. He did, however, succeed in shooting a hole through the hat of a man sitting at the next table. Anyway, the stir set patrons diving in all directions, and Reed pulled his gun (actually the one he'd taken from Teeter) and shot him four times. Teeter died and Reed turned himself in to the law. Instead of being arrested, though, Reed was released and at the coroner's inquest the next day was found innocent by reason of self-defense. However, it appears that Teeter got the best of old Reed in the end. His oversized gravestone lies prominently in the Truckee cemetery, while Reed lies quietly in the same cemetery, condemned to an unmarked grave.

Touch of Evil

Twins Reggie and Ronnie Kray, two of England's most infamous gangsters, loved a good punch-up at the local pub. Reggie spent hours perfecting his "sucker punch," whereby he'd offer a man a cigarette with one hand, and crack the guy's jaw with the other.

_02:: John Wayne v. Randolph Scott

Car chases and bar brawls are staples of certain genres and the viewing public plays an important role in what survives the director's cutting room. And while a real-life bar brawl might take just minutes to complete, picture-perfect re-creations take a little longer. The movie *The Spoilers,* for instance, was rereleased five times with different leading casts, the 1942 version starting John Wayne and Randolph Scott. In fact, the flick is well known for having the longest and most complex bar brawl in cinema history. The six-minute fight scene involved over *30* experienced stuntmen and acrobats, and the bar (understandably) was completely trashed by the end of it. And to get the scene just right, the actors went through their paces breaking everything in their paths: from fake breakaway furniture to mirrors to doors, and just for good measure (and cinematography) they slammed each other against walls, too. The scene actually took 10 days to wrap up, much to the satisfaction of John Wayne, who was quite happy to perform some of the stunts himself.

_03:: The Ugly American in Paris

Following World War I, French–American relations weren't exactly improved by the racist behavior of white American tourists. So in 1923, in a desperate effort to appease wealthy white American tourists, a number of French bars and dance hall owners defied national laws and refused admittance to blacks, including French blacks. Despite government warnings, a group of white Americans drinking one night in a bar in the Montmartre district demanded that two black men who had entered the bar be removed. When the men refused, the ignorant Americans responded by physically throwing them out. The next day the French press announced that Kojo Tovalou Houénou, a prominent leader of the Pan-African movement in Paris and a renowned philosopher, was one of the victims. Outraged and disgusted, President Raymond Poincaré denounced the scandal and ordered the bar closed—a warning that any French bar trying

Just the Facts

THE HUNGRY DUCK BAR BY NUMBERS

Since the Hungry Duck Bar opened in Moscow, Russia, in 1995, the civilized world hasn't been the same. The bar is notorious for its rowdiness and raunchiness, as the numbers show. In fact, the Hungry Duck is the only bar ever denounced by a national parliament, but the club continues to pay "favors" to stay open.

256: Cases the Moscow police have had involving the bar

8: Number of bullets that have been fired inside

2: Number of bomb threats

8-plus: Number of times the police have raided the establishment

5: Number of owners

4: Death threats each owner has received

1: Kidnapping attempts made

2: Number of full-time carpenters employed by the bar on account of all the regularly broken bar stools

40-plus: Number of customers that have had to receive medical treatment from falling off the bar while dancing

2: Types of draft beer available

0: Food items on the menu

to exclude blacks, French or otherwise, would be immediately shut down.

Prophets on the Edge

People are always a little skeptical of prophets. After all, when you're telling the world that God's decided to use you to pass on His message to the masses, or to lead people to some promised land, you're bound to get a few strange looks. Of course, your chances of being believed get even slimmer when you're preaching the gospel of semiautomatics and mass suicides like the following folks did.

_01:: David Koresh (1959–1993)

Best known as the leader of the ill-fated Branch Davidians, David Koresh led a short life as a prophet of doom. Born Vernon Wayne Howell (which didn't quite have that same son-of-God ring to it), Koresh joined the Branch Davidian sect in 1981. Founded in the 1930s by Ben and Lois Roden, the Davidians believed the return of the Messiah was imminent. Soon after joining, Koresh had an affair with Lois Roden, who by then was in her late 60s. While on a journey with Koresh to Mount Carmel in Israel, Roden died, and a power struggle for control of the group took place between her son, George, and Koresh. Shortly thereafter, David returned with seven followers, a great amount of conviction, and a couple of semiautomatic assault weapons (for good measure) to back up his claim. Choosing violence over, say, putting it to a vote, David Koresh attacked George Roden, wounding him in the chest and hands. At a subsequent trial, the seven were acquitted and Koresh's case was declared a mistrial. Believing that he was now the head of the biblical House of David, Koresh moved with his followers to Waco, Texas. Of course, living by the sword (or in this case, the rifle) also meant dying by

it. In 1993, Koresh and 74 of his followers perished in a fire during a shootout with federal agents.

_02:: Amos

Once upon a time, the Old Testament character Amos was satisfied to herd his sheep and tend to his sycamore trees. But the part-time prophet, as he saw himself, accepted "the call" and quickly became a thorn in the side of the religious establishment. At the time, part of Judea was true to Yahweh, while the religious establishment in Bethel worshiped Baal and the Golden Calf. Yahweh had decided to punish them and famous Amos got the job of providing the bad news. First, Amos accused the wealthy Judeans of being greedy, oppressive, and exploiting the poor. Then, he went after the rich who used their money to bribe judges and political officials. Finally, he accused them of perverting the true Israelite religion by moving the temple to Bethel and worshiping the Golden Calf instead of Yahweh. Not mincing any words, Amos told the leaders that Yahweh wasn't bluffing about the imminent punishment and that they'd better get their act together pretty soon. After that, Amos was no longer welcome at most banquets of the wealthy, with most townsfolk wishing that he'd just go back to his sheep and sycamores.

Touch of Evil

David "Moses" Berg, founder of the Children of God, developed "flirty fishing" to support his flock. Female acolytes had sex with wealthy men for money to earn funds for the church. Of course, any detractors who cried "Prostitution!" were labeled as not having enough faith.

_03:: Edgar Cayce (1877–1945)

Known as "the Sleeping Prophet," Edgar Cayce must have been a real bore at social gatherings. Considered to be one of America's greatest psychics, Cayce would close his eyes and appear to go into a trance before making his prophecies. A story has it that an angel appeared to Cayce at the age of 13 asking him what his greatest desire was, to which he allegedly replied that it was to help people. Another story has Cayce placing books under his pillow and absorbing the contents while he slept. Not bad for someone who was illiterate. However, Cayce was best known for his medical prognostications, performing thousands of medical readings for his legion of followers. While there was little or no scientific proof that anyone was actually cured by Cayce's clairvoyance, his followers were quick to spread the word. However, there was an interesting catch: Cayce's followers claimed that if one doubted the mystic his diagnosis wouldn't work. If only Miss Cleo had had such foresight.

_04:: Ezekiel

Talk about a genuine fire-and-brimstone preacher; today's ragamuffin evangelists would run a distant second to the Old Testament prophet Ezekiel. Consider how the guy gave solace to the exiled Israelites. When the bunch found themselves exiled in Babylon, far from their holy city of Jerusalem, Ezekiel didn't hold a pity party. Instead, the sweetheart prophet told the captives that they were directly responsible for their own exile and needed to change their ways if they ever hoped to return home. Probably not the comforting words the people wanted to hear. He also did something entirely revolutionary: he put God in a chariot throne, thus giving Him the mobility to get out of the temple and visit His people in Babylon. The idea of the chariot came to old Zeke in a vision that looks like something straight out of *Independence Day*. As described by the prophet, the glowing chariot emerged from a large storm cloud with fire flashing all around it, and couched in the middle of all the action was a fiery humanlike figure. To religious scholars this was obviously Yahweh coming in loud and clear on a mobile throne (can you see Him now?), though one still wonders if Ezekiel hadn't just had the fiery dream as the result of late-night indigestion.

_05:: The Reverend Jim Jones (1931–1978)

Hanging around with the Reverend Jim Jones was certainly detrimental to more than a few people's health. As an ordained minister in the Disciples of Christ denomination, Jones created a large congregation of followers among the poor in the San Francisco Bay area. Proclaiming himself a prophet and one who could raise the dead, Jones quickly became a local religious celebrity and his congregation numbered over 8,000. But by the early 1970s, a number of local newspapers published articles accusing Jones of using church money to buy political influence. Then, in 1976, another article was published accusing Jones of performing fake healings and coercing church members to sell their possessions and give the money to the church (clearly he was better at raising funds than the deceased). With the pressure on, Jones and a group of his followers moved to Guyana and set up a compound modestly named Jonestown. Things came to a nasty halt in November 1978 when, feeling trapped (especially after killing U.S. congressman Leo Ryan), Jones ordered his followers to down a grape drink laced with cyanide. Over 914 people died in the mass suicide, including Jones. Contrary to popular belief, though, the drink was not Kool-Aid, but one of its competitors.

You Say "Potato," I Say "Nuclear Annihilation": Close Calls in the Nuclear Age

There's a formula for fun: Arm two superpowers to the teeth with thousands of nuclear warheads. Make sure they are deeply hostile and suspicious of each other. Now, cut off diplomatic communication, stir in about 50 smaller countries with their own agendas on each side, and—voilà!—cold war in a jiffy!

_01:: Suez Crisis

On November 5, 1956, during the Suez crisis, the North American Aerospace Defense Command (NORAD) received warnings that seemed to indicate that a large-scale Soviet attack was under way: a Soviet fleet was moving from the Black Sea to a more aggressive posture in the Aegean, 100 Soviet MiGs were detected flying over Syria, a British bomber had just been shot down in Syria, and unidentified aircraft were in flight over Turkey, causing the Turkish air force to go on high alert. All signs pointed to the ominous, except that, not long after, each of the four warnings was found to have a completely innocent explanation. The Soviet fleet was conducting routine exercises, the MiGs were part of a normal escort—whose size had been exaggerated—for the president of Syria, the British bomber had made an emergency landing after mechanical problems, and, last but not least, the unidentified planes over Turkey? Well, they turned out to be a large flock of swans.

_02:: SAC-NORAD Communication Failure

On November 24, 1961, all communication links between the U.S. Strategic Air Command (SAC) and NORAD suddenly went dead, cutting off the SAC from three early warning radar stations in England, Greenland, and Alaska. The communication breakdown made no sense, though. After all, a widespread, total failure of all communication circuits was considered impossible, because the network included so many redundant systems that it should have been failsafe. The only alternative explanation was that a full-scale Soviet nuclear first strike had occurred. As a result, all SAC bases were put on alert, and B-52 bomber crews warmed up their engines and moved their planes onto runways, awaiting orders to counterattack the Soviet Union with nuclear weapons. Luckily, those orders were never given. It was discovered that the circuits were not in fact redundant because they all ran through one relay station in Colorado, where a single motor had overheated and caused the entire system to fail.

_03:: U2 Spy Plane Accidentally Violates Soviet Airspace

U2 spy planes were high-altitude aircraft that took pictures of the Soviet Union with extremely powerful long-distance telephoto lenses. During the Cuban Missile Crisis of 1962, U2 pilots were ordered not to fly within 100 miles of the Soviet Union to avoid antagonizing the Soviets. However, on October 26, 1962, a U2 pilot flying over the North Pole made a series of navigational errors because the shifting lights of the aurora borealis prevented him from taking accurate readings with his sextant. As a result, he ended up flying over the Chukotski Peninsula in northern Siberia, causing the Soviets to order a number of MiG interceptors to shoot his plane down immediately. Instead of letting him be shot down, however, the United States responded quickly by sending out F-102A fighters armed

with nuclear missiles to escort the U2 back to American airspace and prevent the MiGs from following it. Unbelievably, the tactic worked. Even more amazing: the decision whether to use their nuclear missiles was left to the American pilots, and could have easily resulted in a nuclear conflict.

_04:: When Camping, Make Sure to Hide Your Food and Your Nuclear Weapons

On October 25, 1962, again during the Cuban Missile Crisis, a security guard at an air base in Duluth, Minnesota, saw a shadowy figure scaling one of the fences enclosing the base. He shot at the intruder and activated an intruder alarm, automatically setting off intruder alarms at neighboring bases. However, at the Volk Field air base in Wisconsin, the Klaxon loudspeaker had been wired incorrectly, and instead sounded an alarm ordering F-106A interceptors armed with nuclear missiles to take off. The pilots assumed that a full-scale nuclear conflict with the Soviet Union had begun, and the planes were about to take off when a car from the air traffic control tower raced down the tarmac and signaled the planes to stop. The intruder in Duluth had finally been identified: it was a bear.

_05:: A Terrifying Crash

On January 21, 1968, fire broke out on a B-52 carrying a nuclear payload near Greenland, forcing the crew to bail out. The unmanned plane then crashed about seven miles from the early warning radar station in Greenland. The damage done could have been remarkable. The plane exploded, as did the explosives surrounding the radioactive core of the nuclear weapons (which require conventional explosives to detonate). Given the state of nuclear weapons technology at the time, this type of unintentional detonation of conventional first-stage explosives could have theoretically triggered the second-stage fission reaction, resulting in a nuclear explosion. Luckily for the world, it didn't. The resulting explosion would have not only severed regular communications between the early warning station and NORAD, it would have also triggered an emergency alarm based on radiation readings taken by sensors near the station. The only conclusion at NORAD headquarters, in this grisly hypothetical but very plausible scenario, would have been that the Soviets were launching a preemptive nuclear strike, and the United States would have responded in kind.

Senator Charles Percy, who happened to be at NORAD headquarters during this event, said the reaction was one of overwhelming panic and terror. Justifiably so.

Touch of Evil

Western intelligence analysts believe that by the end of the Cold War, the Soviet Union—shortly before it went broke—was spending approximately $350 billion, or a third of its gross national product (GNP), on military spending. The United States, by comparison, was spending only 6 to 7% of its GNP at that time.

_06:: Comp Fear

On November 9, 1979, four command centers for the U.S. nuclear arsenal received data on their radar screens indicating that the Soviet Union had launched a full-scale nuclear first strike on the United States. Over the next six minutes, planes were launched and nuclear missiles initialized for an immediate retaliatory strike. The president's National Emergency Airborne Command Post—an armored jumbo jet with radiation shielding and advanced communications capabilities, meant to allow the president to remain in contact with the government and armed forces during a nuclear war—was also launched, though curiously without the president aboard. However, the alarm was canceled because no sensors or satellites detected an actual Soviet missile launch. The alarm had been caused by computer software used for training exercises depicting a nightmare scenario Soviet first strike.

_07:: Comp Fear, Part 2

Electronic displays at NORAD, the SAC, and the Pentagon included prominent, highly visible numeric counters showing the number of enemy nuclear missiles detected. They normally displayed four zeros—"0000"—indicating that no nuclear missiles had been launched. However, on June 3, 1980, at 2:25 in the morning, the counters started randomly substituting the number "2" for "0." As a result, crews manning bombers carrying nuclear weapons were ordered to begin to warm up their engines, Minuteman missiles were initialized for launch, and airborne command posts were also launched. It was determined that this first event was a false alarm, but three days later it happened a second time—causing the entire emergency response procedure to start rolling once again. The problem was eventually traced back to a single faulty computer chip combined with faulty wiring.

An Eye for an Eye: Charming Episodes of Violence from Medieval Iceland

The sagas of early medieval Iceland (written down between 1100 and 1300) are some of the great works of Western literature. Heck, they've got it all: lust, envy, large-scale violence, widespread failures. Plus, these charming tales are all set in a time when a man just had to do what a man (generally with anger-management issues and a club) had to do.

_01:: Hallgerd the Petty (Njal's Saga)

One of the bloodiest feuds in Icelandic history arose from the seating chart at a wedding, when Bergthora asked Hallgerd Hoskuldsdattir to move over at a banquet to a less prestigious seat. It only makes sense that the slighted Hallgerd took the instruction as a deadly insult. Unfortunately for Bergthora, though, Hallgerd knew how to hold a grudge. After all, this was the same woman whose husband, Gunnar, once slapped her for stealing from one of his enemies. Then, years later, when besieged in his home by his enemies, Gunnar begged Hallgerd to give him a lock of her hair to repair his bowstring, and she refused, reminding him of the slap he'd given her. Gunnar was killed, and Hallgerd was finally happy. Bergthora wasn't any luckier. Despite the attempts of Njal, Bergthora's husband, to make peace, things quickly got out of hand. Eventually, a gang attacked Njal's family on their farm and set fire to the farmhouse, killing everyone inside except for a brother-in-law, a Viking who didn't take kindly to his in-laws being barbecued. In response, he cobbled together a small army and successfully wiped out most of the conspirators before finally ending the bloody feud as all good feuds end . . . with a strategic marriage.

_02:: Hrafnkel's Comeback (Hrafnkel's Saga)

Hrafnkel was the perfect villain: a callous chieftain who murdered without paying compensation (this being rather bad manners at the time). Overthrown but spared by the kinsmen of a man he had killed, Hrafnkel was banished to the life of a penniless vagrant. But he managed to learn from past mistakes, gaining wisdom, kindness, and followers while his enemies grew weak and complacent. And while the wisdom and followers would definitely help him in his greater plan, we're not quite so sure we buy the kindness. Hrafnkel waited seven years for the opportunity to serve his revenge ice cold. And when it finally came, he killed the most dangerous of his enemies, then chased the rest out of his former holdings.

_03:: Thorstein Replaces the Men He Kills (The Tale of Thorstein the Staff-Struck)

What's a poor farmer to do when his honor is insulted by three servants of a wealthy landowner? If you're Thorstein Thorarinsson, you kill 'em, announcing your actions after the fact in accordance with Icelandic custom. Luckily for Thorstein, the three he killed were so worthless that their own boss didn't particularly want to avenge them. Thorstein and the chieftain, Bjarni, fought a rather halfhearted duel, punctuated by frequent water breaks, pauses to examine one another's weapons, and even stops to tie their shoes in midbattle. Finally, they reached a settlement: Thorstein, who was strong enough to do the work of three men, became the perfect replacement for the three he had killed. Downsizing, Icelandic style.

_04:: Egil Rewrites a Poem in His Head (Egil's Saga)

Egil was a raider, a pirate, a murderer, and, oh so predictably, an accomplished poet to boot. On his way to deliver a poem to King Athelstan of England, he fell into the clutches of Eirik, the Viking king of York. This was most unfortunate, as Egil had made a career of being quite a pain in Eirik's royal rear. Given one night's reprieve while the king decided the method of execution, Egil stunned everyone by delivering, in perfect meter, a poem in praise of Eirik. He was released well before anyone realized that he had just replaced "Athelstan" with "Eirik" (the Old Norse form), maintaining the rhythm of the poem and saving his own neck. Long after he died of old age, Egil's grave was excavated and his abnor-

Lies Your Mother Told You

REMEMBER THE *MAINE*

In full, the U.S. battle cry during the Spanish-American War of 1898 was "Remember the *Maine*, to hell with Spain!" It referred to the sinking of the U.S. battleship *Maine* in Havana Harbor in February of that year. But it's never been shown that Spain—then fending off a Cuban independence movement—attacked the ship. Sent to protect U.S. interests, the *Maine* was preparing to leave when it exploded. In reality, though, Spain had nothing to gain by provoking the United States, and much to lose. Many think the onboard explosion was accidental. Or maybe Havana rebels planted a bomb, hoping to bring America into their fight. If so, the tactic worked. U.S. newspapers—especially those owned by mogul William Randolph Hearst—took up the "Remember the *Maine!*" cry and agitated for war. It worked out well for the U.S. government, though...the United States came out of the fight with the Philippines, Puerto Rico, and Guam, while Cuba was happy to win its independence.

mally bulky skull was discovered, proving that you can have a thick head and still do some quick thinking.

_05:: Gudmund Negotiates a Deal (Gudmund the Worthy's Saga)

When a chump named Skaering had his hand cut off by Norwegian merchants, he turned to his kinsman Gudmund to get him justice. Ever helpful, Gudmund arranged a monetary settlement, but as soon as he left the scene the Norwegians refused to pay. Summoned back, a rather annoyed Gudmund made the following proposal: "I will pay Skaering the amount that you were judged to pay, but I shall choose one man from among you who seems to me of equivalent standing with Skaering and chop off his hand. You may then compensate that fellow's hand as cheaply as you wish." Not surprisingly, the Norwegians quickly coughed up the money, no doubt to the sound of Skaering's one hand clapping.

Quit Your Day Job:
Dictators Who Worked Their Way to the Top

In the dreary monotony of daily life, the best most of us can hope for is a promotion and 3% raise. But a small subset of the human population dreams big—of bloody coups and secret torture chambers, personality cults and absolute power. Frankly, it's enough to turn us off ambition entirely. Just imagine if Idi Amin had remained an assistant cook in the British colonial army. Or if these folks hadn't thought to quit their day jobs.

_01:: Pol Pot, the Frustrated Teacher

Before he became a world-famous war criminal, Pol Pot was named Saloth Sar. As a young man, Sar studied carpentry and radio engineering, but proved a poor student so he became—what else?—a teacher. (And you thought *your* classrooms were scary.) From 1954 to 1963, Sar taught at a private school in Phnom Penh before being forced out because of ties to communism. Ever fond of alliteration, Saloth Sar became Pol Pot and devoted himself full-time to Cambodia's Communist Party, eventually becoming the party's leader, and by 1975, his Khmer Rouge guerrilla army had overthrown the same government that once fired him. In his four years of rule, Pot killed more than a million Cambodians. When the Vietnamese came to the rescue and invaded Cambodia in 1979, Pot retreated to the jungle, though he continued to orchestrate guerrilla attacks until his arrest in 1997.

_02:: Hitler, the Frustrated Painter

As a child, Adolf Hitler attended a monastery school and harbored dreams of becoming a priest, but he dropped out after his father's death in 1903. By then, Hitler had a new career in mind: professional artist. And though the Führer's precise but emotionless landscapes showed moderate promise, he was rejected twice from Vienna's Academy of Fine Arts. Bitter, poor, and lonely, young Adolf moved between boardinghouses and hostels, earning a meager living painting postcards. Oddly enough, he might have been just another failed artist had it not been for World War I. Turning in his paintbrush for a pistol, Hitler volunteered as a runner for the German army. Turns out he enjoyed that world war so much that, a few decades later, he decided to start another one.

_03:: Mussolini, the Frustrated Author

Many dictators were also authors. Stalin wrote scintillating screeds like *Building Collective Farms;* Mao's *Little Red Book* is considered to be the second-best-selling book of all time; and Hitler's *Mein Kampf* made him a millionaire. Even Saddam Hussein found a little time to pen two horrible bodice-rippers while performing his duties as president of Iraq. But the most famous dictatorial romance is *The Cardinal's Mistress,* written by Benito Mussolini. Before becoming the world's first fascist dictator, Mussolini worked for a socialist paper, *Il Popolo d'Italia,* for which he wrote a serial later published as a novel. *The Cardinal's Mistress* tells the tragic story of, you guessed it, a 17th-century cardinal and his mistress. And boy is it bad. It's the sort of book where "terrible groan[s] burst forth from" characters' breasts, and characters ask one another to "cast a ray of your light into my darkened soul." No wonder Il Duce gave up his day job.

_04:: Papa Doc, the Frustrated Doctor

Unlike Doc Holliday (brilliant gunfighter and amateur dentist) and Elmer Fudd (inept gunfighter known to Bugs Bunny as Doc), François "Papa Doc" Duvalier was, in fact, a doctor—although we can only imagine his bedside manner. Favoring hypocrisy to the Hippocratic oath, the dangerous dictator was first a physician in Port-au-Prince for nearly a decade before immersing himself in politics full-time in 1943. Even more surprising, he actually rose to power in a legitimately democratic election. And though he was voted in as president in 1957, Duvalier promptly showed his gratitude to the Haitian nation by killing anyone who expressed the slightest opposition to his government. By the mid-1960s, Duvalier had established himself not only as President for Life but also as a quasi-divine manifestation of Haiti's greatness (he claimed to have supernatural powers; Papa Doc even said he placed a curse on John F. Kennedy that resulted in Kennedy's assassination). Incidentally, his son, "Baby Doc" Duvalier, who ruled from Papa Doc's death in 1971 until 1986, was not a doctor. Just a dictator.

_05:: Castro, the Angry Ballplayer?

Persistent rumors would have you believe that old Fidel was a talented baseball player who once tried out for a major-league team in America . . . which is completely untrue. The fact is, Castro did play a little ball back in school: he seems to have been the losing pitcher in a 1946 intramural game between the University of Havana's business and law schools. But the point here is that he was in law school not so much to win ball games as to study law. Castro graduated and practiced in

Havana between 1950 and 1952, when he failed miserably in his first attempted coup d'état. After a brief stint in prison and a few years exiled in Mexico and the United States, Castro and his army finally took control of Cuba in 1959. Just goes to show you, there's more to life than sports!

War, What Is It Good For? Well, Things, Actually

3

War gets a bad rap. Sure, it's often fatal and frequently unnecessary. But if war is so terrible, why do we keep on trying it? Hoping to shed some rosy light on the fog of war, we've collected a few possible, if minor, benefits to starting one.

_01:: Medicine

It seems like nothing brings about a good medical breakthrough like a solid war. Antibiotics, anesthesia, and countless advances in surgery were all discovered or perfected during wartime. In fact, one of the most interesting war-related medical breakthroughs came from Dr. Charles W. Drew, an African American doctor in World War II, who helped pioneer technology allowing the preservation and transfusion of blood plasma. Drew worked from 1940 through the end of the war, and his efforts saved the lives of thousands of soldiers who otherwise would have bled to death. Drew himself, however, was not so fortunate. After falling asleep at the wheel in North Carolina years after the war, Drew sustained massive trauma and bled to death. A persistent rumor claims that Drew was given poor treatment at the hospital because of his race, but friends with him that fateful night vehemently deny it.

_02:: Engineering

War can also bring technological advances. Believe it or not, the phrase "civil engineering" wasn't coined until the 19th century because before that "engineering" had been exclusively a military endeavor. It's common knowledge that math and science have both civilian and military implications, but one prominent example of the type is cybernetics, the mathematical field pioneered by the unfortunately named Norbert Wiener. Cybernetics is the study of control within complex systems, and our boy wonder (Wiener actually got a Ph.D. in math from Harvard when he was just 18) began by applying it as a World War II tool. Amazingly, he used the science to figure out how best to aim artillery fire at speeding airplanes. But he didn't stop there. Wiener went on to write about the nonmilitary political and social uses of cybernetics in his best-selling *The Human Use of Human*

Beings (1950). Today cybernetics helps thermostats anticipate rising and falling temperatures. Do better artillery fire, finely tuned air-conditioning, and one good book make a war worthwhile? Well, that brings us to . . .

_03:: Literature

Peace just doesn't have the same ring as *War and Peace*. And quite frankly, it couldn't get *All Quiet on the Western Front* until after things had gotten awfully loud. From *The Iliad* to Tim O'Brien's *The Things They Carried,* good yarns have often used war as their setting. It's good for visual art, too. Picasso's *Guernica* and Delacroix's *Liberty Leading the People* would have been impossible without the Spanish Civil War and the French Revolution, respectively. Sometimes, in fact, good art is all that emerges from a battle. Kurt Vonnegut wrote the best-selling *Slaughterhouse-Five* about the firebombing of Dresden, an utterly superfluous attack that Vonnegut witnessed as a prisoner of war in 1945. Of the bombing, Vonnegut once wrote: "Only one person on the entire planet got any benefit from it. I am that person. One way or another, I got two or three dollars for every person killed."

Angry Authors and Even Angrier Critics

Nothing sours a literary friendship quite like a bad review. The Irish playwright Brendan Behan once said, "Critics are like eunuchs in a harem; they know how it's done, they've seen it done every day, but they're unable to do it themselves." Whether warring writers keep their feud on paper or let things escalate to physical violence, a great literary feud is always entertaining.

_01:: Amis v. Amis

You'd think that the father-and-son dynamic duo of contemporary Brit lit would stand by one another, but Kingsley Amis (1922–1995) was awfully hard on his son, Martin (1949–   ). Kingsley, most famous for *Lucky Jim,* once told *The Guardian,* "If I was reviewing Martin under a pseudonym, I would say he works too hard and it shows." (Kingsley received his own bad reviews—the novelist Robertson Davies called his work "an awful bore.") But Kingsley's critique was nothing compared with attacks on Martin since. In one of the snarkiest reviews of all time, author Tibor Fischer wrote that reading Martin Amis's *Yellow Dog* (2003) was akin to "your favourite uncle being caught in the school playground, masturbating." Martin responded by calling Fischer "a wretch." So much for British politeness.

_02:: Keats v. *Quarterly Review*

Before he became a central figure in British Romantic poetry, John Keats apprenticed with a surgeon. When he published the now-classic

Profiles in Carnage

PRINCESS OLGA OF KIEV

Olga the Widow: In 945, Prince Igor of Kiev took an army to the land of the Derevlian tribe. The Derevlians weren't exactly amused by Igor's demands for tribute so they defeated his forces and murdered him. In a great display of chutzpah, they then suggested that his widow, Olga, marry their ruler.

Olga the Agreeable: Surprisingly, Olga consented and invited the Derevlian leaders to Kiev to discuss the arrangements.

Olga the Hostess: Arranging a ceremonial steam bath for her guests, Olga had them burned alive inside. She then led an army against the Derevlian capital. When the Derevlians offered her tribute to leave, Olga showed her magnanimity by only asking for three doves per household.

Olga the PETA Nightmare: Their relief turned to horror when she had the birds set on fire (PETA not being around at the time); the doves returned home and set the town ablaze. The survivors were enslaved.

Olga the Saint: As for the Kievan princess, she had a fairly happy ending. She later converted to Christianity and is venerated today as Saint Olga.

Endymion at the age of 23, one critic wrote that Keats ought to go back to medicine, arguing that it's better to be "a starved apothecary than a starved poet." The widely respected *Quarterly Review* was even harsher, using adjectives like "absurd" and "unintelligible." Keats seemed largely unaffected by the criticism—the following year, he wrote his most famous poems, including "Ode on a Grecian Urn." But fellow Romantic Percy Bysshe Shelley later claimed that the bad reviews hadn't just angered Keats; they'd killed him. That led Lord Byron to write in *Don Juan* that Keats had been "snuffed out by an Article." Nice rhetoric, but in reality, Keats was snuffed out by tuberculosis. Immune to the critics, he remained a poet to the last. His entire last will and testament, in fact, was a single line of perfect iambic pentameter: "My chest of books divide amongst my friends."

_03:: Voltaire v. Fréron

In spite of his so-called passion for rationalism, Enlightenment stalwart Voltaire held ferociously unreasonable grudges. He once published a pamphlet claiming Rousseau had abandoned his children, and he even called Shakespeare "a drunken savage." But Voltaire's greatest literary feud was with Élie Fréron, founder of the literary journal *Année littéraire*. Fréron virulently attacked both the underlying philosophies of the Enlightenment and Voltaire's writing. Not one to take it lying down, Voltaire quickly fought back, penning the play *L'Écossaise* to ridicule Fréron. "A serpent bit Fréron," Voltaire said. "But it was the serpent that died." (Incidentally, the play is widely regarded to be one of Voltaire's very worst.) The rivalry didn't exactly die down. In fact, the bitterness seemed to last a lifetime: for example, Voltaire kept a painting in one of his dining rooms depicting a bunch of demons horsewhipping Élie Fréron. How's that for rationalism?

_04:: Gore Vidal v. Norman Mailer

While Norman Mailer and Gore Vidal were serving as commentators for ABC at the 1968 Democratic National Convention, their private feud became fairly public when Mailer called Vidal a "queer." Of course, he had his reasons—after all, the openly gay Vidal had just referred to him as a "crypto-Nazi." End of round one. Three years later, Vidal (most famous for his historical novels) compared Mailer's view of women to that of Charles Manson in the *New York Review of Books*. Mailer, whose gritty *The Naked and the Dead* established his reputation, *was* a misogynist—he once remarked, "I don't hate women, but I think they should be kept in cages." Even so, he didn't appreciate the Manson comparison. Just how much didn't he appreciate it? In the *Dick Cavett Show* greenroom a few months later, Mailer headbutted Vidal, who cleverly responded with a punch to Mailer's gut. The show itself was a disaster, with Mailer insulting both Vidal and Cavett while Vidal stared blankly like, well, like someone who'd just been headbutted.

Touch of Evil

After e. e. cummings' poetry collection was rejected 14 times, he borrowed $300 from his mom and printed it himself. Titled No Thanks, the book's dedication listed all the publishers that had turned him down, arranged on the page in the shape of a funeral urn.

When Nature Is a Real Mother: Natural Disasters Explained

6

There's nothing quite as frightening as when Mother throws one of her temper tantrums. Mother Nature, that is. And while there's some comfort in knowing that at least there's a little science in her madness, the explanations are enough to keep you up at night.

_01:: Krakatoa's Really, Really Big Bang

The terrible tsunami that devastated Indonesia in December 2004 wasn't the first time nature had vented its fury on the South Asian nation. At 10:02 a.m. on August 27, 1883, the volcano on the island of Krakatoa, in the Sunda Strait between Java and Sumatra, erupted. More accurately, it exploded. The detonation threw smoke and ash 17 miles in the air. In fact, the ferocity of the burst echoed so loudly that the sound of the explosion was heard on Rodriguez Island, nearly 3,000 miles away (imagine being in New York and hearing a boom from *San Francisco!*). The pressure wave caused barometers to twitch as far away as London seven times as the shock bounded and rebounded around the globe. But the eruption itself wasn't the worst of it. The explosion sent tsunami waves over 100 feet high toward Java and Sumatra. Ships were carried a mile and a half inland and dumped in the jungle. The disruption was so great, the tide actually rose several inches *in New York*. In all, more than 36,000 people were killed by the tsunami, and most of the nearby coasts of both islands were laid waste. As for Krakatoa, the island blew itself out of existence. It reemerged years later, the result of continued volcanic activity in this turbulent part of the Pacific "Ring of Fire."

_02:: "Bring Out Your Dead!" The Black Death

Between 1347 and 1351, a plague raged through Europe. Arriving in Messina, Sicily, on a Black Sea merchant ship, the disease was initially thought of as solely an animal sickness—like bird flu or mad cow disease. But somehow fleas managed to transmit the condition from rats to people. Called the Black Death because of the dark spots that appeared on victims' skin, the pandemic wasn't just the bubonic plague. In fact, the vicious strain was actually a lethal combination of four variations of plague: bubonic (causing buboes, or inflammations of the lymph nodes), enteric (intestinal), septicemic (an infection of the blood), and pneumonic (filling the lungs with fluid). Quadruple yuck. Even worse, the Black Death worked fast. People who were perfectly healthy at midday were dead by sunset. And the staggering death toll reflects it. An estimated 12 million people in Asia and 25 million in Europe (or one-third of Europe's population) were wiped out. An indiscriminate killer, the disease destroyed rich and poor alike, though only one reigning monarch is known to have died: King Alfonse XI of Castile, who refused to abandon his troops when plague struck his army.

_03:: Russia Dodges a Bullet from Space: The Tunguska Blast

At 7:17 a.m. on June 30, 1908, a 15-megaton explosion (more than 1,000 times that at Hiroshima) flattened a massive part of the Tunguska region of Siberia. The devastated area was 57 miles across, and the explosion shattered windows 400 miles away. A real investigation of the event wasn't undertaken until 1927. But that's not the weird part. The strangest fact about the incident is that there was no impact crater. An entire forest flattened, but there was no hole, meaning the object had exploded *in the air*. Scientists now believe that the object was an asteroid or extinct stony comet; the pressure of its descent simply blew it apart before it hit the ground. But the mysterious nature of the event has led to a whole literature of ludicrous theories, blaming the blast on everything from a black hole passing through the earth to a chunk of antimatter to an exploding UFO to—we love this one—an energy death ray built by Nikola Tesla and test-fired from the Wardenclyffe Tower on Long Island. Whatever they believe, scientists have shuddered and thanked their lucky stars, contemplating what might have happened had the object decided to explode over, say, Central Park. Due to the remoteness of Tunguska, not a single person was killed by the blast.

_04:: The Day the Little Conemaugh Got Much Bigger

Lake Conemaugh lies 14 miles up the Little Conemaugh River from the town of Johnstown, Pennsylvania. On May 31, 1889, the dam that held back the lake waters burst after two days of torrential rain. The results were devastating. A wall of water 60 feet high, moving at 40 mph, crashed down on the unsuspecting people of Johnstown, and the water and debris it carried all but flattened the entire town. In an utterly tragic twist, the town was downstream from a wire factory that was also flattened by the water. Many townspeople caught in the deluge got so entangled in barbed wire that they couldn't escape. In the end, 2,209 people were killed, including 99 entire families. But Mother Nature was not wholly to blame for the tragedy. The Lake Conemaugh Dam was the property of the South Fork Fishing and Forestry Club, which had turned the area into a mountain retreat for the wealthy. However, the club had neglected proper maintenance on the dam. Despite its culpability, though, it was never held legally responsible.

_05:: From the People Who Brought You World War I: The Flu

Just as the Great War was ending and the world looked like it might finally get back to normal, the influenza pandemic of 1918–1919 struck. The pandemic most likely originated in China, but its huge and devastating impact on Spain's population earned it the name "Spanish flu," while the French called it "La Grippe." Even such luminaries as President Woodrow Wilson caught the bug, in his case while attending the Versailles Peace Conference. In the end, one-fifth of the world's population would become infected, and more people would die—some estimates are as high as 40 million—than had during four years of fighting in the First World War. Ironically, the war can be held partly responsible not only for spreading the flu, but also for checking it. Populations were weakened, and thereby made more susceptible, by shortages and rationing and the fact that many of the strongest and healthiest members had been killed in some trench or no-man's-land. But the war had also advanced medical learning and germ theory, and steeled people to hardship. They were used to self-sacrifice and putting the nation before the individual. So they were more calm and cooperative with the measures taken by their public health departments, some of which were tremendously restrictive.

Touch of Evil

"Typhoid Mary" Mallon wasn't quite the walking natural disaster she was made out to be. Although she did spread typhoid to 33 known victims, only three of those died from the disease. The 1903 spread of typhoid through New York was caused by several different carriers.

_06:: Yellowstone National... Supervolcano?

So what exactly is a supervolcano? Just picture a volcano with 10,000 times the explosive force of Mount St. Helens. And unlike Mount Fuji, supervolcanoes aren't available in nice cone shapes. Rather, these extreme volcanoes form in depressions called calderas, where the magma gets so thick that gas can't escape. The pressure keeps building and building until all hell literally breaks loose. We have our very own supervolcano (U-S-A! U-S-A!) under Yellowstone National Park. The *entire* park. In fact, the caldera under Yellowstone is so big—

4,000 square kilometers—no one knew it was there until satellite images told us so. By all estimates, it erupts about every 600,000 years, and the last eruption was 640,000 years ago. We're due. So what happens if it blows? The last eruption of a supervolcano was at Lake Toba in Sumatra 75,000 years ago. So much ash was released into the atmosphere that the sun was blocked out, the global temperature dropped 21 degrees, and three-quarters of all plant life in the Northern Hemisphere died. Ice age, anyone? Hopeful geologists contend that we may be saved by the venting that occurs at Yellowstone through geysers like Old Faithful, relieving a bit of pressure from the caldera. Let's hope they're right.

_07:: Better Disasters through Science: The China Syndrome

OK, so it's not *technically* a purely natural disaster. But it involves a lot of physics and stuff, and it would certainly *cause* one heck of a natural disaster. The name (from the film *The China Syndrome* of 1979, the same year as the Three Mile Island snafu) comes from the theory that, in the event of a meltdown, molten nuclear material would be so hot that it would melt all the way through the earth and come out in China. Of course, we all know that's just plain silly. But experts do tell us that a melting reactor core would be able to sink about 15 meters into the earth's crust, at which point it would hit the water table. The resulting massive release of hot steam would then throw the material back out of the earth with tremendous force, causing the radioactive fallout to be spread across an even wider area. Feel any better about it? We certainly don't.

Leaders Who Murdered Family Members to Get Ahead

Sometimes passive aggression will only get you so far. But is straight aggression really the key? Hey, sometimes you've got to get a head to get ahead. The following are three achievers who'd kill for their relatives' jobs.

_01:: Attila the Hun Gives Brother Bleda the Ax

When Rua, king of the Huns, died in 434 he left an empire to be coruled by his nephews Bleda and Attila. At first the brothers made a good team, negotiating a new treaty in which they agreed not to attack the Eastern Roman Empire (the part that became the Byzantine Empire, based in Constantinople) in exchange for a fee: an annual 700 pounds of gold. Not a bad deal, since it was twice what the Eastern Romans had been paying Uncle Rua. But when Constantinople failed to fork over the protection money, Attila attacked. On his rampage, the Hun destroyed every town and city (including Belgrade) along his way in a succession of battles that devastated the Eastern Roman forces. Finally, Constantinople cried "uncle" and in 443 the city agreed to pay the Huns 6,000 pounds of gold in a lump sum and to triple the annual tribute. Perhaps all the success went to Attila's head because two years later he murdered brother Bleda and took over as sole ruler of the Huns. Why kill Bleda? Historians aren't sure, but it's likely that with all the loot coming his way, Attila wasn't big on sharing.

_02:: Enrique the Fratricide Takes It to Pedro the Cruel

Born in 1334, Enrique de Trastámara was the illegitimate son of Alfonso XI, king of Castile (before Castile became part of a unified Spain). Of course the illegitimate bit brought up a legit concern: the issue of the crown. When half brother Pedro succeeded Alfonso on the throne, it didn't sit so well with little Enrique. With reinforcements from France, he invaded Castile in 1366 and took over, getting himself crowned king. But Pedro, known as "the Cruel," wasn't easily shoved aside. Securing help from England and, with Edward the Black Prince in his corner, Pedro regained the upper hand in a bitter civil war. So, Enrique responded. Rounding up even more French, he captured his brother, then personally murdered him (no one's sure how, exactly) on March 23, 1369. As Enrique II, he became known as El de las Mercedes ("He of the Largess") for awarding a new class of noble titles (with estates included) to his loyal followers. Those still loyal to Pedro's line, however, called the new king Enrique el Fratricida ("Henry the Fratricide") or simply El Bastardo.

_03:: Richard III Snuffs His Nephew

When England's Edward IV died in the spring of 1483, his brother Richard, duke of Gloucester, was appointed protector of the realm. That's because old Eddie's son, the new king Edward V, was only 12. Not only did Richard chafe at the idea of doing Ed V's job, but he didn't get along with brother Ed Sr.'s widow, Elizabeth Woodville. In fact, he thought she and her family had become too powerful, so he arrested and executed a bunch of Woodvilles and locked up his two nephews, young Edward V and Eddie's nine-year-old brother. Then he got priests to annul his brother's marriage to Elizabeth, which unseated her son Eddie as king. Guess who took the throne in the boy's stead. In August of that same year, the two little princes disappeared. Nobody knows for sure what Richard III did with them, but in 1674 workmen repairing a stairway at the Tower of London discovered the bricked-in skeletons of two boys.

Animals Subject to 'Roid Rage

The hormone hydroxy steroid ketone—better known as testosterone—is considered the biological font of maleness. And though it's often linked to muscle-headed gym dwellers, the hormone/drug actually works in pretty mysterious ways when it comes to aggressive behavior. From elephants to monkeys to the tremendously masculine antbird, check out what too much "juice" does to creatures with slightly larger brains.

_01:: Musth You Be So Aggressive?

In 1995, rangers at South Africa's Pilanesberg National Park began finding dead rhinos, brutally battered and mutilated. An investigation was launched, and it led them to a surprising realization: that the raucous culprits behind the beatings were actually teenage bull elephants. Many of the thuggish elephants were turning increasingly violent, and had added rhino murder to their rap sheets. But why all the charges? Apparently, the young bulls were entering a period known as musth, or heightened aggression related to mating, at a younger age and for longer periods than normal for teens. Wildlife biologists realized that the youngsters in the park—populated by relocated animals—lacked the biological and social structure they needed. When a few older, and perhaps wiser, bulls were added to the park, it forced the young'uns to return to their place in the elephant hierarchy. But not only did the adult supervision give them a bit of social order; it actually repressed the teens' testosterone levels, delaying and shortening musth. The elephant-on-rhino crimes stopped soon after.

A Row Is a Row Is a Row

THE CAMPBELLS AND THE MACDONALDS

In the Ring: In one corner we have Clan MacDonald, descendents of half-Viking warrior Somerled and hereditary lords of the western Highlands and isles of Scotland. In the other there's Clan Campbell, lords of Argyll and pets of the Scottish kings, rightful or not.

Round 1: Early 1300s. Robert the Bruce makes his play for the Scottish throne, supported by the Campbells. The MacDonalds (mostly, except for one smart son) support the other claimant, John Comyn. Bruce wins. MacDonalds rebel and lose their lands, many of which are given to the Campbells.

Round 2: 1692, Glencoe. After adhering to the laws of hospitality and sheltering several Campbells through a winter storm, 38 men, women, and children of the MacDonald Clan are massacred by their guests. Three MacDonald chieftains escape to spread news of the massacre and carry on the hatred.

Round 3: The Jacobite Rising of 1745. The MacDonalds are Jacobites (supporters of Catholic claimant Charles Edward Stuart, or "Bonnie Prince Charlie"). The Campbells fight alongside the redcoats of the earl of Cumberland, son of King George II. The two forces meet outside Inverness on April 16, 1746, at the Battle of Culloden. The exhausted Jacobites are driven off and all the wounded are slaughtered, many by the Campbells, while the fugitive prince is secreted "over the sea to Skye" by the brave Flora MacDonald. Punitive laws soon put an end to the Highland way of life.

Last Laugh: To this day, some descendents of Clan MacDonald refuse to eat Campbell's soup.

_02:: Fight Winner Gets (Monkey) Girl and a Hormone High

Surprisingly enough, scientists have measured the testosterone in rhesus macaque monkeys before and after a fight, and found that testosterone levels don't necessarily trigger violence. What they did find, however, was that aggression and violence definitely affect testosterone levels. For instance, if a male macaque sees an attractive, approachable female, his testosterone spikes. Then, if another male challenges monkey number one for that female, both will experience a sudden surge of testosterone. After the juices have been flowing for a while, and the fight's gone a few rounds (by the way, macaques have long, sharp canine teeth, so things can get pretty ugly), the winner's testosterone level will remain high. In fact, it might even rise higher than during the fight and stay high for 24 hours. The testosterone level in the loser, on the other hand, plummets and stays low for a much longer period.

_03:: Homebody Birds Rise to Testosterone Challenge

In migrating birds, the testosterone level is rather low—at baseline—except in the spring when the birds settle into new territories and compete for, well, chicks. On the other hand, testosterone levels of birds that don't migrate rise less, spiking only during their short mating season. But in at least one case of nonmigrating *aves,* the spotted antbirds of the Panama rainforest, males can actually raise their testosterone levels in the off-season when they need to be aggressive against territorial invaders. In fact, the sight or sound of an intruder—or even a tape of an intruder's song, played by scientists—will cause the antbird's testosterone levels to spike, and for a short period he'll become aggressive. Even odder than that: Though his gonads manufacture the hormone, they won't "come to life" sexually until the correct season.

_04:: "Bad Dad" Hormone Gets Bad Rap

What makes male mice go so bad that they need to attack and kill their own young? Strangely, it's not excess testosterone, but another steroid hormone, progesterone. Although essential to the female reproductive system, and present in both males and females, progesterone hadn't been thought to play much of a role in male chemistry. That's because females produce it in much greater volume, as they do estrogen. In 2003, however, scientists in the United States and Canada used both genetic manipulation and drugs to block progesterone receptors in otherwise normal male mice. The results were shocking. Instead of being aggressive, the male mice no longer attacked their young but actually acted tenderly toward them. The results are even more amazing when you consider that three-quarters of a control group of daddy mice killed their own babies, making a strong argument that papas and progesterone just don't mix that well.

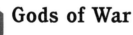

Anger from Above: Gods of War

In many religions, especially some of the older ones, gods tend to specialize. The following deities cornered their respective markets in anger, vengeance, and aggression.

_01:: Huitzilopochtli: You Gotta Have Hearts

According to Aztec legend, Huitzilopochtli's 401 older siblings tried to kill him, but the clever god turned the tables on them and wiped 'em out with his weapon of choice, the *xiuhcóatl* (or for those of you who don't speak Aztec, a turquoise snake). Represented either as a hummingbird or as a warrior with armor and helmet made of hummingbird feathers (not exactly bulletproof), Huitzilopochtli was both god of the sun and the god of war. As such, Aztecs believed that he needed a steady diet of human hearts—preferably of the warrior variety—and human blood. In fact, the need to feed Huitzilopochtli fueled the Aztecs' ambition, and increased their urgency for fighting and conquering other peoples.

_02:: Ishtar: Not Just the Goddess of Box Office Death

Bizarrely enough, Babylon's goddess of sexual love, fertility, and plenty was also a principal goddess of war. Known by the Sumerians to the west as Inanna, Ishtar became one of the most complex and contradictory deities in the pantheon of the ancient Middle East—representing both rejoicing and grief, harvest and devastation. Ishtar also doubled as protec-tor of prostitutes (who probably worked in her temples), and is identified with Astarte, the goddess of war and sexual love worshiped by the Egyptians, Canaanites, and Hittites (a long-ago civilization in what later became part of Turkey). Needless to say, the goddess had nothing to do with the 1987 movie flop that bears her name...unless perhaps she put a curse on it? How else can you explain the eerie flop of a big-budget buddy pic starring War-ren Beatty and Dustin Hoffman?

_03:: Ares: No Dog's Best Friend

Although fiercely warlike, ancient Greeks rarely held Ares, god of war, in high regard. Sure, the guy represented brutality and slaughter—the spirit of war at its most savage. But as an Olympian—that is, among the inner circle of Hellenic deities—he was disliked by his divine peers and even his dad, the great Zeus. So, why the lack of love? Whenever Ares was wounded in battle, he'd come running to Daddy to fix things (mainly bones). And while his pops wasn't always supportive, Ares' sister Eris (Strife) and sons Phobos (Panic) and Dei-mos (Annihilation) stuck by him. All that isn't to say that Ares didn't have any earthly fol-lowers: he was most popular in Thrace, a re-gion to the north of the Greek peninsula. The so-called worship, however, was an SPCA nightmare, as Spartans annually slaughtered dogs in sacrifice to him.

_04:: Mars: The God of Rome Improvement

Unlike Ares, Mars, god of war, carried more clout among Romans than his counterpart had in Greece. According to one story, Romulus, the founder of Rome, was a son of Mars. As such, the fierce battle god was seen as protector of Rome, and the month named for him, March, was festival time, as well as the time to prepare for battle. (Fighting tended to die down over the winter and resume again in spring.) The Mars fan club didn't end with the early Romans, though. In the time of Augustus (around 1 CE) Mars came to be considered avenger of the murdered dictator Julius Caesar (Augustus's great-uncle), and the war god's prominence continued to grow through the early Common Era.

_05:: Tÿr: The Sound of One Hand Pounding

The old Norse god Tÿr governed rules of battle, oaths, alliances, and even treaties. And he did it all with an iron fist . . . but just one of them. According to legend, Tÿr placed his hand in the mouth of Fenrir, a sort of monster-wolf, as a gesture of good faith. Then other gods tied down Fenrir so he could rampage no more. When the wolf realized he'd been duped into being docile for the purposes of being tied down, he retaliated by biting off Tÿr's hand. Of course, Tÿr's image changed from people to people. As envisioned by the Goths, barbarians who were originally from southern Scandinavia but later spread southward, Tÿr wasn't just one-handed but also one-armed. As such,

after a battle, the Goths would hack off the arms of enemy dead and suspend them from tree branches in tribute to their one-armed god. The practice was also pretty effective for terrifying the surviving enemy. While he isn't worshiped with the same vigor today, Tÿr does live on via the calendar, as Tuesdays (Tÿsdagr in Norse) are named for him.

_06:: Skanda: Six Heads Are Fiercer Than One

For early Hindus, the thunder god Indra and his brother, Agni, god of fire, were battle deities until Skanda (also called Karttikeya and Kumara) came on the scene. Devoted to nothing but war and violent adventure, this divine bachelor is depicted as a six-headed, armored archer who rides—what else?—a peacock. According to one myth, Skanda was born only because other gods, including Indra and Agni, needed a warrior to defeat the tyrannical demon Taraka. Since Taraka had been deemed invulnerable against all but a son of the god Siva—a childless, mourning widower—other deities conspired to arouse Siva's interest in the beautiful young goddess Parvatti. It took much meddling to awaken Siva from his mourning, but the matchmaking worked and eventually the six-headed Skanda was born. Enormously strong, Skanda could plunge his spear into the earth so firmly that no one but the god Vishnu could pull it out, shaking mountains and rivers in the effort.

_07:: The Eye Has It

Also called Wotan or Wodan, Odin was the Norse father god—a sort of Teutonic Zeus, but more often identified with the Roman Mercury. (The Latin *dies Mercurii* became Wotan's day, or Wednesday.) The warlike god of a warring culture, Odin presided over Valhalla, where slain fighters went to drink forever in bliss. Odin, often depicted as a tall, long-bearded old man observing the world from beneath the wide brim of his hat, rode an eight-legged flying horse, his cloak billowing behind him. He's also depicted with just one eye, not because he'd lost it riding with scissors, but rather because he'd traded the other in for eternal wisdom. Both wise, and bloodthirsty—definitely the makings of a god you can love.

Historical Figures Who Struck Back with a Vengeance

It's better to give than to receive. But then there's the whole issue of giving back, as in "some of their own medicine." The following are three cases where a little bit of vengeance went a long way.

_01:: The Charlemagne Attraction

On August 15, 778 CE, Charlemagne suffered the only major military defeat of his long reign. The king of the Franks and his army were passing through the Pyrenees when Basque fighters struck the column's rear guard. Why? The attack was simply revenge for the pillaging that Charlemagne had ordered on Basque villages. Among those killed in the skirmish, though, was a young paladin, nephew of the king, called Hrudoland. Today, historians know nothing about the real Hrudoland except for a legend of his heroism that was turned into the 12th-century epic poem *The Song of Roland*. In the poem, the attackers aren't Basque fighters but Muslims, carrying out a plot against Roland hatched by his scheming stepfather. The poet goes on to tell of Charlemagne's victory over the Muslims to avenge

Roland's death, and of the evil stepfather being tried, convicted, then gruesomely executed. A bit of poetic license, to say the least: in history, Charlemagne did gain the upper hand against Muslim rulers of northern Spain, but it wasn't until a decade later. And it didn't have much to do with Roland.

_02:: Murder in the Cathedral

On a Sunday in 1478, a gang led by Francesco de' Pazzi attacked the Medici brothers, Lorenzo and Giuliano, during high mass in Florence's cathedral. The attack on the city's rulers seemed marginally successful at the time, as Pazzi and his pals stabbed Giuliano to death while his other conspirators tried to kill Lorenzo. Wounded, Lorenzo Medici managed to flee the scene. Amazingly, Pazzi's conspirators were wide-ranging, and included the archbishop of Pisa, the duke of Urbino, and Pope Sixtus IV (who wisely stayed in Rome). And while the gang had worked out most of the angles in their plot, they hadn't accounted for the Florentine people's reaction. Outraged Florentines mobbed the attackers, killed them, and dragged their bodies through the streets. When the archbishop tried to take over the government palace, Florentines slaughtered him and hung his corpse on a wall. Eventually, Lorenzo felt he'd gotten more revenge than he sought, and he tried to rein in the people's rage. As for the Pazzi family, business rivals of the Medicis, they lost everything, and many changed their names or dropped out of sight.

_03:: **Russian Reversal of Fortune**

Czar Alexander I hadn't wanted to declare war on Napoléon's France, but what's a czar to do? When France attacked Russia's European allies, he felt obligated to come to their aid. And Russia certainly paid a price. Suffering terrible defeats at Napoléon's hands in 1805 and 1807, Alexander was left with his army decimated, and thus signed a humiliating treaty with France. But Alex, it turned out, had no intention of honoring the bargain. When Napoléon's patience with his "ally" wore thin in 1812, the French corporal decided it would be a good idea to invade Russia. It wasn't. The Russian commander, Prince Kutuzov, devised a controlled retreat, allowing Napoléon to capture an evacuated Moscow—soon destroyed by fire. When Napoléon had to pull back, Kutuzov forced him to return west by the same now-ravaged route he had come, with the fierce winter closing in. The devastating retreat from Russia marked the beginning of Napoléon's end. In March of 1814, Alexander triumphantly entered Paris, vengeance achieved.

All in the Family:
Wars Waged on Familial Insults

Wars can start for all sorts of reasons: to secure trade routes, to capture resources, to eliminate a dangerous rival...but the most interesting wars flare up because of personal insults that lead to family feuds. After all, when a king's starting his speeches with a "your momma" joke, you know trouble's on its way.

_01:: **The Face That Launched a Thousand Ships**

Homer tells the story brilliantly: thousands killed, cities burned and pillaged, and giant equines built out of wood in a country that had barely any trees. And the root cause of the entire affair, as the ancients told it, was a woman: Helen, queen of Sparta. For reasons totally outside her comprehension, she was abducted by Paris, the wimpy prince of Troy. Once thought to be a myth, the story of the Trojan War is being reevaluated by scholars. In the centuries since, documents discovered in Hittite cities in Asia Minor make references to some of Homer's characters and the places he mentions. Did the war really start over the theft of Menelaus' wife? We will probably never know; though control over the lucrative trade routes to the Black Sea probably didn't hurt the cause.

_02:: Sister Pact

After the death of Gaius Julius Caesar, the most important men in Rome were two of his kinsmen, Gaius Octavianus (his great-nephew and adopted heir) and Marcus Antonius (aka Mark Antony). Realizing they could be even stronger with their powers combined, the two united with their good pal Lepidus, and formed a triumvirate that would determine the fate of all Roman territories. But the two needed something to seal the deal, and what better than a couple of marriage vows to do the trick? Octavianus wedded Antony's stepdaughter, and Antony took Octavianus's sister, Octavia, for better or for worse. Of course, for Octavia it was definitely for worse. Once old Mark caught sight of Cleopatra, he wanted a divorce. Meanwhile, this didn't really help matters between Octavianus and Antony, as the two men had remained rivals through their dealings. But news of the Antonys' divorce helped Octavianus decide he'd had enough. The civil war between the two lasted from 33 to 30 BCE. By the end of it, Octavianus was the undisputed ruler of the Roman world; he changed his name to Augustus and became the first Roman emperor. Antony, on the other hand, had committed suicide to avoid capture, having learned the hard way that you just don't mess with a man's sister.

_03:: How a Little Bullying Went a Long, Long Way

Tan Shi Huai was the illegitimate son of a Xianbei (Mongol) mercenary serving the Han dynasty of China. As a result of his low birth, he was considered little better than a slave by his fellow tribesmen. The insults served his way must have stuck in his young craw, particularly given his (as yet unrevealed) ambition, intelligence, and strategic skill. His injured pride may have spurred him on as he gathered a following of malcontents, somehow finagled his way into the supreme overlordship of all Xianbei tribes around 170 CE, and organized a powerful empire north of the Great Wall, even defeating the Huns who had previously ruled the region. Then, in 177, he defeated the Chinese army and threatened the imperial court, though an attack on the capital never materialized because of supply problems. Sadly, however, his empire, which had been held together largely through his own force of will, didn't survive his death. Still, the guy defeated both the mighty Hans and Huns. All because he was picked on as a kid? Makes you wonder how much more effective our politicians could be if we started insulting their families a little more.

_04:: The Great Islamic Schism

Politics in sixth- and early-seventh-century Mecca were dominated by a feud between two clans, the Hashemites and the Umayyads. And though the feud continued into the mid-600s, a generation after Muhammad's rise to power, things really came to a head in 656, when the caliph Uthman (an Umayyad) was murdered. The new caliph, Ali (a Hashemite cousin and a son-in-law of Muhammad), didn't really help smooth things over when he failed (or refused) to track down and punish the assassins. It's little wonder, then, that the Umayyads saw this as somewhat suspicious and, even worse, kind of insulting to their clan. A five-year war broke out, and eventually ended in a truce, but Ali's subsequent murder (not exactly truceful) and replacement by the Umayyad leader Muawiyya (whose kinsmen would rule the Islamic world for a century to come) exacerbated the conflict. Ali's followers, however, have remained faithful to the end. Driven underground, they called themselves Shiat Ali, or "the Party of Ali," and their spiritual descendents are known today as the Shiites. The rift caused by the fiasco survives to the modern day in Islam's two largest sects.

_05:: The Princess Bride (and a Decidedly Less Happy Ending)

In 758 CE, Caliph Abdullah al-Mansur, the titular ruler of all Islam, decided to order one of his nobles to take a royal Khazar bride and bring about some peace (the Khazars had fought two brutal wars to stop Islamic expansion into the Caucasus Mountains and Eastern Europe). To carry out this seemingly easy task, al-Mansur picked the military governor of Armenia, Yazid ibn Usayd al-Sulami, for the great marriage mission. Of course, Yazid was happy to comply, and took home a daughter of Khagan Baghatur, the Khazar leader. Things were going very well when the girl somehow died, possibly in childbirth, though the details are vague. Her attendants, however, didn't need details. They returned home convinced that some Arab faction had poisoned her (not unreasonable, all things considered). Needless to say, Pops got angry, and took his revenge on the Abbasid Caliphate. The Khazars quickly invaded what is now northwestern Iran, plundering and raiding as only nomads can.

SLOTH

⑤ Go-getters Who Found Time to Nap ⑤ Inventions Better Than the Remote ④ Famous Cases of Plagiarism ④ Cats Who Lay Down on the Job But Got Things Done Anyway ⑤ Artists Who Bowed to Beer Pressure ⑤ Lazily Designed Landmarks ④ World Leaders Who Accomplished Absolutely Nothing ⑤ Famous Journalistic Goofs That Could Have Been Avoided ⑤ Laziest Kings of All Time ④ Dates That History Misplaced ④ Famous Tunes Stolen from Other Tunes ⑤ Delinquent Rock Groups and the Chaos They Stirred ④ Famous Figures Who Never Held (Real) Day Jobs ⑤ Bad Nights of Sleep That Led to Drastic Mistakes ④ Laziest Flag Designs ③ Warning Calls History Ignored ④ Figures Who Claimed Someone Else's Fame

Sleeping Giants:
Go-getters Who Found Time to Nap

Call it a power nap. Call it a break. Whatever you call it, don't assume that somebody who sneaks in a few winks in the middle of the day can't also take care of business.

_01:: Thomas Edison: Highly Inventive Napping

Prolific inventor Thomas Edison didn't like to go to bed at night. In fact, he didn't like to take his clothes off or change into pajamas because he thought it somehow interfered with his creativity. The solution? The "Wizard of Menlo Park" chose instead to sleep a few hours at night—often no more than three—then catch naps in the lab around the clock, whenever he felt tired. Colleagues referred to it as his "genius for sleep." After Edison built his laboratory and home together in Menlo Park, New Jersey, in 1876, he could indulge his odd sleep habits with little trouble—except with his wife, Mary, who found his eccentric hours bothersome. But he kept on doing it anyway. Edison loved to stretch out atop a lab table when catching a quickie, but he was known to make do on a stool if nothing more comfortable was handy.

_02:: Warren G. Harding: Late to Bed and Early to Rise

Although he seldom went to bed before midnight and frequently stayed up until 2 a.m., President Harding was not a very late riser. In fact, he always got up at 8. His White House schedule, however, left him increasingly fa-

tigued, perhaps signifying sleep deprivation, but also a sign of the advancing heart disease that would kill him in office in 1923. Friends told Harding that he would be more rested if he stayed in bed in the morning but the president refused, saying that to do so would be "too much like a woman." Irwin "Ike" Hood, chief usher of the White House, recalled that instead, the sleep-deprived president would steal the occasional presidential power nap in the Oval Office.

_03:: Salvador Dalí: Surreal Sleep

Salvador Dalí, the Spanish surrealist painter, arrived at the startling images of his most productive period—between 1929 and 1937—using what he called the "paranoiac-critical method." Apparently, this involved fishing "delirious associations and interpretations" out of his unconscious. It's less than clear how he accomplished this, but he used no intoxicants. "I don't do drugs," he once said. "I am drugs." Dalí wasn't above manipulating his consciousness in other ways, though. He reportedly took odd little catnaps that brought him right to the edge of deep sleep, but then jerked himself out of it. His method was simple: Seated in an armchair, Dalí held a metal spoon in one hand. Then, next to his chair,

It's a Mad, Mad, Mad, Mad Scientist

OLIVER HEAVISIDE REJECTS THE BATH

Maybe it was the scarlet fever he had as a boy that left him partially deaf. Or maybe it was the years he spent isolated in his parents' house studying electricity. Or maybe it was the lack of recognition he received from the scientific community. Whatever it was, something drove British mathematician and physicist Oliver Heaviside (1850–1925) certifiably loony. Heaviside made lots of important discoveries, like operational calculus, impedance, and a layer of the ionosphere now called the Kennelly–Heaviside layer (he's also got moon and Mars craters and a song in *Cats* named after him). But his twilight years were marked by all kinds of kooky behavior, brought on by bitterness and a persecution complex. Oliver refused to bathe, but kept his fingernails impeccably manicured and painted bright pink. He signed all his letters "W.O.R.M.," which stood for…well, worm (how he saw himself or, perhaps, everyone else). And here's the best one: He replaced all the furniture in his house with giant blocks of granite. Yes, really.

he'd place a metal pan. He'd quickly nod off, and as soon as he was relaxed enough to let go of the spoon, it would fall against the pan. The sudden clang waking him up, Dalí was immediately reacquainted with his subconscious, and went back to work.

Touch of Evil

Calvin Coolidge took the oath of office at 2:00 in the morning following Warren Harding's death, but he was rarely up that late during any other night of his term. In fact, he was publicly reported to sleep an average of eleven hours every single day.

_04:: Samuel Goldwyn: Cinematic Snoozer

One of Hollywood's most prominent film producers for over 30 years, Sam Goldwyn believed in hard work. Indeed, he demanded it from his employees. He also believed in taking care of himself. Every day after lunch, Sam would take a siesta, disappearing into a room adjacent to his office, changing into pajamas, and sleeping for an hour. According to biographer Arthur Marx, Goldwyn—the man behind such classics as *Wuthering Heights* and *The Best Years of Our Lives*—believed a 60-minute afternoon nap was the secret to good health. One day he recommended the practice to two writers working on a script for a Danny Kaye picture. "You ought to try it, too," he said. Then, realizing that he didn't want the scribes sleeping on company time, he added, "In your cases, eat a half hour, sleep a half hour."

_05:: Ronald Reagan: To Nap or Not to Nap?

Ronald Reagan supposedly took a nap every day. In fact, it was frequently mentioned in newspaper columns and widely accepted as fact. But First Lady Nancy Reagan vehemently denied the accusations. What he did, Nancy said, was take a short break in the afternoon, away from staff, visitors, and the press. It was, after all, on doctor's orders after Reagan was wounded in a 1981 assassination attempt. Maureen Reagan, the president's daughter, also insisted that Reagan hated to take naps. So maybe the Gipper didn't nap in private, but as a president who was nearly 70 when he took office, he was definitely observed from time to time nodding off in public. Reagan even joked about falling asleep in cabinet meetings and once dropped off in the middle of a speech by Pope John Paul II.

Slacker's Paradise: Inventions Better Than the Remote

Oh, the horrors of the past. Although it's hard to fathom why people bothered to go on living, there was once a time when folks had no choice but to sit up straight in their chairs, fiddle with buttons and zippers, climb stairs, hike to the outhouse, and add numbers with pencil and paper. Below, a paean to the inventions that made it easier to enjoy the simple pleasures of sinful idleness.

_01:: Velcro

Isaac Newton beneath the apple tree. Archimedes shouting "Eureka!" in the bathtub. And Georges de Mestral going for a walk in the woods. The greatest discoveries often stem from mundane observations, and while gravity (Newton) and measurable density (Archimedes) are cool and everything, nothing beats the sweet music of parting Velcro. Mestral, a Swiss engineer, returned home after a walk in 1948 to find cockleburs stuck to his coat. After examining one under a microscope, he noted that cockleburs attach to clothes and fur via thin hooks. Eureka! It took Mestral eight years to develop his product. But in the end, the twin nylon strips worked precisely like a cocklebur on a coat—one strip features burr-like hooks and the other thousands of small loops to which they attach, forming an unusually strong bond.

_02:: Calculator

Ah, the calculator—a handy device that makes 55378008 look like a naughty word when you turn it upside down. Oh, and it also makes math class a whole lot easier. Oddly enough, it was a 19-year-old boy named Blaise Pascal (yes, that Pascal) who invented the first mechanical adding machine. But Pascal's device was cumbersome and couldn't record results, so the vast majority of people continued calculating by hand until 1892, when William Seward Burroughs patented the first commercially viable adding machine. Although Burroughs died before reaping much profit from his invention, his grandson (also William Seward Burroughs) was one sure beneficiary. The younger Burroughs became famous for writing *Naked Lunch,* a book that would likely have been impossible if Burroughs hadn't had all that inherited calculator money to waste on heroin.

_03:: Lay-Z-Boy

In 1928, when he was a mere lad of 21, Edwin Shoemaker forever blurred the distinction between sitting up and lying down by developing the world's first reclining chair. His initial model, a wood-slat chair intended for porches, was fashioned out of orange crates and designed to fit the contours of the back at any angle. It took an early customer, appreciative of the concept but rather unexcited about the prospect of lying down on bare slats of wood, to suggest *upholstering* the chair. Shoemaker and his partner (and cousin) Edward Knabusch then held a contest to name the invention. "La-Z-Boy" beat out suggestions like "Sit 'n Snooze" and "The Slack Back." The next time someone tells you an active lifestyle is the key to long life, reply with this tidbit: The man who invented the recliner lazed his way up to the ripe old age of 91.

_04:: The Toilet

Contrary to popular belief, we do not have Thomas Crapper to thank for the conveniences of the flushing toilet (more on him in a mo-

ment). Toilets with drainage systems date to 2500 BCE, but Sir John Harrington invented the first "water closet" around 1596 (it was also used by his godmother, Queen Elizabeth I). However, toilets never caught on until Alexander Cummings invented the "Strap," which featured a sliding valve between the bowl and the sewage trap. As for Mr. Crapper (1837–1910), he was a plumber who sold, but did not invent, a popular type of toilet, although he did hold several plumbing-related patents. Not surprisingly, Crapper has been unfairly linked to the less-than-pleasant word "crap." The two, however, are unrelated. In 1846, the first time "crap" is recorded as having been used in English, little Tommy-poo was just nine years of age.

_05:: The Escalator

In 1891, Jesse Reno patented the first moving staircase, paving the way for today's world, in which we choose not to use staircases, just StairMasters. Reno's invention was more of an inclined ramp than the escalator we know today; passengers hooked into cleats on the belt and scooted up the ramp at a 25-degree angle. Fairly soon after, he built a spiral escalator— the mere thought nauseates us—in London, but it was never used by the public. Reno's first escalator, however, *was* widely used, albeit not practically. In a testament to how utterly unamusing amusement parks were in the 1890s, 75,000 people rode Reno's "inclined elevator" during a two-week exhibition at Coney Island in 1896. Let's be clear: The escalator was not the means by which one traveled to a ride. It was *the ride itself.*

Say My Name, Say My Name: Famous Cases of Plagiarism

No writer can be fully convicted of imitation except there is a concurrence of more resemblance than can be imagined to have happened by chance; as where not only the thought but the words are copied. And we ought to know a thing or two about plagiarism, since we stole that previous sentence from the great Samuel Johnson (1709–1784), who himself was accused of it. But even by Johnson's strict definition, these folks are all guilty as sin.

_01:: Martin Luther King Jr.: I Heard a Dream (Which Subsequently Became My Dream)

When writing about the Lord God Almighty, one is generally well advised not to break the seventh commandment, but Martin Luther King Jr. managed to turn out pretty well in spite of his tendency to borrow others' words without attribution. King received a doctorate in systematic theology from Boston University in 1955 on the strength of a dissertation comparing the theologians Paul Tillich and Henry Nelson Weiman. In a 1989–1990 review, though, the university discovered that King had plagiarized about a third of his thesis from a previous student's dissertation. And although it was closer to liberal adaptation than outright plagiarism, King's seminal "I Have a Dream" speech was, well, let's say "inspired by" a speech that an African American preacher named Archibald Carey Jr. gave to the Republican National Convention in 1952.

_02:: Stendhal: The Politician's Plagiarist

When asked by Oprah Winfrey about his favorite book during the 2000 presidential campaign, Al Gore cited Stendhal's *The Red and the Black*, a novel set in post-Napoleonic France. The book's protagonist, Julien Sorel, is an ambitious young womanizer who adopts the hypocrisy of his time in order to move up in the world. In his own time, Stendhal, whose real name was Henri Beyle, was most famous not for his novels, but for his books about art and travel. In one, *The Lives of Haydn, Mozart and Metastasio,* Stendhal plagiarized extensively from two previous biographies. Confronted with overwhelming evidence of theft, Stendhal added forgery to the list of his literary crimes, manufacturing correspondence in the hopes of exonerating himself.

_03:: Alex Haley and the Roots of *Roots*

Haley initially gained prominence for being the "as told to" author behind *The Autobiography of Malcolm X* and then went on to publish the epic *Roots: The Saga of an American*

Family in 1976, supposedly a true story that traced Haley's ancestry back to an African man, Kunta Kinte. Haley won a Pulitzer the next year, and the book was made into a wildly popular miniseries (which, curiously enough, featured the PBS show *Reading Rainbow*'s LeVar Burton as Kinte). After the book's publication, though, Haley admitted that he made up large swaths of the *Roots* story and, in a further embarrassment, was sued by author Harold Courlander for plagiarism. Haley acknowledged lifting (accidentally, he claimed) three paragraphs from Courlander's work and settled the suit out of court.

_04:: John Milton: In His Own Words

Was the half-blind creator of *Paradise Lost* a plagiarist? Well, no. But William Lauder, an 18th-century scholar, sure wanted you to think so. Bitter about his professional failures, Lauder published several essays in 1747 claiming to "prove" that Milton had stolen almost all of *Paradise Lost* from various 17th-century poets. One problem, though. Lauder had forged the poems, interpolating text from *Paradise Lost* into the original documents. For a while, many (including the great Samuel Johnson) supported Lauder, but it soon became clear by studying extant copies of the old poems that Lauder, not Milton, was the cheat. And cheating, at least in this case, didn't pay: Exiled to the West Indies, Lauder died an impoverished shopkeeper.

Supine Successes: Cats Who Lay Down on the Job But Got Things Done Anyway

Parents and coaches have the annoying habit of urging people to get up and at 'em. Someone should remind them that the "up" part isn't always necessary.

_01:: Florence Nightingale: Don't Just Do Something, Lie There

As a hero of the Crimean War, nurse Florence Nightingale revolutionized the care of wounded and ill soldiers. And she's been remembered by British soldiers in the Crimea as the tireless "Lady with the Lamp," for patrolling field hospitals all through the night. It's no wonder, then, that Nightingale returned from the Crimea to London in 1856 with enough clout to lobby Queen Victoria for improvements in military living conditions. The next year, however, the 37-year-old healthcare advocate lay down and seldom again got up. Doctors who examined her found her perfectly healthy, with no apparent physical reason for her sudden unwillingness to rise. Living as an invalid for the last 53 years of her life, Nightingale remained inert yet rarely indulged in idleness. She supervised fundraising, advocated better training for nurses and midwives, received official visitors, took care of correspondence, and oversaw substantial projects—such as founding a London nursing school—all from the comfort of her couch.

_02:: Mark Twain: "A Pretty Good Gospel"

"Whenever I've got some work to do I go to bed," said the 69-year-old Mark Twain in 1905. In an interview with the *New York Times,* he explained: "I got into that habit some time ago when I had an attack of bronchitis. Suppose your bronchitis lasts six weeks. The first two you can't do much but attend to the barking and so on, but the last four I found I could work if I stayed in bed and when you can work you don't mind staying in bed." At his mansion in Hartford, Connecticut, the writer—whose real name was Samuel Clemens—ran a rubber hose from the gas chandelier in his bedroom to a gas lamp on his bedside table so that he would have enough light to write by. "Work in bed is a pretty good gospel," he told the *Times.* Of course, this is also coming from the man who said, "Whenever I feel the urge to exercise I lie down until the feeling passes away."

_03:: Winston Churchill: We Will Fight Them from the Bedroom

Britain's cigar-chomping prime minister during World War II conducted considerable state business from his bed. Tucked under the covers, the people's PM would dictate letters, tele-

---

It's a Mad, Mad, Mad, Mad Scientist

THOMAS MORGAN AND HIS FLY PLATE

Thomas Hunt Morgan, the Nobel Prize–winning geneticist whose research with fruit flies established the role of the chromosome in inheritance, was a meticulous thinker, but he was unspeakably sloppy about everything else. So, how sloppy was he? Morgan once wore a length of string as a belt and often sported shoes and shirts with holes in them. In his Columbia University laboratory, which smelled of fermented bananas (food for the insects), Morgan's staff threw discarded fruit flies into a jar of oil that they called "the morgue." Their boss, by contrast, simply smashed his flies against the white porcelain plate he used for counting them. He would leave the accumulating mess for days, even weeks, until someone—often the wife of one of his graduate students—felt compelled to wash the plate. Need more? His mail, which was usually unopened, lay in a massive pile that cluttered his lab table workstation until somebody else threw it away.

---

grams, and speeches—including his famous "Battle of Britain Speech" of 1940—to his secretaries until the early hours of the morning. He worked so late that secretaries were given sleeping quarters in the official residence, 10 Downing Street, so that one would always be on hand. In the morning, Churchill breakfasted and read the newspaper in bed, then would dictate again, to a secretary sitting on the end of his bed. If he had no meetings scheduled, he stayed in bed, working all the while, until noon. Then he would rise, bathe, and go to the House of Commons.

_04:: Hugh Hefner: All Play Is All Work

Given the subject matter of *Playboy* magazine, publisher Hugh Hefner could have claimed the most enjoyable hours spent in the revolving circular bed of his mansion as work time. Nice work if you can get it. That's not what got him on this list, however. Especially in the swingin' 1960s, when his home and headquar-

ters was the 70-room Playboy Mansion on Chicago's Gold Coast, the workaholic's office wear was always silk pajamas, and it wasn't unusual for him to sprawl across that hedonistic bed along with stacks of photos to select from or copy to be reviewed for the next issue. In 1971, Hefner ditched midwestern winters in favor of southern California, where he brought his style of relaxed labor to a Playboy Mansion in Beverly Hills.

Touch of Evil

Xaviera Hollander, famous prostitute and author of The Happy Hooker, *still makes her living in the sack, kinda. She owns a bed-and-breakfast in Amsterdam.*

Hooked on Tonics: Artists Who Bowed to Beer Pressure

Asked to give advice to aspiring writers, novelist William Styron once said, "You ought not to drink; you ought to write." The advice is a lot easier given than followed.

_01:: Patrick Branwell Brontë: Black Sheep in a Snowy Flock

As a boy, Patrick Branwell Brontë (called Branwell) created an elaborate imaginary world with his big sister Charlotte. Including younger sisters Emily and Anne, the Brontë children of Haworth, Yorkshire, spun fantasies that fueled the girls' later careers as novelists.

Branwell wrote, too, but never published anything beyond a few poems in local newspapers. A gifted musician and artist, he opened a portrait studio, hoping to thrive as a painter. Lacking commissions, though, he spent more time in pubs than at the easel. Fired from the few jobs he tried—either for incompetence or (in the case of one tutoring position) questionable behavior toward his employer's wife—Branwell Brontë took to drinking more and to opium. By many accounts as promising a creative force as his sisters were, Branwell died a failure at 31.

_02:: F. Scott Fitzgerald: The Sodden Side of Paradise

Famed novelist (and the guy responsible for plenty of required high school reading) F. Scott Fitzgerald died of a heart attack in L.A. in 1940, believing himself a failure. Aside from his first book, 1920's *This Side of Paradise,* his works had not sold well. That included the critically well received *The Great Gatsby.* Fitzgerald did, however, earn good money writing stories for magazines, but had not saved any. His glamorous marriage had gone adrift upon a sea of alcohol and, in wife Zelda's case, insanity. Although an alcoholic, Fitzgerald typically wrote sober, before his first cocktail of the day. Free of alcoholism, however, he would likely have completed many more novels and may even have been able to hold his family together. When he died, Fitzgerald was writing a novel, *The Last Tycoon,* and it was going well—largely because he was staying away from the bottle. Too bad he never finished the book. After he died, scholars placed Fitzgerald among the best American novelists.

Touch of Evil

Original KISS drummer Peter Criss won an out-of-court settlement after the Star depicted him as a homeless drunk living under a Santa Monica bridge in 1991. The person photographed wasn't Criss but a look-alike alcoholic.

_03:: John Barrymore: Good Night, Sweet (Hiccup!) Prince

Decades before granddaughter Drew appeared on the scene, matinee idol John Barrymore was the most celebrated member of a show business dynasty, along with brother Lionel, a character actor, and sister Ethel, a leading lady of the stage. The three grew up as theater royalty, since parents Maurice Barrymore and Georgiana Drew were 19th-century stars. John took after his famous father, and the resemblance extended to their drinking—a trait that killed them both. When drunk, John made public scenes. He flew into screaming rages. He urinated in public. And the effects played into his career. In his final decade, John—once considered the greatest actor of his time for roles such as Hamlet—was reduced to taking degrading parts in trashy films. His mind was so riddled by booze that he couldn't remember his lines and he often had to read them from a blackboard off camera. A tragic ending for the brilliant talent, he died in 1942 at the age of 60.

_04:: Dylan Thomas: "Do Not Go Gentle..."

Precocious Welshman Dylan Thomas caught the attention of the London literary world when he was only 20 with the publication of his first book, *18 Poems,* in 1934. The Celtic rhythms of his English verse, and their themes—gnawing at elusive love and inevitable death—came across as startlingly full of feeling. Thomas, who had quit school at 16 to become a newspaper reporter, was a writer for the rest of his 39 years, producing poetry, prose, and drama, but he was also a heavy drinker. Constantly in debt to the Inland Revenue (Britain's counterpart to the IRS) and frequently broke, Thomas used alcohol for solace and inspiration. When away from wife Caitlin on a visit to London or on a speaking tour of U.S. universities, the poet was almost certain to get roaring drunk. It was on just such a trip that he died in New York, in 1953, of acute alcohol poisoning.

_05:: Charles Bukowski: When Life Inebriates Art

Some artists lose precious years of their productive life to the bottle. Bukowski, on the other hand, drank as he wrote and wrote as he drank. The prolific Los Angeles poet, who also wrote short stories (collected in the volume *Notes of a Dirty Old Man*) and novels (such as *Post Office*), wrote about drunks, prostitutes, and down-and-outers. His frequent main character, the hard-drinking and often pathetic Henry Chinaski, was a thinly veiled portrayal of Bukowski himself. The violence and graphic frankness in his work flowed from a dissolute life that Bukowski embraced, exposed, mocked, and—in an odd way—romanticized. His one screenplay, for the 1987 movie *Barfly*, was a love story featuring alcoholics on skid row.

If I Had a Hammock: Lazily Designed Landmarks

Attention do-it-yourselfers: You aren't the only ones to ever screw up a project. And you can take comfort in the fact that, most likely, your botched projects aren't on public display. Here are five high-profile screwups that don't have the luxury of anonymity.

_01:: Don't Lean on Me: Pisa's Towering Problems

The best known of the world's landmark blunders, the famed Leaning Tower is actually a *series* of blunders. Begun by Bonanno Pisano (whose name, ironically, means "A good year in Pisa") in 1174, the tower started leaning almost immediately, due to the incredibly poor soil conditions beneath it. Only three floors were completed before Pisa's frequent wars halted construction for 94 years. Then, by the time construction resumed in 1272, the lean was considerable. Of course, rather than de-molishing it and starting over (preferably on more stable ground), the builders decided to *correct* for the lean by building the rest of the tower at a compensatory angle. Which is why, today, the tower doesn't just lean. It actually curves.

_02:: That Sinking Feeling: The Story of Folsom Library

The goof-ups in the construction of the Folsom Library at upstate New York's Rensselaer Polytechnic Institute are made even more ironic by the fact that they occurred at an engineering school. The library's floors were originally intended to bow upward slightly, so the weight of the books would level them. Unfortunately, the construction crews were a little foggy on this concept and built them nice and level. Like floors should be, damn it! Once the books were added, though, the floors developed a pronounced sag. RPI legend also has it that the contractor hired to design the foundation did so without knowing the building was a library, so he didn't account for the weight of the books. The resulting wimpiness of the foundation causes Folsom Library to sink about one inch every year. It's one of several buildings on campus that are sinking, sagging, or moving, phenomena the students refer to generally as "sliding down the hill into Troy."

Touch of Evil

Less than three years after appearing on the "state quarters" series, the New Hampshire natural rock formation known as the "Old Man of the Mountain" crumbled. Of course, the same force that originally crafted the site was to blame for its collapse: Mother Nature.

_03:: Foul Ballpark: Houston's Disastrous Dome

OK, for its time it was pretty amazing. But the Houston Astrodome had some major problems when it first opened in 1965. Proclaimed a masterpiece of engineering and "the Eighth Wonder of the World," its original roof was made of clear Lucite panels. All of which sounds fine, but actually caused such a bad glare that outfielders routinely lost sight of the ball. So the roof panels were painted to block out the sun. Also not a bad idea, except that it caused the

Lies Your Mother Told You

DON'T THROW RICE (THROW BUTTERFLIES?)

Under the sway of the widespread but ridiculous myth that wedding rice poses a threat to birds, thousands of newlyweds have sought out rice alternatives, with questionable results. One of the more popular, ostensibly eco-friendly solutions is butterflies: They're pretty, they're totally natural, and they'll make you—a terrorist? So say the generally genial folks at the North American Butterfly Association, who argued in 1999 that releasing butterflies into the wild amounted to "environmental terrorism." Nonnative butterflies can cause a host of problems—introducing new parasites to native populations, interbreeding, and messing up migratory patterns. Some lepidopterologists (yes, there's a word for butterfly scientists) have even expressed concern that the growing popularity of butterfly releases has led to overharvesting of wild monarchs, the world's most popular butterfly species. Popular alternatives for true environmentalists include bubbles and rose petals. Or, you know, rice also works.

grass on the field to die almost immediately (its life may have been prolonged by the notoriously leaky roof, which let in so much rain during a game on July 30, 1972, that ushers handed out plastic rain shields). What to do? Officials replaced the grass with a new invention: a green carpet called AstroTurf, an abomination that can be blamed for enough wrenched ankles, torn anterior cruciate ligaments, and "turf toes" to fill a Hall of Fame. Texas tidbit: When the stadium was originally proposed, the team was called the Houston Colt .45s. The groundbreaking was performed by city commissioners firing real Colt .45 pistols at the ground (they used blanks).

_04:: Tacoma Narrows Bridge Is Falling Down

Motorists noticed movement of Washington's Tacoma Narrows Bridge on windy days almost immediately after it opened, quickly dubbing it "Galloping Gertie." But it would take a degree in structural engineering to understand precisely what went wrong on November 7, 1940. That's the day old Gertie shook herself to pieces and crashed into Puget Sound. But it can be summed up (kinda) by saying that strong winds induced vibrations in the bridge's rigid steel side girders that started out as vertical oscillations and then became torsional nodes. Got that? In short, it twisted itself to smithereens. At the worst extremity of the twisting motion, the sidewalk on one side of the bridge was 28 feet higher than on the other. Remarkably, there was only one casu-

alty in the collapse: a three-legged, paralyzed black spaniel named Tubby, who was stranded in a car when his owner, Leonard Coatsworth, fled the bridge. Tubby's death earned Coatsworth $364.40 in compensation from the Washington State Toll Bridge Authority. Not too shabby; he only got $450 for the car.

_05:: Putting Your Hancock Where You Shouldn't: Boston's Most Notorious Building

The tallest structure in New England, Boston's John Hancock Tower is a shimmering geometric tower of 10,000 squares of reflective glass. Designed by I. M. Pei, the world-famous architect who created the Rock and Roll Hall of Fame, the controversial addition to the Louvre, and many other structures, this Beantown creation was unfortunately snakebit from the start. After completion in 1976, the building became a menace as pressure differentials and poor securing techniques caused its huge glass panels to routinely pop out and plummet the 62 stories to Clarendon Street below. The high Boston winds caused an inordinate amount of swaying. And the tower's weight caused nearby buildings, including a historic hotel and church, to sink and suffer structural damage. Eventually, all 10,000 glass panels had to be replaced to correct the sway. During the process, it earned the nickname "Plywood Place."

"Fortunate Son": World Leaders Who Accomplished Absolutely Nothing

Inept people in positions of power? So many to choose from, so little space. Ah, well. Here are four to get you started.

_01:: Commodus (161–192 CE)

Commodus has the dubious distinction of being one of the worst Roman emperors—and that's saying something. He was cruel, sadistic, vicious, and crazier than an outhouse rat (perhaps that's all par for the course). He also renamed Rome, as well as days of the week, after himself, thought of himself as the reincarnation of the demigod Hercules, dressed in lion skins, and killed hundreds of animals and people in the gladiator arena in rigged fights. Need more? Commodus was so swept up in the Hercules/gladiator thing that he let others run the empire, until they showed too much competence. Then he'd have 'em killed. As for his own life, Commodus was strangled by a wrestler while taking a bath. In his wake came a long line of really lame emperors, and one not-so-lame movie, as 2000's *Gladiator* was very loosely based on the Commodus administration.

_02:: Pope John XII (937–964)

There were a lot of bad popes in the Middle Ages, but this guy, whose birth name was Octavian, was a pip. As Daddy's little boy (and son of the secular ruler of Rome), John XII was given the keys to the pope-dom at just 18. But things didn't exactly start off on the right foot. After a disastrous military expedition against a rebellious lord in the Papal States, John XII settled for less ambitious pursuits. In the eight years to follow, John XII was guilty of rape, fornication, looting the church treasury, and gambling. After being briefly (and rightly) deposed, John struck back at his deposers with even more unholy behavior . . . by killing some and mutilating others. Good Catholics can be comforted in knowing that he died with almost as little grace as he lived: John's less-than-saintly life was ended in 964 by an enraged husband, who caught his wife being given more than just the sacrament. John's reign accomplished only one thing: it ensured the pope's office would become politically trivial during the rest of the Middle Ages.

_03:: Edward II (1284–1327)

Lazy and incompetent, Eddie II got to be king of England only because his three older brothers all died. Quite an honor indeed! Taking the throne in 1307, Edward abandoned his father's efforts to work through the nobility to get things done. Instead, he chose to irritate them by conferring power to a guy from France who was his best friend and possibly his lover (not the best decision). Edward also had his royal rump handed to him by the Scots, who were fighting under Robert the Bruce at the time. But that isn't the worst of it. Edward finally agreed to a set of limits on his authority imposed by English nobles, but reneged. His disaffected wife, a French princess, then invaded England with her new boyfriend. Ever incompetent, Edward was deposed, imprisoned, and eventually murdered. A tough end, even for a nincompoop.

_04:: James Buchanan (1791–1868)

Whenever there is talk of America's worst presidents, Buchanan's name is almost sure to come up. Which is too bad, even if warranted, because old James had one of the best political pedigrees. When elected in 1856, Buchanan had been a legislator, congressman, U.S. senator, minister to Russia and Great Britain, and secretary of state. Unfortunately, he was also a Northerner with Southern sympathies at a time when America was rife with sectional

Touch of Evil

Before his death, George V predicted that once his son took the throne, he would "ruin himself in 12 months." He was wrong, however, as Edward VIII abdicated the throne to marry divorcée Wallis Simpson two months before the full year was up.

tensions, thus pleasing no one. Thoroughly incompetent in the post, President Buchanan cleverly confronted the tensions over slavery by doing nothing. Of course, the economic depression triggered by a bank panic didn't really help matters. It's no wonder Buchanan didn't run for reelection on the Democratic ticket. One good thing did result from his incompetence, though. Buchanan's paralysis caused a split in his party, which helped ensure the election of a Republican candidate in 1860: a fellow by the name of Lincoln.

The Inconvenience of Fact-checking: Famous Journalistic Goofs That Could Have Been Avoided

There's an old adage in journalism: "If your mother says she loves you, check it out." Here are five instances in which journalists forgot to call someone other than Mom.

_01:: The Amazing Tasaday

They lived in caves, wore leaves, used stone tools, and had no word in their language for "enemy." At least that's what Manuel Elizalde Jr., the Philippine government minister who "discovered" them in 1971, said. The "Stone Age" tribe of about 25 was called "the anthropological find of the century," featured on the cover of *National Geographic* and idealized by media around the world. They were also declared off-limits by Philippine dictator Ferdinand Marcos. That is, until Marcos was deposed in 1986, and journalists and anthropologists got to revisiting the Tasaday. This time, tribe members had a slightly different story: that they'd been coerced by Elizalde into posing as primitives. While some scientists still insist the Tasaday are unique in some ways, no one claims they're the 21st-century version of the Flintstones, as they were originally hailed.

_02:: A Cooked-Up Tale

In journalistic terms, it was a world-class "weeper"—the story of an eight-year-old heroin addict named Jimmy. In fact, the September 28, 1980, story in the *Washington Post* was so good, magazines and other newspapers reprinted part or all of it. And the mayor of Washington, D.C., even ordered city police to find the poor kid. It's no wonder, then, that the reporter, Janet Cooke, won a 1981 Pulitzer Prize. Of course, her spoils proved to be her undoing as well. The publicity quickly raised questions about her background, and it soon became clear she'd fudged the story from her imagination. An embarrassed *Post* fired Cooke and gave the Pulitzer back. Where to go from here? Cooke took a job as a $6-an-hour department store clerk. But in 1996, she did sell the movie rights to her tale. Presumably it's based on a true story.

_03:: Hitler's Diaries

"I've got to have a really serious talk with Eva," read one entry. "She thinks that a man who leads Germany can take as much time as he wants for private matters." According to the German magazine *Der Stern*, that quote was from Adolf Hitler's secret diaries, and the magazine was willing to fork over 5 million big ones to a guy named Konrad Kujau, for the pages. Supposedly discovered in East Germany, the diaries were authenticated by the eminent

Just the Facts

SLUMBER BY THE NUMBERS

60 million: Number of American adults who suffer from inadequate sleep

77: Percentage of American adults who drink coffee on a daily basis

100 billion: Estimated annual loss in dollars because of sleep-deprivation-related problems in the United States

100,000: Number of fatigue-related traffic accidents per year in the United States

65: Percentage of Americans who lose sleep due to stress

32: Percentage who lose sleep due to stress on a weekly basis

18 million: Number of Americans who suffer from sleep apnea

8.6: Average number of hours of sleep Americans got daily in 2000

1: Ranking of Honolulu, Hawaii, in 2003 survey as best U.S. city in which to get a good night's sleep

2: Ranking of Fresno, California, in same survey

British historian Hugh Trevor-Roper, and the London *Sunday Times* even agreed to buy the reprint rights. But much to everyone's chagrin, the German government revealed the diaries were a rather amateurish fraud. Kujau and the *Der Stern* reporter who arranged the seven-figure deal went to jail. And in 2004, one of the fake volumes sold for $7,741 at a Berlin auction. Go figure.

_04:: The Scoop

The *New York Post* will never be confused with the *New York Times,* at least not by anyone who can read. But the *Post* had a big scoop on July 6, 2004: Democratic presidential candidate John Kerry had picked Congressman Richard Gephardt as his running mate. Of course it was wrong—Kerry had picked Senator John Edwards. Trying to manage the damage done, the *Post* apologized the next day for their error, while the *Times* gleefully reported that the source of the scoop was none other than *Post* publisher Rupert Murdoch. Of course, Murdoch hotly denied it. Whoever was to blame, the *Post*'s July 6 edition quickly took its place in history alongside the *Chicago Tribune*'s 1948 "Dewey Beats Truman" headline and was selling for $10 and up on the Internet within days, all of which says something about accuracy being its own reward.

_05:: A Rather Bush Story

Well, they looked authentic, unless you looked pretty closely, and CBS didn't. Instead network news anchor Dan Rather reported on September 8, 2004, that CBS had obtained documents showing President George W. Bush had received special treatment while in the Texas Air National Guard. And for nearly two weeks, CBS and Rather steadfastly defended the story, despite almost immediate doubts raised about the documents and their source. Finally, on September 20, the network cried "uncle" and Rather apologized for airing the story, confessing his staff had failed "to properly scrutinize the documents" or properly check out the sources behind them. Subscribers to the "liberal media conspiracy" theory had a field day, and the incident gave the network a black eye. It also left an indelible mark on Rather's long and storied career.

Royal Bums: Laziest Kings of All Time

When you're born with a silver spoon in your mouth, it's no wonder you grow up expecting someone to pull said spoon out, pile it high with delicious food, then put it back where they found it. The following are just a few of the spoiled royals who managed to get away with doing nothing, both for themselves and their doting subjects.

_01:: Louis XIV and His Shirt-Sighted Attendants

Louis XIV may have gotten a lot done in his life, but he seems to have been profoundly lazy when it came to personal care. According to contemporary accounts, to get up in the morning Louis XIV required the assistance of literally hundreds of servants and favored courtiers, who helped him bathe, dress, and shave. It was a great honor to hand the king his shirt, and courtiers and sycophants vied with each other for the singular prestige associated with forking over the emperor's new clothes.

_02:: Charles II: A Royal Drain on England

Charles II is on record as one of the laziest kings to rule Britain. And sure, he played an important role just by showing up, since his restoration to the throne signaled a return to peace and tranquility after a bitter civil war. But once he got there, Charles didn't do much of anything. A contemporary English chronicler, Samuel Pepys, described Charles as "a lazy Prince, no Council, no money, no reputation at home or abroad." Not the best PR. Even worse, a common saying at the time had it that Charles "never said a foolish thing, and never did a wise one." Ironically, the high point of Charles's popularity came when he survived an assassination attempt during the "Rye House Plot," named after the place where the would-be assassins allegedly wanted to kill him...after a lifetime spent not doing things, not getting killed was Charles's biggest accomplishment.

_03:: Ethelred the Unready

With a nickname like "the Unready," old Ethelred's place in history is pretty obvious. The poor royal seemed unable to make any decisions by himself, and generally found it easier to put them off. And sure, this governing-byprocrastination strategy worked just fine when England was at peace, but not so well when it was attacked from abroad, which is exactly what happened in 1009, when Sweyn Forkbeard and his Danish Vikings invaded England. The Danes had given plenty of warning, threatening England for several years, but rather than organize an army to fight them, Ethelred thought it would be less work to just buy them off. Unfortunately, the easy loot only encouraged the Danes, and they demanded successively larger sums. When finally pushed to make a decision, the one Ethelred made proved to be the wrong one. By ordering the slaughter of Danish settlers in 1002, he simply provoked the Danes even further. Truly unready in the end, it's no wonder he was deposed by Sweyn Forkbeard in 1012.

_04:: Sultan Selim II: Lazy Like a Fox

Sultan Selim II, "the Drunk," is generally considered one of the most disgracefully lazy rulers of the Ottoman Empire, which is no small accomplishment. But perhaps his indolence was even more noticeable because of the contrast with his father. Selim's pop, Süleyman the Magnificent, ruled from 1520 to 1566 and in that time conquered much of the Middle East and North Africa. His progeny, on the other hand, preferred to spend almost all his time in the harem, never once led his army in a campaign, became an alcoholic, as his nickname suggests, and generally withdrew from all administrative duties. Historians of the Ottoman Empire often mark the beginning of its decline from his completely useless reign.

Touch of Evil

Were King Kong of normal size, perhaps he wouldn't have been so hyper. Gorillas sleep about 13 hours a night, and sometimes nap during the day as well.

_05:: Nicholas II and His Royal Ramblings

Nicholas II, the last czar of Russia, was a bit slow and didn't care for the tasks of government at all. He did keep a diary through most of his reign, though, and it's remarkable to read how little time he seemed to spend on affairs of state compared with, say, the latest news about his dogs. The journal is filled with entries like "At about 6 my dog Shilka whelped 2 puppies whose father was Iman. It caused a lot of fuss in the house." Looking for something deeper? Try this: "I've been hanging pictures upstairs in the new bedroom with green furniture." Or this: "The 3 of us had dinner together at 8:30. We were awfully hungry after our trip and . . . I stuffed myself in an indecent way." Even more remarkable than his complete lack of competency, after the Russian Revolution of 1917 he spent most of his remaining time happily working in his small garden. That is, until he was shot.

Next Time, Mark It Down:
Dates That History Misplaced

From Momma's birthday to the Wilkersons' anniversary to, you know, the time Eadweard Muybridge figured out that horses have all four of their hooves in the air while running, there are just some dates that you know are important...but somehow end up being a little harder to remember.

_01:: October 24, 1942: Smithsonian Admits Its Plane Wrong

For decades children have been taught that Wilbur and Orville Wright were the first to fly a machine-powered airplane. However, for more than a couple of years the Smithsonian Institution thought differently. The fact is, an inventor named Samuel Langley unsuccessfully attempted to fly over the Potomac River in an airplane he'd designed nine days before the Wright bothers made their famous Kitty Hawk flight. A few years later, though, after Langley had passed away, a number of his colleagues repaired the crashed plane and displayed it in the Smithsonian as the first manned flying machine. For two decades, a bitter debate ensued with the Wright broth-

ers, who by then had loaned their original aircraft to the Science Museum in London. Finally, on October 24, 1942, the Smithsonian apologized to Orville Wright (Wilbur had died years before) and declared that he and his brother were in fact the first to fly a machine-powered aircraft. With history corrected, Orville donated his airplane to the Smithsonian.

_02:: October 13, 1307: A Terrifying Friday for the Templars

While there are tons of stories about how the dreaded Friday the 13th date came about, the one with the most historical significance happened on October 13, 1307. During the previous century, a religious order of warrior monks had sprung up in France to fight in the Crusades. Known for their religious piety and courage in battle, the Knights Templar soon became wealthy and actually served as Europe's first banking system. Meanwhile, the French king Philip IV, needing money to run his kingdom, turned on the Templars after coercing the pope to drop their protected status. Then he craftily sent out secret orders to every bailiff in his kingdom. Under penalty of death, the documents were to be opened on October

Touch of Evil

"I am apt to believe it will be celebrated, by succeeding Generations, as the great anniversary Festival." John Adams wasn't talking about July 4, though, but July 2, when the Continental Congress first actually declared American independence.

12 and executed the next day, Friday, October 13. The orders demanded the arrest of any and all Templars and the forfeiture of all their possessions to the king. As a result, over 2,000 Templars were arrested and tortured into making confessions. Interestingly, a couple years later, Jacques de Molay, the Templars' grand master, while being burned at the stake, cursed Philip and the pope, saying that they would both join him in death within the year. They both did!

_03:: June 15, 1878: Muybridge (and a Horse) Invent Motion Pictures

The photographer was Eadweard Muybridge and the horse was Abe Edgington. Commissioned by Leland Stanford (the railroad tycoon and the cofounder of the university bearing his name), Muybridge was attempting to photograph the horse running in full stride to see whether all four of the horse's hooves left the ground at the same time. Twelve box cameras, fitted with special trip wires, were placed 21 inches apart along the track; the cameras essentially recorded what was too fast for the eye to see. Not only did this prove that horses become airborne while running, but the camera technique became the foundation for motion pictures. Despite a quick run-in with the law (Muybridge was also known for tracking down a journalist and shooting him for allegedly having an affair with his wife and fathering his son—later ruled a justifiable homicide), Muybridge continued to experiment with motion photography, and even earned the title "Father of Motion Pictures."

_04:: March 3, 1879:
The Supreme Court Finally
Listens to a Woman

On March 3, 1879, Belva Ann Lockwood won the right to plead a case before the U.S. Supreme Court, thereby becoming the first woman admitted in the court. The case involved the right of Samuel Lowery, an African American attorney, to practice law. However, this wasn't the first "first" for Ms. Lockwood. After moving to Washington, D.C., at the end of the Civil War, Lockwood applied to law school only to be told that, as a woman, her attendance would be an "injurious diversion" to the other students. Eventually she did receive a law degree from National University Law School, but the school refused to award her a diploma. She then wrote to President Grant, the titular head of the school, telling him to either award her the diploma or take his name off the letterhead. Two weeks later she got her diploma. In 1884, as the candidate for the Equal Rights Party, she became the first female to run for president, receiving 4,000 popular votes (women weren't allowed to vote) and two electoral college votes. Lockwood also may have been the first to foresee the Beltway gridlock as she was frequently seen riding a tricycle through the streets of Washington, D.C.

Songs in the Key of Trite:
Famous Tunes Stolen from Other Tunes

Ever had a catchy song you just couldn't get out of your head? Well, have you ever taken said song, thrown in a couple of new lyrics, and told everyone it was your own? That's just what these cats did, and it landed them in a boatload of trouble. The following are four cases where imitation was a pretty expensive form of flattery.

_01:: "My Sweet Lord"/
"He's So Fine"

After a pretty successful run with the Beatles, George Harrison recorded his solo album *All Things Must Pass* in 1970 and released "My Sweet Lord" as its first single. The song quickly became a big hit. The problem was that back in 1962 a group called the Chiffons had recorded a hit song by Ronald Mack in the United States called "He's So Fine." Actually, the problem wasn't just that the Chiffons had released a song, but that the songs sounded pretty much the same. In early 1971, Mack and the Bright Tunes Music Corporation filed suit against Harrison and his American and British music companies. In order to settle the lawsuit, Harrison initially offered to purchase the entire Bright Tunes catalog, but it wasn't agreeable to Bright Tunes. The company countered the suit with a proposal whereby Harrison would surrender the copyright to "My Sweet Lord" and they'd share 50% of the royalties on the song with Harrison. Neither side gave in and the suit went on for years. Finally, the suit was settled with Harrison admitting that he "unknowingly" plagiarized the melody.

_02:: "Ice Ice Baby"/"Under Pressure"

On his 1990 album *To the Extreme,* Vanilla Ice sampled some very identifiable riffs in his hit "Ice Ice Baby" from the Queen/David Bowie song "Under Pressure." While it's a pretty common technique to hook audiences and generate sales, the problem was that Ice didn't bother to license the song or give Queen or David Bowie any credit. The album's liner notes credit Vanilla Ice and two others as the composers, and while it goes on to thank other artists, there's no mention of either Bowie or Queen. Although the case never went to court, Vanilla Ice was threatened with a lawsuit, which he settled for an undisclosed amount. Interestingly enough, Queen rereleased "Under Pressure" as part of its 1992 *Classic Queen* album. The liner notes stated that not only was the song a hit in the U.K., but that in 1990, the bass and piano were featured again in Vanilla Ice's number one single "Ice Ice Baby."

_03:: "Avalon"/*La Tosca*

Using someone else's musical composition isn't just an epidemic of the rock era. In 1920, the song "Avalon" was introduced to the American public by Al Jolson. Considered a classic American love song, it was later recorded in 1937 by the Benny Goodman Quartet and featured in at least five movies. Of course, the music and lyrics are attributed to Vincent Rose

and Al Jolson (aka "the Jazz Singer"). And while it wasn't common for Jolson to take credit for many of his hit songs, in this case he probably wished he hadn't. Soon after the song was published, the Italian composer Puccini and his publisher filed suit against Jolson, claiming that the melody was plagiarized from the aria "E Lucevan le Stelle" from his opera *La Tosca.* Puccini won the case and all future royalties. He also received settlement of $25,000, not a small sum for that time.

Touch of Evil

While the Beach Boys' "Surfin' USA" seemed like an obvious update of Chuck Berry's "Sweet Little Sixteen," Berry was only credited on the label after initiating a lawsuit.

_04:: *Ghostbusters/* "I Want a New Drug"

Is the Stay Puft Marshmallow Man the new drug that Huey Lewis & The News were looking for? Say it ain't so! When the movie *Ghostbusters* came out in 1984, the theme song ("Who You Going to Call?") sounded very much like Lewis's "I Want a New Drug," and Lewis quickly decided he was going to call his lawyer. Understandably, the suit was settled out of court in 1995, and while Ray Parker never admitted that he copied Lewis, he did agree to pay Huey an undisclosed amount. However, the story doesn't end there. In 2001, as part of a *VH1: Behind the Music* segment, Huey Lewis, in discussing the battle over the *Ghostbusters* tune said, "They bought it," referring to Parker and the settlement. Of course the segment gave Parker some ammunition of his own, and Parker filed suit against Lewis for violating their agreement, whereby the fact that money had changed hands was never to be made public.

Riot Back At'cha:
Delinquent Rock Groups and the Chaos They Stirred

Just because you're a big-shot, world-famous rock-and-roll band doesn't mean you have the right to play with people's emotions. At least, that's probably what these rock bands' moms told them after they came home stoned (we're talking bruised from having rocks pelted at them, not high on drugs!).

_01:: Guns N' Roses— December 6, 2002

The rock group Guns N' Roses had a history of canceling concerts, or just plain deciding not to show up for 'em. On December 6, 2002, however, South Philadelphia fans struck back. When the group didn't arrive as scheduled, the warm-up act continued to play for close to two hours. Understandably, the crowd grew increasingly irritated, and unlike the GNR anthem, they didn't "have a little patience." Tempers quickly moved toward the boiling point when the crowd saw the warm-up group removing their equipment from the stage and nothing was being set up in its place. Unknown to the crowd of 20,000, Guns N' Roses had canceled right before the show because their lead singer, Axl Rose, was "too sick" to perform. No one told the audience, though, and after standing around for even more time, they quickly realized their own "Appetites for Destruction." Chairs, drinks, and even ceiling tiles were tossed as the crowd went berserk. In fact, it took over 100 police officers to restore order, and while no one was arrested, a number of individuals did require hospital treatment. Interestingly, concert officials denied that there was any trouble and claimed the fans left in an orderly fashion.

_02:: Creed—December 29, 2002

Some musicians show up at a concert but aren't really there. And while Bob Dylan's been accused of it for years, it was definitely the case with Scott Stapp, the lead singer for Creed, in Rosemont, Illinois. Once onstage, Stapp was so under the influence of alcohol and drugs that he was unable to sing the lyrics to any of the group's songs. On a number of occasions he actually left the stage and didn't return for several minutes. When he did choose to return, he fell to the floor and rolled around in pain; then it appeared like he'd passed out. Many angry fans left the arena, but four of them decided to take things into their own hands. By filing a class action suit against Creed and their promoters, the fans sought over $2 million in refunds for the 15,000 concertgoers attending that night. The group later apologized for what they called their "most unique" experience and reminded the fans that it's only rock and roll, even if you don't like it.

_03:: Punked in Montreal— October 2003

Fans weren't exactly happy when organizers canceled a midweek punk rock show in Montreal in mid-October 2003. After all, the concert attendees had already gathered to hear their bands, Total Chaos and The Exploited, play when they received the bad news. Of course, a different sort of total chaos did eventually show up: police reports indicate that at roughly 8 p.m., when they were informed of the cancellation, hundreds of punk rock concert fans immediately expressed their anger by rioting, smashing windows, overturning cars, and setting things on fire. In fact, the Canadian press reported that one city block had 24 cars and at least six stores with smashed windows. When things finally calmed down, an unknown number of people had been arrested and two police officers had sustained injuries. The French-language TV channel LCN said that the band had to cancel after Canadian customs officials had barred some members of The Exploited band from entering the country.

_04:: Jefferson Starship— June 17, 1978

The Jefferson Starship was known for inciting their fans to riot when they did perform at concerts. Unfortunately, things didn't change much when they didn't. In Germany, as part of a European tour, the Starship was scheduled to play at the Lorelei Amphitheater outside Wiesbaden when Grace Slick (the group's lead singer) allegedly became ill and stated that she wasn't going to perform. Without Slick, the group couldn't go on, and decided to cancel the concert. Of course, the crowd of over 10,000 didn't quite understand. They had, after all, waited for a couple hours, and when the announcement came they erupted. Angry fans started throwing bottles and rocks at the stage, injuring one of the crew. When the crew finally gave up trying to save the band's stuff, the crowd attacked the stage and destroyed over a million dollars' worth of equipment. And whatever wasn't torched was thrown over a cliff into the Rhine! Apparently, the fire could be seen from miles away, and when the fire brigade showed up they were pelted with bricks and forced to flee the scene. As for the police, they never did show up.

_05:: Hot Fun in the Summer Sun— July 21, 1973

The city of Milwaukee runs an annual 11-day festival called Summerfest. And in the summer of 1971, Sly and the Family Stone caused a riot among the 100,000 fans in attendance when they failed to show up on time (something they were known for doing). Essentially, the old pattern of a crowd getting rowdy and police making numerous arrests occurred. Unfortunately for the Summerfest, though, lightning did strike twice. On July 21, 1973, the group Humble Pie failed to show up on time and the large crowd went even crazier, this time throwing bottles and cans, torching food tents, and stealing barrels of beer. The crowd then set bonfires using chairs and fences as the fuel. And then they took their show on the road, going over to a nearby circus, beating up two workers, and swinging on the trapezes. In the end, police managed to clear the area using nightsticks and tear gas, though seven officers were injured in the event, and damages totaled in the thousands.

Born Retired:
Famous Figures Who Never Held (Real) Day Jobs

What do these dictators, witty writers, spiritual leaders, terrorists, and philosophers all have in common? Well, there's one thing they didn't have: a job.

_01:: Oscar Wilde (1854–1900)

"Cultivated leisure is the aim of man," Oscar Wilde once famously said, and he certainly lived his life by that dictum. Wilde was brilliant, winning a gold medal in Classics at Trinity College in Dublin in 1874 before earning a scholarship to Oxford. When his father died, however, Wilde left the family's finances to his older brother Henry, and worked only once in his life, a brief two-year stint as the editor of a women's magazine called *The Woman's World,* from 1887 to 1889. Wilde spent the rest of his time writing, giving lectures on aesthetics, coining pithy epigrams, and generally being a wit. Sadly, Wilde was forced to do hard labor near the end of his life after he was found guilty of immoral conduct for homosexual activities. A broken man, he died shortly thereafter, in 1900.

_02:: Socrates (468–399 BCE)

Aside from a possible brief stint as a sculptor, Socrates seems to have spent most of his hours ambling around the *agora*—the gymnasia where Athenians exercised, which was also Athens's central public meeting place and marketplace. When he wasn't milling about the town, the old philosopher could be spotted going to parties and loitering in taverns where citizens and foreign guests gathered. All this isn't to say the poor guy enjoyed the lush life. Socrates lived and dressed simply, wore neither shoes nor shirt, and owned only one coat. He also ate poorly, lived hand to mouth, relied heavily on the charity of his friends, and refused gifts when they were offered. Like, for instance, the time his friend Charmides offered to give him slaves who could have made money to support him. He also refused to accept presents from powerful leaders of Greek cities, not wanting to ever compromise his integrity. When the great philosopher was put on trial for allegedly teaching sacrilege, Socrates tweaked the Athenian assembly by suggesting that far from being a criminal, he deserved free room and board at their expense. Unamused, they condemned him to death.

_03:: Buddha (ca. 563–483 BCE)

Buddha, like Socrates, was a full-time thinker whose schedule of meditation, contemplation, and conversation didn't leave any time for work. Born around 563 BCE, Siddhartha, as he was called when young, was the son of a king who ruled a small kingdom in the northern floodplains of the Ganges River in India. The young prince led a life of leisure in his early years before growing disgusted with the materialism of the royal palace. Instead of sticking around, Siddhartha wandered off into nature at the age of 28, and after seven years of travel, meditation, and conversation with Hindu mystics, he attained enlightenment under a *Bodhi* tree. Receiving visitors and teaching students from under the tree, he spread the message of moderation and separation from material want that became Buddhism—and never did get a job.

_04:: Osama bin Laden (1957–   )

Before he started fighting for his own violent version of Islam, terrorist Osama bin Laden led the life of a playboy. Born around 1957 to a wealthy Yemeni father and Syrian mother, bin Laden was heir to part of the massive fortune his billionaire father had accumulated in the Saudi construction business. As such, he squandered his days, acquiring a reputation for drinking too much and womanizing in his teens and early 20s in Beirut, which was then a cosmopolitan tourist hot spot. In fact, he didn't become a firmly committed, full-time Islamic radical until he went to fight the Soviet invasion of Afghanistan in 1979. That's where Osama began his improbable transformation from a rakish ladies' man to a mass-murdering zealot, never having worked a day before then.

Less-Than-Golden Slumbers:
Bad Nights of Sleep That Led to Drastic Mistakes

"To sleep, perchance to screw up." OK, we'll admit that's not exactly what the good bard said, but it does fit these five slices of somnambulistic history.

_01:: A Christmas Wake-up Call

Colonel Johann Rall was a proven fighter, having already led his Hessian, or German mercenary, troops in successful battle against the American rebels. But he was contemptuous of his foe, and boy did he like to drink. In the end, the happy juice proved to be his undoing.

On December 25, 1776, Rall ignored warnings that rebels under General George Washington were on the march toward Trenton, New Jersey. Instead, he got drunk and went to sleep, as did many of his 1,400 soldiers. Washington, meanwhile, made a daring predawn crossing of the ice-choked Delaware River. At daylight on December 26, the rebels attacked and routed the Hessians. Rall, who was under the covers when the battle began, got dressed just in time to be killed . . . proving that some days it really doesn't pay to get out of bed.

Touch of Evil

Cyril Evans, the wireless operator aboard the Californian, *forgot to set the automatic signal detector in his haste to catch some shut-eye. As a result, the ship didn't receive any warnings from the nearby* Titanic, *and (despite being the closest to the wreck) failed to lend a hand until far too late.*

_02:: "Get the Phone, Eva, I'm Schnoozing"

The weather seemed too rough over the English Channel the evening of June 5, 1944, to launch the greatest military invasion in history. So Adolf Hitler figured, "What the hell, I'm going to bed." Der Führer took a sleeping pill and left orders not to be disturbed. Big mistake on old Adolf's part: D-Day was several hours into effect before aides got the courage to wake Hitler up to get his permission to mobilize needed troops and equipment. Even then, the dictator dallied. He had tea, took a nap, and met with the premier of Hungary. Finally, about 5 p.m. on June 6, he issued orders, mostly bad ones that kept German generals from being able to move reinforcements to the invasion area. Good thing for the Allies that he woke up.

_03:: Asleep at the Switch?

During a clear, sunny morning, February 8, 1986, the 114-car Canadian National Railway

It's a Mad, Mad, Mad, Mad Author

ONE WORD, TWO WORDS

The charming children's books (and wartime propaganda) of Theodor Seuss Geisel (Dr. Seuss) have entertained young and old alike for generations. One commentator described his work, which included *If I Ran the Zoo, Horton Hears a Who!, How the Grinch Stole Christmas,* and *The Cat in the Hat,* as wonderful stories of "ludicrous situations pursued with relentless logic." Starting in 1957, Seuss's work becomes noticeably laconic: the number of different words drops considerably. With *Green Eggs and Ham,* Seuss won a bet with his editor, who wagered that he couldn't write a book using fewer than 50 different words. Brilliance or laziness? You decide.

freight train rolled west near the small town of Hinton in the province of Alberta. Rolling east was a passenger train. But because the freight train's three-man crew missed a stop signal, the two trains were on the same track. The result was a horrific collision, killing 23 people, including the freight train's engineer and brakeman. Just why the crew missed the signal has never been resolved. What was reported, however, was that the engineer had worked 26 of the 30 days before the wreck, and the crew had had little sleep. In the wake of the tragedy, the rail company introduced sweeping measures to combat crew fatigue.

_04:: Oil on the Waters

The reef was well marked on the charts, the weather was OK, and the 984-foot-long *Exxon Valdez* had all the latest navigational equipment. But the oil-laden ship still went aground on Prince William Sound just after midnight on March 24, 1989. The result—only the worst oil spill in American history, which led everyone to ask the same question: What happened? Despite the popular notion that it was caused by a drunken captain, the U.S. National Transportation Safety Board attributed the spill to other causes. Among them was that the third mate, who was at the helm at the time of the accident, was "impaired by fatigue," as was the rest of the crew. Exxon, it turned out, had a policy of increasing crews' workload to save money. The spill cost the company $2.2 billion, which translated into a lot of overtime.

_05:: "I Object: My Attorney's Asleep"

Calvin Burdine was scheduled to die on April 11, 1995, 12 years after being convicted of killing his boyfriend in Houston. But a federal judge stopped the execution a few hours before it was scheduled. What prompted the justice's change of heart? Well, among other things, he was troubled that Burdine's lawyer had slept through portions of the trial. Amazingly, a three-member federal appeals court panel overruled the judge, reasoning that a defendant had no constitutional right to a conscious attorney. Fortunately for Burdine, a full appeals court ordered a new trial, and the U.S. Supreme Court concurred. As of 2004, Burdine was doing life in a Texas prison after a plea bargain. And lawyers all over the country were trying to stay awake.

What's That You're Flying? Laziest Flag Designs

Flags are an important reminder of who we are and what we stand for, so it's surprising how often a flag design is chosen in a seemingly careless manner, with little attempt at originality of appearance. What follows is a list of just four of the many, many lazily designed flags that have still waved proudly from masts across the globe.

_01:: Libya: It's Ridiculously Easy Being Green

In 1977, Libya left a federation of Arab states (the other members were Syria and Egypt) that had all used a pan-Arab banner with horizontal stripes of red over white over black. As part of an effort to forge a new, uniquely Libyan identity, the ever-wacky Muammar al-

Gadhafi unveiled a new flag design for the "Socialist People's Libyan Arab Jamahiriya." The flag, representing Islam and fertility, was completely green.

Touch of Evil

The flags of Denmark, Finland, Iceland, Norway, and Sweden are all nearly identical in design; each depicts a cross with its intersection in the first third of the field.

_02:: Haiti: Get the White Out

The modern Haitian flag features two horizontal stripes, blue over red. But the original version, adopted upon independence in 1804, featured two stripes arranged vertically like those on the French flag. The flag originated when Jean-Jacques Dessalines, a leader of the Haitian revolt against France, tore the white stripe out of a French flag and told his goddaughter to sew the two remaining stripes together. Ironically, while Dessalines meant this as a gesture of contempt for his country's former white masters (many of whom were massacred by their former slaves during the fight for Haitian independence), the color white in flags traditionally stands for peace, something Haiti unfortunately has known little of in its 200 years as an independent country.

_03:: Alaska: The Best Darn Artist in the Whole Eighth Grade

Alaska had been a U.S. possession since 1867 and a territory since 1912, but apparently nobody ever bothered to make a flag for the place until 1927, when the territorial government of Alaska farmed out the responsibility of flag design to the Alaska Department of the American Legion. The Legion, in turn, decided flag design was too important to leave to anyone but teenage children, and so sponsored a contest. The winner, John Bell Benson, was a 13-year-old boy. He actually did a fair job, all things considered—the flag is dark blue, with eight five-pointed gold stars in the shape of the Big Dipper and a larger gold star representing the North Star, Polaris. The lazy, lazy inhabitants of Alaska even let Benson pick the state flower—he chose the forget-me-not.

_04:: China: Getting By with a Little Help from Communist Friends

The Chinese Communists developed their own flag during the terrible decades-long civil war with the Nationalists and various warlords. The clever design featured a red background with a golden hammer and sickle. The only problem: This flag was identical to that of the Soviet Union, minus a star. Not to be outdone, the later Communist parties in Vietnam and Laos adopted their own flags. For some reason, however, these were simply copies of the Chinese version. This intrepid spirit of innovation would serve the Communists well in defeating Western democracy and capitalism in the cold war. Oh, wait...

The Sound of Sirens:
Warning Calls History Ignored

Tsk-tsk! If you hear the warning bells a-ringing (or see that a certain group has been looting and plundering your neighbors and is now making a beeline for your home), maybe it's time to put down the remote and start planning your defense. Of course, if you're too lazy to make a move you could always cross your fingers and take your chances. Unfortunately, that genius tactic didn't work out so well for the following folks.

_01:: Beware Macedonians Bringing Gifts

Demosthenes (384–322 BCE) was a brilliant Athenian orator, though apparently he was pretty good as an oracle as well. Throughout the 340s BCE, he begged, harangued, and pleaded with the feuding Greek city-states to unite against what he saw as the growing threat of Macedon, under its brutal, one-eyed King Philip. But Philip wasn't without his charms, either: the wily warlord threatened, flattered, and bribed the city-states until they were either too scared, too vain, or too rich to risk fighting the Macedonians. When they finally realized the danger, it was a little too late. With the evidence all pointing to Philip's plot for total domination, Demosthenes did finally succeed in scrounging up a coalition against him, but they lacked the time and resources to prepare. At Chaeronea in 338 BCE, Philip and his son Alexander (a few years shy of being "the Great") destroyed the united Greek armies. Demosthenes lived on until 322, giving him plenty of time to tell his fellow Hellenes, "I told ye so."

_02:: Norse by Norse-West: The Vikings Arrive on the Scene

In 789, Viking marauders made their first appearance in the British Isles. Then, four years later, a major force of Norsemen sacked the famous monastery at Lindisfarne. Doing pretty darn well for themselves, the Vikings' raids became a regular part of life in England, Scotland, Wales, and Ireland over the next few decades. Across the Channel, the nobles of what is now Germany and France heard of the attacks and tried to build up their defenses, but the Carolingian rulers opposed such efforts, fearing (not entirely without reason) that nobles could use these bases to rebel. By the

Touch of Evil

No one blinked when Swedish scientist Svante Arrhenius predicted a global warming scenario that would cause problems around the world. Maybe it's because his alert came about a hundred years too early, in 1896.

Lies Your Mother Told You

THE "SURPRISE" PROTESTANT REFORMATION

Teachers often describe the Protestant Reformation as if it came out of nowhere, but Martin Luther and Ulrich Zwingli were hardly the first to take stabs at reforming the increasingly corrupt Catholic Church. From about 1300 until the rise of the Protestant movement, would-be reformers popped up everywhere—John Wyclif in England, the fire-and-brimstone Savanarola in Florence, and Jan Huss in Bohemia. Though they tried to effect change from within the Church, most of these folks ended up burning at the stake or meeting some other sticky end. Simony (buying a position in the Church), nepotism (riding on your relatives' coattails), and indulgences (buying forgiveness for your sins) all continued unabated, eventually sparking the Reformation and the splintering of Western Christianity.

mid-800s, entire provinces were in the hands of Scandinavian marauders; and Carolingian monarchs, too, had to pay vast bribes to keep them happy. One group of these pirates was even granted land in northwestern France; the province of Normandy is named after these "Northmen."

_03:: Winnie Prophesies Doom

Winston Churchill, dismayed by the rise of Hitler, was reported to have said that "the hottest part of hell is reserved for those who, at a time of grave moral crisis, steadfastly maintain their neutrality." During the 1930s, Churchill did his best to alert his fellow Britons to the danger on the horizon, but no one was particularly interested, since everyone was focused on the Depression. When Prime Minister Neville Chamberlain signed a peace deal with Hitler, Churchill told the House of Commons, "You were given the choice between war and dishonor. You chose dishonor and you will have war." The irrepressible Churchill was right, of course—within months Germany had unleashed war, and Britain and France were caught with their proverbial pants down.

Resting on Someone Else's Laurels:
Figures Who Claimed Someone Else's Fame

When "'Tis a far, far better thing he does than you'll ever be able to do" happens to be the case, maybe you should take a page out of these guys' playbook. After all, it's a great thing to be able to produce something that will be remembered for all time. It's even better to let some other chump do the work while you just steal the credit.

_01:: Darius "I'm the Greatest" the Great

In 522 BCE, the Persian king Cambyses died while at war, and the relatively young Persian Empire erupted into rebellion. The Persian prince Darius became the new king after leading six other conspirators to kill off the most prominent challenger. And while Darius did succeed in arranging the end of the various rebellions (largely through the efforts of said six coconspirators), the age of Persian expansion was largely over. Sure, old Darius defended the empire well, but his best-known foreign campaign, the invasion of Greece in 490 BCE, ended in defeat. But that didn't stop the Persian from stealing a bit of glory for himself. On a monument erected in his honor in Behistun (in modern Iran), Darius claimed the kingship of 23 nations, virtually all conquered by his predecessors.

_02:: Pope Gregory's Calendar

In 1582, Pope Gregory XIII ordered the Catholic world to adopt an adjustment to the old Roman "Julian" calendar then in use. And while many people can tell you the new "Gregorian" calendar corrected some of the misplaced leap years of the old system, which had resulted in the year being slightly too long, few people knew the identity of the real inventor. The calendar was actually designed by Aloysius Lilius, a Neapolitan doctor. And Lilius himself had relied upon the calculations of Roger Bacon, a 13th-century English philosopher who had once been incarcerated by the Church for heresy. Not surprisingly, Pope Gregory got all the credit because the system change was mandated in the papal bull *Inter Gravissimas*, but we're pretty sure he didn't mind too much.

_03:: The Many Inventors of the Telescope

Most people credit Galileo Galilei (1564–1642) with the invention of the telescope. But then most people are wrong! Until recently it was believed that Galileo was the first to use the telescope for observation of the heavenly bodies, and that Hans Lippershey (1570–1619) was the first to build a workable telescope. This conventional view, however, may be mistaken as well—various cryptic remarks in Leonardo da Vinci's (1452–1519) notebooks, which discuss the science of optics, actually seem to refer to the use of telescopic devices to study the moon. And in 1938, Domenico Argentieri discovered a previously ignored diagram in a Leonardo manuscript that appears to depict the plans for a primitive telescope. Chalk another great invention up to old Leonardo.

Touch of Evil

After Hank Ballard failed to show up on American Bandstand to promote "The Twist," host Dick Clark asked his protégé, Chubby Checker, to record the tune for the program. He did, and it became the biggest dance record of its era.

_04:: Morseward Bound

Forget what you learned in grade school: Samuel Morse was at the least a second placer when it came to the telegraph. Instead, set your sights on the true champ, Sir Charles Wheatstone (1802–1875). It's true! The British inventor built the first practical electric telegraph in 1837 or 1838, at the very least four years before Morse received his U.S. patent (and around the time he was conducting his early experiments with electric telegraphy). Even in America, though, Morse's "invention" of the telegraph is fraught with controversy: a friend, Dr. Charles Jackson, accused the inventor of stealing his idea (which could move Morse from second into third place). Also in dispute is the extent to which Morse's assistant, Alfred Vail, contributed to both the design of his telegraph machine and the development of the "Morse code," which was originally called the "Morse-Vail." (Does that even leave Sammy in the running anymore?) Well, whatever the case, you can always trust that the telegraph system will forever bear the good old Morse name.

About the Editors

For the first 22 years of their lives, **Will Pearson** and **Mangesh Hattikudur** were really well rounded, in the "wow, nice résumé" kind of way. Joining and starting any clubs they could, doing anthropological research in Tibet, trying to save whales, wetlands, and any other bumper-sticker cause they saw. So, what happened to those days? Now they're only well rounded in the "you should really slow down on the chips and queso" kind of way. Ever since the duo started *mental_floss* as Duke University students, all they want to do is talk trivia. In fact, it's kind of a problem. If anyone knows of a good trivia-addicts support group, please contact the *mental_floss* staff immediately.

mental_floss presents: Forbidden Knowledge is their fourth book together. The pair also worked on *mental_floss presents: Condensed Knowledge, mental_floss presents: Instant Knowledge,* and *Lolita,* published under the pen name Vladimir Nabokov.

Elizabeth Hunt was not a trivia buff—for years she felt compelled to share her SAT scores to look smart at social gatherings. Then Mangesh introduced her to *mental_floss,* and she discovered that trivia knowledge is even more impressive than high school achievements. Now she often opens bar conversations with the classic line "So...did you know that beer is made by bacteria feeding on yeast cells, then defecating?" *mental_floss presents: Forbidden Knowledge* is her second *mental_floss* book. When she's not flossing, she works as a book editor at the International Reading Association.

mental_floss magazine, currently available at newsstands everywhere, was founded in 2001 with the mission of blurring the lines between education and entertainment. The magazine has received rave reviews in a variety of publications, including *Newsweek,* the *Washington Post,* the *Chicago Tribune,* and *Entertainment Weekly.* The *mental_floss* staff has contributed to more than 80 segments on CNN *Headline News* and recently released its first board game, *mental_floss: The Trivia Game.* Daily trivia and the *mental_floss* store are easy to find online at www.mentalfloss.com.

About the Contributors

Erik Sass is a freelance journalist in Brooklyn, New York, covering American foreign policy, New York's immigrant communities, and anything else that strikes his fancy. His interests include geography, espionage, guerrilla warfare, and microbrewed beers from around the world. He's good at the history questions in Trivial Pursuit but is completely clueless about sports, science, and entertainment, so don't choose him as your partner.

John Green writes for *Booklist* magazine, where his reviewing niches include books about Islam, Christianity, boxing, and conjoined twins. John's background in religious studies prepared him for a lifelong study of sin, which culminated in his work for this book. Besides writing for *mental_floss* and regularly contributing to NPR's *All Things Considered,* John is also the author of the novel *Looking for Alaska.*

Christopher Smith is a regular contributor to *mental_floss* magazine and also contributed to its first book, *mental_floss presents: Condensed Knowledge.* As a writer and creative director in the advertising field, he has written for some of the industry's best-known brands, including Motel 6, Home Depot, 7-Eleven, Red Lobster, Chick-fil-A, Red Roof Inn, and Bennigan's. Since 1997 he has performed with Ad-Libs, one of America's most successful comedy troupes. A native of upstate New York and graduate of Penn State, he lives in Dallas with his wife, Heather, and their toddler, Clara, who, at the time of this writing, is looking forward to the expected addition of twin baby brothers.

Steve Wiegand is a senior writer for the *Sacramento Bee,* where he specializes in covering vice—sex, drugs, and gambling. Wiegand's 30-year newspaper career has also included stints at the *San Francisco Chronicle* and the *San Diego Tribune.* He's the author of two books, *Sacramento Tapestry* and *U.S. History for Dummies.* In his spare time he's a woodworker, and plays blues harp and sings with the nearly legendary Sacramento band Deadline.

Brian Gottesman is (he assumes) the only contributor to *mental_floss presents: Forbidden Knowledge* to be put in apprehension of imminent attack by a feral reindeer while hiking in Iceland. He is a Phi Beta Kappa graduate of the University of Rochester, where he earned a B.A. in history, and of Harvard Law School. An aficionado of the obscure (he enjoys reading Icelandic sagas, and his college thesis was on Eurasian nomad tribes so obscure that they are widely thought to be mythological), Brian is making his first contribution to a *mental_floss* project. He is the author of *The King of Zion: A Tale from the Age of Faith,* as yet unpublished, and *Lords of the Steppe,* a work in progress. Brian practices law in Wilmington, Delaware.

Peter Haugen (rhymes with "now then"), author of *World History for Dummies* and a contributor to *mental_floss presents: Condensed Knowledge,* has been theater critic of the *Sacramento Bee,* a regional news editor of the *St. Petersburg Times,* and a contributor to *mental_floss, History Magazine,* and *Psychology Today,* among many other publications. A Phi Beta Kappa graduate of the University of California, Berkeley, he once held a job stacking wet turkey feathers with a pitchfork (really). Trained in journalism at the Defense Information School, he was awarded the Keith L. Ware Award and a Meritorious Service Medal during his hitch as a U.S. Army journalist. He has taught journalism at the University of Wisconsin and at California State University, Fresno. He lives in Madison, Wisconsin, with his wife, two sons, and assorted pets of various species.

Bill Hauser, Ph.D., contributed to *mental_floss presents: Condensed Knowledge,* and is currently an assistant professor of marketing and an adjunct professor of sociology at the University of Akron in Akron, Ohio. After two decades of directing market research for Fortune 500 companies, Bill is currently fulfilling his lifelong dream of teaching, research, and writing.

Index

Exclusive offer for
FORBIDDEN KNOWLEDGE READERS!

If you liked *Forbidden Knowledge*, you're going to love *mental_floss* magazine. Hip, quick, quirky, and fun, *mental_floss* is the perfect antidote to dull conversations. Jam-packed with fascinating facts, lucid explanations, and history's juiciest secrets, *mental_floss* uncovers everything from black holes to the Dead Sea Scrolls, and laces it with just enough wit to keep you grinning for weeks. So, go ahead and pick up a copy. And an hour later, when your kids are tugging at your pant legs and your spouse is burning dinner, and you're busy wondering just where the time went, you'll realize that *mental_floss* doesn't just make learning easy, it makes it addictive.

Save 50% off the cover price of this wonderful magazine. Go to www.mentalfloss.com/ forbiddenknowledge or complete and mail the form below.

Please enter my subscription to mental_floss magazine immediately!
__ 6 issues (1 year) $14.95
__ 12 issues (2 years) $27.95
(Canadian orders add $10.00 per year; payable in U.S. funds)

Name: _____

Address: _____

Apt / Suite #: _____

City _____ **State** _____ **Zip** _____

Check enclosed _____ **Please charge my Visa/MC** _____ **Exp:** _____

Signature _____   **WHCCK**

Mail this form to:

mental_floss
P.O. Box 1940
Marion, OH 43306-1940

HarperCollins*Publishers* is not a party to this offer and is not affiliated with *mental_floss* magazine.

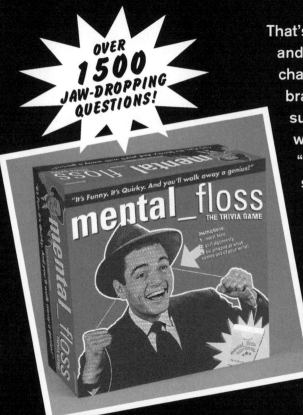

Get Your Knowledge On!

0-06-056806-2

0-06-083461-7

Jam-packed with fascinating facts, lucid explanations, and history's juiciest secrets, the **mental_floss** books uncover everything from black holes to the Dead Sea Scrolls, and lace it with enough wit to keep you grinning. Curious? Then go ahead and nurture your inner smart aleck today!

0-06-078475-X

mental_floss *presents*: *Condensed Knowledge*

Want to know what four things Einstein got wrong, which scandals rocked the art world, or which tiny nations don't really belong on maps? Filled with meaty trivia and hearty facts, *Condensed Knowledge* is everything you learned in school but forgot—in convenient book form!

mental_floss *presents*: *Forbidden Knowledge*

Discover just how sinfully delicious learning can be in this wickedly smart guide to the dirtiest, darkest corners of history. From evil schemes to hoaxes to tasty creatures that we've eaten into extinction, *Forbidden Knowledge* is filled with facts to soothe your mischievous side.

mental_floss *presents*: *Instant Knowledge*

A pocket-size A-to-Z guide to all the facts and intellectual tidbits you need to discuss hundreds of topics. In this handy format, you have a veritable ace up your sleeve for cocktail parties or the next dinner with the boss!

Available Wherever Books Are Sold.

Visit www.AuthorTracker.com for exclusive information on all your favorite HarperCollins authors.

 Collins *An Imprint of HarperCollinsPublishers*
www.harpercollins.com